DOCTOR WHO

SUPERIOR BEINGS

NICK WALTERS

Published by BBC Worldwide Ltd,
Woodlands, 80 Wood Lane
London W12 0TT

First published 2001
Copyright © Nick Walters 2001
The moral right of the author has been asserted

Original series broadcast on the BBC

Doctor Who and TARDIS are trademarks of the BBC

ISBN 0 563 53830 9
Imaging by Black Sheep, copyright © BBC 2001

Printed and bound in Great Britain by Mackays of Chatham
Cover printed by Belmont Press Ltd, Northampton

For Paul Vearncombe

Contents

Chapter One
Almost Human

As she stared out over the curving sea, a light breeze messing with her hair, Aline Vehlmann felt better than she had for days. More herself, more *human*. She was tired, her back ached, she was a little drunk, and she felt homesick. On top of this she was beginning to feel daunted by the size of the project she'd taken on. Once more she wondered if it had been too early to return to work – not that this current assignment was anything like real work. More like an extended holiday, an unending splurge of indulgence. Her Eknuri hosts seemed to forget that her human-basic body wasn't used to unfettered hedonism. Her poor human mind couldn't handle Eknuri levels of stimulation. Her therapist hadn't foreseen that when she'd suggested this as a good way of resuming her career with minimal risk to her still-fragile psyche.

Aline looked down at her feet, pale hostages to the strappy bondage of Eknuri fashion. A thought kept bothering her: it just wouldn't go away. What if this 'gentle easing back' turned out to be a violent wrench which threw her right back to square one?

Making a conscious effort to lighten her thoughts, Aline filled her vision with ocean, as if to cleanse her mind. The pronounced curvature of the horizon was an alarming and constant reminder of the tiny size of the planetoid. And of the brio, bordering on arrogance, with which the Eknuri deployed their technology.

The artificial air was zingy and fresh and Aline felt her head beginning to clear, her thoughts crystallising into a plan. Maybe she would pull out of the party, go back to Eknur 4, write up her notes. But that meant real work, and really thinking about the alien-ness of the Eknuri. She felt almost afraid of both, and the prospect of leaving the little pleasure-world saddened her. She looked down at the white strip of beach below, the slow unfurling of the waves. The sight soothed her, postponed any decision, helped her relax in the moment.

Then she sensed a presence behind her and whirled round, startled.

An Eknuri towered over her, all bare flesh and bonhomie. Aline found her eyes drawn to the tattoo on his broad chest, and the almost-but-not-quite-indecent leather thong that barely hid his manhood.

Athon. The host of the party. The man who wouldn't take 'No' for an answer – or more precisely, the man who wouldn't take 'Get *lost!*' for an answer.

Aline found herself backing against the low balustrade, arms folded in front of her like a barrier. 'Hello, Athon. Party going well?'

He smiled, revealing – what else? – perfect white teeth. 'Yes, wonderfully!'

Behind Athon a sheer curtain of red stone cliffs rose to meet rose-pink sky. They were standing on the outermost edge of an intricate network of balconies of smooth white stone, inlaid with shifting mosaics, arranged around a waterfall that fell in a shimmering ribbon from a shallow V in the clifftop. The focus of the party was an auditorium through which the Eknuri had managed to persuade the water to fall in a complex double spiral symbolising their augmented DNA. They liked to boast, but in such a beautiful way.

Athon took a step towards her, suddenly serious. 'I'm a little concerned you're not enjoying yourself to the full.'

Not again. Aline smiled and slipped sideways along the balustrade, out of his reach. Fear began fluttering away in the pit of her stomach. 'Athon,' she said, her voice harsher than she meant it to be. 'I'm just a little partied out, that's all. I would prefer to be left alone for a while.'

'Partied out?'

From where Aline stood, the shimmering corkscrew of the waterfall seemed to disappear into the top of Athon's head of dark curls, making his confused expression all the more comic.

'Just a term we have back on Earth. I'll be all right in a minute.'

He'd moved closer to her, the tattoo on his bronzed chest

shifting like a living thing. 'I hope you're going to rejoin us soon. The storm is on its way.'

'I wouldn't want to miss that.' Aline was distracted by a sudden light pressure on her body. She looked down. Athon's hand was like a thing carved out of brass and marble, his fingers moulding her ribcage, dwarfing it. Aline was swamped by feelings of panic and helplessness. Fear gathered strength, creeping over her like pins and needles. Making an effort to control herself, she looked him in the eye – she had to crane her head back to make contact – and shook her head. 'Athon, I thought I'd told you. I thought you understood.' Her voice wavered, betraying her unease.

He took his hand away and stepped back, staring at his sandalled feet, like carved wood blocks on the shifting mosaics.

Once there was some distance between them Aline felt herself begin to return to normal. *They may look human*, a voice inside her mind insisted, *but they're not*. Another taunted, *It's not working – you'll be living in fear for the rest of your life*.

Aline shook her head, dismissing her inner demons. Easy enough in the sunlight but she knew they would return once she was alone in the dark.

Athon's handsome features were clouded with hurt. Aline felt guilty, as if she'd been in the wrong. 'I thought I'd explained that I don't want to participate in the more intimate Eknuri customs. I'm here as an observer, remember?'

He nodded, dark curls bobbing. He looked like a guilty child. 'I'm sorry, I'm just curious. It's just that I've never met an Earthwoman before.'

Aline doubted this – there were plenty of curious Earth visitors to Eknur 4, and tourists were becoming a bit of a nuisance. 'That's all right, Athon. Just try to control yourself in future.'

He flashed her a boyish smile. 'I will. Come and join us soon – don't miss the storm.' Then he was gone, out of her sight in just a few strides.

Aline felt absurd, as if she had been a mere mortal admonishing a God. Which wasn't too far from the truth, she reflected. There was something classical about the Eknuri physique. Their limbs were long and sinewy, their waists narrow, shoulders wide. Their features were handsome rather than beautiful. They'd be a worrying prospect, a potential über-race bent on domination, if they weren't all pacifists. Or, more accurately, hedonists, thought Aline. The pursuit of pleasure, not glory or power, was the Eknuri driving force. She could go with that – up to a point.

They still unsettled her, which was stupid, she knew. All her life she had worked so hard to contact aliens, to be with aliens, to be inside alien minds – and now she was terrified to be with a bunch of overgrown kids who were hardly different from humans. She told herself it wasn't her fault, it was the after-effect of the Encounter. But hadn't that event come about precisely *because* of her desire to know, to understand? Was the pursuit of knowledge ultimately destructive?

Aline became aware that someone was watching her, from further down the crescent-shaped balcony. A tall, dark figure was leaning against the staircase which led up to the waterfall, arms folded across her chest. She frowned. How long had Taiana been watching her? Had she seen Athon's little misdemeanour? The last thing she wanted was to be the cause of jealousy or resentment. After all, she was trying to maintain an academic distance from her subject.

Taiana unfolded herself and loped across the flagstones. She was the strangest Eknuri that Aline had met so far. An athlete, one of the best Eknuri sprinters and zero-g gymnasts, Taiana was literally super-human. Her skin was almost jet-black, there wasn't an ounce of fat on her lithe body and she wore a shining black garment that fitted her like a second skin. Her eyes were orbs of gold, and she wore a skullcap that shifted with colours like a patch of oil. There seemed to be three podgy flies buzzing around her head, orbiting like crazed satellites. Servitors, Aline knew, linked to Taiana's cortex, with access to the Eknuri datanet. Taiana carried them everywhere with her. She liked to keep in touch.

Taiana came to a halt before Aline. 'Athon been at you?'

Her voice was flat and featureless, making everything she said sound like a statement. It took a second or so for Aline to work out what she meant. 'Yes, but he didn't mean it.'

Taiana snorted, turning her bullet-black head towards the sun and squinting. 'He means it all right. Watch yourself.'

Aline felt a stir of annoyance. Despite her problems, despite only being human, she wasn't an invalid. 'Has he ever "been at" you?'

Taiana's head whipped round like a weapon sight. 'He wouldn't dare,' she intoned.

Aline felt she was on the verge of something interesting. Sex, to the Eknuri, was a communal event, almost a sport. They didn't bond for life, and as they were all physically compatible there didn't seem to be preference for one mate over another. Eknuri sexual customs were going to form a large part of her paper, but this was something new. Animosity between a male and female Eknuri? (They didn't change sex as far as Aline knew.) Evidence that, for all their incredible advances, human emotions such as jealousy and contempt still churned in their breasts?

Aline was about to form a question when the air was filled with a sudden, violent sound which seemed to pull at her mind. A roaring, tearing, rising-and-falling noise straining towards an eternally out-of-reach climax. She was unable to move – the sound awakened emotions she thought she'd locked away for good. She felt that she was about to be shown something so big her mind couldn't take it – not again.

Aline tried calling out to Taiana but her voice was stuck in her throat, like in those dreadful nights of sleep-paralysis that used to plague her. In slow motion, she saw Taiana run to the inner curve of the balcony that overlooked the central auditorium. Aline tried to follow but her feet wouldn't budge.

Then, with a jolting sensation, all was back to normal. Aline almost fell after Taiana, her senses jangling, slapping her hands on the balustrade just as the noise began to spiral away into the upper registers of her hearing.

In the exact centre of the auditorium, in front of the aperture through which the waterfall spiralled, something was forming. A ghost shape.

Aline held her breath. She felt as though she was on the verge of discovery – and madness. A small part of her was resigned to it, always knew she would fall again. She'd always suspected her sanity was temporary.

Aline screamed, a whoop of terrified exhilaration, as before the waterfall, watched by a gathering crowd of cheering, applauding Eknuri, a strange blue box solidified into existence with an echoing thump.

The TARDIS was home now. Peri had come to accept that. But sometimes it really freaked her out, like the way the layout seemed to change around without her noticing. One day the third door on the left from the console room would lead to her room, another time it would lead to the john. Even creepier, from time to time objects would appear in her room – items of clothing, ornaments, books – that she couldn't remember fetching for herself. The Doctor swore blind he didn't put them there. He'd never go into her room without her permission anyway and she trusted him on that. She had to trust him on everything. Lucky for her he was such a charming guy and so easy to get along with. Hard to believe he was a centuries-old alien. Most times he seemed as human as she was.

So if it wasn't the Doctor leaving her little gifts (a first edition of *The Catcher in the Rye*, a small cactus in a glazed earthenware pot, an ice-cold can of cream soda), then either there was somebody else living in the TARDIS, or the ship was somehow doing it by itself. Creepy. The Doctor had assured her there was no one else in the TARDIS, as far as he knew, and told her not to worry about the gifts. 'Probably the TARDIS's way of welcoming you aboard,' he'd said, frowning. 'She doesn't leave me presents any more. Better let me know if anything else appears – you never know if these things are important.'

Hardly reassuring, but the Doctor hadn't seemed too worried, so Peri began to get used to the TARDIS's little quirks. At times she wondered if the ship was trying to tell her something, but it beat her as to what. Like dreams – hard to work out whether they really meant something or whether they were just a load of unrelated junk the mind was sorting through. She wondered if, somehow, the TARDIS was reading her dreams, providing her with objects it found within her sleeping mind...

She decided to test this theory. She'd left her only pair of sunglasses in Lanzarote and so as she settled down to sleep every night she'd bring them into her drowsy mind, hoping that the TARDIS would provide in the same way it had obliged with J. D. Salinger. But the TARDIS proved no Tooth Fairy and so one morning Peri set forth into the wardrobe to dig out a pair for herself.

This time it only took her three attempts to find the wardrobe. The first door she opened led into a potting shed, occupied by a solitary garden gnome, the second into the laboratory, but the third time she came up trumps.

The wardrobe was mind-boggling. There were no walls, only a white nothingness, and the racks of clothes stretched in parallel lines into infinity, surrounded by jumbles and piles of stuff. There were hat-stands, shoe racks, tie racks, tailor's dummies and even a half-dozen wedding dresses suspended from a wire frame, like some bizarre mobile. She was sure that hadn't been there on her last visit. Something to ask the Doctor about.

Despite the wardrobe's vast size, Peri soon found what she was looking for. A pair of genuine Ray-Bans were perched on the nose of a rather dilapidated-looking teddy bear.

'Hey there, little guy,' said Peri, picking it up. 'One cool dude bear.'

The toy felt heavy and soft in her hands. Comforting. It had an old, musty smell. She wondered how long it had lain neglected, who had snuggled up to it on cold winter nights. The Doctor? Peri giggled at the image. Supporting the bear in the crook of her arm, she slid the sunglasses off its face. She gasped in dismay. The bear had no eyes, just limp threads of frayed cotton.

Shuddering, she put it back where she'd found it, on a deckchair beside a looming mahogany chiffonier. Next to this monstrosity the bear looked forlorn, its arms drooping in its lap, its sightless gaze somehow seeming to reflect on the infinite space within the wardrobe.

Peri looked around. Was this deliberate or was the TARDIS fooling with her again? And if it was deliberate what possible event could a teddy bear with no eyes prefigure? She shook her head, telling herself to stop analysing everything and just go with the flow. She fiddled with the Ray-Bans. No wonder someone had seen fit to cover up such a sad disfigurement. She avoided the bear's sightless gaze. How could she wear them now, and deprive the toy of its dignity?

Then she had an idea. There had to be a billion buttons in this place – all she had to do was find a couple of shiny black ones, some needle and thread and she could restore the bear's sight.

She slipped the shades into the pocket of her cotton shirt and was about to stride off into the endless alleyways of diverse couture when the Doctor's voice rang out.

'Ah – there you are!'

He was standing at the entrance to the wardrobe, looking serious, brisk, excited and annoyed, all at once.

Peri grinned. 'Yep, here I am!'

The Doctor looked around curiously, as if he'd never seen the contents of his own wardrobe. 'What are you doing in here?'

She felt herself blushing, not wanting to tell him about the bear. 'Doctor, I'm a nineteen-year-old girl.' She waved her hand around the racks of clothes. 'We have this thing called fashion?'

The Doctor stared over her shoulder, his eyebrows disappearing into his fringe of blond hair. 'I try not to think of some of the things I've got in here. Come along, we've landed.'

Peri's gaze flickered to the blind bear and back to the Doctor. 'Where?' She found it odd that their voices didn't echo in such an enormous space.

The Doctor frowned. 'I'm not sure exactly where but we've got quite a reception committee.' He made to turn away, then whirled back with a flap of fawn coat, as though he'd suddenly remembered something. He wagged a finger and said awkwardly: 'You know I think that outfit really suits you.' And then he was gone.

Peri grinned. He hadn't the faintest idea how to treat an American girl in her late teens, but his attempts were so sweet.

The bear's sightless gaze caught her attention and her smile faded. No time to fix you now, she thought. She picked it up and gave it a cuddle. Then, telling herself not to be so sentimental, she followed the Doctor's receding footsteps, squeezing past a rack of ball-gowns, rustling silk shirts and ghastly sequinned things that could never have been fashionable, at any time, on any planet, ever.

Chapter Two
Uninvited Guests

The Doctor looked up as Peri entered the console room. 'Who were you talking to just then?'

'No one. Myself.' She still didn't feel like telling him about the bear.

'Well, make up your mind.'

Peri didn't answer – she'd caught sight of the scanner screen. It showed a crowd of tall, tanned people in a bewildering variety of exotic gear moving around a courtyard, their manner languid and relaxed. Some of them had stopped to look at the TARDIS, and were clearly debating it, though they didn't seem surprised at its sudden materialisation.

'Who are they?'

'Eknuri.' He frowned. 'Which is odd, as we're nowhere near Eknur 4.'

Something about their build looked wrong – no, different. They were like bodybuilders, or statues come to life. All were wearing elaborate head-dresses or had sculpted hair; their bodies were adorned with jewellery and clothed with strange clinging silks and intricate laces. It was hard to tell the two sexes apart – and that was assuming there were just two. Travelling with the Doctor was forcing Peri to rethink almost everything she'd come to accept as the norm back on Earth.

Her gaze was drawn to one guy wearing way less than the others. His bronzed body was bare apart from a skimpy thong and a crescent-shaped tattoo on his chest, and his unadorned hair was a glossy golden-brown tangle. He was talking to a skinny woman in a black dress, who was staring at the TARDIS with unnerving intensity.

'Are they aliens?'

'Extremely advanced humans. They've pushed the arts and sciences to the very boundaries.' There was a ring of admiration

11

in the Doctor's voice. 'They've used genetics, physics, philosophy, literature, er, sport, all to enhance the basic human condition and elevate it to the highest level. Something much more than human.'

'Sound like a bunch of big-heads to me.' The tattooed guy was laughing at something and Peri found herself smiling at the screen. There was something natural and carefree about him that was attractive even if he was a big-head.

'You'd think that, wouldn't you?' the Doctor tapped at the TARDIS console again and to Peri's irritation the screen faded to white. 'I've met countless races of super-beings with an over-inflated sense of their own importance. The Eknuri aren't like that, though. They possess the rare gift of humility. They know how microscopic they are in the universal scheme of things. It doesn't exercise them as it does the more immature, militaristic races. Shall we go and meet them?'

Peri thought of the tall golden-skinned guy. She smiled at the Doctor. 'Why not?'

Aline wasn't surprised that the Eknuri were now more or less ignoring the strange blue box. Nothing seemed to faze them. She idly wondered what you'd have to do to put one over on the Eknuri. Crack open their home planet with your bare hands, probably. She'd overheard a couple of them chatting and they seemed to think the box was some kind of party trick. Athon had demurred, of course, but that only reinforced the view.

Now Aline felt even more isolated from the party. It was as if the arrival of the blue box was some sort of omen. For some reason it reminded her of her Encounter. Maybe her past was reaching forward to claim her. Aline went up to the box and touched it, swallowing her fear. It seemed to tingle beneath her trembling fingers, as though it were alive.

She looked round at the Eknuri, their babble of conversation and relaxed manner going some way towards calming her. She touched the blue box again, looking at it closely, opening herself up to wonder. Her initial flood of fear subsided and she found her old curiosity returning, the analytical areas of her mind beginning to creak into action. The thing could have teleported in, which meant high technology, but its appearance gave the lie to this. The wording on the top was even in Old Earth English! Could it be *that* ancient? Perhaps it was a facsimile. Perhaps it *was* a party trick. She fell to watching it from a distance, sipping from a glass of wine, turning over the possibilities in her mind.

She was the only person watching when the door opened.

Her hand flew to her throat and she let out an involuntary gasp of surprise. In an instant she realised how complacent the Eknuri were. This could be the spearhead of an enemy invasion. Then she remembered that the Eknuri had no enemies. Then two humans – or at least, humanoids – stepped from the box and her fears subsided. A little.

They weren't Eknuri, that was certain. The man was tall-ish, with fair hair and an inquisitive, pleasant face. The style of his clothes looked as antiquated as the blue box, but they were pristine, unsoiled. The girl was a real looker, with a bell of black hair, dark green eyes and sharply defined, wholesome features. She was wearing knee-length blue shorts and a white shirt tied up at the waist. The man had a protective arm on her shoulder, but the rest of his body leaned away from his companion. Curious.

Their sudden appearance had recaptured the interest of the Eknuri. A babble of laughter and comment broke out. Daeraval struck up an impromptu song about magic boxes on his vihuela, his voice rising like a kite into the salmon-hued sky. Athon strode up to the new arrivals, arms outstretched, welcoming them to the party. The girl's eyes shone as she drank in Athon's undeniable physical beauty.

Aline allowed herself a small, wry smile.

She knew she had to speak to these people, find out who they were, where they were from. A crowd of Eknuri had gathered around them, barring her way for now. She'd have to pick her moment. She felt excited, and afraid, because her lifetime's experience of alien cultures told her that despite his outward appearance, the man was alien, certainly more so than the Eknuri, maybe even as alien as...

She shuddered.

Nothing could be that alien, ever again.

Peri usually enjoyed being the centre of attention, but as the group of tall, imposing Eknuri pressed in around the Doctor and herself, she couldn't help feeling a little intimidated. She stood her ground, though, putting on her most winning smile, squarely meeting the eyes of the giants crowding her, trying to form a sense of their surroundings. They seemed to be on a courtyard suspended on the side of a cliff. Behind the TARDIS, water fell in a graceful, impossible spiral. The air was full of strange, exotic scents. Music that sounded like something between a harp and a guitar came to a flourishing finish somewhere beyond the crowd, followed by clapping and cheering.

The Doctor introduced them, not at all bothered by the beings that towered almost a foot above him. 'Hello, I'm the Doctor and this is Peri.'

As if that explained everything.

The tattooed Eknuri smiled, revealing a row of even white teeth. 'Welcome! My name is Athon. I usually frown on gatecrashers, but you arrived in such incredible style.' There was a general babble of agreement. 'I hope you'll stay for a while and enjoy my party.'

A party! Neat. Peri found herself grinning widely at Athon while her mind groped for something to say.

'Of course we will,' said the Doctor, raising his eyebrows at Peri. 'For a while.'

Athon indicated the TARDIS with a sweep of his bronzed arm which showed off his muscles to great effect. 'I have to say, great trick!'

'The TARDIS is no trick-box, I can assure you.' The Doctor sounded hurt.

'Then what is it?' asked a woman with green eyes and long, shining black hair.

'It's a time machine,' Peri blurted out.

The Doctor shot her an admonishing glance, and then smiled at

14

the Eknuri, who had been momentarily silenced by Peri's revelation. 'Well, it is.'

'How quaint,' said the green-eyed woman. 'I've always thought of building one. But there are so many more interesting things to do.'

Peri could see what type this one was – the sort of woman who'd never admit to being impressed no matter what you did.

'Such as what?' the Doctor sounded genuinely concerned.

'Come on, Seryn, admit it – this is *real* art!' The speaker had a handsome, chiselled face and long silver-grey hair which strangely didn't make him look old at all.

'Just think, Daeraval,' said a woman with braided yellow hair and pale blue eyes. 'We could go back and meet the Eknuri founders, show them how well it's all turned out.'

'That would give them a shock!' said Daeraval.

'Quite,' said the Doctor, raising his eyebrows at Peri.

Everyone – even Athon – was looking at the TARDIS and Peri was beginning to feel left out.

'Oh, ignore Yuasa,' said Seryn, green eyes glittering. 'She's our resident historian. Can you blame her for getting all excited?'

'Not really,' stammered Peri, looking for a way out of the crowd.

The woman called Yuasa collared the Doctor and began interrogating him about the TARDIS. She seemed amused rather than amazed by the prospect of time travel. Peri smiled. The Doctor was proud of his TARDIS, and often enjoyed being the centre of attention too.

Peri felt a strong yet gentle arm around her shoulders as Athon began to lead her away from the crowd, his hands a gentle pressure on her body. Despite his almost overpowering maleness there was a feminine grace in the languid way he moved.

'A traveller in time,' he said softly. 'The things you must have seen...' He sounded envious.

'Well, I haven't been travelling long.' Peri winced. Her own voice sounded so brittle, so *banal*.

'How long?' he asked. Peri couldn't help noticing that he wasn't wearing much, apart from sandals, thong and tattoo.

'Hard to say – time travel's a confusing business.' It was

something she'd heard the Doctor say and she bit her lip in embarrassment.

To her relief he laughed, a full sound like a tolling bell.

He led her up a flight of steps that led away from the courtyard to a balcony overlooking the bottle-green sea. The horizon curved so wildly that Peri staggered under a wave of giddiness. Athon fell quiet, allowing her time to drink in the view.

After a moment she turned to him. 'So why the party?'

Athon shrugged, muscled globes of shoulders heaving. 'No reason,' he said. 'We just like to get away every now and then.'

Below, a beach of pure white sand stretched into the misty distance. She could hear the slow crashing of the waves, smell the salt in the air. She took the Ray-Bans out of her pocket and slid them on. 'Great place you have here.'

'Yes it is, isn't it?' Athon said, as if it was the first time he'd realised. 'I wanted to have it on the beach or in the sea but Seryn persuaded me to put it here, because of the view. Oh well, I could always move it later.'

Peri was dying to ask how he could move such a seemingly permanent-looking structure, but she didn't want to appear naive – she was, after all, a fascinating time-travelling babe. She leaned on the balustrade, her elbow coming up against a bump, which tingled against her skin. Alarmed, she looked down to see a small white cone, about the size of a quarter. There were several of them, spaced evenly along the balcony.

'Forcefield generators.' Athon must have noticed her curious frown. 'They're for later.'

Suddenly the steeply curved horizon took on a threatening aspect. Peri stepped back from the balcony. 'Why, are you expecting an attack?'

'Attack? Here? The very idea.' His eyes widened and he grimaced at his unconscious rhyme, reminding Peri so much of the Doctor she had to take a breath.

Athon went on. 'We've seeded a real sky-bruiser of a storm. And we're going to be right on the edge of it.'

'A storm...' Peri remembered being terrified of hurricanes when

16

she was a kid. Hiding in the basement of her uncle's farm as a typhoon scoured the landscape. As if God's great vacuum-cleaner was out for a final clean-up.

'We're hoping for particularly fine lightning effects, and serious precipitation. At least six inches.' He smiled down at her. 'Don't worry, the forcefield will protect us. Not even a single drop will dampen our spirits.'

Peri couldn't imagine it ever raining here. She could feel the heat rising from the flagstones in waves. Maybe she should nip back to the TARDIS for her bikini, the lemon yellow one with black piping. But she didn't feel like leaving Athon. He might get away.

They started walking again, up a narrow staircase which led up through the waterfall. As they reached it, the waters parted like a curtain to let them through.

From up here the view was incredible, the curvature of the horizon even more disorienting. The TARDIS stood almost directly below her, but there was no sign of the Doctor.

She remembered what the Doctor had said. 'So this isn't your home planet, then?'

'This is my little retreat. Somewhere to come and let off steam.' Athon frowned and looked away, as if remembering something unpleasant. He looked back at Peri, opening his mouth as if to speak, and then changed his mind and smiled. 'And this is just a small bit of it!'

Peri found his hands on her shoulders, his arms stretching out, framing her vision like bronze balustrades, his chest-tattoo rippling like a tapestry of snakes. 'There's an arctic zone, with ice palaces, a whole mini-continent of rainforests – it's beautiful!'

The soft, firm-but-light pressure of his palms on her shoulders through the fabric of her shirt was making Peri's legs quake, her heart hammer in her chest. His eyes were so deep, so expressive, more full of life and emotion than any she'd ever seen. 'You – you say there are forests?'

'I can show you if you like.' He grinned, and leaned towards her like a conspirator. 'I've brought my favourite skyboat with me.'

Peri put her hand over her mouth, suppressing a laugh. She looked out over to sea. No sign of dark clouds yet, but Peri knew how quickly a storm could break, especially on the coast. 'Won't we get caught in the storm?'

Athon waved a hand. 'Oh, we'll be back long before that! You won't believe how fast my skyboat can go.'

Peri had to admit she was tempted. Rainforests, skyboats, hunky alien guys – and talking of alien guys...'OK – but I'd better check with the Doctor first.'

'Check what with me first?'

There was a hissing swish from behind them. Feeling Athon's hands slide from her shoulders, Peri turned to see the Doctor framed against the plunging wall of water. She felt guilty, then angry at herself for feeling guilty. 'Nothing.'

The Doctor had a familiar enthusiastic gleam in his eyes. 'I've been invited back to Eknur 4. A place I've always wanted to visit. One of the wonders of the universe!' He could barely contain himself. 'Yuasa wants me to give a series of lectures on temporal physics. How can I refuse such an offer?'

There was something about the way he was looking at her, something calculating in his gaze. Peri frowned. Had he been eavesdropping? She found the idea unpleasant. 'Hey, great! Well, you can go on your own, can't you? We've only just got here.'

The Doctor looked put out. This was going to be a struggle. 'Aren't you interested in seeing one of the wonders of the universe, Peri? As a student I thought you'd have an insatiable thirst for knowledge.'

He was trying to manipulate her. She didn't want to fall out with him, but she had to stand her ground. 'I do have an insatiable thirst for knowledge.' She looked for Athon, but he'd gone – tactfully absented himself, she supposed. 'Athon's going to show me the rainforest zone. Botany, my field.'

Touché.

The Doctor's mouth twitched in an uncharacteristically humourless smile. 'Well, off you go then. I'll wait here for you, there's no rush to get to Eknur 4 really.' Despite the breeziness in

18

his voice, he sounded piqued. And parental.

Something occurred to Peri. 'Hey, you're not jealous, are you?'

He turned to her, smiled, and then frowned. 'Whatever makes you think that?'

Peri felt herself blush. 'Well, that I want to spend time with other people.' She bit her lip. Like she was married to the Doctor!

The Doctor's expression remained set in his familiar puzzled frown, then he turned away. 'Of course not.' There was a slight edge to his voice, something Peri couldn't quite identify. Anger? Then Peri realised what it was. The Doctor was embarrassed. Hiding his true feelings – whatever they were. A silence developed between them, like an invisible eavesdropper.

Just then Athon appeared, fingers steepled before his chest-tattoo, every inch the solicitous host. 'Everything all right?'

'Yes,' said the Doctor. 'Everything's fine.'

He looked upset and Peri felt a pang of conscience. Perhaps she should ask him to come with her and Athon. But she stuck by her decision. Why should the Doctor have her all to himself? Peri set her mouth in a resolute pout, a delicious feeling of rebellion swelling her heart.

Athon took her arm and led her away. Peri didn't look back in case the Doctor tried to guilt-trip her.

Much to Aline's annoyance it took her quite some time to corner the Doctor. She'd been at the back of the crowd of Eknuri as the visitors had held court. She'd laughed when the girl had announced that the blue box was a time machine, but then the Doctor had confirmed it, seemingly in all seriousness. If he was in earnest, then he must be one of only two or possibly three species. If he was what she thought he was, perhaps he'd seen some of the things she had seen. Perhaps he could explain them to her.

She floated around pretending to enjoy the party for a while, drinking more wine and trying not to feel too giddy. She felt as if she was in a waking dream of lecherous gods and time machines.

At last she caught a glimpse of a fawn coat disappearing round the side of a pagoda. She darted after him, her small body moving with ease through the crowd of languid giants.

She found the Doctor on the outermost ribbon of the balcony, where she'd been standing when the blue box had materialised. He was staring, not out to sea, but inland. There was no sign of the girl, Peri. Lovers' tiff? No, the bond between them – as far as Aline could tell in the brief sight she'd had – had seemed platonic, like father and daughter. No, that was wrong. Teacher and pupil?

Aline went to stand beside the stranger, taking the opportunity once more to enjoy the vista of sea and sky.

He didn't seem to notice her, but he must have known she was there. She followed the line of his gaze. She could just make out the distant dot of a skyboat.

Athon. In an instant Aline grasped what must have happened.

The Doctor ran a hand through his straw-blond hair and gazed out to sea. He started muttering to himself. 'Why can I never seem to hold on to them? I try to understand them.'

Aline decided reassurance was in order.

'Don't worry, your friend's in safe hands. Athon's an experienced flier.' And not only that, she thought, but tactfully decided to keep quiet.

He seemed to notice Aline as if she'd just materialised out of nothing. He looked embarrassed. 'Is she now?' His gaze was intense, from his deep-set eyes squinting in the sun to his bared teeth.

Aline was taken aback. 'Well, yes. I think so.'

His voice and his expression softened. 'Then she probably is.' He smiled. 'Hello, I'm the Doctor.'

'I know.' They shook hands. 'Aline Vehlmann.'

He narrowed his eyes. 'I've heard of you – wait a minute, not *the* Aline Vehlmann, renowned xenologist and bio-astronomer?'

Aline backed away, feeling herself withdraw from his eager enquiry. 'Not any more,' she said in a small voice. He looked puzzled, so she coughed and shook her head. 'Sorry, actually, yes I am. I've been in retirement for a while.'

'Retirement? Surely not! Why?'

His look of concern made her feel queasy, and angry with him. The last thing she wanted was sympathy – she wasn't an invalid. 'I'd rather not talk about it.'

A brief flash of colour out towards sea caught her attention. Dozens of glittering rhomboids were scooting round the sky, darting and chafing at each other, their vanes rippling and clattering as crowds of Eknuri gathered below waved and cheered. Duelling kites. They looked like alien creatures of the air, battling for territory.

Aline shuddered and looked back towards the Doctor, who was admiring the kite-play with full enthusiasm, hat held against his chest in an oddly reverent stance.

Aline felt resentful that he'd recognised her. Only the Institute knew she was here, and the self-centred Eknuri didn't care who she was, so who was he to turn up out of the blue – literally – and chum his way into her life? 'I'm still enough of an expert to know that you're not human. Your pretty friend, maybe, but not you. What are you?'

He seemed a little taken aback by her direct approach and it gave Aline a small thrill to see how she'd rattled him. 'I, er, we're travellers,' he fudged.

'That's no answer,' Aline persisted, smiling waspishly up at him, fighting down a rising feeling of fear. 'Come on, you're a *Time Lord* and that blue box is your TARDIS, admit it.'

The Doctor flicked a small pebble from the balcony. It sailed in a steep arc, soon lost to view against the blinding whiteness of the beach. 'Right first time. Your retirement must have been a great loss to your profession.'

Aline didn't want the conversation to return to herself, but she felt too shook up to even speak. Here before her was a *Time Lord*! As ancient and alien as – she shook her head, shying away from thoughts of her Encounter. Anyway, the Doctor seemed benign enough. He'd more or less leapt right into her lap, like a friendly cat. Scrap the Eknuri paper – no one had ever published anything on these mysterious Lords of Time. She had to stick by him, at all costs. It was risky, given her state of mind since the Encounter, but it would more than justify her decision to return to the field.

The Doctor broke the silence. 'I do hope she's all right.'

'Peri? She'll be fine.' Aline was still trying to work out their relationship. Definitely not teacher–pupil; stronger than that. 'She's human, isn't she? Not a Time Lord like you.' She felt embarrassed asking but she was a bit out of practice.

The Doctor laughed. 'Oh yes, she's human all right.' He seemed to gather his thoughts. 'What am I worried about? She's quite capable of taking care of herself and no possible harm could come to her.'

He seemed to be trying to convince himself, like an over-protective parent on the eve of his teenage daughter's first date. 'You seem very close to Peri.'

The Doctor coughed. 'Well, I may not be for much longer. I've been a fool, totally misjudging her. She may leave me already. You know, she hasn't been with me for any time at all, really.' He spun around, throwing his arms out wide. 'I can show her all of time and space but I can't,' he slumped, 'I can't give her what humans really need. Especially one of her age.'

This was getting interesting. 'Which is?'

The Doctor looked away. 'You're human. You tell me.'

Aline could almost feel his embarrassment – it emanated from him like a wave.

'But I'm not of her age. I was once. Perhaps you could take me into your TARDIS and turn me into a teenager again.'

The Doctor smiled and put his hat back on. 'And go through all that angst and acne again?'

'I could handle it.' There were so many questions she wanted to ask him, she hardly knew where to start. 'What brings you here?'

'Oh, blind chance, as usual.' He smiled, as if revelling in his seeming lack of control of his own TARDIS. Aline was beginning to feel more relaxed around him. Despite being an immensely old and powerful alien, he seemed very human, more so than the Eknuri.

His face brightened, sunny in an instant. 'I'm quite pleased to have bumped into the Eknuri. You know they've invited me to lecture back on their homeworld?'

'Well, that is good news.' And so it was. Looked like Aline wouldn't have to try too hard to stick with her new subject.

She noticed that the Doctor had a stick of celery pinned to his lapel. No, not pinned – it was just *there*, clinging on somehow. Maybe it was some sort of symbiont, Aline wondered half-seriously. Or maybe he just fancied a nibble every now and then.

He seemed to notice her staring at the celery, and started fiddling with its stem. 'You haven't told me what you're doing here.'

Aline sighed. She was going to have to give something away, it seemed. 'People back home are very interested in the Eknuri, Doctor. They're seen as a beacon of hope for humanity. I'm putting together a paper on them for the Hamilton Smith Institute. My thesis is classification. Are the Eknuri still "human" in the strictest sense? Or are they so far removed as to be a separate species?'

'Good question,' said the Doctor. 'They seem all too human to me.'

They began to walk back down the balcony to the central courtyard. It was empty apart from the Doctor's TARDIS – the sight of which still sent a thrill of fear through Aline – and two Eknuri: Seryn, draped on a chaise-longue, and Taiana, sending her servitors chasing up and down the spirals of the waterfall for no apparent reason. Most of the others were crowded on the outer balconies and upper ramparts, watching the antics of the duelling kites, or waiting for the coming storm, or were inside having sex. Daeraval's sparkly refrain filtered up from somewhere below.

The Doctor walked up to the TARDIS and patted its side, looking around himself as if at a loss what to do next.

Aline went up to Seryn. She was certainly the most conventionally attractive Eknuri that Aline had met. Her pale, oval face had a gentle humanity lacking in many of the Eknuri females. Her hair was long and black, hanging with an airy lightness around her bare ivory shoulders, and her eyes were the most striking green Aline had ever seen, like sunlight falling on leaves.

'Hello, Seryn,' said Aline, crouching down next to her.

The woman paid her no attention, just lay leaning on her arm, long legs crossed under her shimmering gown.

'Suit yourself.' Aline stood up again, fighting down the hot feeling of embarrassment. Not the first time that had happened. Sometimes the Eknuri seemed to retreat inside themselves, as if pondering ultimate questions and naked truths.

But one look at the set of Seryn's lips told Aline that she was doing neither of these. She was sulking! But over what? Maybe Athon... Aline had noticed the pair talking together earlier, even kissing. Now Seryn was trying not to look bothered that Athon had run off with a human-basic. So even if Eknuri didn't bond for life, they could still get jealous, still get hurt by relationships.

In which case they were still human, as the Doctor had said. There was hope for them yet.

Something tall and hard bumped into her. Rubbing her shoulder, Aline stepped back to let Taiana pass. The tall Eknuri wandered into the middle of the courtyard, her feet falling over one another as if she was drunk, servitors circling her oil-slick head. Then one of them shot off with a noise like water thrown on a fire.

The Doctor moved to intercept Taiana, his hands reaching up to steady her shoulders. 'Are you all right?'

Taiana seemed to come to her senses. 'Yes. Of course I am.'

Aline went up to the mismatched pair – one (relatively) small and fair, the other like a slice of night come to life. She'd seen Taiana like this before, in communion with her servitors, her mind swamped with too much information.

A situation Aline could sympathise with all too well.

'What is it, Taiana? News from home?'

Taiana shook her head. 'Closer than that.'

The Doctor was instantly on the alert. 'Peri and Athon?'

Taiana waved a languid hand. 'No. Something else.' Her voice was flat and emotionless, her eyes inscrutable gold discs. 'An unanticipated vessel has entered the atmosphere, that's all.'

Chapter Three
Earth Girls Aren't Easy

Peri leaned back dazed as the desert rushed below them at insane speed. Hot, dusty air blasted around the windscreen, pulling her hair back from her face. She kept hold of her shades with one hand, the other gripped the dashboard, and her legs were braced against the chassis. It was terrifying. And there were *no seatbelts*.

She loved it. Every part of felt totally alive. She wanted to scream for the sheer hell of it. So she did.

Athon laughed. 'Isn't this wonderful?' He had to shout over the roar of the wind and the high-pitched whine of the skyboat's engine.

Peri yelled again. 'Yee-hah!'

Rushing headlong into the unknown with a complete stranger – especially a hunk like Athon – was thrilling in ways time travel could never be. She'd fallen in love with the skyboat as soon as she'd seen it. It looked so Fifties – like a speedboat crossed with a Pontiac, all silver tailfins and chrome finishing. Athon had said he'd 'invoked' it himself, whatever that meant. Peri resolved to get him to invoke one for her, when she left. If she left...

There was only one glitch. Since they'd taken off, Athon had talked exclusively about himself, showing no interest in her whatsoever. The first disillusionment. Now he was waxing lyrical about his skyboat. 'The others don't know what they're missing.' His hair was blown back from his face in a rippling stream. 'Relying on safe, sterile old warpfields. They'll never appreciate the joys of antigrav engineering.'

Thrilling though the journey was, there was a point to it, or so she'd thought. They'd been flying for what seemed like ages and there was still no sign of any vegetation. 'Are we there yet?'

'Depends on where you want to go.'

Peri looked sideways at Athon. His face was deadly serious and there was an unmistakable gleam in his eyes.

'What do you mean? I thought we were going to see a rainforest.'

Athon smiled. Peri was uncomfortably aware that he wasn't looking where they were going.

'There's plenty of time for that later.'

No there wasn't – the Doctor was probably already tired of waiting for her. Then she remembered that she was in the middle of an admittedly rather childish act of rebellion, so she leaned towards Athon. 'Where else do you suggest?'

Athon grinned. 'I have a place in the mountains, where I entertain my special friends.'

Peri felt a weight on her bare leg. She looked down to see Athon's hand cupping her right knee and smoothing upwards towards her inner thigh.

His voice sounded close to her ear – too close. 'Take those glasses off so I can see your eyes.'

Peri shrank away. 'Hey!' she cried, slapping his hand. 'Get off me!'

He took his hand away and returned it to the steering wheel, his face indifferent.

Peri found herself vainly trying to pull the hems of her denim shorts further down to cover up her legs. She folded her arms and glared at Athon. 'Well, aren't you going to apologise?'

He shrugged, his muscled arms flexing. 'What for?'

Peri's lips curled in disgust. The second, major, and final disillusionment. Right now Athon looked uglier than anything she'd ever seen. 'You're supposed to be the peak of human evolution, but you're not even half a step up from the dumb jocks I had to put up with in college. All you're interested in is fast cars, talking about yourself, and getting laid!'

She sat back, feeling flushed and self-righteous. 'Take me back to the Doctor. At least I know I'm safe with him.'

'If that is what you wish.' He seemed unconcerned, which only made Peri more angry.

'It certainly is, buster.'

'I think you're being rather foolish, over nothing.' He flashed her a smile which made her flesh creep. 'Perhaps the Doctor neglected to inform you of our customs. I've bonded with all the women back at the party – Seryn, Yuasa, Taiana, even the Vehlmann woman. It's just something we do, for fun.'

'Yeah, well, where I come from we have customs as well. Not treating women like lumps of meat is one of them.'

'Well, I'm sorry you don't understand.'

He sounded totally insincere but at least he was doing what she'd asked. They were banking in a wide arc. Suddenly there was a low beeping sound from the dashboard.

Athon frowned. 'We seem to have visitors.'

Wary in case this was a ploy to give him another chance to feel her up, Peri craned round.

Above the silver tailfin of the skyboat the pink-white sky rippled in an exhaust haze through which Peri could make out the omnipresent peaks of the mountains. And something else. A dark shape, about level with them, approaching fast. Its angular outline reminded her of the spy-planes she'd seen on TV. Those things had always given her the creeps. Ships of silent death.

She turned back to Athon. Maybe there was a simple explanation. 'More party guests?'

'Maybe. Don't recognise the vessel. Could be Orchios, he loves big ships and things.' Athon frowned. 'Thought he was away strato-surfing on Voriakaan, though.'

Peri turned round again. The thing was nearer now, its central mass spanning the tailfin, its presence accompanied by a low rumble of powerful engines. 'Shouldn't you try hailing them, or something?'

Athon shrugged. 'Already tried. Whoever they are, they want to play.' To Peri's alarm he turned round, taking both hands off the wheel, waving his arms at their pursuers. 'So you want to race, friend?'

Peri leaned over and steadied the steering wheel. Not that they could bump into anything several hundred feet above ground, but it made her feel more secure. As Athon clambered back into position her hand accidentally brushed his buttocks.

He grinned. 'Seems like they're not the only ones who want to play.'

Peri shrank away from him. Hadn't he got the message? 'Hell will freeze over first.'

Athon hunched over the wheel. 'Let's give them a run for their money.'

If Peri had thought they were going fast before, now they were practically supersonic. She yelled as the small skyboat leapt forwards in a crushing blast of acceleration which seemed to leave her guts way behind.

It had stopped being fun. Something told her they were rushing headlong into danger. 'Athon, slow down!'

Athon's wild laughter merged with the shrieking whine of the engine. The view ahead was a streak of white and pink. The wind screamed in her face. Suddenly Peri's shades were snatched from her head, gone for ever.

'Great,' she muttered, squinting in the suddenly-bright desert light.

And then they were in shadow.

Peri looked up and saw a scarred rust-red underbelly so near she thought she could touch it.

'Come on!' cried Athon, though whether he was urging on his skyboat or taunting the dark shape which bore down on them Peri couldn't tell.

This was no game, she knew it. 'Get us out of here!' she screamed, not caring any more how fast they were going, her voice subsumed in the shrieking of engines and buffeting roar of the wind.

Suddenly there was a crack like a gunshot and the skyboat began to plummet like an out-of-control lift. Peri gripped on to the sides of her seat as she felt herself being yanked bodily upwards. Her stomach turned over again and she retched, bringing a sour taste of bile into her mouth.

Athon was wrestling with the steering wheel, his eyes at last showing some trace of fear, though his mouth was twisted in a grimace of concentration. The engines were cutting in and out, there one second, gone the next. Ahead, an endless white sheet of sand rushed up to meet them.

Peri wiped her mouth and filled her lungs, ready to scream again. An image of the eyeless teddy bear popped into her mind, then the Doctor's face, then her room in the TARDIS. Certain she was going to die, she struggled to think of something profound, make peace with the universe, but they were going too damn *fast* and the air was tearing at her clothes and oh God she was gonna barf again and –

They hit the ground with a bump that jolted all the breath out of Peri and made her bite her tongue. The taste of blood mingled with bile and made her feel even more sick. They bounced into the air a few times. Hot stinging sand dashed into Peri's face and she covered her eyes with her hands. Now everything was a red blur. She felt herself thrown violently from side to side as the skyboat skidded and swerved over the rippling sand. She could hear Athon laughing – did the guy have no concept of danger? – and the swish and bump of the desert beneath them. Blinking rapidly, she cleared the gritty sand out of her eyes at the same time that Athon let out a full-throated yell.

She saw something looming directly ahead of them – a fang-like rock. There was no way they were going to avoid it.

Athon spun the steering wheel and grabbed Peri, forcing her across his lap.

'Hey!' she cried, her voice muffled against his tight stomach. Then she realised what he was trying to do – use their weight to swing them round the rock. Suddenly there was a jarring impact and the vehicle flipped away from under Peri, sending her flying through the air, arms and legs windmilling. She hit the ground face down, stunned, eyes gummed shut with tears and sand, body numb with shock, no sound in her ears but the roaring of her own blood.

She lay immobile for a few moments, and then rolled over on her back in her self-made trough of sand, feeling the heat of the sun press down on her with almost physical weight. She felt weak and woozy. Was anything broken? Where was Athon?

Peri sat up and wiped the sand out of her eyes, wincing in the desert glare. The first things she saw were her knees, blooded and grazed by her fall. Beyond them, the ground levelled away into the heat-haze.

Through which a line of tall figures were marching, shimmering black phantoms.

Another line of figures seemed to be drifting above them.

Peri squinted. Was it an illusion caused by the heat-haze? Or was she concussed? She could hear a mechanical chattering that sounded somehow familiar.

She scrambled to her feet, trying to get a grip on things. This could still be a jape by Athon and his pals – or it could be trouble. What did she have to lose by assuming the latter? Only her dignity, and by the state of her that was already pretty well shot. She backed away from the advancing figures, still trying to make them out. They were tall, with long muscular legs and elongated bodies. Humanoid, not human; their V-shaped heads had pointed ears and long snouts. She could hear the growling and snickering of their voices – they didn't sound friendly. They were carrying large, gun-like objects – no, to hell with it, those *were* guns.

This was no game.

As for the ones in the air, she hadn't been hallucinating. Above their heads, rotor-blades whirled in a shimmering blur. Like miniature personal helicopters...

Peri didn't wait to see or hear any more. She turned and ran, stumbling as her feet sank into the yielding sand. Her heart leapt with relief when she saw Athon sprawled by the side of the skyboat. It looked miraculously intact, its gleaming silver surface as pristine as the moment she'd first seen it. Perhaps it had some sort of self-repairing forcefield – she sure wished she did.

As Peri staggered towards him, Athon sat up and got unsteadily to his feet.

'Athon!' she cried, indicating the line of advancing figures with a wave of her hand.

In answer there was a distant click, like the release of a safety catch. Something whistled past her ear and thudded into the side

30

of the skyboat. It glinted in the sun, a gleaming metal bolt.

Cackling laughter from behind told her that they had meant to miss. They could easily have hit her. They were toying with her.

She was close enough to see Athon's face now, contorted in fear, his mouth hanging open, eyes unseeing. He was shaking his head. To her utter disbelief, he scrambled into the skyboat.

Peri ran faster, brushing stinging sweat from her eyes. 'Hey, you bastard!'

But it was too late. The skyboat lifted vertically from the ground, slowly and gracefully, and began to move off. She could hear its engines, the note wavering and falling. It must have sustained some damage after all.

Peri ducked as a chattering, whirring sound came from directly overhead.

Two of the fliers bore down on the skyboat as it came about. She could see their dangling legs and brush-like tails. She got a good look at one of them in profile as it turned to bark a command to its colleague. It looked like a fox or a wolf, with reddish fur and black-pointed ears.

She could see Athon's terrified face framed with his sand-caked golden-brown hair as he looked over his shoulder. The skyboat picked up speed, but it wasn't enough. The two fox-creatures swooped – their rotor-blades churning the air dangerously close to each other – and reached down in unison, plucking Athon from his seat.

The skyboat flew on, gaining height but not much speed. Perhaps it was on autopilot, heading back towards the party. A party that now seemed like a distant memory.

Peri sank down on her knees, mouth agape. The creatures drifted apart, stretching Athon between them. His mouth was open but she couldn't hear his screams over the sound of the rotor blades. They bore him off into the distance, where Peri could see the dark shape of their pursuer hovering above the sand.

Footsteps scuffed behind her. Peri twisted round, getting to her feet, ready to run some more.

But there was no point in running. There was nowhere to run. There were too many of the creatures standing in a ragged circle around her, tongues lapping out of their black-lipped jaws, tails swishing from side to side. Their eyes were golden-yellow and slanted, shining with purpose and hunger, a wild evil glee at being alive. There was no pity in them, nothing she could appeal to.

Suddenly the smell of the creatures hit Peri in an almost solid wave, a heady animal musk. She retched again, spots of bile darkening the white sand.

The creatures barked with laughter at this.

Well, if she was gonna die, she was gonna die as Peri Brown, not some cowering wretch. Still feeling sick and light-headed, Peri got to her feet and folded her arms. 'If you're going to kill me, get on with it.'

One of the fox-creatures stepped forwards. Peri tried not to shrink back. It thrust its face right down to hers. To Peri's disgust and confusion, it leaned forward and licked her face, from her neck right up to her hairline with a tongue as long as her forearm. Its soft wetness slithered over her face like a gigantic slug, leaving her coated with stinking juices. She gagged at the fetid smell of the creature's breath as it wheezed over her, its saliva dribbling into her eyes. What did this mean? Were they going to kill her, eat her, or – she felt afraid of hoping – spare her?

The chattering laughter came again, and the creature stepped back, its eyes lustful, licking its lips, relishing the taste of Peri's sweat. Peri felt her eyes drawn to its teeth. Unlike those of a fox or wolf, they were clustered closely together, rooted in grey gums spotted with black, and had a polished blue-white sheen.

There was a definite air of anticipation among the others. They were crowding closer, licking their lips, drool pooling on the sand.

The leader swung round and hissed at them. They backed off, tails swinging.

The leader turned to face Peri again. Slowly, it reached into a pouch on its waist and drew out a small, stubby pistol.

Peri sighed. Well, at least they weren't going to eat her alive.

It raised the gun.

Peri thought of the blind bear back in the TARDIS. Now it would never get its shades back. Perhaps it had been a warning – maybe it meant that you could never tell the future, never see what was going to happen next.

The smiling fox-creature pulled the trigger. Peri felt a sharp stinging in her side, and then her body turned to lead and everything went black.

Chapter Four
Taken by Storm

'Oh, it's probably a joke.' Seryn's green cat-eyes flashed up at Aline, and then narrowed their aim on the Doctor. 'Or more gatecrashers.' She stretched and yawned, almost falling off her chaise-longue.

Which was overdoing the utopian languor a bit, thought Aline.

The Doctor ignored her and addressed Taiana, his voice urgent, expression intense. 'Tell me more.'

'There's nothing more,' said Taiana. 'It's small, fast and heading down towards the desert some miles away.'

The Doctor shook his head in disbelief. 'Aren't you even slightly curious?'

'A little,' Taiana admitted, lips parting to reveal the pale pink tip of her tongue. 'But we'll find out who it is when they get here. Anyway, I've sent a servitor to intercept it.' Her golden eyes narrowed to slits as, for the first time, Aline saw her smile. It wasn't pretty, like some devil mask. 'We're in no danger.'

The other Eknuri murmured their agreement. Somewhere below, Daeraval began a new song.

No danger. How could there be, in such a tranquil haven? But Aline felt her old fears swirling around the back of her mind, ready to leap out and take over. Since the Encounter, she'd always been able to sense things. The presence of someone behind a closed door, a friend's image popping into her mind a few minutes before they called, always knowing exactly what the time is, all sorts of seemingly commonplace coincidences. She'd undergone psych-testing without ever thinking she'd rate above the norm, but she had. Far above. Her therapist had a theory that her Encounter had awakened Aline's latent psychic abilities. Half-intrigued, half-scared by this revelation, Aline had never tried to develop these powers, and tried to suppress them most of the time, but sometimes she couldn't help it.

Like now. Something was coming, she knew. Something that wasn't the storm. Something far more powerful, more destructive...

And she could almost see the Doctor thinking, his mind racing ahead of everyone else's. Since Taiana's announcement his relaxed manner had fallen away and he'd become animated, driven by his exasperation with the Eknuri and concern for Peri.

'Is there any other means of transport on this planetoid?'

Seryn and Taiana exchanged amused glances.

'Only Athon's skyboat,' said Seryn. 'And your little time machine.'

The Doctor swung away, mouth closed in a thin line.

Perhaps he sensed something, too. Aline went up to him. 'Can you feel it?'

'Feel what?'

Aline felt suddenly embarrassed. 'A sense of oppression.' She winced. She always found it difficult putting into words what her mind was trying to tell her.

He peered into her eyes. 'Are you sure you're all right?'

Aline smiled and tried not to think of how false it looked. 'Fine,' she lied. 'Whoever these visitors are, we're safe enough here. Eknuri technology will protect us.'

He put his arm around her and led her to one side. 'Do you really believe that?'

'No.' Aline was surprised to realise that this was the truth. She looked nervously up into the sky, then out to sea, realising how vulnerable they were. At any moment, a warship could come screaming over the top of the cliff, or skimming across the sea. But all she could see was a darkening sky above them, clouds growing imperceptibly thicker by the minute. The kites had been stilled in anticipation of the coming storm.

She turned to the Doctor. 'What do you think we should do?'

'Gather all available information and await further developments.' His gaze seemed to reach into her mind. She turned away, looking out to sea again. But this time it failed to soothe her. It looked threatening, an arena into which at any moment an aggressor might step.

Aline ran a hand through her wind-blown hair and looked over at Seryn. 'Their complacency gives me the creeps. How can they be so sure it's nothing?'

'They've never been at war, they exist within a technocracy which protects them from the vagaries of life, unlike us lesser mortals.'

Aline looked at him narrowly, amused that he could consider himself as such. 'Think how I feel.'

The Doctor suddenly snapped into life, pacing around, one finger raised. 'This planetoid hasn't any defences as such – they're relying on some sort of subspace warp to whisk them all home at the first sign of trouble, yes?'

Aline remembered her brief but disorienting journey through the Eknuri warpfield. Cleverer and more elegant than traditional matter transportation but just as stomach-churning. 'Yes, and if the worst comes to the worst the whole place can be tucked away into hyperspace. Or the Eknuri can bring their "big guns" through the warpfield.' Aline didn't have any clear conception of the Eknuri defence system, except that it was silent, invisible and terrifyingly effective.

'So even if we are attacked, we've got nothing to worry about,' said the Doctor. His optimistic words were laced with acid sarcasm.

Aline smiled. 'Maybe. Except this whole party seems to me like a group of children who've gone into the woods without telling the grown-ups where they're going.'

'Well, it's about time someone started acting *in loco parentis*.' The Doctor darted back across the courtyard to where Taiana sat hunched on a stone bench. 'Any word from your servitor yet?'

Taiana shook her head and frowned. 'No.'

'Taking rather a long time, isn't it?'

Taiana shrugged.

'Well, can't you get in touch with Athon's skyboat?'

Seryn's mouth curled in a smirk. 'Already tried. He's cut it. Obviously enjoying your young friend.'

Aline winced.

The Doctor's mouth twitched, but he made no comment. Instead he turned back to Taiana. 'What about the forcefield? I noticed some generators around here earlier.'

Taiana rolled her eyes heavenwards.

'What's wrong with it?'

'It's decorative – won't be any defence against energy weapons,' explained Seryn.

'Decorative?' The Doctor looked perplexed.

Aline sidled up to him. 'They've whipped up a storm for their entertainment. The forcefield's to keep the rain off, nothing more.'

Already the light, strained through the tailor-made clouds, had taken on a dusty, tired aspect which only added to Aline's feeling of doom.

The Doctor raised his eyebrows. 'Such frivolous use of technology. Anyway, I advise you activate it until we know if these visitors are peaceful,' he glanced at Aline, 'or otherwise.'

Taiana dipped her chin towards the tiled floor. 'Whatever.'

'Well, go on then!'

Taiana flashed him a look of golden fire, and flexed her fingers to indicate the two servitors orbiting her head. 'It's done.'

'And I also suggest you activate your warpfield in case we need to escape.'

Taiana stood, like a black piston thrusting upwards. 'We are more than capable of taking care of ourselves. Thank you for your concern.'

The Doctor sighed, thrust his hands deep into his coat pockets and whirled away.

Aline hid a smile behind a pale hand. Sarcasm, now – nice to know the Eknuri weren't above the lowest form of wit. Then, as she brushed away a stray lock of hair, she saw, out of the corner of her eye, a black speck following the line of the cliffs, too far away yet to make out any detail.

She hurried up to the Doctor and grabbed his sleeve, pointing with her other hand. 'Look.'

The Doctor and Aline watched as the speck approached, grew larger. Aline winced as it flashed bright silver in the sunlight.

A flat voice from beside her. 'Athon's skyboat.' Taiana had come to join them, her face a mask of concern. At last an Eknuri was paying more than cursory attention to the situation. Aline felt reassured by her statuesque presence, as if Taiana could bring the Eknuri defences to bear with just a snap of her long black fingers.

The Doctor stepped up to the edge of the balcony. 'It's heading right for us.' He frowned. 'It's damaged.'

Aline could hear its engines now, a low complaining whine.

'It's out of control,' said the Doctor. 'Taiana, is there any way your servitors can gain control of the skyboat?'

Even as he spoke one of the bee-sized AIs zipped away towards the approaching vehicle, passing through the forcefield with a noise like a whiplash. The one remaining in orbit around Taiana's head looked to Aline rather lonely.

The skyboat was on a level course with them now, and only a hundred metres away. Aline couldn't see the servitor. Taiana's mouth moved wordlessly as the AI sent streams of information back to her.

'Can't – lock,' shouted Taiana suddenly. 'Down!'

Strong fingers gripped Aline's shoulder, pulling her towards the ground. She couldn't stop herself from looking up, to see the skyboat skim the edge of the forcefield. There was a crackle and a flash, and the skyboat skimmed away, careering down towards the beach.

Aline leaned over the balustrade in time to see the skyboat hit the ground some fifty feet below, a little way along from them. It sent up a fan of white sand, skimmed across the beach and came to rest upside-down, half-in and half-out of the water. Wavelets lapped at it like investigating fingers.

'Come on,' said the Doctor.

'Where are you going?' said Taiana, her head tilting in a curious weaving movement as the other servitor returned to its orbit. 'It was empty.'

The Doctor's face was flushed red. 'I know. Don't you care about Athon?'

Taiana shrugged, her voice dull, but with a sullen, threatening edge, like distant thunder. 'He's done this sort of thing before. Last time we were here he trapped some of us in some kind of replicating web. Crystalline duplicates of ourselves everywhere. If we go to investigate, something similar will happen.'

The Doctor's face darkened and he stepped right up to Taiana. 'Show me how to get down to the beach. Then go and ready everyone for immediate departure.'

Taiana blinked, her golden eyes going on-off-on like tiny lights, and her mouth opened in a silent gape of astonishment.

Seryn yawned, eyes scanning the horizon. By now the sky was a dark lead-grey belly of clouds, casting an immense shadow over the sea, and over the party. A nagging wind had whipped up from nowhere. Seryn shivered. She had gone up to the highest point of the installation, right next to the waterfall, for some reason which for the moment eluded her drink-dazed mind. Everyone else was crowded below in the main courtyard. Servitors orbited each other in the stream of water below Seryn, ready to fully invoke the warpfield. It didn't have to be this complicated; people took the warpfield for granted and Seryn had wanted to make them think about it, so she'd programmed the servitors to invoke the field within the water itself so that the party guests would appear to step out of the waterfall as they arrived. A rebirth from water.

Seryn looked out to sea again. Nothing but a bruised cloudscape and an ocean agitated by the beginnings of the storm. It would be a pity if they had to leave before the weather event. She'd spent a long time programming it with Athon. It was all this Doctor's fault. She was sure he was a friend of Athon's, sent to work an elaborate trick on them all. She wondered what it would be this time. A fake alien invasion? That would be fun!

So why did she feel sick inside? What had made her come all the way up here?

Athon. Seryn realised, with a slow dawning sense of surprise, that she was worried about him. She laughed nervously, the sound catching in her throat.

'Share the joke, Seryn!'

She spun round. Daeraval had stepped through the waterfall, long grey hair lifting in the wind, eyes twinkling.

'There's no joke,' she blurted out. 'Something's wrong – I can feel it.'

Daeraval laughed. 'It's just the storm affecting your head.' He extended a hand. 'Or the wine! Come back down and join us. You'll miss the fun when all is revealed.'

Seryn wasn't sure it was all a joke any more, but she took Daeraval's hand anyway, allowing him to lead her back down the narrow staircase. Made more sense to stay near the warpfield if there was really anything wrong.

As she stepped into the courtyard Yuasa handed her a goblet of wine, from which she took a grateful gulp.

Yuasa and Daeraval exchanged amused glances.

'You're hitting it hard,' said Yuasa. 'Anything wrong?'

'She senses something wrong,' said Daeraval, wiggling his fingers at Seryn.

Seryn shook her head and smiled, trying to play things down. 'The only thing wrong is your dreadful singing,' she drawled.

Daeraval looked mortified for a second, then laughed. 'Seryn, for that I will serenade you all night!'

Just then, Taiana pushed her way through the crowd towards them. She cannoned into Yuasa, sending her flying.

'Hey!' cried Yuasa, grabbing on to Daeraval for support.

Seryn reached out and touched Taiana's shoulder. 'Are you all right?'

Suddenly Taiana grasped her head and folded to the ground, letting out a strangled, keening whine that made Seryn feel cold inside.

A circle formed around Taiana as she writhed on the floor, her long body curling and folding like a wounded serpent.

Seryn felt as if the world was dropping away from her. She knew for fact now that something was badly wrong.

Everyone was looking at everyone else, not really knowing what to do. Illness was virtually unknown. Servitors did all the diagnosis and healing that was necessary. Seryn glanced over at Taiana's servitors, still whirling away in the spiral waterfall. Then with a sudden burst of steam they exploded, sending the crowd screaming and running for cover. At the same moment a shadow closed over the courtyard like a lid.

Seryn looked up and gasped, her legs turning to water, hair flailing in a sudden hot wind. Something was falling from the clouds, something dark, a progeny of the storm. She heard Yuasa screaming. She'd never heard anyone scream before, unless in pleasure or abandonment. Never in fear. The sound rooted her to the spot, fascinated her. Yuasa's face was stretched, distorted, the eyes mad and wild. Screaming, running figures jostled Seryn and she fell on to the mosaic she'd invoked only a few hours earlier. Legs and feet bumping her, Seryn crawled for cover. Above, the dark thing hovered, roaring and shuddering. There were gunshots and screams.

Seryn reached the edge of the courtyard and stood up, back against the wall. She could see the dark thing more clearly now; some kind of ship of horribly ugly design. Figures descended from it, abseiling down on ropes or flitting about on portable helipacks, firing on her friends, her lovers... She saw Daeraval fall, clutching his chest, disappearing from view in the milling throng.

Seryn felt her legs tremble. She wanted to run, but there was nowhere to run. This couldn't be happening. Where was Athon? Why was this happening? Why here, why now, to her?

Through streams of tears mingled with rain she saw Yuasa in the grip of one of the brutes, its head darting forward, jaws clamping around her neck. Blood began to flow in thick spurts down Yuasa's robe, over her weakly flailing arms.

Seryn stared in fascination at the creature. It was as tall as her, possibly taller, a thing of stinking blackness, red fur and pitiless eyes. It had Yuasa in a grotesque parody of a hug now, huge shoulders obscuring her face, head shuddering as it worried at her throat. Yuasa's screams descended into an obscene liquid gargle. Then the creature released her and she dropped to the ground like a broken doll. Three of the beasts crowded round her, dropping to all fours, their teeth flashing in the dull light. Seryn heard the rip and shred of Yuasa's clothes, the growling of the creatures as they fed.

It had all happened in seconds. Now Yuasa was gone for ever, torn from life as easily as a page from a book. And just as irreplaceable.

Seryn fell to the ground and curled up, willing reality away, hoping against hope that this was all some drug-induced hallucination.

Something hit her in the back, hard, and hands grabbed her, turning her over. She opened her eyes and screamed. A pair of feral yellow eyes burned into hers, alight with hunger. It snorted, spraying her with mucus. She felt a crunching pain in her ribs as it kicked her. Seryn cried out, suddenly indignant – what gave this filthy thing the right to hurt her? Then it kicked her again, harder. She curled around the pain, gasping, hoping that this was some joke, that suddenly she'd be whisked back to Eknur 4, that she wasn't going to die like Yuasa.

And then the storm broke, with a peal of distant, disapproving thunder. A forgotten entertainment, the rain began to stream down but the attacker's ship prevented even one drop of it from falling on Seryn.

Chapter Five
A Taste of Rain

Aline had left her strappy shoes on a shelf of rock at the foot of the cliff. The sand was warm on her bare soles. It was cooler down on the beach, a long insistent gust of wind sweeping diagonally across the sand to bother the cliffs. The Doctor seemed preoccupied, intent on the crashed skyboat that lay on the shore ahead of them like a beached sea-creature. He'd managed to whip up a token sense of urgency in the Eknuri and the warpfield had been invoked on standby, ready to whisk them all off at the slightest hint of danger.

As they walked side by side, a sickening thought occurred to Aline. What if the Doctor was behind it all? The fear returned, gripping her insides like frost. She knew it well enough to catch it early and prevent it warping the facts. Time Lords never interfered, that was one fact. They certainly never harmed anyone. That was another. Aline forced herself to relax. Everything would be all right - they'd find Peri and Athon and they could all go back and have some more wine.

They were almost upon the skyboat now. Empty, Taiana had said, of anything living. Aline tried to make out if she could see anything in the shadows beneath the upturned vessel, and shuddered.

She stood back as the Doctor ran up to the crashed skyboat. He leaned down and peered underneath. Aline bit her lip.

He stood up again, shoulders slumping, hair blown back by the wind. 'Empty,' he said. Then his eyes widened. 'Oh, no.'

Suddenly, the sound of engines boomed along the cliffs like a peal of thunder.

The Doctor ran up to Aline, grabbing her shoulders and whirling her round, her black dress flapping around her in a sudden breeze. She heard his voice close by her ear. 'The "unanticipated vessel"...'

From the ceiling of clouds that now pressed down over the clifftops, an alien ship descended like a great black bird, its wings curling down over the party installation, angular figures streaming down from it like spores of death. Aline saw an Eknuri leap over a balcony, only for two of the figures to descend upon him, bearing him to the ground. She saw a trio of women herded into a corner by a brace of the attackers. She heard their screams. She turned away, her whole body shuddering.

The Doctor looked at the azure crystal crescent in his palm – their link to the warpfield – closed his fist and shook it angrily in the air. 'Why haven't they activated the warpfield?'

If they had, they wouldn't be standing on the beach any more. 'Perhaps they were overcome... no time to react.' Aline found herself staring at the ship, its engines screaming as it maintained its predatory position. More of the attackers were descending from it now. Something about the shape of their heads was familiar...

The Doctor's face was a grimace of pain. 'Oh, Peri...' he breathed. He tossed the warpfield crystal on to the white sand where it lay like a lost jewel. Then he turned to Aline. 'Whoever they are, their intentions are clearly hostile. We can't go back for the TARDIS, so there's only one thing to do. Hide.' He pointed up the beach, where black cave-mouths gaped. 'If we're quick, they might not notice us.'

The caves looked a long way away. Aline felt rooted to the spot, like a statue in the sand. She became aware of a strange sensation, cool pinpricks on her face and arms. She looked up. The sky had now completely clouded over; the seeded storm was about to bear fruit.

'Come on,' urged the Doctor. He started haring across the beach, sending up white puffs with each stride. Aline followed, toes digging in the sand, shoes forgotten, as heavy spots of rain began to fall from the leaden sky.

Hunt Marshal Veek glared down at the fallen human, her lips curling back in a low snarl. The creature just lay there, in a pool of its own urine, like the sack of meat that it was. The pungent scent filled Veek's nostrils, almost overwhelming her.

It was good to be hunting, to be free, however briefly. Pity this prey was hardly worth the hunt. It hadn't even tried running away. Veek hunched down, hauling its head up by its hair, causing it to moan in pain. It was in shock. Pathetic. Wide unfocused eyes shimmered in an oval of damp pink flesh. Veek could feel her salivary glands squirting with bloodlust. However pathetic, at least it was meat – real meat.

Veek released the creature's head and stood up, swivelling around, always alert for any threat though she was certain there could be none from such a pallid, cowering lot.

All around, hunters were snaring the last of the prey, toying with them, goading them into paroxysms of fear before loosing their stun-darts. Veek let them have their fun. They would be returning to the long sleep soon, a prospect none of them relished, Veek least of all.

The creature at her feet had started moaning again, and was trying to crawl away, its cold wet eyes fixed on Veek. A sour anger curdled in Veek's powerhouse heart. This would be their last hunt before the next stage and she'd prayed for it to be a planet full of prey, diverse and sinewy, putting up a good fight, promising stringency and flavour. Not these useless cubs. Even more pathetic than the usual type of human.

At least there had been fire in the eyes of the beast they'd caught out on the plain. At least that one had run, and there had been defiance in its glare when Veek had shot it. But *this* thing! Now it had crawled under a stone bench and was sobbing like a vixen in labour. Irritated, Veek reached under the seat and dragged it out, hissing at its frantic struggles. She shot in the back of the neck. It was still in an instant, its panting subsiding into the deep breaths of slumber.

Her anger barely spent, Veek kicked the prone sack of meat. Though her every instinct screamed at her to fall upon this creature and devour it, she knew she had to preserve the thing. Her long jaw twisted in a dark-hearted grin. When the prey woke in a hundred or so years' time, the first and last things it would see would be Veek's eyes burning with hunger, Veek's sharp teeth sinking into its own worthless flesh. She couldn't wait to gulp down its blood, drink in its screams, drown in its pain.

She sensed rather than saw something move above her and looked up to see the skirmisher lift away, off to find a landing-place. The sky it revealed was stone-grey, and Veek felt heavy splashes of rain spatter her face, making her blink. She opened her mouth, feeling the raindrops hit her tongue and run down her throat, little rivulets of water, cool and fresh.

The sensation awoke something within Veek; an image of home, of green fields and forest seen through sheets of rain. She shook her head, dismissing the mental picture. She'd probably never see home again, she told herself. Had to get used to it. A sacrifice they all had to make.

Quick footsteps behind her. She swung round, harpoon-gun at the ready, then relaxed. 'Hunter Flayoun.'

Flayoun was her mate, a heavy-built hunter with a pleasing green tint in his yellow eyes and a flash of white across the top of his head and left ear. Raindrops beaded his whiskers, which was cute. Veek grinned. The fur around his mouth was dark with blood; unlike her, he'd been unable to resist indulging his bloodlust. She let it pass; that was why, after all, she was Hunt Marshal. She was able to resist temptation. Most of the time.

She stepped close to Flayoun and licked the blood and rain from his face. The image of her homeworld returned, stronger this time: she saw the valley in which she was born, the warm, dry den from which she used to watch the rain as a cub. Sometimes she'd run outside with the other young hunters and chase prey through the fields, their hot blood keeping their drenched bodies warm.

With this memory came a longing so sharp it was almost pain.

Fighting away emotion, she stood back from Flayoun, and pointed down at the unconscious human. 'Take that back to the skirmisher with the rest.'

With one scoop of his arm, Flayoun hauled the body over his wide shoulder.

Veek looked around. 'Any more?'

Flayoun shook his head 'All rounded up – except a few.'

'What happened to them?'

Flayoun's eyes glittered through the rain. 'Hunters hungry.'

Veek gave him a brisk nod. That couldn't be all, could it? They'd detected only one settlement on this ridiculously small world, and this was it. The humans they'd snared out in the desert had been a bonus. But Veek sensed there were more of them, hiding somewhere near.

She leaned over the balcony. There, half in and half out of the water, was the tiny vessel they'd shot down. From it, a double line of footsteps led to the foot of the cliffs some distance to the left, blurring slowly in the thickening rain.

Veek turned to Flayoun. He was still holding the stunned human. She licked her lips. 'Dump that. Let's hunt.'

The Doctor and Aline had wormed their way to the back of the smallest cave, little more than a vertical slit in the sandy rock. It was dark and dry, the entrance shrouded by the rain which had begun to fall, slowly at first and then with greater intensity.

Aline sank into the shadows, clutching her knees, heart still pounding from the exertion of the run. She couldn't remember the last time she'd run in fear. The last time she'd tried was during her Encounter, only there had been nowhere to run then. And there was nowhere to run now, only a shivering wait in a dead-end cave.

The Doctor stood against the smooth rock wall, eyes intent on the entrance. His voice was a whisper. 'With any luck the rain will wash away our tracks.'

Aline began to laugh, then found herself unable to stop, her whole body seized in a juddering fit. Tears made her vision swim. She pressed her hands on to her face, the palms crushing her lips against her teeth, fingers massaging her streaming eyes.

When she surfaced again the Doctor was before her, eyes searching her face. 'Are you all right?'

The banality, yet sincerity, of the question made Aline want to cry again. She answered in kind. 'Yes, thank you.' She could hardly speak, her throat constricted with fear.

His eyes showed understanding and suddenly Aline felt that she could confess to this alien who wore the shape of a man. His hand covered hers, a warm dry presence like the pages of a much-loved book. She felt some of her tension ebb away.

'Aline, did you manage to get a good enough look at them to determine their species?'

Aline nodded, sending drips of cold water down on to her bare shoulders. 'Yes. I hope I'm wrong, but I don't think I am.'

The Doctor leaned towards her eagerly, shrugging off his jacket and folding it around her. The lining was still dry and she snuggled into it, grateful for the warmth.

'Go on,' he whispered.

Aline closed her eyes, but there was no way to avoid reality. She had to face it.

She'd realised what the creatures were as they'd raced across the wet sand. That realisation had spurred her on so she'd overtaken the Doctor and beaten him to the cave.

'They're Valethske. A race of hunters, probably nomadic; no one knows where they're from.' She remembered the Institute's woefully brief XENOLOG entry. 'There are stories of them popping up out of nowhere, hunting humans for food, going back centuries.'

The Doctor sat back on his haunches, his face lost in shadow. 'Anything else?' His voice was barely audible above the hiss and rush of the rain.

'They live to hunt, they have a highly developed sense of smell,' she shrugged, the movement jerky with fear. 'I've not studied them in depth and don't particularly want to.'

'They can't hunt only humanoids,' said the Doctor, looking down at himself. 'Not much meat on us, for a start.'

'They're sadists – they enjoy the looks of terror on people's faces.' Aline imagined Seryn and Athon cowering before a snarling Valethske, and then wished she hadn't. 'They probably hunt herd animals for meat on their homeworld, I don't know. I'm only going by what the stories say and the stories say they hunt and kill – us.'

The Doctor's face was in shadow, Aline could just make out his furrowed brows. Just make out his words, framed in a tense outrush of breath. 'Oh Peri, I'm sorry.'

He regarded the shining curtain of water at the cave entrance. When he spoke his voice had regained some of its breathless vivacity. '"If I were called in to construct a religion, I should make use of water."'

Aline frowned. 'Pardon?'

The Doctor turned to her. 'Be thankful for the rain. Hopefully it'll mask our scent. We'll wait here until we can be absolutely sure they've gone.'

His blind optimism was beginning to get to her. 'Or until they find us and kill us.'

'Shh!' admonished the Doctor. He leaned closer to her again. 'We'll wait until they've gone, then go back to the TARDIS. I may need your help and I need to know that I can rely on you.'

It had been a while since anyone had needed her. Aline didn't appreciate the pressure and looked away. 'I'm afraid you can't.'

His voice was a hot breath in her ear. 'Why not? You're a xenologist, one of the best in your field. I've heard tales of you braving situations that would warp the mind of a less well-trained individual.'

He was intruding again, and this time Aline gave in. Why not tell him? They were going to die soon anyway, so what did it matter? Drawing the Doctor's coat around her, she huddled into herself. 'That's just what happened to me. I encountered something no amount of training could ever have prepared *anyone* for. It had a rather drastic effect on me. It drove me insane. But I'm all right now – as long as I avoid anything alien.' She smiled without humour, wanting to get this confession over with and get back to waiting to be killed.

'Well, I'm an alien and you seem to be getting on fine with me,' said the Doctor.

'But you *look* human,' said Aline, closing her eyes, ashamed to look at him. 'That's the worst thing. Since the Encounter I've not been able to face the alien. Anything varying from human-basic sends me into shock.' She opened her eyes to see the Doctor's face a mask of concern and pity. 'I've turned from a xenologist into a xenophobe.'

The Doctor reached out and grasped both her hands in his. 'Your reactions are beyond your control, you can't help it.'

'I know,' said Aline. 'And I'm getting better, or so my therapist says. At least I'm off the medication now.'

'Now I understand the Eknuri assignment,' said the Doctor. 'Studying a humanoid species is your way of getting back in the swing of things, hmm?'

'Right.' Aline nodded. And bagging a Time Lord into the bargain. 'But I didn't bank on an alien attack. Not here, not now.'

'Quite.' His hand brushed her knee. 'Quiet.'

Aline followed the line of his gaze, and had to stifle a scream.

There was a dark shape in the rain beyond the cave entrance.

Veek ignored the insistent bleeping of her comm-unit, scanning the cave-mouths through the sheen of rain, Flayoun at her side. The rain was heavy, heavier than anything she'd known on her homeworld. Somehow, it seemed unnatural, forced. As if the Gods themselves were trying to drown her.

Snarling at her lapse into superstition, Veek switched off her comm-unit and moved towards the entrance of the nearest cave. From the echo of the rainfall she could tell it was deep, maybe going back fifteen, twenty metres. The sort of place panicking prey would hide, not thinking that they were walking into a trap. She smiled, licking rainwater from her lips.

A hand on her shoulder. She turned, irritated at the distraction.

Flayoun shook his head, sending droplets of water flying off in a rainbow arc. She saw he'd answered the incoming signal, and growled in irritation.

'The Vale Commander orders our immediate return to the ship.'

'Tell him we're about to snare more fresh prey,' said Veek. Beyond Flayoun she could see the skirmisher settling down on the beach, the hatch opening. Fools, so impatient to return to the long sleep. So dedicated to the Great Mission. Had they forgotten what it was like to hunt, what it meant to be Valethske?

Flayoun had already taken a few steps towards the skirmisher. Loyalty and dedication to the cause, and fear of what the Vale Commander would do if he caused any delay, had snared him as surely as any trap.

'He orders our immediate return,' said Flayoun, his voice husky with tension.

'Tell him...' began Veek, and then, suddenly, a new and exciting possibility popped into her mind. What if she stayed on this rainy little world, dropped out of the Great Mission? It was a dangerous thought. If she stayed, the Vale Commander would find her, and have her eviscerated and eaten. Even if she somehow escaped that fate, there was no guarantee she'd ever see her homeworld again.

And that, she realised in a flash of insight, was what she wanted more than anything, more than the success of the mission.

To return to Valeth Skettra...

She'd somehow always known it, but it was the first time such a thought had formed crystal-clear in her mind. It shocked her – and thrilled her.

'Hunt Marshal? Veek?'

But any action would have to wait. She would have to guard her words and deeds carefully so they wouldn't betray her thoughts.

Veek shook her head, dislodging droplets of water from her fur, and followed Flayoun back to the skirmisher. The prospect of the long sleep rose like a stone slab on her mental horizon, cold and senseless.

Chapter Six
A Cold Day in Hell

The rain had washed most of the blood away. At least Aline could be thankful for that.

Of the Eknuri themselves, or their attackers, there was no sign, bar the odd scrap of torn clothing, discarded baubles of jewellery, a lone sandal. The waterfall still spiralled down from its cleft in the cliff, sparkling in the sunshine which seemed even more vivid after the brief intensity of the storm. The air bore a fresh, metallic tang, obscenely clean, like a freshly scrubbed mortuary.

The Doctor stood in the middle of the courtyard, hands cupped to his lips. 'Anyone there?'

His voice echoed around the stone courtyard and along the receding perspective of cliffs until it was swallowed up in the ceaseless sighing of the surf.

No reply came.

The Doctor's face was ashen, hands hanging impotently at his sides. 'Nothing.'

Aline shivered. The sun was just beginning to dry her wrecked dress and her messed-up hair, both of which clung to her like clumps of kelp. Her shoeless feet ached from the run back.

They had waited until the shape in the mouth of the cave had retreated. Waited until the sound of engines screamed away into the sky like a fading nightmare. Aline wanted to wait until the storm passed, but the Doctor insisted on getting back so they ran pell-mell through the streaming rain which seemed as though it was never going to end. Even underneath the Doctor's coat, flapping around her like an unruly second skin, Aline had got soaked.

Now the Doctor, his sodden coat slipped back over his surprisingly broad shoulders without a second's thought, was crouching to examine the shattered remains of the servitors, which had fallen by the parapet of the opening through which the waterfall spiralled its unfeeling way. 'They didn't manage to invoke the warpfield, so...'

Aline hugged her damp chest. 'The Valethske must have taken them.'

The Doctor's look was accusing, as if he resented her voicing the dreadful possibility. 'You said there were reports of them hunting humans.'

Aline shook her head. 'Not actual, verifiable reports. Travellers' tales, stories, legends, that sort of thing, it's hard to say how much is based on fact. They all tell of Valethske raiding parties taking whole colonies away with them, harpooning babies for sport, keeping people alive for days while they chew on their extremities. That sort of thing.'

'No one's ever studied them, worked out what makes them tick?'

Aline shook her head. 'I never really believed they were real until now. Just stories.'

'Oh they're real enough, unfortunately for us,' said the Doctor. He walked quickly over to his TARDIS, fishing in his inside coat pocket and drawing out a small key on a long golden chain. 'We've wasted enough time here.' A glance back over his shoulder. 'Are you coming?'

Aline realised what he meant, and felt a thrill of fear and anticipation shudder through her. The blue box looked so ordinary, so mundane, that it was hard to believe that it was one of the most powerful machines in the known universe. A bit like the Doctor – homely and innocent on the outside, but inside? She felt guilty thinking about it, but this was the chance of a lifetime. She tried to forget that people had died, that by the grace of little more than blind luck she was the only survivor. But hadn't she always tried to turn any situation, however dire, to the good?

'Come on, come on!' said the Doctor, thrusting the door open and beckoning her on. 'There's no other way off this planetoid, unless you want to wait for the Valethske to come back for seconds.'

Overcome with a sense of fearful curiosity, Aline allowed herself to be manhandled inside the Time Lord's TARDIS.

After a moment of disorientation, she found herself standing blinking in a brightly lit room, swaying slightly on her bare feet.

The Doctor darted around the console that dominated the room, and fell upon a bank of switches. The column in the centre began a gentle rise and fall. 'I haven't got time for you to be overwhelmed, just accept that it's bigger on the inside than it is on the outside,' he straightened up, his hair flopping down over his brow, 'and get on with it.'

'Don't worry, I can accept it,' said Aline, padding towards the console, fighting down a feeling of disappointment. She'd been expecting a glittering crystal-cathedral, or an echoing Gothic chamber of flickering shadows, or something she couldn't possibly imagine that would take her breath away. Not just a big white room with roundels on the walls, a six-sided console and a wobbling hum right on the edge of her hearing. 'Get on with what?'

He whirled away from the console and ushered her towards a door in the far wall. 'You need to clean up and change into something more practical. Wardrobe's down there, second door on the right, bathroom's opposite. Usually.'

Aline fought free of his gentle but insistent persuasion. 'Where are we going?'

'After the Valethske. Now please hurry, I've got to track that shuttle.'

He all but shoved her through the door.

Aline bathed and changed in panicky haste, resisting the temptation to explore the seemingly infinite wardrobe, finding for herself a rough approximation of what she used to wear in the field. And would again, she told herself, when she came out the other side of this. But every time she closed her eyes, she could see the jackal heads of the Valethske, distant and terrible against the clouds. As she washed the sand from between her toes and dried her rain-soaked body she felt herself verging on a panic attack – a feeling of constant awaking, a heart-thumping rush, just like when she tried coming off her medication too early. She was about to go with this *alien* into a nest of other *aliens* vicious *aliens* who would surely kill her what was she *doing*?

It was with a bitter, helpless anger that Aline dressed herself, forcing her body – drenched again, this time with sweat – into sturdy boots, khaki trousers with lots of pockets, a thick dark-green cotton shirt, and an ancient-looking brown leather jacket. Strangely, it had all been laid out for her on the back of a chair, almost as if the Doctor had known she was coming. Wait – what if he had? What if this was all some sort of plot?

'More likely a delusional episode,' she told herself. 'Time Lords, Valethske, what next?'

Perhaps...

No. She'd never meet their like again. And if she did, that would be the end, for sure. Her mind wouldn't be able to take a second Encounter.

Aline shook her head, banishing such thoughts, and tied back her black hair with an equally black ribbon. Since her unburdening she felt empty, lost, as if telling the Doctor had removed an important part of who she was. No one, except those directly involved, and senior people at the Institute, knew about what had happened, and she hadn't spoken about it to anyone bar her therapist for years. Telling the Doctor had been a good idea when faced with what at the time seemed like certain death, but she wasn't so sure now.

Anyway, she hadn't told him everything. She didn't know everything herself, so how could she?

Back in the console room, the Doctor was waiting for her, arms folded, smiling the painted-on smile of someone with bad news to break.

Aline was instantly on her guard. 'What is it?'

'Like the jacket. Belonged to Amelia Earhart, I think.'

Aline knew hedging when she heard it. 'I thought we were madly chasing the Valethske shuttle?'

'Oh we are, we are,' he came up to her, his eyes searching her face. 'But this is a time machine.'

He seemed to be awaiting a reaction, but he'd totally lost her. 'What do you mean?'

'I mean,' said the Doctor, leading her towards the disappointingly low-tech console, indicating a tiny screen with a jabbing finger, 'that there's no immediate rush.'

The display showed a parabolic arc linking a cluster of figures. A small dot was moving along the arc. It meant little to Aline. The figures seemed to be co-ordinates of some sort, but the display was meaningless. 'Why, what's happened?'

'We were too late. Before we even got back to the TARDIS, the shuttle had docked with its mothership. And by the time we dematerialised the mothership had engaged some sort of faster-than-light drive.' He frowned. 'Not *much* faster-than-light, though, which doesn't say a lot for Valethske technology.'

Aline folded her arms, the jacket creaking in protest. She had an uneasy feeling about what was coming. 'Get to the point.'

He spoke quickly and breathlessly, the words tumbling over each other. 'The point is, the Valethske mothership is heading for a solar system some hundred and thirty light years away. It's going to take them a while to get there and, to survive the journey, the Valethske must be putting themselves into some sort of suspended animation. Probably very rough and ready, judging by the evidence we have so far of their technology. I wonder why they're putting themselves through all this?' He paused, frowning, momentarily lost in thought.

'They may have frozen their prey, too,' said Aline. 'Peri. The Eknuri...'

The Doctor paced around the console. 'As the Valethske ship is in FTL, I can't risk attempting a landing now. The only chance of rescuing Peri and the others is to try to materialise the ship just as it emerges from FTL, before the Valethske wake up.'

'So that means...'

'Yes,' said the Doctor, coming to a stop in front of Aline. 'Travelling approximately one hundred years into your future, into a very dangerous situation indeed.' He sighed. 'There's no way of knowing what's waiting for us on the Valethske ship.'

A feeling of feathery lightness took hold of Aline. This was almost too much to take, on top of everything else. What had started as a gentle reintroduction to the field of xenology had mutated into a headlong flight towards her worst fears.

The Doctor rested a solicitous hand on her shoulder. 'Are you all right?'

It was the second time he'd asked. Aline hugged the jacket to her, relishing its musky smell, taking comfort in its solidity. 'Yes, I'm fine.'

'Good! I waited for you to change so you could have the choice. We haven't left your time-stream yet – I could either put you down somewhere inhabited now, and you can get on with your life, or you can come with me.'

Her life. Her brothers in the Senate, her mother, her therapist, the astrophysicist she'd started a peripatetic affair with, all the people that cared about her –

- would all be dead in a hundred years. It would almost feel as if she was killing them if she went with the Doctor.

'Given what you've told me, I thought I'd better let you choose. I wouldn't want to force you into a situation where you wouldn't be able to cope.'

The Doctor's words wormed their way deep into Aline's mind, reaching down to the brilliant young student she had been, the confident and renowned xenologist she'd become. How many first contacts did she have to her name? How dare he suggest that she wouldn't be able to cope!

But you won't cope, came her inner voice. *You proved that back on the planetoid. The only thing that motivates you now is fear.*

'Aline?'

On the other hand, there's nothing like facing your fear.

And if she left the Doctor now, she'd be running away. She'd probably never get the opportunity to study a Time Lord again. Though the prospect frightened her more than she could begin to imagine, she came to a decision.

'Doctor, it would be a very bad idea if I came with you. I'd much rather not.'

'Oh,' the Doctor moved to the console, then paused, picking up the inflection in her voice.

She fixed him with her most sincere, compelling stare. 'But I have to.'

Peri Brown didn't believe in Heaven or Hell. Not as real places, anyway. As concepts, as metaphors, fine. You do good, you go to Heaven, you do bad, you go to Hell. She'd believed it when she was too young to know any better, the same way she'd believed in Santa Claus and the Headless Horseman. At college and in the years before she'd had her whole world-view turned upside down by the Doctor, she'd believed that doing good was an end in itself. Helping people was its own reward, plus they'd hopefully do the same for you some day. And you did bad, sometimes, because it was fun – little bad, like teasing boys, stealing from stores or lying to her stepdad. As long as she did enough good to balance it out, Peri figured, it was OK. This even held true on alien worlds and in situations she would never have dreamed of in a million years. Being on the Doctor's side was like doing the ultimate good. Just hanging out with him seemed to have some positive effect on the universe. Keeping the balance tilted in favour of light.

Perhaps that was why she was in Hell – or as close to it as she could imagine – because she'd defied the Doctor and run off with a real handsome devil. Perhaps she was being punished for abandoning the Doctor. It was a hell – huh – of a flimsy theory – but she needed to rationalise what was happening to her *real* bad.

Rationalise waking up with a jolt to find herself being dragged along on her back over dusty earth, her feet juddering along in her wake, catching glimpses of fiendish hound-faces, all gleaming teeth and yellow eyes. A white mist curling around her and vast walls of scarred metal closing in. One of the hounds had noticed she was awake, and bent to lick her face. She'd passed out.

Rationalise waking again, to find herself strapped to an upright gurney, a bright light lancing into her eyes. She'd tried screaming but her voice wouldn't work. She glimpsed pointed ears, a row of white teeth bared in a terrifying grin, a flash of yellow eye. Then she'd passed out again.

Rationalise waking to find herself blind, unable to move or speak, unable to feel even the beating of her heart.

And cold. So cold that each breath seemed to reach down inside her and slice at her lungs. So cold that she could feel the tears freeze to her face.

She began to dream. Dream of swimming in the sea at Lanzarote, the warm water caressing her body. Dream of wandering lazily around the Boston Botanical Institute with her mother when she was eleven. Dream of being anywhere but in this Hell.

But Hell was meant to be hot, not cold. Hadn't she told someone not too long ago Hell would freeze over before... before what? She couldn't remember. The Doctor... she couldn't remember his face.

Then suddenly there was a mechanical clunk, a blast of burning ice in her face – over her whole body – and she stopped remembering anything.

Chapter Seven
Rescue

The dark hulk of the Valethske ship had been sleeping for over a century. Now it was coming to life. Its waking was not a sudden return to consciousness, but a flickering, piecemeal event, like an orchestra of rusted, obscure instruments tuning up for a concert in a rusty scrapyard the size of a mountain – though if it was a concert, the music was steeped in blood, its composer long turned to dust, its meaning long scattered to the interstellar gulfs.

Signals sparked in tottering relay. Multitudinous systems and servo-mechanisms spluttered, coughed, yawned, creaked and pinged into life, jittery and spiky after a hundred years of downtime. The sleep cells and the engines took heed of this flutter of activity and amended their functions accordingly. The cells began to revive their occupants, sending nanites coursing through their bloodstream. The engines began to slow the ship as yet another destination zero clicked into register.

In the midst of this waking gestalt, unnoticed by the still-drowsy surveillance systems, something ancient and powerful performed keyhole surgery on time and space and extruded itself obstinately into reality.

Aline stepped from the TARDIS, holding the torch before her like a protective talisman. It was next to useless, illuminating only a tiny too-bright circle, throwing everything else into a shadowy profundity in which anything could be lurking. All she could hear was her own breathing, amplified by the oxygen mask, which had a foul rubbery smell.

Trying to look everywhere at once, she grabbed the Doctor's sleeve. 'Are you sure they're all still – asleep?'

'For now,' came the Doctor's muffled voice, then he moved on, sending the beam of his pen-torch probing ahead, a gaudy carpet-bag held in his other hand.

Aline followed, trying not to imagine what might be in the fiendish shadows that flicked at her from every side, keeping as close to the Doctor as she could without bumping into him. The twin canisters and straps of the oxygen pack looked incongruous against his coat. He looked like a tourist exploring a famous cave system, not someone on a shockingly dangerous rescue mission.

But that was the thing about the Doctor – he wasn't at all what he seemed, such as in his attitude to herself. Sometimes he was attentive and helpful, almost painfully considerate. The way he'd waited to ask her before lunging off into the future had touched her. That such a being as a Time Lord could be concerned about a solitary human life. It would be like Aline working in the dark so as not to tempt moths to a false moon. At other more preoccupied times, like now, he almost seemed to relish making her feel nervous. She recognised the process from her days under therapy; tough-love, burning the comfort blanket. Well, she could see through that.

She couldn't see much of anything else, though. They appeared to be walking on compacted soil, dull orange-brown in the beam of her torch. Motes spun in the shaft of light like interstellar flotsam. Ahead, the Doctor's torch picked out leaning walls of rusted metal. He was flicking it around casually, yet quickly, as if trying to catch an errant child. Suddenly he sent the beam straight up, its weak light barely illuminating gantries and shapes of folded, cowled machinery, like mechanical bats waiting to swoop. Aline could hear distant groans and shrieks – which she hoped were mechanical rather than organic in origin – and now and then the ground below would heave and shudder, sending grit dancing around her boots. It didn't feel as if she was inside a ship at all. How big was this thing? The TARDIS scanner screen had just shown a blackness against the stars, like an asteroid or a black hole.

Aline found it hard going keeping up with the Doctor's long strides. Amazing to think that the ship had been travelling for over a century. Their voices, their footfalls, were the first to break the silence of decades. She shivered. The chill air of the Valethske ship had crept in to the gaps between her clothes and body. 'Do you know where we're going?'

'I'm doing what I always do, following my nose,' said the Doctor, neatly evading giving an answer. Then: 'Aha!'

They came to a gap in the sloping wall, more like the result of damage than an intended opening, which led through to a wide area roughly circular in shape. The ground sloped down to a railing which bordered a circular pit filled with a ghostly bluish glow.

The Doctor hared over to the railing, Aline following close behind.

Ranged in concentric circles descending into the pit were hundreds of alcoves, each one harbouring a clot of frozen fog that bled soft blue light. Walkways criss-crossed the pit, which narrowed down to a knot of total darkness.

The Doctor placed the carpet-bag on the earth floor and began to climb down the nearest ladder. Aline followed, wishing she had gloves – the rungs were ice-cold to the touch.

At the nearest alcove, Aline and the Doctor peered at the frozen shape trapped within. Behind the pane of frosted glass set crudely in the crumbling earth wall of the chamber, Aline could make out the naked, sleeping body of a Valethske, its fur dusted with frost. Silver tubes snaked around its torso. Aline jumped as an eyelid flickered. How long before they awoke? How long after that before they were able to hunt, to attack, to kill?

'Let sleeping dogs lie is what I always say,' said the Doctor, the words almost inaudible beneath his mask.

Aline followed him back up the ladder, only too glad to be away from the pit of slumbering killers, and along more earth-floored metal canyons. By now the groaning of the waking ship was almost constant, and a white mist had begun to seep down from somewhere high above, lending the whole place ghostly illumination.

'Oxygen,' said the Doctor. 'While the Valethske are in suspended animation the ship doesn't need to maintain an atmosphere. Now it's beginning to manufacture one in readiness for their awakening. We haven't got very much longer.'

In the receding gloom Aline could make out angular, ugly shapes; ducts like giant snakes, cowling like the armour of stag-beetles, buttresses like the shoulders of giants. Although the total darkness had been terrifying, it was infinitely preferable to the emerging nightmare of the ship's interior.

They soon came to another pit, a little way down the main canyon from the sleeping Valethske. As Aline climbed down another frosty ladder after the Doctor, torch jammed in a pocket of her trousers, she realised with a sense of sick dread that the Valethske pit lay between themselves and the TARDIS. Already it seemed to be getting warmer. When the Valethske woke up, they'd undoubtedly be hungry. Ravenous.

Aline stopped trying to prevent her teeth chattering, her limbs from shaking with fear, and let her body get on with being terrified as her mind tried to concentrate on the task in hand.

Touching down, she peered into the nearest alcove. Inside, an indistinct but recognisably human shape. A man, clad in some kind of uniform, complete with beret. Not an Eknuri. Aline turned and peered over the rail. The concentric circles of gantries and alcoves presented a giddying prospect.

How were they going to find their friends in this lot? There must be hundreds of bodies frozen in suspended animation. How many other planets had the Valethske raided?

Aline straightened up. It was definitely getting warmer. She looked around for the Doctor. He was standing on the metal gantry about thirty degrees around from her, peering at each alcove in turn. The alcoves spilled a bluish, icy light into the pit and strands of mist were winding their way down the walls.

Suddenly the Doctor gave a satisfied shout. When she joined him he was already tapping at the pad of instrumentation by the side of the alcove. The person inside was Peri, there was no mistaking her bell of hair, her young features, arms raised as if to fend something off.

Aline moved on to the next alcove, and her heart leapt in a pang of recognition. Athon! Equally unmistakable. Despite everything she felt a smile take over her face. How great it would be to be back on the pleasure-planetoid, fending off Athon's advances and glugging down glass after glass of Eknuri wine. Suddenly she felt she knew what it was to be human, to be alive, and almost burst into tears of mingled joy and terror. If she ever got out of here, she vowed, she'd treasure every second of experience and never, ever be scared again.

'Are you all right?' came the Doctor's voice, his hand on the elbow of her jacket.

That question again! 'Never felt better.'

He looked offended by her sarcasm. 'We have to hurry.'

Aline could hear a musical dripping as the ice on the ladders and gantries began to melt. The Doctor passed her the carpet-bag. 'I'm going to try to revive them. As they come out, you know what to do.'

A few more taps at the panel, and the door of the alcove slid back. Peri fell into the Doctor's arms, her lips blue, her dark bell of hair speckled with ice. The Doctor caught her and gently began to remove the silver tubes from her arms and neck. She couldn't see the Doctor's expression beneath the mask, but his eyes told her he was overjoyed to see Peri again. Then he frowned, eyes darkening, maybe realising that they had a long way to go before they were safe.

Aline helped him set Peri down on the cold metal gantry. He cradled her head in his hands in a curiously loving gesture. Peri's mouth opened in a gasp, her lungs desperately trying to extract sustenance from the thin air. Aline unzipped the bag and took out an oxygen pack, fixing it to Peri's body as quickly as she could. Once the mask was in position the Doctor nodded to Aline, and then stood up, hurrying over to the next cubicle.

Aline knelt over Peri, cradling her head in her lap, extracting a hypo and locating the carotid artery below the girl's jaw. She pressed the impeller. A neuro-stimulant, the Doctor had explained, to speed up recovery. Nothing happened for a few seconds, and then Peri convulsed, her back arching like a violin bow. Aline soothed her as rasping breaths tore in and out of the young girl. She'd seen this sort of suspended animation before, a kind of crude cryogenics where simple anti-freeze glycoproteins lowered the blood's freezing point and nanites worked constantly, repairing cells and preventing organ damage. It usually took hours for subjects to recover – while the stimulant would help, Aline and the Doctor still had to work quickly.

First Athon, then Taiana, and then two people Aline didn't recognise were hefted from their alcoves, fitted with masks and ministered to.

Aline went back to Peri, checking her pulse. Slow, erratic, but there, and though her hands were still ice cold, Aline could see colour returning to her lips and cheeks. It would be a while, though, before she regained consciousness.

The Doctor came over to her. 'This is one of the most painful decisions I'll ever have to live with, but we must leave now.'

Aline blinked. 'What about Seryn? Yuasa?' All the others...

The Doctor shook his head. 'We've only got seven oxygen masks. Help me try to bring Athon and Taiana round – they can carry the others.'

Taiana was stirring, her head lolling from side to side. Her skull-cap was gone – torn off, maybe, by a Valethske – her short golden hair, matching her eyes, was matted with blood.

The Doctor went over to her and helped her to her feet.

'Taiana!' he shouted right in her face.

Dark eyelids flickered, revealing golden slits.

'Can you hear me? Can you walk?'

Taiana nodded, then slumped against her alcove, legs folding beneath her.

Aline went to Athon, who was sitting with his head between his knees. 'Athon?'

He looked up, brown eyes vacant, tears frosted to his face. 'Aline?'

'Yes, it's me. Don't ask me how you got here, don't even think for a while, we need your help.'

Athon blinked. Had he understood her? She recognised the look on his face. She'd seen it on her own in the mirror often enough, in the dark years. Fear blotting out everything, numbing, paralysing. On Athon's usually relaxed, complacent features, it was ugly, almost obscene.

Aline gripped his shoulders, digging her fingers into the cold brown flesh, desperate to get through to him. 'Athon, can you hear me?'

There was the glimmering of recognition. A blur of movement from the side – Taiana was lifting up a tall silver-haired man in military uniform, draping him across her shoulders like a stole. The Doctor had already picked up Peri, cradling her in his arms with surprising ease.

He called to her, voice muffled by the mask. 'Come on!'

Using all her strength Aline helped Athon to his feet. He swayed a little, still drowsy – maybe that was a good thing, the last thing she wanted was for him to panic. With agonising slowness he stooped and picked up the other stranger, a petite young woman in military garb with short red hair.

The Doctor turned to lead the way, Taiana and Athon shuffling after him with their charges.

The journey out of the pit was a nightmare, and seemed to take an age. At one point Athon, still woozy from the after-effects of the cryogenic treatment, slipped on the rungs, sending Taiana and her charge sprawling to the bottom of the ladder.

Once out of the pit, progress was easier, but they were running out of time. All around them, the ship was coming fully to life. Some of the leaning metal walls began shifting, opening up to reveal walkways leading to Gods knew what further pits. Chunks of light shone down from beyond the gantries above, and the mist had all but cleared. The Doctor took off his mask and called back to them. 'The atmosphere's stabilised now, but don't throw away your masks. We might have to cross an area of depressurisation.'

Aline kept up the rear, to make sure the Eknuri didn't drop their charges.

At last, they came to the main passageway. Surely the TARDIS couldn't be far away. She didn't fear it now. It was the closest thing to home in this new century.

The Doctor came to an abrupt halt. 'Oh, no.'

He was staring at a bulkhead just in front of them.

'Don't tell me we're lost,' said Aline.

'Oh, we're not lost,' said the Doctor, regarding Aline with a look she could only describe as haunted. 'The TARDIS is on the other side of that.' He indicated the dead end with a nod of his head.

'What?' Aline couldn't believe it. To have come so far...

Setting Peri upright on the ground and indicating for Aline to steady her, the Doctor ran up to the bulkhead.

Aline concentrated on holding Peri. She was heavier than she looked. Her eyelids were fluttering; she was just below the surface of consciousness.

The Doctor pounded a fist against the shield of pitted, scarred metal. The impact sounded depressingly solid. 'Repressurisation!' said the Doctor, turning back to them. 'The ship's sealing off the areas of itself which don't need an atmosphere. Just my luck to have landed the TARDIS in such an area.' He looked around for a control panel, but there was nothing, only the rust-hued metal. He glared at the shielding, as if he thought his gaze could melt the way through to the TARDIS. 'If only I still had my sonic screwdriver.'

'What's happening?' said Taiana, her voice more slurred than usual.

'Yes, would you mind explaining just what is going on?' said Athon, walking up to the Doctor, the young woman's head lolling against his shoulder, seemingly forgotten. 'I mean, I like party games, but...' he caught sight of Peri, and frowned. Then the colour drained from his face. 'I remember now. Those creatures...'

The Doctor raised his hands in a shushing gesture. 'There will be time for explanations later.' He whirled around. 'We have to find another way off this ship.'

The soldier in Taiana's arms began muttering something.

'Shuttle bays.' His voice was cracked and weak. He opened his eyes. They were blue and unfocused. 'Shuttle bays.' He raised a wobbling finger, pointing back the way they had come.

'Brilliant!' said the Doctor. 'Lead the way, Mr…?'

'Captain. Captain John Melrose.'

'What about the TARDIS?' said Aline.

The Doctor looked pained. 'We have to get away from here. The TARDIS won't be any use if we end up dead.'

Taiana took the lead, carrying Melrose in her strong arms like a baby. It was a bizarre sight; the tall, dark-limbed woman cradling the barely conscious six-foot soldier. They had to stop and listen to Melrose at each junction as he muttered directions and pointed the way with a shaking hand. In this fashion they wormed their way through the Valethske ship, coming eventually to a vaulted hangar-like area. Ranged along the walls were sleek wedge-shaped vessels of varying sizes, some of which Aline recognised as the same as the one that had attacked the Eknuri.

The Doctor led the way to one of the smaller shuttles, putting Peri down gently against its hull and motioning for Aline to steady her. After a tense moment fiddling with the controls, a hatch hissed open, revealing a dark interior. The Doctor scrambled inside and after a few seconds, harsh interior lighting snapped on.

The Doctor emerged and ushered them all in. Athon went first, carrying the female soldier; then Taiana with Melrose.

The Doctor picked Peri up once more with surprising ease. 'After you,' he said to Aline.

'Thank you.' His politeness in such a situation made Aline smile, and she ducked inside, following the sound of Taiana's voice along a short companionway to the flight deck. It was small and cramped, and Aline wondered how the Valethske – being as tall as the Eknuri – could stand such confinement. She helped Taiana and Athon make sure that Melrose and his comrade were safely strapped in, then the Doctor appeared with Peri.

'Won't the Valethske know about this little hijack?' asked Aline.

'Probably,' said the Doctor as he strapped Peri in to a seat.

He motioned for Aline to take the co-pilot's position and she strapped herself in as tightly as she could. She heard him tap away at the console in front of them.

'I mean, won't the flight log show it? Won't there be alarms, security?'

The Doctor grinned at her from the pilot's seat. 'I've just made friends with the flight computer and told it that we're a party of Valethske on a scouting mission. Their technology is –'

'Not very advanced,' finished Aline. 'Thankfully for us.'

'Indeed,' said the Doctor. He craned round to look at the others. 'Is everyone ready?'

There were murmurs from Athon and Taiana, but the others were still unconscious.

The Doctor raised his eyebrows at Aline. 'Well, here goes.'

He reached forward and took hold of the shuttle's controls, which consisted mainly of chunky levers and buttons. They looked as brutal and simple as the creatures they were designed for.

Nothing happened for a few seconds, then Aline felt herself pressed back into her seat as the shuttle plunged downwards and outwards, as if the ship was spitting them out like a pip.

She couldn't believe it. They'd escaped. They were free.

Well, almost all of them...

She tried not to think about Seryn and the others. And the Doctor's TARDIS, trapped in the bowels of the ship.

The dark hulk of the Valethske ship had been sleeping for over a hundred years, and now it was fully awake. Its damage log showed interference with the sleep cells, and there was some confusion over the skirmisher complement – minor troubles. At least this time the sleep cells had functioned: none of the occupants, Valethske or prey, had perished, and there had been no major failures of any systems. The ship was fully tuned up now, ready to play its killer song.

It came to a complete halt, between the orbits of the two inner planets of the destination system, as it had been programmed to, thousands of years ago.

And then waited for its masters to awake.

Chapter Eight
Lust for Life

The first thing Hunt Marshal Veek felt on waking was a pitiless gnawing in her guts, a demand for sustenance she couldn't ignore. Then cold: ice cutting down to the bone, burning her throat as she gasped for air. She tried to move, couldn't; tried again; couldn't. Always this paralysis, always the mind waking before the body. All she could do was think. And all she could think of was food, of sinking her teeth into the quivering flanks of a calfling, of ripping open the abdomen of a human and sinking her face into its slippery guts. Her hunger seemed to Veek like a living thing, racing through her veins like wildfire. She knew it was really the nanites working their magic in her bloodstream, helping her back to consciousness, but she liked to think it was her hunger, her lust, her driving force, which dragged her from the long sleep.

At last, with a great effort, Veek was able to open her eyes. Made no difference; everything blurred, foggy. She arched her back, feeling her spine stretching, muscles complaining. The stiffness slowly thawed out of her and she half-stepped, half-fell from her alcove, dimly aware of the mewling and growling of the other waking hunters. She staggered forwards, stumbling against the railing, yawning, strands of spittle trailing down on to her teats. Below them, her stomach growled like a sick cub. Had to eat, had to eat *now*. Always this way, after waking. Always this insatiable hunger. As she wiped the sleep from her eyes, her vision returned. She glared back at the alcove that had been her prison, remembering the rainy planetoid, over a century in the past yet seeming only like yesterday.

Another span of forfeited time, pushing them further away from home. How far had they travelled, through both distance and time? Did home even exist any more?

Groans and mewls of pain echoed around the pit as her fellow hunters clawed themselves back to reality, naked, their red fur frosted, their eyes open but as yet unseeing, feeling their way along the gantries, bumping into each other and having pathetic, blind tussles. Was this any way for Valethske to behave? Where was the dignity? After so long, what was the point? Dangerous thoughts, Veek knew – but as she watched the waking hunters, she wondered if any of them thought this way. Or if any of them thought at all.

Veek growled and tore her gaze away from the scene, padding hastily along towards the exit ladder, wanting to be first to reach the fresh prey. The Commander's Vale Guards, always the first to be woken after the long sleep, would have sated their hunger on disgusting, pallid, synthetic flesh, lit the fires in the pit and prepared some of the ship's store of fresh prey for the hunters. The prey would be waiting now in the pit, terrified, shivering in deliciously sweet fear-sweat, wondering what was going to happen to it.

Veek was going to happen to it, Veek and all the other hunters were going to gorge themselves and there was nothing the prey could do about it. There was nowhere to run, nowhere to hide. For once, the thrill of the chase didn't matter to Veek – sating her hunger was more important.

Now more of the hunters had regained enough of their senses to act upon the hunger that gnawed at their guts. They were scrambling up the ladders, fighting to be first, uttering yelps and shrieks of anticipation.

Veek heaved herself up out of the pit and staggered to her feet, feeling her legs take control and propel her across the earth floor.

Suddenly something grabbed her legs and she went sprawling headlong in the dust. Feet thumped past her as other hunters made headway for the prey. She rolled over, snarling and coughing, eyes watering, to see Flayoun crouched before her in a fighting stance, his eyes gleaming with lust.

The sight of his body sent a thrill of anticipation through Veek. She'd almost forgotten him in her haste to eat. He looked a mess: fur matted and dull, ichor running from the corners of his eyes, claws long and untended. But that didn't matter. It was good to see him.

'Flayoun,' she murmured, stepping closer, rubbing his chest, teasing him. 'Shall we fight, frisk or feed?'

The lust in his eyes sharpened, he put his hands to his belly, and wailed. 'We feeeeeeed!'

Veek felt her own hollow stomach growl again, demanding sustenance. How many times had they gone through this ritual? She pulled her lips back, revealing the sharp teeth she knew he admired. 'I'll take a bite out of you, hunter!'

Flayoun roared and lunged for her.

Veek leapt backwards with a shriek, spun round and dived after her fellow hunters, Flayoun close behind, snatching at her tail.

Soon, she told her hunger, soothing it as if it was an embryo cub growing inside her, soon you shall be satisfied.

Scuttling and scampering, the Valethske hunters obeyed their impulses and swarmed towards their prey.

Seryn woke to the sounds of crackling fire and the moans of the wounded. So it hadn't been a hallucination. It had all been real. She took in her surroundings as quietly and as calmly as she could. What she saw made her want to scream, but she bit her lip until it bled.

She was in a cage suspended over a pit in which fires burned. She wasn't alone; there were three other Eknuri with her. She called their names, but they were still unconscious. That – or dead.

Her dress was torn, ripped off crudely at the waist, her shoes were gone, and her body was slick with sweat. It kept running down her forehead, stinging her eyes. She ached in every possible way and her left arm felt as if it had been wrenched out of its socket, as if she'd been carried like a doll.

Painfully, she turned to lie on her belly, looking down through the grid of the cage at the bonfires. Oily smoke curled upwards towards her. Seryn could make out other cages, suspended at differing heights from a ceiling criss-crossed with gantries, the occupants slumped within. Around the walls of the pit, dark mouths of tunnels gaped. Could she hear a distant shrieking, a bestial yapping above the constant crackle and pop of the fires? She strained her hearing, heart hammering, eyes fixed on the nearest entrance.

How had she got here? She dimly remembered waking, freezing cold, and being taken half-blind and stumbling through a maze of earth-floored passages. She remembered trying to speak to the beasts, plead with them, ask them why they were doing this to her and her friends. In reply they'd beaten her and she'd passed out. Now her whole body ached, and sitting on the jagged, rusted grid of the cage floor didn't help. She tried standing, but her legs were too weak and any movement made the cage lurch beneath her.

She looked down at the orange pools of light cast by the fires, squinting to make out shapes. There, fifty feet or so below her cage, lay one of her shoes, next to a pile of bones. Human bones by the look of it. She coughed as a wraith of smoke passed through the cage. Surely they weren't going to *eat* her? It was absurd. She laughed out loud. The sudden crazed sound frightened her, so she clamped her hands over her mouth.

Her laughter caught the attention of one of her fellow captives. He raised his head, dull eyes staring from beneath a floppy fringe of grey hair, mouth sagging open. Daeraval, the musician. A man of cheerful heart, charming wit, incredible musical versatility and wondrous voice. Seryn remembered how he'd sung at Athon's party, his voice seeming to soar into the air like a kite, a sound of pure freedom and joy.

Now, his tunic shredded, bare arms showing deep furrows of claw-marks, Seryn could hardly bear to look at him.

On a sudden mutual impulse, they shuffled towards each other, the cage swinging wildly in response to their movement, its supporting chains creaking in protest. They held each other tightly, Seryn burying the man's head in her breast. Great swathes of emotion surged within her. She had never felt the need for the company so much as now. She kissed him with more passion than she'd ever kissed anyone before, as if she was trying to suck the life out of him.

She knew then she was going to die. This intensity, this passion, was all there was now, all that was left. They held each other for a long time before they spoke.

'Seryn?'

'Yes?'

'What's happened to us?'

Seryn smoothed his hair. 'I don't know. Part of me still hopes it's all some elaborate joke.'

'Seryn, this is real. We've been stupid, letting ourselves be caught off guard like this. These creatures, whatever they are, will soon be very sorry for what they've done.'

Seryn leaned back, regarding his face. He looked fevered, his skin pink-orange in the fireglow. 'What do you mean?'

'We'll be missed, don't you worry. Our friends will be after us. And they'll send these beasts shrieking into the heart of a black hole. Wipe them all out!'

His voice had sunk to a terrifying hiss.

'Daeraval, calm down. Help me look for a way out of this cage.'

'Already tried. There is no way out.'

Seryn slumped against him. There was nothing either of them could do but wait. Or maybe there was something. 'Daeraval, this may sound mad, but could you sing for me?'

He turned to look at her, eyes wide. 'I can't.'

She squeezed his hand, sticky with sweat. 'Please.'

He shook his head, eyes wide. She realised that he was looking over her shoulder, beyond her, to the tunnel entrances in the pit walls. 'They're coming.'

She spun round.

From the dark entrances, vulpine shapes were pouring in their dozens, their claws scrabbling on the dirt. She could hear their panting and growling, fancied she could almost feel the heat of their breath. But it was only the heat from the fires below.

The cage gave a sudden jerk, and started to descend.

Seryn held Daeraval to her and screamed.

Suddenly the cage rocked under a heavy impact. Seryn looked up to see one of the creatures spread-eagled on top, teeth champing at the bars.

Screams from somewhere to her left. She looked to see the nearest cage, almost hidden under a writhing mass of fur, crash to the floor of the pit, its occupants spilling out.

She looked away but couldn't blot out their screams.

The cage bottom suddenly swung open beneath them and they fell, spinning a short distance before thumping into the ground. Seryn lay stunned, her whole body thrumming with pain.

The two unconscious Eknuri smacked into the ground nearby and she heard the snap of breaking bone.

Daeraval rolled into a nearby fire, screaming as his tattered tunic burst into flames. Soon two of the creatures were on him and his screams intensified. Seryn watched them rip at his throat, watched his arms flailing to push away the beasts, watched the dark spray of blood splatter on fur, hardly daring to believe it was happening.

But it was.

Seryn scrambled into an area of darkness away from the fires. She was crying, her vision blurring and her chest heaving, but inside she was calm. Perhaps it wouldn't hurt that much, perhaps it was only the small pains of life – cutting a finger, stubbing a toe – that hurt, and death wouldn't be too bad.

Soon enough she felt rough paws on her arms and legs, claws digging in. The pain wasn't too bad. Then a heavy weight on her chest as one of the beasts pinned her to the ground. As it began to rip at her throat and face, drinking down her lifeblood, Seryn realised she had been wrong. It did hurt, it hurt worse than anything, it was agony and she *screamed*...

Veek drank down the human's blood and screams with gusto. She remembered this one; the terrified creature that had tried to crawl away from her at the last hunt. Senseless with fear, the prey didn't put up any resistance and Veek was able to eviscerate it with ease, filling her mouth with great clumps of its flesh. She tossed the liver, kidneys and heart on to the rocks surrounding the nearest fire, preferring the taste of cooked internal organs.

Her immediate hunger sated, Veek lay back, watching her fellow hunters feed. Vale Guards watched from the gantries above, eyes gleaming in the firelight, lusting after the prey – but they would have to wait, until they trained as hunters. If that ever came to pass, on this madness of a mission.

The Great Mission. All too soon the Vale Commander would be calling them to the briefing. All too soon they would have to embark on yet another pointless survey, with not even the promise of fresh prey at the end of it. All too soon they would have consumed all their live prey and be reduced to subsisting on synthetic flesh like the Vale Guards.

Flayoun appeared before her, fur streaked with blood. Veek grinned. *All too soon*... but there was still time to sate other appetites.

In the light of the fires, in the pools of spilled blood and entrails, as Seryn's internal organs cooked slowly on the hot stone, Veek and Flayoun's bodies came together and the pit rang with the piercing screams of their mating.

Chapter Nine
A Well-Tended Paradise

Peri sat up, opened her eyes and realised she had absolutely no idea where she was. As she took in her surroundings, her mouth fell open in awe. Wow. Had she died and gone to botanist's heaven? Her head reeled with a sense of disorientation as she tried to take it all in.

She was sitting at the top of a shallow slope, gazing out over a complex landscape of gardens that spilled out in a dazzling panorama all around her. From her elevated position, she could see lanes of tall, silvery trees, leading off into the hazy distance like spokes of a giant wheel. Between them, an ordered sequence of fields and flowerbeds stretched towards the horizon. Over all this was sky of such startling blue Peri felt she could almost taste it. Someone had propped her in a sitting position against a tree whose leaves cast dappled shade around her, protecting her from the blazing sun.

Her palms brushed the short, inch-long grass, and she examined it, fascinated. It wasn't like anything she'd ever seen on Earth or any of the other planets she'd visited so far. It was dark green, almost black, shading to purple at the root, and the blades had square, sheared-off ends as if recently mown.

She turned round, feeling the smooth silver-grey bark of the tree with curious hands. Behind her a whole forest of similar trees crowded the top of the small rise. It wasn't like any forest Peri had ever seen. The trees were evenly spaced, their thin branches bearing heart-shaped, golden-hued leaves whispering like lovers conversing in secret. It looked way too neat to be natural.

She turned back, eyes exploring the vista more methodically. Was that movement out there, in a garden some miles away? Or were her eyes playing tricks on her? She tried to stand, but a lurching feeling in her stomach forced her on to all fours and she vomited, off-white bile splattering the uniform grass. Muttering apologies to whoever kept this place so trim, she tried to control her retching spasms, her fingers digging with little resistance into the soil. It was soft, dark, gritty, and a rich peaty smell rose to her nostrils. Not natural, then. Cultivated, treated. Like a garden – but *what* a garden!

As her heavings subsided she tried to remember how she'd got here. Hadn't she been on the way to look at some alien plant life, with... the Doctor? No. She'd been running away from the Doctor, for some reason. Running away, with...

She felt the gentle pressure of hands on her shoulders, easing her into a sitting position. She wiped the tears from her eyes, focusing on the face that was staring intently into hers. A tanned face with wide-set brown eyes, under a fringe of glossy brown hair. There was a name attached to that face, she knew, and it suddenly sprang into her mind. The guy she'd temporarily dumped the Doctor for. 'Athon?'

His eyes narrowed in concern. 'Are you all right?'

'Yeah, I'm fine, now.' She remembered the skyboat, the breathtaking flight over the desert. And more. His hand on her leg. His crude suggestion. And then the attack from out of the blue and the way he'd abandoned her to the hunters. Galvanised by a sudden surge of anger, she shoved him in the chest, the balls of her fists connecting with the breastbone beneath his tattoo. 'Get away from me!'

Athon rolled backwards down the slope, arms flailing. 'Hey! I'm sorry!'

He made to scramble back up towards her, but Peri set her face into a glaring mask. 'You left me to die, Athon.'

'But we're safe, now,' he said, spread arms indicating their peaceful surroundings. 'We're alive.' He tried to smile, but the expression froze into a grimace. Clearly he knew what he'd done. Equally clearly he wanted her forgiveness. Well, he could whistle for it.

'So we're safe. I bet you had nothing to do with it,' she said. 'Where's the Doctor?'

'Not far. Come, I'll take you.' He stooped over her, offering his hand, hope gleaming in his dark brown eyes.

'Just point me in the right direction and get lost,' said Peri, getting to her feet. Underneath her nausea, a hollow hunger gnawed.

Head hung low, Athon pointed to the forest border to Peri's left, and then slunk off into the trees.

Trying to ignore the shooting pains in her legs and the throbbing in her head, Peri set off in the direction he'd indicated.

She stopped, and found herself staring at the horizon as if it meant something to her. Then she realised – it was flat. So they couldn't be on the Eknuri planetoid. She began to remember more, how she'd been fascinated by Athon, thrilled even. She felt disgusted with herself. What had she been thinking? But that was before she'd found out what a creep and a coward he was.

She wished she could remember more, but the period between getting shot and waking up in this fantastic garden had the fleeting quality of a dream. Hadn't she been taken to some freezing pit, inside a hell of rusted metal and earth? Whatever, she was free now, someone had saved her – probably the Doctor, she thought with a pang of guilt. Well, he'd be able to explain everything. He usually did. She hurried along the perimeter of the forest, eager to get the apologies and explanations over.

The Doctor was arguing with a tall guy with short silver hair in a crumpled grey and black uniform. Other people stood or sat in the shade of the trees. A tall black-skinned woman, probably an Eknuri, lounged against a tree, her long body the only bit of darkness against the silvery-green forest. The black-haired woman with the staring eyes was sitting cross-legged watching the argument with morose intensity. On the edge of the small group, keeping watch over the vista of gardens, a bulbous, alien-looking gun held at the ready, was another woman, in the same type of uniform as the guy arguing with the Doctor, with the same style hair only copper-red.

None of them had noticed Peri – all of them except the red-haired woman were intent on the Doctor and the grey-haired soldier. They were shouting, the Doctor sounding frustrated. He pointed at the gun the soldier held loosely between them, then at the panorama of gardens and trees. His meaning was clear: *What use are guns in paradise*? He'd gone beyond pleading and was now in full-on exasperation mode. He once told Peri he never got on with soldiers, now she could see why. With his blond hair, youthful looks and bizarre outfit the Doctor must look like the ultimate draft-dodging peacenik.

Peri walked right up to the Doctor and the soldier, ignoring the stares of the others, and tapped the Doctor on the shoulder.

The Doctor broke off from his conversation and turned round, face flushed and frowning. 'Not now, Aline, can't you see I'm rather busy?' As he spoke his face cleared and he broke into a beaming smile. 'Peri! How are you feeling?'

They hugged each other like old friends – which Peri supposed they were. She could almost feel the glare of the soldier burning into her but she ignored him.

They disengaged. There was a moment of unease.

The soldier looked about to speak again but the Doctor held up a hand. 'Captain Melrose, will you please give us a moment?'

The soldier looked as if he was about to protest, but he nodded assent, giving Peri a hard stare, and went to confer with his comrade.

The Doctor handed her a bar of chocolate and she wolfed it down, not caring where he had got it from.

'You've been unconscious for hours,' she heard him say. 'Any side effects?'

The chocolate made her feel a whole lot better, but she was still hungry. 'Well, I was sick a little back there and I ache all over but apart from that, I'm OK. Look, Doctor, about running off with Athon –'

The Doctor put both hands on her shoulders. 'Don't apologise. If anyone's sorry, it's me for letting them take you.'

She was about to argue with him, demand the right to apologise, when she saw in his eyes that it didn't matter. She was forgiven. Obviously things had moved on a whole lot since she'd been captured, and the Doctor had more important things to worry about than their little tiff. She swallowed, still feeling sick. 'Doctor, what's happened? How did we get here?' She frowned. 'And what did you call me just then?'

'When?'

'Just then, when I tapped you on the shoulder.'

'Ah yes, you haven't met Aline, have you?' said the Doctor, indicating the dark-haired woman, who had stood up and approached them. 'Aline Vehlmann, renowned xenologist. She's been very brave – without her help you'd still be on the Valethske ship, wherever it is.'

Aline had watchful brown eyes which looked a little too large for her face, and a pale complexion that looked like it had never seen the sun. She'd tied back her shoulder-length black hair which made her look even more severe.

'Hi,' said Peri, shaking her hand. Her fingers were slightly stubby, and there was a resolute set to her jaw. Peri somehow got the feeling that this was a woman who had been to the edge and back.

'I'm very pleased to meet you,' said Aline. She had a cultured, know-it-all kind of voice, and a rather haughty smile – and one of Peri's favourite jackets – but if what the Doctor said was true then Peri was pleased to meet her too.

Something else the Doctor said. Vale something. 'Who or what are the vale thesk?'

'Valethske,' corrected the Doctor.

Aline opened her mouth to speak but was interrupted by the return of Captain Melrose. 'Murdering vermin,' he said. He had a deep, clear voice that sounded used to being obeyed. Officer class to a T.

'Peri, meet Captain John Melrose,' said the Doctor. 'Also instrumental in our escape from the Valethske ship.'

Melrose smiled. It seemed genuine enough, and he extended a great slab of a hand towards Peri. He had a pink, fleshy face, with a prominent nose and a high forehead. His blue eyes looked raw, bright, as if they'd seen too much. His hair was light grey, cut short but just beginning to grow out. His handshake was predictably harsh and Peri did her best to return it, impatient to get these introductions over and find out just exactly what was going on.

'And his comrade-in-arms, Lieutenant Lornay Meharg.'

On hearing her name, the small woman turned round and gave them a curt nod. She had a small, heart-shaped face and, even with brutally short red hair, she looked rather elfin to Peri. Like her senior officer, the young soldier's eyes bore a haunted look.

'This is Taiana and you already know, Athon, wherever he is,' said the Doctor, looking round with a baffled expression.

'Yeah, hi,' said Peri, waving briefly at Taiana, whose golden eyes burned from the shade of the trees. 'Look, Doctor, where the hell are we, how did we get here and,' she had a quick look round for a familiar blue shape, but couldn't see it anywhere, 'where's the TARDIS?'

The Doctor's face clouded. 'I think we'd better have a little chat.'

After the Doctor had explained everything – well, everything that he could – Peri stared up at him, amazed at how calm he seemed, seeing like they were probably stranded for ever in this weird well-tended paradise.

'You did all that just to save me?'

He peered at her quizzically, and then looked away, seemingly embarrassed. 'Well, it was nothing, really. Just a quick hop in the TARDIS and the usual last-minute dash.'

Peri picked up on the strain in his voice when he mentioned the TARDIS. 'But the TARDIS...'

'I shouldn't worry. The Valethske won't be able to harm it, and they're probably in this solar system somewhere, maybe even on this planet.'

Peri shivered. The Doctor's explanation had filled in the gaps in her memory. She now knew how close to being on the menu she had been. But all the other poor souls on that ship... 'That isn't a comforting thought.'

'Quite,' said the Doctor.

Something else was bothering Peri. The aching in her bones, the fog in her head, the sickness – she knew the cause of it now, but that was no comfort at all. 'You say I was on that ship for a *hundred years*?' She still couldn't quite take it in. This was a different sort of time travel, harsh and disturbing. The thought of her sleeping body, hurtling across light-years of space year upon year, gave Peri the creeps. What made it even more weird was that it seemed like only yesterday that they'd landed at Athon's party.

'Give or take a year or so.' He peered intently at her face. 'But don't worry, you look great for a hundred and nineteen-year-old!'

'Huh, thanks a lot!' But she knew that in trying to make light of it, the Doctor was letting her know that she'd come to no harm. And she was safe, for now. Athon had been right. Impossible to believe there was any danger in this paradise.

They were standing some way from the others, at the edge of the forest. The Doctor had pointed out the dark wedge of the Valethske shuttle in which they'd made their escape, parked in the middle of a field of dry, fallow grass. To prevent its owners tracking it, the Doctor had disabled the flight computer. That was what the Doctor and Melrose had been arguing about – who had custody of the shuttle's control chip. The Doctor had won that one, but had been unable to dissuade Melrose from taking the two Valethske guns they'd found on the shuttle and keeping them to himself. So much for making a peaceful approach to any ETs they might meet on this strange garden-world.

Peri looked at the gardens surrounding their hill. 'Doesn't seem real, does it?'

The Doctor smiled his familiar curious half-smile. 'You're right, it doesn't. What makes you say that?'

'Well, it's obvious,' said Peri, indicating the vista of flowerbeds, the impossibly neat forest stretching behind them. 'It's all too neat to be natural.'

'Anything else?'

Peri thought for a second. 'No insects. No birds, either. An ecosystem of just plants on their own is, well, impossible, isn't it?'

'Nothing's impossible, Peri. Depends on the edaphic and biotic conditions. One thing's for sure – someone or something tends these gardens. This grass doesn't cut itself, someone planted those trees in a regular pattern.'

Peri shivered. 'So where are they?'

'Questions, questions, and no answers. Come on, let's get back to the others before Melrose starts shooting at the trees.'

'Doctor, glad you're back. Is Miss Brown appraised of the situation?'

'Yes, I am,' said Peri.

This didn't look good. Melrose had everyone standing in a line before him, his lieutenant by his side.

'As the senior officer here, I am assuming command of this party, which is now under the auspices of the Korsair Military Corps.'

'Now hold on a minute...' began the Doctor.

Melrose ignored him. 'The shuttle we took from the enemy ship is a short-range vessel. It hasn't got sufficient fuel to make it to any other planet within range, certainly not to the next system. More to the point, any attempts to activate it could attract the attention of the enemy.' His cold blue eyes took on a new intensity as he warmed to his subject. 'Our first priority is therefore to establish contact with any indigenous life, obtain their assistance, contact Korsair command, and take out the enemy.'

'We don't even know for certain if there is any sentient life on this planet,' implored the Doctor. 'And as for contacting Korsair command, I've got some rather distressing news for you.'

'Silence!' barked Lt Meharg, bringing her stolen weapon to bear on the Doctor, her piercing blue eyes zeroing in on him like weapon sights.

The Doctor backed away, hands raised to ward her off. 'Now let's not be too hasty.'

Taiana, Athon and Aline sidled slowly away from the Doctor and Peri.

Lt Meharg advanced towards the Doctor. Melrose looked on, his face impassive.

They're taking refuge behind what they know, realised Peri.

She'd seen the similar looks on the faces of Vietnam vets. The thousand yard stare, the haunted look – whatever these two had been through at the hands of the Valethske, they were now taking it out on them, taking command, while they could. The feeling of power must be exhilarating, almost overpowering.

As if they didn't have enough problems.

Then Melrose spoke. 'At ease, Lieutenant.'

Sighs of relief from everyone.

'Now, where was I?' muttered Melrose.

'In the middle of setting out a plan to take on an entire shipload of Valethske.'

The Doctor's sarcastic tone wasn't lost on the soldier. 'Well, what would *you* suggest?'

The Doctor stepped forwards, eager to take centre stage. 'I assume democracy existed – exists – on Korsair, so let's take a vote on it!'

'I have already stated, this unit is under Korsair command!' shouted Melrose. His voice lowered to a dangerous growl. 'Martial law, Doctor.'

The Doctor sighed. 'Look, is anyone else going along with this? Taiana, Athon – surely you can see the folly in what he's saying?'

Both Eknuri still looked dazed from their hundred years' sleep. Athon had a puzzled half-smile on his face, as if still expecting this all to be a joke, and the perpetrator to pop out from behind a tree at any moment.

Taiana's golden eyes were serious. 'Yes, in principle,' she said slowly. 'There is no need for aggression. But I agree with Captain Melrose's basic idea. We should try to make contact with the inhabitants of this planet.'

'Well I don't agree,' blurted out Athon. 'I think we should get back to the shuttle, take our chances. Someone might pick us up.'

'Yes, the Valethske,' said Melrose through gritted teeth, narrowing his eyes at Athon. 'You really are as stupid as you look.'

'He's been through rather a lot,' said the Doctor, voice hard-edged with anger. 'Leave him alone. It's only human to panic.'

Melrose came right up to the Doctor. 'Been through a lot? I've seen my whole squadron killed by the Valethske. Good soldiers, shot down and ripped open before my eyes. They kept me alive for days, teasing me, seeing how many of my troopers they could tear apart before I cracked. I had to listen to their dying screams, Doctor, I had to hear them crying for their mothers, and I had to take it and show nothing. I didn't crack then and I won't crack now. And I won't rest until that ship of hell-hounds is no more than drifting interstellar dust!' Melrose was shouting now. 'So what do you suggest we do, Doctor?'

The Doctor looked at a loss for a second, glanced at Peri, and then sighed. 'I suggest we go along with your plan.'

Peri gaped, but one look from the Doctor was enough to tell her he was biding his time. Let the soldier-boys do all the shouting while the Doctor worked everything out in the background.

'Right!' said Melrose, sounding pleased with himself. 'I suggest we head for the structure Lt Meharg sighted a few hours ago.'

'What structure?' asked Peri.

The Doctor led her a little way off, and pointed along one of the avenues of trees. In the distance, a good few miles off, something rose into the clouds, like a fairytale castle, only more organic-looking.

'It's a fair guess that it's a centre of civilisation,' explained the Doctor. 'Let's hope the natives are friendly.'

Melrose called for everyone's attention, but another, softer voice cut across his hectoring tones.

'Before we set off, there's something you all should know.'

Everyone turned to look at Aline.

Her pale face looked strained with tension. She had her arms folded in front of her, hugging the leather jacket to her.

'What's the matter, Aline?' said the Doctor.

Aline took a deep breath. Peri could see there was a lot going on behind those large brown eyes. 'Ten years ago, I headed up a contact mission to investigate a new life form, which hadn't responded to any attempts to communicate with it. I had – I have – wide experience of all types of alien species, so I went in. This creature... I can't begin to describe it and it's not important now.

It sensed I was receptive to it and tried to mentally bond with me. It was too much for my mind – for any human – and I – well, I lost my mind for a while.' She tried a smile which looked ghastly. 'But I'm all right now.'

'You have my sympathies,' said Melrose, in a voice which implied the exact opposite, 'but is this relevant?'

'It may be,' said Aline, brushing a strand of hair away from her eyes. 'When we first got here, I sensed a presence.'

Melrose snorted and Lt Meharg gave a short sneering laugh.

'Why didn't you tell us before?' said the Doctor.

'I wasn't sure, there was too much else going on – landing the shuttle, getting everyone away...'

'What sort of presence?'

'I don't know, but it was similar to the thing that drove me out of my mind.'

'Similar in what way?'

Aline's dark eyes were fixed on the Doctor as she spoke. 'Old. And powerful. And more alien than anything any human has ever encountered.'

Chapter Ten
The Sleeping Beast

Vale Commander Kikker stood among the flickering shadows on a gantry above the pit and watched his hunters feed and copulate. Over a third of the ship's store of prey had been broken out for the hundred-plus hunters. There would be enough left for this survey, but after that they'd need to replenish their stocks. More hunting, more delay – but Kikker knew he couldn't deny his hunters the pleasure of fresh, living flesh.

Kikker gazed into the embers of a fire far below. Perhaps there wouldn't need to be another stop. Perhaps, after so long, this was it, their long search over at last. The prospect filled Kikker with surges of pride, followed quickly by a sinking sense of disappointment. What would he do, once he'd completed the Great Mission? It had been going on so long he could hardly remember Valeth Skettra. Better, perhaps, if it never ended – but no. Kikker wanted the honour. Maybe, once the Great Mission was over and Kikker's immortal glory was assured, he'd take his own life. It would be the perfect point at which to end.

Kikker took a bite from the chunk of synthetic flesh he carried with him and chewed absently, trying not to notice the dismaying lack of taste. Another reason Kikker wanted the Great Mission over. Unlike his loyal Vale Guards, he was entitled to fresh prey, but to set an example he'd taken a vow to abstain until the successful conclusion of the Great Mission. This sent a strong message to Vale Guards and hunters alike – Kikker, bloodthirsty veteran of a thousand hunts, was so certain of the success of the mission that he was willing to forgo the greatest pleasure known to Valethske.

To Kikker, success would have a real taste – the taste of warm blood and soft, succulent flesh.

He turned away from the feast below, trying vainly to stop himself drooling. He dared not let any of the hunters see him like this. There had been several challenges to his command, and he'd bested them all, but if any of the hunters saw the merest hint of weakness in him they'd be on him like a pack of cubs on a tender roasted boar.

Unable to keep the thought of food far from his mind, Kikker angrily thrust more of the synthetic meat into his mouth, gagging at the rubbery texture. Vats deep within the ship's bowels grew the stuff from cultures prepared centuries ago, an unending source of bland sustenance. If he'd been a harsh leader, and a stupid one, he could put an end to the hunts, force the hunters to eat the synthetic stuff and concentrate solely on the Great Mission. But that was no way to treat hunters. They needed fresh prey.

If only one of the two viable planets in this system showed signs of mammalian life. That way, they could combine the search with the hunt. He'd only find out after the ship completed its first survey of the planets.

Uneven footsteps rang along the gantry, and Kikker wolfed down the rest of the food, wiping the drool from his lips, instantly angry.

A tall, stooping figure limped towards him, clad in a simple tunic, his yellow eyes gummy with age.

'Ruvis,' hissed Kikker. 'Why do you disturb me? The mission briefing isn't for another hour, after the initial survey!'

Ruvis blinked at him, licking his lips. 'I make no apology for disturbing you.'

Kikker ignored his insolence. Ruvis had the respect of the hunters, but paid none to their Commander. He had once been a hunter, but instead of taking the honourable way out for an old hunter – volunteering for one of the Great Vale's glorious suicide missions – Ruvis had instead opted to join the technical elite. The coward's way out, Kikker always thought, but on balance, the Valethske needed technicians and engineers to manufacture their machines of war and destruction. And Ruvis was no coward – he refused to be intimidated by Kikker, however much the Vale Commander tried. If his role in the Great Mission had been less important, Kikker would have killed him long ago. 'Then what you have to say had better be of the utmost importance.'

Ruvis bowed his head, but his voice was mocking. 'That's for you to decide, Vale Commander.'

Ruvis popped a piece of synthetic flesh in his mouth and chewed, his jaw whirring. Kikker knew he preferred it to living flesh. Sometimes he wondered if the cancers that had ravaged his body – or the treatment that had eventually burned them away – had warped the technician's mind. Ruvis was one of the few survivors of a disastrous skirmish with the Sontarans. He'd spent three lunar cycles stranded on a derelict ship with nothing to eat but Sontaran flesh, which was notoriously tough, tasteless and highly carcinogenic. His left leg and lower jaw had been eaten away by disease and subsequently replaced by prosthetic equivalents. His mechanical jaw whirred with servo-mechanisms as Ruvis spoke, but his voice was still as smooth and deep as it had ever been.

'When the Vale Guards began the revivification process, they noticed that five prey had already been revived. They were nowhere to be found on the ship. And one of the short-range skirmishers is missing.'

Kikker hurled the lump of ersatz meat into the pit. 'What?'

Ruvis went on. 'The computer log indicates that it was taken by a pack of hunters for a scouting mission, but this is obviously impossible. I suspect sabotage.'

Kikker's mind raced. 'So five prey escaped. Not enough for the hunters to notice.' He bared his teeth and flattened his ears, moving closer to the technician. 'It is best that no one hears about this, Ruvis.'

Their eyes locked. Ruvis didn't back down, but he gave a tiny nod. Kikker relaxed. Ruvis may not respect the Vale Commander but he knew what was best for the Great Mission.

'So what happened?' asked Kikker. 'A breakdown in the cryogenic equipment?'

Ruvis shook his head. 'As with the flight computer in the skirmisher, that had also been tampered with. We have had intruders.'

This was unprecedented. 'How? The hull is unbreachable!'

'They left something behind,' said Ruvis. 'I think you'll find this interesting.'

With a last look at the hunters, many of whom were now relaxing in the glow of the fires, the smell of burning human fat rising to his nostrils, Kikker followed Ruvis from the gantry down to the main access tunnel of the ship and to one of the holding bays. At the far end, a tall blue box stood behind a cordon of Vale Guards. The young Valethske looked edgy, and seemed very relieved to see their Commander.

Kikker dismissed them with a wave of his hand and approached the strange object. 'What is it?'

Ruvis shrugged. 'I don't know.' A rare admission of ignorance.

Kikker walked up to the blue box, wondering at its strangeness. It seemed to be a manufactured thing of squares and straight lines, but its purpose was unclear. He reached out to touch it, claws chafing the worn blue surface. There was the strangest sensation, as if he was caressing a sleeping beast.

There was something familiar about it, something which nagged at him. He was sure he had seen it somewhere before, maybe in the century-long dream of the long sleep, maybe in reality.

Kikker drew back his hand and turned to Ruvis. The old technician was staring at the object, eyes misty, lost in contemplation.

'An alien artefact, obviously,' said Kikker, letting his tongue explore his formidable set of incisors. 'Equally obviously, it must have penetrated the ship, using some sort of teleport.' Pleased with this hypothesis, Kikker glanced slyly at Ruvis.

Ruvis's jaw whirred. 'In which case, what is it doing still here? If it teleported in, it could teleport out.'

That was a point. 'Maybe it was meant to remain here. Maybe it's some sort of explosive device, planted by our enemies to destroy us. Maybe even the Gods themselves...'

They looked at each other, and Kikker noticed the unease in Ruvis's old eyes. Kikker knew that Ruvis, although a technician, believed in the Gods as much as he did. All Valethske believed.

Their existence was a historical fact. Whether or not they still existed, it was up to Kikker and his crew to discover. Could this strange object have been sent from the Gods? Could the Great Mission, after so many centuries, be over at last?

Kikker could see similar thoughts passing behind Ruvis's gummy eyes. At length the old technician spoke. 'We cannot rule out that possibility. Though if it was sent to destroy us, would it not have been a little less ostentatious? It was discovered within minutes of the Vale Guards' waking. And surely, it could have detonated while we all still languished in the long sleep.'

Then Kikker remembered where he'd seen it before. 'Ruvis – remember the last hunt, before the long sleep?'

Ruvis nodded, his tail curling up against his spine. 'Yes, the planetoid. Slim pickings, I hear.'

Kikker pointed at the blue box. 'That box was there, right in the middle of things! And it was still there when we left!'

'You're sure?'

Kikker bunched his fist and punched the side of the box. 'Of course I'm sure! Which means that...' he tailed away, not really knowing what it meant.

Ruvis's jaw whirred. 'It must have followed us. It couldn't have teleported in before the long sleep, as we would have detected it. It must somehow have come here while we were in flight.'

Kikker snarled. 'That's impossible, the speed we were going!'

'I know,' said Ruvis. 'That leaves only one possibility. It must have come aboard when we came out of faster-than-light speed. Which means... by Azreske!'

Kikker met Ruvis's astonished gaze.

'A time machine?' they both said at the same time.

Kikker looked back at the blue box in wonder. Could it be?

'If we gain access to time travel we will be invincible,' whispered Ruvis.

Kikker growled. 'You mean, more invincible than we already are.' The implications spun in his mind. With a time machine, the Valethske could proliferate throughout the universe. The possibilities were endless. Kikker's place in the Hall of Glory was as certain as the breath in his body.

'Of course, this might not be the same object,' mused Ruvis. 'It could be another of its kind.'

'It's the same, I know it,' said Kikker. He came to a decision. 'Prepare a skirmisher, take this artefact to a safe distance beyond the blast range of a thermonuclear device of this size. We'll investigate it once this phase of the mission is over.'

Ruvis saluted and went away to prepare transport for the strange blue box.

Kikker stayed for a while, regarding the box intently, as if he hoped that just by looking at it he could divine its secrets. His hunter's instinct knew that whatever it was, time machine or not, it would be vital in this mission. It was an omen, a sign that the end was in sight, that the objective set hundreds of years ago by the Great Vale would finally be reached, and Valethske honour satisfied.

And then, thought Kikker, eyes closing gently in a dream of flesh, he would taste living meat once more.

Chapter Eleven
Shock Tactics

As the creature advanced Aline stood her ground, even though her legs felt as if they were going to crumple beneath her, even though she wanted to scream her lungs out and run for the trees. Two things prevented her from embarking on such an undignified course of action: her training, and the reassuring presence of the Doctor at her side.

'Fascinating!' came the Doctor's voice of indefatigable enthusiasm. 'Completely autonomous, motile plants – I've never seen such a degree of specialisation.'

Aline felt herself nodding in agreement, her eyes fixed on the creature before her. Its pale-green appendages did indeed seem suited for a number of tasks – there were many-fingered 'hands', digits rippling like the fronds of a sea-anemone; thick, trowel-like leaves, surely intended for digging; sharp, lethal-looking pincers that reminded Aline bizarrely of secateurs; and other, obscurer forms, their purpose unclear. Aline was close enough now to see that the joints in its limbs were barely half an inch apart, making them extremely flexible. As they curled and waved against the blue sky, they made a clicking sound.

'Hey, don't *shoot* them!' Peri shouted from somewhere near the edge of the garden.

Aline tore her gaze away for long enough to see Captain Melrose and Lt Meharg crouching against the neatly trimmed hedgerow, Valethske weapons targeting the creature. Peri, Athon and Taiana stood nearby, the two Eknuri trying not to look out of their depth, Peri looking on anxiously. Further along, another of the creatures worked on the hedge, seemingly oblivious to the drama being played out around it, pincers busily snipping at the leaves.

The creature stopped just in front of the Doctor and Aline, swaying slightly on stilt-like legs, its great flowered head raised up as if in fanfare to the golden orb of the sun. Its many appendages came to rest, looping back against the central stem. Aline realised she had hold of the Doctor's hand, and as she turned to him he smiled in reassurance.

That was enough to shake Aline out of her fear-trance and remember who she used to be. Who she would be again: Aline Vehlmann, renowned xenologist, veteran of countless first contact situations. Just like this.

She let go of the Doctor's hand and stepped towards the alien creature. It was beautiful, in a bizarre kind of way. Its limbs – which numbered above a dozen, though they were so complex and spindly Aline found it hard to count them – sprouted from a gourd-like central mass roughly the size of a human torso, dark green, mottled and gnarled like old tree-bark. Its half-dozen 'legs' were complex, stilt-like appendages which bore the body a good six feet clear of the ground, and which ended in leaf-like 'feet'. From the top of the body rose a thick green stem which widened out into a trumpet-like flower-head, rather like an orchid, which towered over ten feet from the ground, dwarfing even Taiana. This one was pale creamy-white shot through with bright-red veins; beyond it, and around the garden, stalked other creatures with different colorations.

'Tempting to think of the flower at the top as the creature's head,' came the Doctor's reassuring voice, 'but its sense organs are probably in the tips of its appendages. A unique life form...'

Aline discerned a gentle urging in the Doctor's raised eyebrows, his half-smile. Saw what he was up to. Her therapist would have pronounced it madness for Aline, in her current state of recovery, to attempt contact with a totally new alien species. Hence the Eknuri assignment. But there was a gentle wisdom in the Doctor's eyes, telling Aline that he knew better; there was no point hiding, no point running away. Best to confront her fears. Best to confront the alien – the obviously and outrageously alien, like this plant-thing, not beings like the Doctor who hid their difference beneath a mask of seemingly human flesh and blood.

Not that the Doctor would risk her life by thrusting her towards something dangerous. He'd let her make up her own mind about going with him to the Valethske ship – and there was always the possibility of a second, closer and possibly fatal encounter with that species – so he must be sure the plant-creature posed no threat.

With a last look at the Doctor, Aline squared up to the alien plant. She didn't smile or spread her arms wide in welcome – a novice error: any gestures made in first contact are open to interpretation. Instead she kept her expression relaxed and open, her mind calm and focused, one sentient being reaching out to another.

The great orchid-like head swept round in an arc, limbs clicked and moved, and, with a gentle lurching motion, the creature stepped around Aline.

She turned to watch it go, to see it stoop above a bed of tulip-like blooms and begin to extract weeds deftly from the dark-brown soil and toss them into its trumpet-like mouth.

It had completely ignored her!

Unable to stop herself, Aline collapsed in a fit of laughter, grabbing on to the Doctor for support – and then burst into tears of relief.

When Aline recovered from her laughing/crying fit, she realised that everyone was staring at her. Peri was gaping at her openly, incredulous; the two soldiers were looking at her as if she was mad and the Eknuri looked embarrassed, as if she'd committed some serious social *faux pas*.

Only the Doctor seemed unconcerned by her reaction. There was genuine pleasure in his eyes, as Aline wiped her tears away and turned to face him.

'Well done,' he said. 'You're well on the road to recovery.'

Peri couldn't see what the all the fuss was about. She'd faced up to the Valethske – been chased, shot and frozen by them – without once cracking. But if all it took to throw Aline was a giant walking pansy then Peri didn't hold out much hope for the woman. And she seemed over-friendly with the Doctor. What had they been up to while she'd been stored away on the Valethske ship like a Thanksgiving turkey? They'd had plenty of time to become the best of chums. Now the Doctor was cradling her in his arms as she cried. Yuck.

Peri turned away and went across the garden to where the creature was at work weeding a bed of blooms, a trowel-like appendage making flowing, precise movements. Flowers tending flowers. Cute, thought Peri, but what the hell was it all for? The purpose of flowers was to attract insects, the intermediaries of pollination. Peri bent and cupped one of the dark orange tulip-like blooms in her hand, putting her nose into its cool cup of petals and sniffing. No smell. No pollen. No point! There was a tap on her shoulder, and she looked up. The towering plant-creature loomed over her, its clicking tendrils gently easing her away from the flowerbed.

'Hey, OK, I get the message,' cried Peri, walking back to the others.

They had spotted the creatures a few hours after they had left the hilltop forest and followed a long avenue of silvery-barked trees in the general direction of the strange castle-like thing. Melrose had wanted to make first contact but the Doctor had miraculously persuaded him to let Aline have a go. Much good she'd been.

Aline had more or less recovered now and was standing by, arms folded, as Melrose and the Doctor argued again.

Melrose's face was flushed. 'Clearly these – what did you say we should call them?'

'Gardeners,' said Aline with a smile and a glance at the Doctor.

'These "Gardeners" pose no threat, and we can't communicate with them. Therefore, they are of no interest to us. Therefore, we press on, to the structure we identified earlier.' He smiled without humour. 'Do you agree, Doctor?'

The Doctor's eyes were wary, his words carefully chosen. 'I agree that we should go on, but I don't agree that these creatures are of no interest.'

Melrose looked tired and impatient. 'So we go on? Good.' He

turned away from the Doctor, heading back towards the avenue of trees, motioning with his gun for the others to follow.

They did. They had little choice. Behind Melrose's back, Peri saw Athon flash a grin at Lt Meharg. The soldier grinned back with a warning glance in Melrose's direction. Peri felt grimly satisfied. Just you wait, she thought. Or maybe she was just the type to be fooled by Athon's unsubtle ways. Whatever, she was welcome to him.

Peri caught up with the Doctor before Aline could chum up to him again. Unable to think of anything major to say, she said, 'This place is weird.'

'Weird and interesting, Peri, but only to the likes of us and Aline.' He sighed, gaze scanning the seemingly endless colonnade of trees. 'People like Melrose seem to have lost the capacity for wonder. I wonder...'

The Doctor lapsed into silence for a while. Peri began to realise how tired she was. And hungry. That bar of chocolate hadn't nearly been enough. She felt hollow inside, and images of waffles swimming in syrup, hot dogs and ice-cream flitted about her head.

'Wonder what?' she asked the Doctor, half to take her mind off her rumbling tum and half out of curiosity.

He spoke in low tones, so Melrose – or any of the others – couldn't hear what he was saying. 'Melrose is volatile, unpredictable. He thinks he's in control of the situation but really he has no idea of what the situation is yet. He could jeopardise our lives. I've got to have one more try at getting through to him – and I'm afraid it's time for shock tactics.'

So saying, he left Peri's side and fell into step with Melrose, smiling amiably at the soldier. Peri wondered what he had in mind. Behind Melrose, Lt Meharg – Lornay – was chatting freely with Athon, weapon held loosely by her side. She wouldn't be a danger to them, mused Peri. Already she seemed to realise her old way of life lay far behind her, and her eyes had lost their haunted look.

Peri let her gaze drift beyond her fellow travellers through the branches of the trees to the gardens beyond. So much to see. Endless gardens of the most outlandish, fascinating plants. Sunflowers as tall as houses, their heads intent on the sun like radar dishes. Dense patches of gnarled, twisting bushes, bristling with thorns, dotted with berries as big as her fist. Plantations of trees, fruit dangling enticingly from their branches. And things that defied classification, baroque warpings of plant biology, strangely beautiful. Between each field or garden or orchard ran lanes of the now-familiar dark green grass, the occasional neatly trimmed hedgerow, and here and there Gardeners worked, tilling the soil, pruning leaves. In the distance Peri saw a new kind of Gardener, a many-legged thing that hugged the ground, bearing before it a wide mouth that worked at the grass. That explained the neatly cropped stems, thought Peri, wondering again what it was all for. Gardens were kept for pleasure, for walking in, for looking at. But there was no one here to enjoy the beauty of the flowerbeds, or to stroll along the avenues of trees. Except themselves. Were they the first ever visitors to this garden-world?

Peri realised she'd fallen way behind, and forced her legs to speed her up, wincing with the effort. The avenue seemed endless, and her legs were aching badly. She truly felt her hundred and nineteen years. Marshalling her energies, Peri drew level with the Doctor and Melrose.

One look at her flushed face was enough for the Doctor. 'We'll rest, we've been walking for quite a while now.'

'I'm all right,' said Peri, trying to avoid Melrose's piercing stare, 'really.'

'No, you're not,' said the Doctor, gently leading her to the side of the avenue. She sank gratefully on to the grass, cool and springy in the shade, and leaned back against the smooth bark.

Melrose gestured with the barrel of his gun into the patches of blue sky visible through the interlocking branches above. 'We haven't got time. The Valethske could turn up at any minute.'

'Peri needs rest,' said the Doctor, squaring up to Melrose. 'So does Aline, so does Lt Meharg, and so do you. You were in suspended animation just like Peri. However well-trained you are, your body is going to need time to recover.'

Melrose and the Doctor stood glaring at each other for a few seconds, and then with a nod of his jutting chin, Melrose turned away and sat down stiffly in the middle of the avenue, Valethske gun held across his lap.

'As for you, Taiana, Athon, well, your physiology is more resilient than the basic human,' he smiled apologetically down at Peri, 'so please bear with us.'

Taiana leaned against a tree and watched them sullenly from a patch of shadow. Athon sat down on the grass a bit too near Peri for her liking. He gave her a fleeting, hopeful look which she crushed instantly with a stony glare. Lornay sat down right beside him, which seemed to cheer him up a little. Huh.

A silence fell over the party, and once more Peri was struck by how quiet it was. No birdsong, no chirruping of insects, just the gentle whispering of the wind through the trees. There wasn't even the usual feeling of being watched. The planet was ignoring them. That suited Peri. She suddenly felt heavy with sleep.

'Can't be far to that structure now. Wonder what it is?' the Doctor said breezily, trying to kick-start a conversation.

Peri felt her eyelids closing and a blissful drowsiness started to seep through her body. Her hunger pangs receded to a bearable level. Through a dazy fuzz she heard the conversation weave around her.

'Looked like a castle or a palace to me,' said Athon.

'No, it's a ship,' said Lornay. Her voice had a musical Celtic lilt. 'A bio-organic chlorophyll-fuelled starship that's gonna whisk us off this planet.'

If only, thought Peri, beginning to half-dream about a giant flower-powered rocket.

Aline's calm voice drifted from nearby. 'It's neither.'

'Ah, you have a theory!' Peri heard the Doctor snap his fingers... and then she was asleep...

...but Athon's voice jolted her awake again. He was almost shouting. 'It's far too big to be a tree!'

Peri opened her eyes, shifted position. Trust him not to notice that she was asleep and keep quiet accordingly.

'Perhaps it's a city,' said Lornay.

Aline gave her a dark look. 'I think my hypothesis is more likely, given what we've seen so far, don't you?'

Lornay glared at her.

'A giant tree,' said the Doctor. 'Yes, that does seem likely. Doesn't it, Peri?'

'Yeah,' muttered Peri. She felt too tired to care much about anything. 'A giant tree. Must be.'

She closed her eyes again, hungry for sleep.

There was silence for a while, then the Doctor spoke.

'Captain Melrose, you've yet to tell us of how you got captured by the Valethske.'

The tone of his voice told Peri he was up to something – perhaps the something he'd mentioned earlier – and she made herself stay awake to listen.

Melrose sighed. 'There's not much to tell.' He gazed off through the trees, as if searching the skyline for memories. 'Is there, Lieutenant?'

Lornay stared down at the grass, idly toying with the short, uniform stems. 'No, Sir.' Her large blue eyes were framed by a tense frown as if she was trying hard not to remember.

'Anything you can tell us about the Valethske might be of help,' urged the Doctor.

Melrose took a deep breath and began. 'Korsair's a military outpost, formed to police and protect the planets of the Thynemnus System. Colonists arriving all the time, lots of territorial and racial disputes. Without a strong military presence the whole system would have descended into chaos long ago.'

'Racial disputes?' asked the Doctor.

Melrose nodded. 'With the indigents. Some weren't too hot on the idea of co-existence. We had to step in and pacify.'

Peri recognised a euphemism when she heard one. 'I hardly blame them.'

Melrose's blue eyes were cold. 'I do. They get the best out of the deal – superior technology, our protection. Before we arrived they were just primitives grubbing about barely above subsistence level, ignorant of the potential of the worlds they eked out their lives upon.'

The Doctor raised his eyebrows and looked down at Peri with a world-weary expression. He'd obviously heard a lot of crap like this in his long life. 'Where do the Valethske fit in? Was their homeworld one of the planets earmarked for "pacification"?'

Melrose shook his head, picking a blade of grass and rolling it between his fingers. 'No.'

'No one knows where the Valethske homeworld is,' put in Aline. 'Or even if they still have one.'

'Right.' Melrose continued. 'I was overseeing a dispute on one of the newest colonies. The indigents – a bunch of filthy boar-like creatures – had started attacking the colonists. No deaths as yet, but I took a squad in, just to keep the lid on things. We'd been there barely a day when the Valethske turned up. Hit us when we least expected it. Took all the colonists and many of the indigents prisoner, had a big feast that night.'

Peri noticed that Lornay kept her eyes fixed on the ground, her face white, mouth slightly open, reliving the events Melrose was relating.

Melrose closed his eyes. 'I can still see the fires, Valethske cavorting around them, my troopers... Good men and women... torn apart. Sometimes, they'd use – instead of with each other –' Melrose's face writhed in a sudden, uncontrollable spasm of disgust. When it was over his eyes were wide, imploring. 'You've got to understand, there's no bargaining with the Valethske. To them, we're just prey. Walking lumps of meat. Nothing more. So if you're thinking of trying to negotiate with them to get your ship back – forget it.'

The Doctor looked uneasy. 'We'll see about that.'

'No,' Melrose leaned forward, stabbing a finger at the Doctor to emphasise his words. 'Forget it. They won't care. You are just meat.'

'They spared you and Lornay, though,' put in Peri.

Lornay looked up suddenly, dark shadows under her eyes, face pinched in anger. 'I'd rather they'd have killed me.'

Melrose leaned towards her. 'Easy now, Lieutenant – remember you're a soldier.'

Lornay blinked, wiped her face with small hands, trying to control herself. 'I'm sorry,' she gasped through sudden tears. 'It's just – the things I've seen –' She lapsed into silence.

Athon folded a long arm around her.

Melrose appeared to let this pass, for the moment. His eyes were chips of blue in his reddish-pink face. 'Oh, they "spared" some of us all right. Froze us for later.' He leaned forward, looking from the Doctor to Aline to Peri as he spoke. 'I've worked out what they're doing – they're on some immense voyage across the galaxy, looking for a new homeworld, and they need to keep stopping off to restock with meat every now and then. Meat – meaning us.'

Taiana spoke up. 'Perhaps this is it, their new homeworld. A garden for them to play in.' Her voice was bitter and sarcastic, the first time Peri had heard any emotion in her voice.

The Doctor gazed through the trees to the gardens beyond.

'I sincerely hope not. But why would they choose to come here, where there's no meat at all?'

'Except us,' said Peri.

The Doctor shot her an admonishing glance. 'Yes, well, I don't think we actually need to be continually reminded of that, Peri.'

Peri felt embarrassed and looked away. She heard the Doctor address Melrose again.

'Tell me, when did all this happen? I mean, which year?'

Melrose frowned. 'Well, 2594.'

'Ah,' said the Doctor, with a warning look at Taiana, who looked as if she was about to speak. 'How long do you think the Valethske kept you and the lieutenant on ice?'

A shadow passed over Melrose's face. 'Couple of years, maybe more – ten, at most.'

The Doctor shook his head. 'Captain Melrose, it was over five hundred years ago.'

Melrose opened his mouth, but no words came out. He stood up, gun swinging from left hand. With his other hand he reached out, fingers splayed, grasping at air. 'Five hundred *years*?'

'It's true,' said Taiana. 'It's been a century since Athon, Peri and I were taken.'

Lornay looked at Peri, eyes wide in shock. 'This true?'

Peri nodded, trying to look and sound reassuring. 'I'm afraid it is.'

Melrose's eyes were pleading. 'Doctor, you're joking – please tell me you're joking.'

'Does it look like we're joking?' said Aline. 'The Doctor's right, believe it.'

Melrose shook his head. Peri could see a sudden breakout of sweat on his pink, lined brow. 'Korsair command... the colonies...'

The Doctor stepped towards him. 'Now take it easy – the main thing is, you're alive.'

'What's the point?' yelled Melrose suddenly, his cultured tones rising in a strangled yell. 'What's the bloody point?'

Peri rose to her feet as everyone began to back away from Melrose. Everyone except the Doctor. Peri realised that this was it, the time had come, the time the Doctor had been worried about: when Melrose gunned them all down in a moment of madness. Why the hell had the Doctor told him the date? Didn't he guess it would unhinge Melrose?

The Doctor approached Melrose, talking soothingly, trying to calm him. But with a roar, Melrose raised the gun and loosed a bolt of energy at the canopy of leaves above them. Peri ducked as scorched plant material floated down around her like surreal confetti.

In the silent, stunned aftermath of the gunshot, Melrose spoke. 'No one follow me. Not even you, Lieutenant.'

'Where are you going?' asked the Doctor.

Melrose's eyes glittered. 'To find the truth.'

'What truth?'

'The truth about what's going on here.'

'I've been telling you the truth,' the Doctor shouted.

'He has,' added Peri.

'No.' Melrose was emphatic. He panned the gun in an arc

covering all the party. 'I'm going now. No one follow me.'

With that, he turned and ran from the avenue of trees, disappearing into a thick growth of fern-like plants.

The Doctor and Lornay both started after him.

'No, stay here with the others – I'll see if I can reason with him.' Then the Doctor was gone, haring through the ferns after Melrose.

Peri was about to run after when a hand gripped her shoulder.

She turned to see Taiana's dark face. She was shaking her head. 'You heard what he said. We'd better stay here.' Her golden eyes for once showed a glimmer of fear, and Peri realised how traumatised the Eknuri woman was. Who knew what dark images flickered behind that smooth brow?

'OK,' said Peri, deciding to give in for the moment.

'All I want to do is find civilisation and use it to get back home.' Taiana turned and stalked off to stand with Athon.

Chapter Twelve
Forbidden Fruit

Peri walked over to Lornay, who was standing staring at the ferns still settling into place after the Doctor and Melrose's departure.

'Are you OK?'

'Yeah, I'll be fine.' She shook her head. 'The way he looked at me, as if he didn't know me any more.'

'Has he done this sort of thing before?' Aline had joined them.

'No, never. He never cracked, not even when the Valethske...' Lornay's mouth worked in agitation. Then she looked up at Peri. Her frown framed an expression of dawning realisation, as if she had just woken from a bad dream. 'I ought to get after my Captain – ah what the hell. He's old enough and ugly enough to look after himself.'

'So's the Doctor,' muttered Peri. 'Well – he's not ugly but you wouldn't believe how old he is!'

Lornay smiled briefly, revealing tiny, pearl-white teeth. Then she stared at Peri, her expression suddenly challenging. 'Oh yeah? I've had to believe a lot of weird shit today. So try me!'

In that moment Peri saw that Lornay wasn't the type to crack under pressure. She was just a grunt, paid to take orders, not to think. Paid to kill in the name of 'keeping the peace'. The sort of person the Doctor – and by association Peri herself – should cross any gulf of time and space to avoid. Oddly, though, Peri found that she quite liked the young soldier – she couldn't be that much older than herself, Valethske interference notwithstanding.

In contrast Aline remained a distant, forbidding figure. Peri wouldn't have minded chatting to the xenologist about her experiences, but there was something in her eyes that gave Peri the creeps. Something about the way she stood, as if she wasn't listening to their conversation, but to something else, something that none of them but Aline could hear.

With enthusiasm, Peri told Lornay about the Doctor and the

TARDIS, enjoying seeing the young soldier's eyes bug out in amazement. Peri noticed Athon lurking nearby, blatantly eavesdropping, but she ignored him.

'You're mad,' said Lornay when she'd finished. 'Or I'm mad.' She laughed. Then she shrieked as Athon crept up and grabbed her from behind, lifting her off her feet.

Exchanging a wry glance with Taiana, Peri turned away, her gaze running along the line of smooth, silver-grey trunks to a field beyond, a regular square of the usual dark grass, with a hundred or so small, pink-leafed trees, evenly spaced and well tended as usual, their branches almost touching the ground, heavily freighted with large yellow fruit. Three Gardeners towered over the trees, taking fruit in their many-fingered hands, twisting it from the stems and dropping it inside their flower-like mouths, where it disappeared soundlessly. What were they doing? Were they eating it? Peri felt her eyes drawn to the fruit. She suddenly remembered how ravenous she was.

'Hey, Lornay,' she called out. 'You hungry?'

Lornay came over. 'I've been tryin' to ignore it, but yeah.'

'You're not thinking of eating some of the fruit, are you?' Aline's voice was unwelcomingly harsh.

'Why not?' said Peri, moving off towards the trees. 'I've got to eat something soon or I'll just pass out.'

'I don't advise it,' said Aline, stepping in front of Peri, barring her way. 'We've no idea what that fruit actually is – it may contain alien toxins.'

Peri didn't like the tone of her voice one bit. 'Aren't you hungry, though?'

'I may be, but I'm also intelligent.'

The two women stood glaring at each other for a few seconds, at impasse.

Then Lornay said, 'Let her pass.'

Aline shook her head vigorously, more of her black hair coming loose. 'Has everyone gone mad? This fruit is *alien*. It could be poisonous. It could kill you!'

Lornay levelled her gun at Aline. 'And so could I.'

Peri bit her lip. Things had gone too far too quickly. But would Lornay really shoot? She couldn't risk it. 'Aline, if I were you I'd do as she says.'

Aline stared at Lornay, but backed off, hands raised. 'All right, go ahead, but I want no part of this.'

Lornay walked out from the avenue of trees down the small incline to the orchard. Peri followed, her hunger still insistent, but now tainted with unease.

She looked back to see Aline striding off up the avenue, and Taiana and Athon standing watching from the edge of the trees.

Ignoring Athon, Peri called. 'Hey, Taiana, you coming?'

'I can control the enzymes in my gastric tract for much longer before I require food,' called Taiana.

'Suit yourself,' muttered Peri and hurried to join Lornay in the orchard. The trees weren't very tall – the three Gardeners towered over them. Lornay was standing by the nearest tree, gun lying on the grass beside her. She reached out and cupped one of the large yellow fruit in her hands, and just stood there.

Peri walked up and asked her why she was hesitating.

With a jerk of her head Lornay indicated the petalled head of a nearby Gardener rising above the enmeshed branches of the trees. 'Those things give me the creeps. They're watchin' us.'

'They don't even know we're here,' said Peri. She didn't care if they did. All she cared about was eating, making her hunger go away.

The fruit looked even more succulent close up. She could almost hear it speaking to her: 'Pick me.' Peri reached out for the fruit, cupping its powdery-yellow skin in her hand, relishing its heavy coolness. Its stout pear-shape gave slightly as she squeezed it gently; it felt nice and ripe, and from the tree on which it hung heavily along with dozens of others like it, a creamy, musty aroma curled around Peri's head, intoxicating her.

'Are you sure about this?' said Lornay.

'Nope,' muttered Peri, intent on the fruit, fingers running up towards the thick woody stem. God, she had to eat, even if it was poison. In a moment of delirious abandon, mouth watering like crazy, Peri twisted the pear-like fruit from the branch. She raised it to her mouth ready to take a big, satisfying bite, when Lornay yelled out.

'Holy shit!'

All at once there was an urgent thrashing as something moved through the trees towards her.

Lornay grabbed Peri's hand, dashing the fruit to the floor.

The three Gardeners were moving swiftly through the trees like giants wading through a leafy sea, their appendages flailing and clicking, an unearthly hissing emanating from their flower-like heads.

Peri backed away towards the avenue of trees. The Gardeners didn't look so inoffensive now, their appendages flailing like whipcords. In a few strides they were almost upon the two women.

With a cry, Lornay brought her weapon to bear and fired, hitting the leading Gardener at the point where its head met its body. The flower-like head exploded in a burst of pale flame, but the rest of it kept advancing, stilt-like legs carrying it tottering towards Peri.

Lornay fired again, blasting the central body of the Gardener.

It exploded into flames, crashing to the ground amidst a tangle of twitching limbs.

The other two Gardeners paused in their advance.

And then Lornay fired again, and again, until the two creatures were charred, sticky masses of appendages, petals and vegetable mulch. From their remains rose a sweet sickly smell.

Lornay stood panting hard, gun still held at the ready.

Peri grabbed her and dragged her back towards the others, who must have seen it all. Aline's face was a pale mask of disapproval. Peri couldn't meet her gaze.

'I don't think there was any need for that,' said the xenologist.

'You saw those things – they were gonna kill us,' said Lornay.

Aline turned away. 'Oh, here comes the Doctor.'

The Doctor came up to them. He was breathing hard, and his face was flushed.

'Any sign of the Captain?' asked Lornay.

The Doctor shook his head. 'No. Nothing, I'm afraid. He's lost himself somewhere in this tamed wilderness.'

Lornay swore.

The Doctor frowned at her but made no comment. 'My guess is that he's gone back to the shuttle.'

'Then I'd better get after him!' Lornay made as if to run off, but Athon held her back.

'That's just a guess,' said the Doctor. 'Our safest bet is to stick together. Let Melrose come to terms with things on his own.' Then he sniffed the air. 'What's that smell?' His gaze drifted beyond Peri and to the charred remains of the three Gardeners. 'Oh no,' he breathed. 'What happened here?'

Aline went to speak but before she could say a word, Peri cut in.

'It's my fault, Doctor.' She explained what had happened, watching the Doctor's face darken in a disapproving frown. When she finished, she bit her lip. The last thing she needed was a lecture from the Doctor.

But instead he turned to Lornay. 'There was no need to kill them! They wouldn't have harmed you.'

'How do you know?' The skin around Lornay's mouth hardened in anger and her blue eyes glittered. 'You weren't here, you didn't *see* those things turn nasty.'

'They could have some sort of defensive capability,' put in Aline. 'Barbs, thorns, poison...'

The Doctor's face had that look of hurt disapproval, mouth slightly sucked in and eyebrows raised. 'You mean you approve of this?'

Aline's gaze flicked over to the cremated Gardeners and back to the Doctor. 'No. But I can understand why Lornay acted as she did.'

The Doctor took his hat out from his inside pocket and jammed it over his fair hair, shading his eyes from view. 'So can I.' His tone did not indicate approval.

Peri's stomach chose that moment to let out a strangulated gargle of hunger, clearly audible to everyone. The Doctor strode off down the slope.

'Sorry, all right?' she called after him, exchanging an exasperated glance with Lornay. All very well for the Doctor to take the high moral ground when he hadn't been there.

The Doctor had reached the edge of the orchard. 'There's no need to apologise for feeling hungry, Peri.'

'I wasn't!' She glared at the back of his head. 'I don't know...'

Aline went to move towards the Doctor but Peri held her back. The woman gave her a look of total surprise, which made Peri feel even more angry. If anyone was going to make up with the Doctor, it was going to be Peri, not this cuckoo in the nest.

'He's right, you know. There was no need to kill them. A few warning shots would have sufficed.'

'Yeah, we get it,' said Peri, dismissing Aline, resenting the way she was siding with the Doctor.

He stood with his back to them all, hands in his pockets. Peri could tell from his posture that he was deep in thought.

'We've got to eat, and soon,' said Lornay in a low voice. 'Any more of those choc bars?' she added hopefully.

'You ate them all back at the forest,' said the Doctor. He sighed. 'I should have brought more from the TARDIS. But then I hadn't banked on losing the old girl.'

'More to the point, we're going to need water.'

As soon as Aline mentioned it Peri realised how sand-dry her throat felt, how cracked her lips were when she ran a parched tongue over them.

The Doctor turned back towards them. He spoke in stilted tones. 'Fortunately, fruit will stave off hunger and contains enough fluid to keep thirst at bay.'

He walked stiffly over to the orchard, giving the scorched Gardeners a wide berth, and plucked a fruit from the nearest tree.

Peri started down the slope after him, looking around fearfully for any Gardeners. But there were none to be seen.

She saw the Doctor take a big bite out of the yellow fruit and she came to a halt, hand flying to her mouth.

The Doctor chewed, a contemplative look on his face, and then swallowed, his Adam's apple bobbing above the collar of his cricket shirt.

Then he smiled.'We Time Lords have extremely well developed palates – we can detect even the smallest amounts of toxins in foodstuffs.' He held out the fruit to Peri, with a sad glance over at the Gardeners.'This is perfectly safe.'

She took it from him, its warm syrupy juice staining her fingers.

'I suggest you all take your fill before more Gardeners arrive,' he called to the others. He leaned towards Peri, eyes shining from the strip of shade beneath his hat-brim.'There'll be no more killing, not if I can help it.'

He strode off back to the avenue of trees, passing the others who were running down the slope – even, Peri saw with a wry smile, Athon and Taiana; so much for enzymes or whatever.

Peri's stomach growled again. She brought the dripping fruit up to her face and buried her teeth in its flesh, closing her eyes with the sheer pleasure of it, and took a big, grateful bite.

Chapter Thirteen
Inside the Tree

Dusk was falling by the time they neared the tree. Or rather, Tree – something of such size deserved at least one capital letter, thought Aline. The sun was a pale orange ball sinking slowly below the horizon, the darkening sky revealing a twinkling vista of stars. Aline felt a sense of humbling awe when she realised hers were among the first human eyes to gaze upon these constellations. Something she had never lost, even in her darkest days, was her sense of wonder. It was what had got her started on her path, from student to lecturer to renowned xenologist – to her Encounter. And now this strange world, with its mysterious presence she had fleetingly detected. Could she be on the verge of a second Encounter? Her mind balked at the idea, but the seeds of fear were there, churning in her stomach along with the alien fruit.

In front of her, the others walked in a ragged line. Taiana seemed lost without her servitors. She hardly said a word to anyone, and seemed totally unimpressed by her surroundings. Athon and Lornay were shadows in the darkness ahead, moving close together, almost touching. To Aline's amusement but not to her great surprise, they had struck up a friendship that had strengthened since Melrose's abrupt departure. They made a strange couple: Athon was a living statue, Lornay was a sprite.

The Doctor was conjecturing about the possible origins of the planet they had named, by consensus, simply 'the Garden'.

'It's interesting, you know.' He was gazing at the orb of the setting sun. 'It's very similar to Earth's.'

'Luckily for us,' muttered Peri. 'Or we'd fry. That or freeze.'

'Indeed,' said the Doctor. 'Maybe it's artificial, as the Garden seems to be. Which means that whoever built all this had considerable power.'

'A race of skilled astro-engineers with green fingers?' chipped in

Aline, grinning at the image.

The Doctor smiled at her, but his eyes held a different expression, questioning. 'Maybe. I wonder if they're still around?'

Aline held up both hands, the leather jacket creaking. 'Don't ask me.'

Peri made a moue, as if she thought Aline was putting on an air, but of course she didn't know about the Encounter, or indeed anything about Aline.

But the Doctor said softly, 'I won't. But do tell me at once if you sense anything.'

Aline nodded, though she doubted she would. Since the hilltop forest, she hadn't 'sensed' anything and was beginning to doubt if she ever had.

As the daylight faded, the plants began to glow with their own inner light. It was beautiful, calming, this strange silent world of luminous plants under a sky crazed with distant, alien stars. Aline began to feel as if she was walking through a dream world, an entrancing land found only in children's stories.

She saw in the Doctor's open face, his contemplative silence, that he shared her sense of wonder. 'It's hard to believe we're in any danger at all,' she said.

The Doctor's expression hardened, his lower lip sliding over the upper, giving him a look of defiance. 'Even so, we are,' he said, keeping his voice low. He sighed and looked up at the stars. 'Somewhere up there, my TARDIS is in the hands of the Valethske.'

'You're not hoping they're going to come here?' said Peri. The fear in her voice was plain. 'They're hardly likely to hand it over, are they?'

Aline saw him put an arm around her shoulder, and look away to the glowing trees, as if searching for inspiration. 'They can't know what it is. We'll get it back. Somehow.'

Peri didn't look reassured. Aline didn't blame her.

The young girl was keeping her distance from Athon, for some reason, darting him the odd look of obvious hatred. Didn't take a genius to work out what had happened there. Despite his surface geniality and air of innocence, Athon was no gentleman, unlike the Doctor. Aline could quite see why Peri hung around with him. He generated an easy-going atmosphere of friendliness that wasn't intimate and was therefore non-threatening. The perfect platonic relationship. Except humans also needed non-platonic relationships. What if Time Lords needed human company, for some reason? Perhaps the Doctor needed to vicariously live through Peri's experiences. Did Time Lords know anything of love? Aline realised that she was already beginning to mentally map out her paper on Time Lords. Whatever kept her sane.

Not far ahead now, the giant Tree loomed, a spiky silhouette against the darkening blue, framed in the receding perspective of the avenue of lesser silver-barked trees. Aline had been right – it was certainly a tree, but unlike any that had existed on Earth. Indeed 'tree' wasn't enough to describe the enormous growth, implying as it did a single closed organism, discernible from its fellows once you got close enough to tell the wood from the trees. In this case, the wood was the trees and vice versa. Dominating the gardens, which were arranged around it in concentric circles, its main mass consisted of thick, closely intertwined trunks thrusting their limbs into the ground. These bifurcated upwards and outwards into a complex, skeletal network of leafless branches, like fingers clutching at the stars. The extent of the Tree was hard to gauge from a distance, but as they got closer Aline realised it had to be at least a couple of kilometres in diameter. More like a city than a tree.

The allegory was reinforced by the herds of Gardeners that were converging on the Tree like citizens hurrying home before curfew. They ignored the interlopers in their midst, seemingly intent on reaching the Tree. Aline was relieved, if a little perplexed, that no retribution had followed the killing of three of their number. Maybe murder was a new concept for the Gardeners. Before Aline and the others had arrived, death must have been a natural occurrence – no funeral rites, just composting. That had all changed now. Just by being here, they were upsetting the natural order of things, irrevocably skewing the balance of the Garden's ecosystem.

Aline kept this to herself, mainly because they had enough problems without her making them all feel guilty. After all, they weren't here by choice.

Presently they reached the end of the avenue, about a hundred yards from the giant Tree whose mass now spanned the horizon and cast an area of deeper darkness which engulfed them and the Gardeners filing into the gaps between its twisting trunks.

The Doctor took out his pen-torch and flitted its beam around. As on the Valethske ship, it wasn't much help.

'What do you think they're doing?' asked Peri, indicating the clicking, rustling lines of Gardeners.

'You saw them picking the fruit earlier,' said the Doctor. 'Maybe it's not for their own sustenance, and they're taking it to whatever lives inside.'

Peri's eyes glittered as she stared up at the Tree. 'Not more aliens!'

'Perhaps there's a human colony here,' said Taiana. 'Yes – these Gardeners could be genetically engineered servants!'

Athon nodded, his face lit up with enthusiasm. 'Just waiting for us.'

'If they had the technology to create genetically engineered plant servants they would know of our presence on their planet,' said Aline, despairing yet again at Eknuri naivety. Why had they stopped? She wanted to go on, into the Tree. She said as much to the Doctor.

'I suggest we wait until morning,' said the Doctor. 'It will be pitch dark inside – the Gardeners won't need light. We'll make camp here.' He waved the torch beam in the vague direction of a cluster of bushes at the end of the avenue.

Lornay hefted her gun. 'I say we go in. We still go along with the Captain's plan. We make contact with the intelligences controlling this world, get their help.'

'I agree,' said Aline, stepping up to the Doctor. 'We can't waste any more time.'

The Doctor looked dubiously up at the panorama of stars. 'If the

Valethske wanted to find us, they'd have been here by now. They've moved on, somewhere else, taking my TARDIS with them.' His head fell; he was finding it hard to face up to this truth. 'I'm sorry, Peri.'

Peri moved to his side, her smooth young face downcast, deep furrows below her eyes. She muttered something about it not being his fault.

Lornay appeared to give in. 'Right. We rest, then. I'll keep first watch.'

Everyone else sat or lay down, grateful for the rest, even Taiana and Athon. Even the Doctor, who settled himself comfortably against a tree-trunk.

Aline met the Doctor's gaze. 'I'm going for a walk.'

'Don't stray too far,' he said. He pushed his hat down over his eyes but Aline still got the feeling he was watching her.

She walked a little way off, down the avenue towards the Tree. Something seemed to be happening to her mind, thoughts and images forming deep within it, as if there was something inside her using her brain for its own ends.

As if there was something inside the Tree reaching out to her.

The presence she had sensed – it was back, stronger than before. An instant of panic-charged flashback to the Encounter, of the thing reaching out to her and touching her mind – filling it to overflowing with more information than it could possibly handle. A moment of realisation: *what if her mind had been changed somehow by the Encounter*? Not merely by boosting her psychic powers; what if the Encounter had opened up dormant areas of her mind? Areas that advanced beings could make contact with.

As these thoughts flashed through Aline, she felt her body chill to the bone, her breath swelling and sinking with increased rapidity. Butterflies in the stomach. Dry mouth. Yes, she had all the symptoms – but she wasn't afraid. This surprised her more than anything that had happened since Athon's party. She watched the Gardeners as they filed into the tree, their movements creating a background of clicking and rustling.

And then, slowly, almost without realising it, Aline began to walk towards the Tree.

Peri wandered through the gardens, unable to sleep. She was too worried, her mind wouldn't stop spinning. The Doctor didn't usually need sleep but Peri had seen his face, strained and tired. Obviously the loss of the TARDIS was affecting him more than he was letting on.

She came to a chessboard of flowerbeds, alternating orange and blue tulip-like blooms. In the near distance, the Tree loomed. Whatever way she turned, she was always aware of its presence, as if it was watching her. Or something within its tendril maze of branches was watching her. She shuddered, trying to think of something else, without much success.

Suddenly she became aware of soft footfalls on the grass behind her, and turned to see Athon approaching, his bronzed body silvery in the starlight.

Peri folded her arms and gave him her standard glare.

'Peri,' he began. 'I –'

'If you're gonna ask me to forgive you, forget it.'

He raised his hands to his chest, as if in prayer. 'No, nothing like that. I just want to say – sorry.'

It was far, far too late for that. He should have apologised to her the moment – the *moment* – she'd woken up back on the hill. And then he should have done something to prove he wasn't a worthless, spineless creep. Where had he been when Lornay had loosed off against the Gardeners? Hiding behind Taiana, that's where.

Peri turned away. 'Get lost, Athon, I don't want to talk to you.'

But he wouldn't go – and worse, he seemed to have regained some of his arrogant self-regard. 'Peri, we're both stranded here. We haven't got much choice over that. So we should at least try to get on.'

So he wasn't sorry for her sake, he just wanted it easy. 'Why? Give me one good reason. If we weren't stuck here you wouldn't see my heels for dust!'

He changed tack. 'I don't expect you to forgive me, but please try to understand. I'm Eknuri, we're superior to humans in many ways –'

That was it. Without waiting to hear him out, she turned on him. 'Superior? You? That's a laugh riot!'

He backed away, a look of dismay breaking over his face.

'Peri, let me explain –'

Peri sucked in a deep breath and let rip, fists bunching in anger. 'Shut up! The Doctor risked his life to save me, and I know he'd do it again, and I'd risk my life to save him so I guess that makes us superior, you... you...' She spluttered to a halt. There just weren't the words to describe him. 'Just go away, Athon. Go and play with your new friend.'

Athon's eyes hardened and he straightened up, towering over her. 'All right. If that's the way you want it.' His voice was shaking with barely suppressed anger and for a moment Peri was scared of him, of the potential of those bulging muscles coupled to an immature mind. She wouldn't put it past him to lose his rag and hit her.

'Let us speak to each other no more, unless absolutely necessary. And probably not even then.' With that, Athon turned and stomped away through a flowerbed, kicking the blooms and scattering their petals to the night.

A little way off Peri saw Lornay leaning against a tree. She'd probably seen their argument, though hopefully she was too far away to hear anything. She'd taken off her combat jacket and now wore only a skimpy singlet. Athon saw her too and changed course. Gloomily, Peri watched them kiss, Athon bending as if to smell a flower. Clinging to each other, they moved off into the darkness, out of sight.

'You're welcome to him, honey,' she muttered.

'He has a fondness for non-Eknuri women.'

Peri all but jumped out of her skin. 'Taiana! Where the hell did you spring from?'

Taiana's form resolved itself out of the darkness, her figure-hugging black costume gleaming in the starlight. 'Like you,

125

couldn't sleep. Feeling restless.' She sighed. 'And lost.'

'I know how you feel,' said Peri, thinking of the TARDIS – the home she was just getting used to, and would probably never see again.

'My servitors – without them I have no access to the datanet. My mind feels empty.' Taiana's deep voice was dripping with sadness. 'I can't think like I used to. Every thought, every idea, every whim I had was backed up or acted upon by the datanet. Now when I try to think of something, all I get is – nothing.' She folded her arms, her head tilting at a contemplative angle. 'A hundred years. So much would have happened back home. I ache to know.'

There was no tactful way of saying what Peri thought of next, so she just came straight out with it. 'Won't everyone you know have died after a hundred years?'

Taiana smiled sadly. 'Home is still home. And no, not everyone. We Eknuri can live for up to two hundred years. I myself am eighty.'

'That's nothing,' said Peri, 'the Doctor's almost ten times that.'

'Really,' intoned Taiana seemingly without interest. Then her head jerked upwards, her eyes fixed on a point in the sky above the topmost branches of the Tree. 'A shooting star...' she breathed.

Peri looked. It appeared as if one of the stars was moving, a pinpoint of light describing a falling arc against the deep blue of the night sky.

A shooting star – or a star*ship*?

Peri's blood ran cold. 'That's no comet,' she stammered. 'Come on – let's get back to the Doctor and the others!'

Aline jumped as someone tapped her on the shoulder. 'Where do you think you're going?'

Relief flooded through her as she realised that it was the Doctor. 'Nowhere.'

The Doctor stood before her, hands in pockets, his pale tan costume an area of relative brightness in the gloom. 'You were walking towards the Tree, as if you were in a trance.'

How could she explain what she felt? That something inside the Tree was calling her, something she felt would complete her. 'Was I? I didn't realise...'

He saw through her straightaway. 'You've sensed it again, haven't you? The alien presence.' He looked over to the towering mass of trunks and branches. 'And it's in there.'

Aline shook her head, ready to deny everything, but to her surprise, she said, 'Yes.'

He began ushering her back towards the others. 'I don't think it's a very good idea to go in at night.'

She shook free, suddenly angry at him. 'You can't order me around,' she said with more harshness than she felt. 'I'm going in whether you think it's a good idea or not!'

He ran a hand through his hair, exasperated.

'Oh come on, Doctor – don't tell me you're not curious.'

'Oh, I am, I am.' He looked back towards the end of the avenue of trees. 'I suppose the others will be safe.'

Aline saw her chance. 'Yes, they'll be fine.' She began to move off towards the Tree, not looking to see if he followed.

She was glad to find that he did.

'We'll just take a quick look,' said the Doctor. 'That's all.'

Aline took his hand, which seemed to surprise him, and led him across the skirt of grassland that surrounded the Tree. There were still a few Gardeners about, their clicking movements jerky and urgent, as if they were rushing to be on time for something.

Aline and the Doctor followed a trio of the motile plants into a dark gap between two massive trunks, each easily five metres across. Aline was fleetingly reminded of the cave in which they'd hid from the Valethske. The gap led into a soft-floored tunnel that meandered its way into the depths of the Tree. The Doctor had been wrong about the darkness – a phosphorescent moss clung to the walls, bathing everything in a green glow. Above, the 'ceiling' was a knotted fibrous mass, the roots and rhizomes of a profusion of parasitic plants trailing down and brushing against their faces. Aline noticed the Gardeners in front brushing them aside with quick, nervous-seeming movements of their appendages.

Behind them, more Gardeners followed. Aline sensed that there was no threat in the plant-creatures. She'd encountered alien plant species before, and though not usually hostile they all possessed a certain single-mindedness. All they wanted to do was disperse their spores as widely as possible. As for the purpose of the Gardeners, Aline felt she was shortly going to find out, along with answers to bigger, more personal questions.

Caught up in the procession of clicking, swaying plants, the Doctor and Aline moved deeper and deeper into the Tree. The Doctor squeezed her hand as if to reassure her. He must think she was terrified. Aline held back a titter of amusement. She wasn't scared at all.

Presently the tunnel widened, and led into a cathedral-sized chamber, its barked walls bulging and knotted, patched like a luminous map of alien continents with the phosphorescent moss. The far side of the chamber was a convex bulge, like a giant green stomach. Running across its middle was a lipped slit, like the mouth of some prodigious reptile. In front of this Gardeners clustered, their appendages raised above their flower-heads, waving in unison.

As Aline and the Doctor watched, the green mouth opened, and from its dark depths a cluster of mottled purple tongues unfurled, reaching down to the floor of the chamber like ramps.

Aline paused at the edge of the tunnel, eyes fixed on the mouth, on the tongues. Fear returned, swamping her in a sudden tidal wave. She clung on to the Doctor, barely aware of the Gardeners that stepped around and over her.

'Come on, let's get back to the others,' said the Doctor, pulling her away from the scene.

But Aline stood firm. She heard her own voice as if from far below her. 'No. No, I've got to stay.'

The Doctor caught his breath. Did he realise something had changed in her?

'We'll observe for a bit longer,' he said, his voice tight with reluctance.

The rustling of the Gardeners increased in urgency until, in a blur of movement, things scuttled down the tongues. A new genus of motile plant; many-legged, bulbous creatures the size of small cars. As they descended, their pod-like bodies opened like the wing-cases of beetles.

When they reached the floor of the chamber they stopped before the mass of Gardeners, who stooped above them and from their trumpet-like mouths poured the fruit they'd harvested earlier. When full, the pod-like motiles closed and ran back up the ramp-like tongues into the gaping mouth.

Aline found herself moving towards the forest of Gardeners, eyes fixed on the darkness inside the green mouth. Fear had gone, replaced by certainty. She knew what she had to do.

She had to allow herself to be harvested.

'Aline!' cried the Doctor. 'Stop! Try to resist it!'

'I don't want to,' she murmured. 'Can you feel it too?'

The Doctor kept pace with her. 'I can feel something – some sort of psychic signal, emanating from beneath the Tree.' He stood in front of her. 'I can't allow you to go in there.'

'But I want to go,' said Aline. 'I'm not afraid.'

By now they were caught up in the rustling crowd of Gardeners – it was like being inside a living, moving forest. Stilt-like legs leaned and shifted. Appendages curled and whipped and clutched.

The Doctor dodged a questing frond. 'Aline, listen to me. You've told me about your Encounter, how something tried to psychically link with you. It's obviously left some residue of itself buried deep inside your mind, and the thing inside this planet recognises it! It wants to make contact – not with you, but with the thing that destroyed your sanity! This time it'll totally overwhelm you. I can't let you go!'

Aline shook her head, disappointed in the Doctor – he'd got it all wrong. 'Doctor, it's not like that. My Encounter was merely a preparation for this. All my life I've been fascinated by alien species, alien cultures. The thing I Encountered knew this, and wanted to make me see – make me see everything. It prepared me, paved the way. My enforced xenophobia, the Eknuri assignment, my meeting you, the Valethske attack – it was all to get me here, so I could make contact with the being that lives inside the Garden, fulfil my destiny.'

The Doctor looked suddenly furious. 'Aline, you're a scientist!' A green tentacle curled around his waist. 'Listen to the rubbish you're spouting!' A Gardener hoisted him high in the air. His hands clawed frantically at the appendage. 'There's no such thing as destiny!' he cried – then the Gardener flung him across the chamber. He hit the mossy wall and fell to the leafy ground, apparently out cold.

Aline smiled. 'Doctor, I thought you were my destiny, but you were only a part of it.'

She turned away from the fallen Time Lord and walked up to the green mouth. The gateway to her destiny. As Gardeners wrapped their welcoming tentacles around her, hoisting her up towards the mouth, Aline fancied she could see a smile playing around its corners.

Then its lips closed around her and she was in total darkness.

Chapter Fourteen
Fresh Meat

Peri ran back towards the avenue of trees, her feet scattering luminous petals. Taiana sprinted ahead, calling Athon's name in foghorn tones. Why she wanted to find him was beyond Peri. They didn't seem particularly close. But then, Athon was Taiana's only link with the home she'd probably never see again. Peri's one thought was to find the Doctor. How he could possibly save them all from a ship full of insanely ravenous beasts, she had no idea, and didn't really care. She just wanted to be with him, when they came. With the Doctor around, miracles happened, last chances popped out of the blue. Without him she was as good as dead.

She came to a breathless halt beside Taiana, who was looking around, brows knitted in confusion.

'What's the matter?' Peri gasped between gulps for breath.

'There's no one here!'

It was true: no Doctor, no Aline, no Athon and Lornay. Peri peered into the surrounding gloom, but all she could see were patches of glowing fruit that intensified the surrounding darkness. Taiana was pacing around, shouting out Athon's name with increasing impatience.

Loudly. Very loudly. Too damn loudly!

Peri launched herself at Taiana, grabbing at her arms. They were like iron bars. 'Shaddup!' she hissed. 'Do you want them to find us?'

Taiana shook her head, her golden eyes widening with dawning terror.

The two women stood in silence, staring up at the starscape for further signs of movement. But there was nothing, and for long seconds that seemed more like minutes nothing happened. Peri concentrated on listening for the others' voices. But there was no low hubbub of conversation, no snores of the soundly sleeping – and no gasps of passion from lover-boy and soldier-girl, thought

Peri with a mental sneer. So where the hell was everyone? Could the Valethske have got them already?

Taiana pointed to a patch of starry sky above the Tree. 'It must have come down some distance away.'

'We hope.' Something occurred to Peri, and a shameful feeling of relief washed over her. 'Hey, what are we worrying for? It might not even be the Valethske! It could have been a regular falling star, or even a rescue ship of some kind.'

A flicker of hope animated Taiana's face. She was about to speak when something roared overhead, sending them diving for cover. A blast of air followed in its wake, shaking the trees and whipping up a storm of leaves and petals. Peri blundered into what she thought was a tree, but it moved and steadied her with long, strong arms. Taiana. As the thing thundered into the distance, Peri observed it bank around the side of the Tree, its outline clear against the starlit blue.

No mistaking. It was the same as the ship that had shot down Athon's skyboat. She felt a rush of blood rise to her head, and her heart began to pump faster. Run, screamed her mind. You gotta run. *Now*!

Peri realised she was still holding on to Taiana. She let go, brushing bits of leaf and grass from her hair, trying to make up her mind which way to run. Did it matter? Wherever they went, the Valethske would surely sniff them out.

Her eyes came to rest on the Tree, looming into the night sky beyond Taiana, blotting out the horizon.

Taiana's shoulders jerked in a robotic shrug. 'What shall we do?'

'The only thing we *can* do,' said Peri, heading off at a run towards the Tree. 'Hide, and hope.'

Hunt Marshal Veek hung on the threshold, her gaze sweeping across the planet's surface. She knew that somewhere down there among all that useless vegetation, prey scuttled. Beside her, Flayoun adjusted the shoulder-hasps of his copter backpack, a continuous low snarl emanating from deep within his chest.

Veek prepared to jump, outstretched arms resting lightly on the frame of her copter-pack, claws curled around the controls.

'Look at it all!' bellowed Flayoun, his voice rising above the roar of the skirmisher's engines. His eyes were crazed with bloodlust. 'All that plant-stuff! No good to us.' He leaned out of the hatch, answering the roar of the wind. *I want something's flesh!*'

Veek rolled her eyes. 'And you shall have it, my hunter.'

She jerked the control handle. Above her, the rotor-blades unfurled and the engine stuttered into life. Bracing herself against the airframe, Veek waited until the revs reached a level she knew would bear her weight and then she stepped out into thin air. Behind and above, she heard Flayoun's battle-yell as he followed her. She plunged downwards, clear of the skirmisher, the ground rushing up at her, the air roaring around her, her teeth bared in a grin of exhilaration. A stray thought flitted past: *Cut the engine and you'll be out of the Great Mission for good*. She dismissed it angrily. Hunt Marshal Veek's death, when it came, would be honourable, not cowardly.

Straining against the harness that clutched her like the talons of a giant bird of prey, Veek mastered the controls, listening to the complaining whine of the engine, judging her adjustments, as the rotors churned the air, bearing her aloft. Stars whirled about her like bright metal dust.

She came about in time to see the skirmisher bank sharply and disappear round the side of the enormous tree that dominated the area. Swooping down towards her were a dozen hunters in standard sweep-and-search formation, dark shapes against the speckled night-blue of the sky. Flayoun's voice crackled through her comm-unit and she barked out a series of orders. She watched with satisfaction as the hunters broke off in pairs, spreading out over the area. Flayoun headed forwards to join her.

Scans had picked up faint signs of mammalian life, concentrated in one area of the planet, near to where they had located the stolen skirmisher. As Hunt Marshal, it was Veek's job to lead the hunters in the search. She welcomed it as a distraction from the futility of the Great Mission.

Veek and Flayoun swept through the sky, eyes intent on the dark masses of vegetation below. Curiously, it all seemed to be laid out in regular patterns of strips and squares. Patches of it were glowing with soft fire that Veek took at first to be nocturnal insect life, which confused her as the survey scans had detected only plant life and the escaped prey. She heard Flayoun intermittently cursing the plant-life. At times like this, Veek felt disappointed in her mate. At least this world was a contrast to the only other planet in the system – a barren, solid lump of rock, barely more than an oversized moon.

It had taken their instruments mere minutes to map that wretched world, turning up no signs of life whatsoever, intelligent or otherwise. No transmissions of any kind, no surface structures, no sign of mining or underground habitation, nothing at all. Just a rock. The hunters were sorely disappointed, and the Vale Commander nearly had a rebellion on his hands. But Kikker knew his hunters, and he appeased them by releasing all – all! – of their captive prey. The hunters gorged themselves stupid – even Veek, for what Valethske can resist fresh prey? There was a bit of a furore when one of the younger Vale Guards, unable to endure the smell of spilled blood any more, threw himself into the pit and on to the torso of a half-eaten human. Such heresy! Of course, several hunters – including Flayoun – immediately fell on the hapless Vale Guard, and under the unforgiving gaze of Commander Kikker eviscerated him where he stood, passing round his heart, liver and kidneys to be consumed before his dying eyes.

Veek had watched with a sinking heart. That Valethske should be reduced to this. Surely she couldn't be the only hunter immune to the madness this cursed mission had spawned! But as she watched Flayoun and Burzka gulping down the Vale Guard's entrails, she reflected that maybe she was the only sane one among them.

As a consequence of this feast, they had no prey left. All this meant was that before the next long sleep, they'd have to go hunting to replenish their stocks. This prospect pleased Veek but also irritated her, for it would bring only a temporary halt to the Great Mission, and once the sleep cells were full of prey, they could go on. On and on for centuries more. The mission and the future were one. There was nothing else.

She had vowed, as she'd checked over her copter-pack, that this plant-world would be her last stop. Somehow, she was going to escape. Even if it meant desertion and execution.

Veek flew nearer to the ground, the rotor chattering above her, the downdraught from the blades flattening her ears against her head and tickling her whiskers, alert for any sign of movement. She could have deployed her motion-tracker or heat-sensors, but Veek was a true hunter and preferred to rely on instinct. It had never failed her before and it didn't fail her now. There – running low, trying to use the cover of the trees – were two humans, their pale flesh standing out in stark contrast to the dark grass. A shout from Flayoun confirmed that he'd sighted them too. The two hunters circled around the fleeing prey, spiralling closer in, cutting off any chance of escape.

The copter-packs weren't built for stealth – they were meant for speed and terror. Valethske possessed excellent night-vision, so Veek had no trouble zeroing in on the prey. Now she was right on top of them, cruising just above their heads. She snapped on the lights of the copter-pack, drowning the two humans in a sudden blaze of unbearable brightness. She recognised them immediately – the smaller one, the one with short red fur on its head, was one of the soldiers they'd captured and tortured on Thynemnus, centuries back. It would be good to finish off the job. The other, larger one, its dark hair flailing around its face in the blast of the rotor blades, was one of the lumbering, cowardly creatures they'd snared on the last hunt. Veek noticed with amusement that they were both naked. She could smell the musk of the male, the sweet scents of the female. The odours aroused her and she began to drool.

She descended in front of them, killing the power, the blades sighing to a halt.

The two humans clung to each other, blinded by the lights of Veek's copter-pack. Flayoun touched down on the far side of the pool of white light, his mouth hanging open, hunger, as always, in his green-yellow jewels of eyes.

In a sudden blur of movement, the smaller human made a break for it, towards the trees. Before Veek could do anything Flayoun drew his bolt-gun and fired. There was a wet crunch and the female's skull exploded in a messy burst of blood and bone. It dropped immediately, face down, blood pumping from its shattered head. It twitched and shuddered violently for a few seconds, a liquid gurgle bubbling from the ruins of its face. Veek stared balefully at its smashed head, its pale skin laced with its own blood. Its left foot suddenly jerked spasmodically, thudding against the earth as if trying to kick down the doorway to the underworld. And then it was still.

Veek glared at Flayoun. 'Hunter, that was foolish! We need to question this prey.'

She turned to the male, which had sunk to its knees, its eyes fixed on the body of its dead companion. Veek cursed Flayoun once more under her breath. He just *didn't think*, sometimes! Now the male, traumatised by the death of its mate, would be impossible to interrogate.

Nevertheless Veek grabbed its hair and pulled it to its feet. It was large for a human, almost as tall as Veek, but despite its prominent muscles it was shivering in fear. It had defecated, the smell of excrement mingling with the metallic tang of blood and the odours of heat and sweat in a heady cocktail that made Veek reel.

She breathed in its naked skin-face, watching it gag and splutter. 'Where are the others?'

In answer, the prey made unintelligible sounds, and liquid began to pour from its eyes. Useless. Veek took out her dart-gun and stunned it, tilting its body so it fell beside its companion.

She cut the lights and switched on her comm-unit, gathering reports from the other hunters. No sign of any more prey. She looked around. Into the night sky rose the gnarled silhouette of the giant tree. Veek cocked her head at it speculatively then turned to Flayoun. 'Contact Hunters Burzka and Akkia, tell them to take these two back to the ship. Then tell the others to follow us.'

'Where are we going, Hunt Marshal?'

'The only place they could be hiding.' Veek started the motor and the blades began to whirl slowly above her head, gathering speed.

Over the thumping of her heart and the gasping of her breath, Peri could hear the unmistakable chattering of rotor-blades. She felt as if her legs were going to give way any second and willed herself on. Hopefully, in the sprawling shadow of the Tree, the hunters wouldn't be able to see her. It stretched like a vast wall in either direction and its spreading branches blotted out the stars.

Peri stumbled into a patch of darkness at the foot of a massive trunk and looked frantically around. 'Taiana! Where are you?'

'In here!'

Peri followed the sound of the voice into a gap between two of the trunks. She felt hands grab her and haul her inside. She found herself in an earth-floored passageway like a fairy grotto, with glowing green walls and roots and things hanging down, brushing her face.

She peered back out into the dark Garden.

In the sky, way above the tops of the silver-barked trees, she could see figures outlined against the stars. She could hear the chattering engines of the copter-packs, louder now. It took her right back to the desert and the crashed skyboat and she felt sick.

The figures were getting bigger by the second, getting nearer.

She looked at Taiana, and the tunnel beyond. It seemed to lead quite a way back before twisting into the unknown. Good – the twistier the better. Right now they needed to get as lost as possible. 'Ready?'

'What about Athon and the others?'

Peri tried not to think about what might be happening to them. 'We can't do anything for them. Maybe they've come in here too. Come on.'

They moved on down the tunnel, and it wasn't until it had taken a couple of dozen snake-like turns and forked off an equal number of times that Peri began to relax – but only a little. She turned to say something to Taiana when from round the next corner, the Doctor appeared.

Peri stood with her mouth open, too surprised to speak.

He looked hurt; he was limping and clutching his upper left arm with the right. His troubled frown gave way to a smile of welcome when he saw them.

'Peri, Taiana!' Then he frowned. 'What are you doing here?'

'Hiding,' said Peri, 'from the Valethske.'

The Doctor looked from Peri to Taiana. 'They're *here*?'

Taiana nodded.

Without another word, the Doctor turned back and ushered them before him, casting a glance up the tunnel.

'Where's Athon?' asked Taiana.

'I don't know!' snapped the Doctor.

'He'd gone off with Lornay, last I saw,' said Peri. Even though she hated his guts, she hoped they were safe.

That left... 'Hey, what about Aline?'

The Doctor shook his head. 'I wish I knew. I hope she's alive.' He heard Peri gasp. 'I'll explain later. Come on, we've got to find somewhere to hide!'

After a few more minutes frantically hurrying along the tunnels they came to a circular chamber lined with giant translucent pods. Inside each pod Peri could just make out the still form of a Gardener.

'This is as good a place as any,' said the Doctor.

'Let me look at that arm,' said Peri.

The Doctor drew himself away from her. 'Only a bruise.'

What was up with him? 'Are you going to tell us what happened to Aline now?'

The Doctor walked around the chamber, hands held behind his back, looking at the pods absently. 'I wish I could. She's been – harvested. Taken inside the planet by whatever it is that's behind all this.'

'Which is?' said Taiana.

'The presence she sensed, remember? Well, it seems to be real.' His voice was hard, his eyes glaring. 'She wanted to make contact with it and, well, I hope they're very happy together.'

He was angry, but only with himself, Peri realised. She knew he would have tried to save Aline, and wouldn't forgive himself for failing.

'Oh, great,' muttered Peri. Valethske on the outside, strange alien force on the inside, and them sandwiched in between. She went to the nearest pod. Inside, a Gardener was festooned in a network of fibrous roots. Despite their predicament, she was curious.

'They're basically autotrophes, so they need to metabolise energy through photosynthesis,' said the Doctor in a calmer voice. 'But they're so complex they can't obtain all the energy they need from photosynthesis alone. These pods probably provide some other method of sustenance, nutrients from the Tree.'

Peri nodded, feeling as if she was in a dream. Here they were, being hunted to death, and the Doctor was lecturing them on extraterrestrial plant biology. It didn't help. She couldn't keep down the feeling of fear and panic. 'Doctor, what if they find us?'

'They won't,' he said with a smile of reassurance that vanished as soon as it had appeared. 'I hope.'

'Hope isn't enough this time, Doctor,' said Taiana in a dull, flat voice. 'We need a miracle. And as we all know, miracles never happen.'

Peri wanted to argue with her, but this time she felt inclined to agree.

The Doctor perked up. 'I do, however, have an ace up my sleeve – the TARDIS!'

Peri could have kicked herself. 'Oh yeah – if the Valethske are here, so is the TARDIS!'

'Every cloud...'

Then the Doctor's face fell.

In the entrance to the chamber stood two Valethske.

Peri backed up against the pod, hands scrabbling against its smooth glass-like surface, her body still looking for a way out when her mind told her there was none. She bumped into Taiana, and looked up at the tall Eknuri. There was no sadness in her eyes, only resignation in her lowered eyelashes, a longing for home faintly flickering in her golden irises.

Peri could only watch as the Doctor stepped towards the two Valethske, showing them a façade of mild unconcern, his raised eyebrows and chin seeming to say, 'And what are *you* doing here?' - but Peri could see his hands clasped behind his back, fingers twisting nervously together.

The lead Valethske took a loping stride to come face to face with the Doctor. To his credit, he didn't flinch from the beast, which was a good twelve inches taller than him.

Another Valethske moved into the chamber. This one was slightly shorter and had a flash of white fur across its left ear. It was aiming a bulky, square-ended weapon at the Doctor's chest. Behind it, several more of the creatures fanned out around the doorway, levelling an assortment of weapons at them.

The lead Valethske licked its lips and raised a stubby silver pistol that Peri recognised all too well. She realised that this creature was the same one that had shot her, back on the planetoid. It had the same hungry gleam in its eyes. And the same musky, animal stench.

The Doctor held up his hands. 'Don't shoot! I have some information that is of vital importance to you.'

Every Valethske in the chamber hissed and cackled in unmistakable laughter, but kept their guns trained on their captives.

'I have, really!' said the Doctor, indignant. 'You'll have come across a blue box, somewhere on your ship.'

The Valethske snarled and shoved the Doctor in the chest. He staggered backwards, winded.

'Silence, prey! I know nothing of any blue box.'

Its voice was at once gruff and sibilant, dripping with evil cunning.

'You must have found it,' muttered the Doctor, regaining his composure. 'Listen to me, it's very important!'

'Are there any more of you?' snarled the Valethske.

The Doctor shook his head, glancing back at Peri and Taiana, without seeming to see them. 'No, ah, this is it. We're the only people on the planet.'

The Valethske cuffed him across the face. 'You lie, but that does not matter. We have already found and snared two others.' Its yellow eyes met Peri's, burning with belligerent glee.

And then, with a casual flick of its hand, it fired. There was a sharp hiss, a soft thud, and the Doctor fell backwards, clutching his chest.

'Doctor!' cried Peri.

Another hiss, close to Peri's side – and Taiana fell, sliding down the smooth surface of the pod.

The Valethske closed in upon Peri. There was recognition in its eyes. 'You have come far, prey – through space and time. But you will never escape us.'

Peri stood her ground as she had done in the desert. 'Gonna try.'

Peri held its gaze, pouring all the hate and defiance she could muster from her eyes. Inside her, a small hope flickered: *It's only going to stun you and freeze you. You might be rescued again...* but one look at the Doctor out cold crushed that hope. The Valethske held all the cards.

The Valethske levelled its weapon and fired. Peri felt a dull thump in her chest, a heavy feeling spread out through her body and then nothing.

Chapter Fifteen
Bargain

Captain John Melrose had walked himself to the point of exhaustion, until he dropped and passed out under the unforgiving sun. He was woken by a raging thirst and by the prodding of a trio of Gardeners. He leapt to his feet, scrambling around their stilt-like legs, grabbing his gun and swinging it up to cover the towering plant-creatures. They recoiled, appendages briefly flailing, and then walked slowly and serenely away. Curious. They seemed to recognise the gun, realise that it could cause them harm.

Uninterested in the implications of this, Melrose wandered further through the gardens, dogged by his thirst, dazed by the endless uniformity of the terrain. He longed to see an untended field, undergrowth running wild, but it was all neatly tended flowerbeds and orchards, partitioned by hedges and grass avenues. He was hopelessly lost. There was nothing on which to get a bearing. He couldn't even see the giant tree towards which they had been headed until...

Until he'd cracked.

Melrose dropped to his knees, fingers clawing at his overheated head, remembering how he had acted. He saw the Doctor's face, serious and calm. Lt Meharg, her young face a mask of distress. The others, their appalled faces shutting him out. Controlling himself with an effort, he realised that he couldn't go back to the others, couldn't face Lt Meharg again. He recalled her eyes, wide with – with *pity*. He'd behaved in an unsoldierly manner in front of a subordinate. How could he ever command her respect again? By his own actions he had excommunicated himself from the way of the soldier. He was fit only for early retirement on medical grounds. As for the Doctor and the others, he didn't care about them. Bunch of misfits, as far as he could tell. He felt a spark of lust as he remembered the curveaceous body of the girl, Peri, and her bold, spirited nature. The kind of woman he could imagine wanting to get to know, after the end of his tour of duty.

But the certitudes of military life were shattered now. If the Doctor was right, five hundred years lay between what he used to be and what he had become. The Valethske had taken him out of his own life and now he was only a reprise, a footnote. Far better that he had fallen fighting them than to be alive now, scrambling lost around an alien world, dying of dehydration under a burning alien sun, with no plan, no chain of command, no hope.

Melrose stumbled on weakening legs through the gardens, head swimming with the delirium of thirst. By blind luck, he stumbled upon a canal, its mirror-still surface almost level with the grass banks. He slaked his thirst, splashing water over his whole body. Afterwards, he followed the canal through the endless gardens, figuring that it might lead to a centre of civilisation and therefore a way off the planet. Dusk fell as he walked, but Melrose was blind to the beauty of the starlit night and the softly glowing blooms. He walked himself into a reverie in which he dislocated himself from his actions and was born again into the garden-world, his dishonour erased. At times he would surface from this trance and face the reality, and sit sobbing for a while, clutching the Valethske weapon to his chest as if it was the thing most dear to his heart.

It was as he sat gazing mournfully at the constellations reflected in the dark surface of the water that he became aware of a sound. A distant rumble, similar to thunder but more controlled. The sound of engines.

Getting slowly to his feet, he swivelled round, peering into the night. There, on the horizon, he saw a mountain settling itself on a pillar of fire.

A ship. No, not any ship – the Valethske mothership, huge and dark and jagged, a giant inverted cone.

He smiled. Now there was hope – one hope. Revenge. What remained of his soldier's instinct told him the Valethske would be after their stolen shuttle, despite the Doctor's assurances that he had disabled its flight computer. He cursed as he remembered that the Doctor was still in possession of the craft's control chip.

A small glitch in the plan that was forming slowly in the back of his mind.

Melrose felt much better. More like a soldier again, now he had something real to fight. It didn't really bother him that he'd probably die in the attempt. It didn't seem to matter any more.

Peri rolled nearer the warmth, not wanting to wake, wake and remember, wake and confront reality. Heat played across her body, comforting, reassuring. Like those big Thanksgiving fires back when she was a kid... *don't get too close*... She could see the pulsing orange blur of flames through her eyelids, and smell oily, acrid smoke. Her eyes and mouth felt dried up and the side of her that faced away from the source of the heat felt cold and clammy. In the distance, she could hear clanking, rumbling machinery, sudden metallic crashes, and something that sounded like dogs yelping. Beneath her, earth. Dirt and dust and grit, sticking to her stomach and thighs where sweat had broken out in response to the crackling flames.

In a surge of movement, sudden panic jerking her to full wakefulness, Peri sat up and opened her eyes. To her right a substantial bonfire roared, its orange brightness bruising her eyes. Fresh sweat broke out on her forehead and she scrambled away from the flames, her bare feet and buttocks scraping on the loose dirt.

She realised with a shock that she was naked.

Instinctively she drew her legs up to her breasts, wrapping her arms around her knees. She looked around for her clothes, but all she could make out was bonfires and the patches of darkness between them. She tried to work out where she was and how she had got here but her mind was a tumble of faces and places. She knew terrible things had happened to her but her mind shied away from the details. Gradually she began to make sense of her surroundings. She was in a steep-sided earth-walled pit, illuminated by bonfires in various stages of conflagration. Far above her was some sort of ceiling, criss-crossed with walkways. There were cages hanging from chains, spinning slowly in the rising heat, their bars reflecting the orange light of the fires.

Where was – where was the Doctor? In a flash she remembered him confronting the Valethske, his body slumping to the floor. She remembered the Garden in all its bewildering beauty.

Nothing like this hellish place. Had to be the Valethske ship. After the Doctor had gone to all that trouble to rescue her... He shouldn't have bothered. Peri got the feeling that she was always going to have ended up back here.

She stood up, swaying on unsteady legs. A short distance away she caught sight of Athon, sitting with his head in his hands. As far as she could tell he was naked too. By his side lay Taiana, flat on her back, hands lying palms upwards as if relaxing in a yoga exercise, her long body like an ebony statue in the flickering light.

Peri moved towards them, looking around fearfully for any sign of Valethske. Her foot nudged something smooth and round. A human skull, jaw hanging open in a gaping parody of a grin, eye sockets as black and deep as despair.

She grimaced and backed away, realising with revulsion that the whole area was littered with human bones and scraps of clothing. She swallowed, her dry throat rasping. So this was it. Any moment now, Valethske would leap out of the flickering shadows, bear her to the ground and sink their teeth and claws into her and it would all be over. She clenched her fists, gritted her teeth and screamed at herself mentally to get a grip. No good if she gave in to fear. No good if she stopped remembering who she was. She was Peri Brown and she would never ever be mere fodder for anything.

Athon looked up bleakly as she approached, his eyes red from weeping, trails of tears staining his face. There was no animation in his expression, not the slightest indication that he'd noticed her nudity. She almost wished he'd letch at her – at least that would mean he was himself.

She crouched down beside him, putting a hand on his broad shoulder. 'Athon, what happened? How did you get here?'

He looked at her with blinking, defeated eyes.

'Where's Lornay?'

At this he looked away, mouth twisting in a grimace of pain. 'They... they killed her.'

'Oh,' said Peri, trying to think of something to say. But there was nothing she could say. 'I'm sorry.'

She didn't ask him what the Valethske had done to Lornay. She really didn't want to know.

She went to move around his cowed bulk to see if Taiana had woken, but a restraining hand held her back.

Athon fixed her with a pleading, terrified stare. She was reminded of news reports of children in wartime, their faces too young to be shattered by grief, too smooth to be worn down by horror, their eyes wide and full of fearful incomprehension, and perhaps a dawning realisation of atrocity.

His big hands gripped her forearms, fingertips pressing painfully down. 'Why? Why are they doing this to us?' His voice was distant, child-like, as if it was coming from the point within himself to which he had retreated.

Peri licked her cracked lips. Her head was throbbing, maybe an after-effect of the sedative the Valethske had used. Or maybe they'd kicked her about a bit. *Why? Because they're gonna kill us and eat us,* she wanted to yell at him. But instead she smiled as best she could, gently disengaged herself and patted his hand. 'Don't worry, it's gonna be OK. We're gonna find the Doctor, find the TARDIS and get out of here. We're gonna be OK.'

Athon's mouth twitched in a brief smile, though his eyes remained haunted beneath his tangled fringe. Not totally convinced by her words, then.

But then neither was Peri herself. For all she knew, the Doctor could already be dead. She closed her eyes and counted to ten, banishing such defeatist thoughts. Then she went over to Taiana, who was just coming round, eyes golden slits behind purple-black lids.

A sound from above distracted Peri and she peered upwards through the inverted forest of chains, cages and walkways. She could just make out two long-eared figures, staring down at them. There was something in their stance that struck Peri as odd. They weren't regarding herself, Athon and Taiana with the usual Valethske bloodlust, but something else – an air of expectation, almost of impatience. What did they want of them?

One of the watching hunters moved, leaning over the edge of the walkway. Its companion turned towards it, the low growling tones of its voice echoing over the pit.

Peri prepared to run – then realised the Valethske were staying put. There was no sound of running feet, no yelps of anticipation. No hunters skittered from the tunnel entrances that ringed the pit.

She turned back to Taiana, who had come fully to her senses and was looking around with a dazed expression.

'Where are we?' she asked. Her voice was even duller and deader than usual.

'On the Valethske ship,' Peri replied. 'Don't think much of their economy class accommodation.'

Taiana didn't respond to the joke – or perhaps she just hadn't understood it. 'At least they haven't frozen us.' Taiana's eyes widened as she realised she was naked, her hands running up and down her torso. 'What's going on?'

Several possibilities flitted through Peri's mind, none of them particularly pleasant. 'I don't know. Perhaps they enjoy ogling naked people.'

She turned away, eyes following the patterns of the flames. With a pang of dismay, she saw the arm of her white shirt poking from the flames, as if flung out to save itself from immolation. The bastards had burned their clothes! Peri felt even more naked now. Her clothes were the last connection with the TARDIS, with the Doctor, with her life. Without them, she was cut off, adrift – and to the Valethske, just another walking lump of meat.

Then she saw something nearby, something black and shiny. A shoe.

She scrambled over and picked it up. It was beautiful, its marbled patent-leather upper glittering in the firelight. On an impulse Peri brought it up to her nose and sniffed, getting a faint odour of perfume mingled with the biscuity tang of feet. Much too big for her – easily a size ten or eleven, which meant that it was probably Eknuri.

Soft footfalls in the dirt behind her. She turned to see Athon standing there, the orange light from the fires making him look like a bronze statue. Her eyes flicked down, then up to his face.

His gaze was fixed on the shoe that Peri still clutched in one hand. She raised it slowly. 'One of yours?'

He shook his head, his bottom lip beginning to tremble. He spoke, the words forcing themselves from him, each syllable a grunt of pain. 'No – was – Ser-Seryn's.'

Peri remembered the black-haired, haughty Eknuri woman. Her vivid green eyes. Her calling the TARDIS 'quaint'. All the other Eknuri – superior beings, every one, the pinnacle of human achievement.

Nothing but bones on the ground and torn scraps of clothing now.

Peri started to cry at the pointless loss of life. She tried to control it but she couldn't.

Athon stumbled towards her, also weeping. He took the shoe from her and held it up to his face, muttering Seryn's name over and over in a tortured lament.

Peri reached out and embraced him and they held each other, their bodies meeting, her head resting against his broad tattooed chest, his arms enfolding her. It didn't matter now what he had done to her, it didn't matter what she thought of him. They were two human beings in pain and they needed each other.

Veek was beginning to lose her patience. 'We've tried this before,' she said, glaring at Ruvis, who was intent on the prey in the pit below. 'It never works.'

Ruvis's jaw whirred loudly, but it couldn't hide the smugness in his voice. 'This time, I'm more certain of success. These specimens are in their prime. Look at the pale-skinned female's pelvis! Built for child-bearing.'

'Look,' said Veek, trying to sound reasonable. 'Even if we do get them to mate, humans gestate for nine months. And their young take well over a decade to reach maturity! It's too slow, Ruvis – far easier to hunt mature prey.' And more in keeping with our nature, she thought.

Ruvis tore his eyes away from the humans. 'If we could establish a breeding stock, we wouldn't need to hunt. We'd have a stable population of prey and we could devote all our energies to the Great Mission.'

That was all very well for those who couldn't hunt any more. 'Ruvis, you were a hunter once – you must know that the hunt is life itself!'

Ruvis's old eyes glittered in the light of the fires below. 'Hunt Marshal Veek, you knew when you volunteered what this mission would entail. You knew the priorities.'

Veek tensed. She'd forgotten for a moment that Ruvis was as dedicated to the Great Mission as the Vale Commander. She'd forgotten that as far as she knew, she was the only dissenter. She had believed in their goal, centuries ago when they had set out – but that was before she realised the futility of the Great Mission. She had never really grasped the sheer size of the galaxy before. Hard enough to find something concrete, something solid, in its infinite reaches, but they were chasing legends, hints, myths...

She chose her words carefully. 'Of course I knew. And my devotion to the Great Mission is absolute. But you should also know – as the Vale Commander does – that hunters need to hunt, and if we are denied, the mission is in jeopardy. You won't have any hunters left to do your surveys! They'll desert, find a world rich in prey and start a new colony.'

Ruvis waved a hand dismissively. 'Oh, you'll still be able to hunt, within the ship – Azreske knows, it's big enough.' He leaned over the railing, jaw whirring as he spoke. 'I have a new plan – what if, during the long sleep, we let these humans breed within a closed environment? Something more conducive to their needs than the pit in which we – or rather you – consume their fellows.'

There was a trace of bitterness in his voice and Veek knew then that he still dreamed of the hunt, despite his old ruin of a body.

'Then, after a century or however long it takes to reach our next destination, we'd have a couple of generations of prey ready and waiting for us.'

'You proposed that before,' growled Veek. 'There are too many problems. We couldn't be sure they wouldn't escape and try to destroy us. Or kill themselves rather than comply. And how many do you expect to breed from a mere two females?'

Ruvis sighed. 'The Vale Commander has agreed.'

Veek wasn't sure she'd heard correctly. 'What?'

'Look – the male and the white-skinned female are embracing!' Ruvis leaned forwards with interest.

But Veek could hear their sobs. 'Ruvis, they're still in shock. Intercourse will be as far from their minds as we are from home.'

Ruvis's ears twitched. 'Perhaps some form of drug therapy...'

Veek decided not to comment. This was madness. By agreeing to Ruvis's futile experiments, the Vale Commander was losing touch. Maybe it was about time she challenged his leadership, as she almost had after the survey of the barren planet. Others had tried – and Kikker had defeated them easily. But at least it would be an honourable death.

Ruvis's comm-unit bleeped. He listened for a while, and then looked at Veek, his damaged face alive with excitement. 'That other prey – the one you said spoke of the blue box. It has come round at last!'

Veek couldn't understand what he was getting worked up about. What was so important about this prey? Then she saw Ruvis's expression; he'd averted his eyes, as if he'd given away too much.

He turned and limped along the walkway.

'Wait, Ruvis!'

He paid no attention and carried on. With a last look at the prey in the pit – they weren't mating, not that she'd expected them to be – she hurried after the old technician. Her instinct told her that there was something going on, something Ruvis didn't want her to know about.

Something about this blue box...

* * *

Kikker paced up and down before the prey, tail swishing with impatience, watching its pale, fleshy face for any signs of life. He could hardly wait for it to regain consciousness – he hadn't conducted a decent interrogation in centuries. The last had been the soldiers on Thynemnus – they had resisted well, providing him with hours of satisfaction. He remembered slicing one open and tossing its innards to some Vale Guards, who had scrambled like starving whelps for the rare treat of fresh meat. Even then the prey had not screamed – it had died without even a whimper. This one, though, looked nothing like a soldier – its clothes were civilian, its hair fair and fine, visible flesh unmarked by battle-scars. It looked sleek and well-fed. Young and firm-limbed. Kikker couldn't help himself from drooling, and he once again cursed his no-flesh pledge.

Behind him stood the same two Vale Guards, their eyes already glimmering in anticipation, standing to attention on either side of a trolley on which instruments of torture were laid out. Kikker was pleased to see that they had been cleaned, sharpened and polished so that they gleamed in the dank, watery light of the brig. On the vitreous walls, between the pale glowglobes, hung racks of larger equipment – cudgels, swords, impalers, peelers, piercers, scrapers, prods and spikes. These had not been cleaned – instead, they were deliberately left crusted with the blood of previous victims, to help instil dread in the latest. The smell rising from them was old and rank, sour and tarry, but it still made Kikker's mouth water.

In the centre of the room was the chair – a fiendish device of torture and a testament to the ingenuity of Valethske martial engineering. Once strapped in, the victim's body could be harmed in a number of exquisitely painful and interesting ways. Needles hovered above tethered wrists ready to inject poison or drain wearying quantities of blood; electrodes waited to send arcs of agonising energy through the victim's convulsing body; straps bound the chest, arms and legs, ready to be tightened; the whole chair could be spun on its axis, or slowly immersed in a pool of acid beneath the brig, or made to crush, twist, stretch or snap selected limbs. Even though it hadn't been used for hundreds of years, it was still in excellent working condition. Kikker made sure of that.

Suddenly the prey emitted a groan. Kikker stopped pacing. Its eyelids flickered – and then opened, revealing typically weak, milky human eyes. It strained against its bonds, looking around, eyes widening as it realised where it was.

Kikker's lips widened in grim mirth. Now came the fear, the begging, the pleading for mercy. He stepped closer, the better to hear its pathetic mewlings.

Its tiny, weak mouth moved as it spoke. 'Short back and sides, please.'

Kikker snarled, bending over the prey. 'Fear me!' he hissed, reaching out and twisting the flaps of its ears. 'By the blood of the Great Vale, you have reason to!'

Kikker was rewarded with a grimace of agony. It would have to do for now. He turned to the Vale Guards. 'Summon Technician Ruvis.'

Then he turned back to the prey. It was regarding him levelly, without fear.

That was something new to Kikker.

'Where are my friends?' it said.

There was strength in its voice – how foolish. Soon Kikker would bring home the utter futility of its situation. 'They are being – utilised.'

The prey strained against its bonds. 'If they're harmed in any way...' Its voice tailed off as it realised it was in no position to threaten him.

'Then what?' roared Kikker.

'Then I won't tell you what you want to know.' It nodded and raised its eyebrows. 'Yes, I can see from your eyes – you've found the TARDIS, haven't you!' It smiled – the first time Kikker had seen anyone in the chair ever do so. 'I thought as much.'

Kikker hissed in anger. 'Silence, or I will open your face.' He turned to the table of torture implements.

He was interrupted by the arrival of Ruvis, who limped into the brig, hardly able to contain his enthusiasm. To Kikker's surprise, Hunt Marshal Veek followed him.

'Ruvis,' said Kikker, nodding at the technician. 'And Veek – shouldn't you be overseeing the survey?'

Veek saluted. 'Vale Commander.' Her eyes closed with his. There was a spark of defiance in their yellow-green fire. Veek was a skilled and lethal hunter, the best Hunt Marshal that Kikker had ever worked with. She knew the ways of the hunter, her instincts were infallible and her bloodlust insatiable.

But Kikker also knew how dangerous she was. Hunt Marshals were always sniffing after promotion. Kikker had already bested the two Hunt Marshals who had challenged his authority. Veek was now the only Hunt Marshal on the mission. She carried her responsibilities well, and was always fiercely loyal, but he could see cool calculation behind her green-yellow eyes, and suspected that she was awaiting her chance to challenge his leadership. He almost relished the prospect; a close fight with a vixen as lithe and supple as Veek would be a stimulating experience.

'I wanted to know about this strange blue box the prey babbled about when I captured it,' said Veek. 'I thought it was merely a ploy, but Ruvis confirmed that there is such an object.'

Ruvis cringed, then regained his composure. 'What does it matter that the hunters know of the box?'

Kikker fumed. 'It might endanger the Great Mission!'

Ruvis inclined his head. 'In what way, exactly?'

'What's this "Great Mission"?' said the prey.

Kikker ignored it. 'We'll find out, when this specimen tells us exactly what it is.'

The three Valethske surrounded the chair, towering over the shackled form of their prisoner, who still appeared exasperatingly unconcerned about his plight. 'Well, since you're all so interested, I'll tell you,' it said. 'It's a time machine.'

Kikker gave a curt nod of satisfaction. 'We had already guessed as such.'

The prey looked deflated, as if it had expected Kikker to be impressed. It started blabbing again. 'I'll make a bargain with you

– you can have the time machine, if you let my friends and myself go free.'

Kikker snarled. 'Valethske do not make bargains with prey!' He picked up the chair's control panel, itching to hear the human scream in agony. Now they had its machine, it could die.

Ruvis snatched the control panel away. 'Listen, Vale Commander. Listen to what the prey is saying.'

Fighting down a wave of anger, Kikker forced himself to listen. It was talking quickly, breathlessly – talking for its life. 'Now this may sound like I'm playing my get out of jail free card, but I'm the only one who can operate this time machine. Kill me and you'll be forever denied its powers.'

Veek was staring at the prey, her mouth hanging open. She licked her lips. 'I suggest we kill it now,' she growled. 'It's only trying to save its own worthless life.'

Kikker agreed – prey, if it could talk, would say anything to postpone death.

'Let me take it to the hunters,' said Veek. 'Let them tear it to pieces!'

'No, no, no!' groaned Ruvis. 'What if it speaks the truth?'

'You've got nothing to lose,' said the prey. It smiled up at Kikker. 'You can always kill me later.'

Kikker bunched his fists, but restrained himself. He mustn't let his anger get in the way of the prize of time travel.

'Let me show you the time machine,' said the prey. 'And then you can decide.'

'Agreed,' said Kikker, beckoning the Vale Guards. 'Free him – but keep him closely guarded. Also, free the other prey. Put them to good use – they can assist with the excavation.'

Kikker noticed Veek's eyes on him.

The guards did as they were instructed. To Kikker's irritation Ruvis started chattering to the prey almost as an equal, asking questions about the machine. He felt sick as the prey shook hands with the old technician and introduced itself as 'the Doctor'.

Ruvis saw Kikker's disapproval and met it with a glare of defiance.

Veek drew him to one side. 'With respect, Vale Commander, this seems like a trick of the most obvious kind.'

Kikker nodded. 'Good counsel, Hunt Marshal Veek. But we must take the risk. A time machine would set us up among the Gods.'

He could see in her eyes that she knew it too.

Nevertheless, she persisted. 'Let me go into this TARDIS with him. We cannot risk the life of our Vale Commander.'

Kikker shook his head slowly, keeping his eyes fixed on hers. What was she planning? 'You are needed to oversee the excavation. Make sure the Doctor's companions come to no harm.'

Veek's eyes widened and her tail thrashed about like a trapped animal. 'You are letting prey go free?'

Kikker grinned at her. He felt a glow of shameful, perverse pleasure in denying the hunter the meat that he himself had not tasted for centuries. 'Only until we have learned the secrets of its time machine. Then you can do what you like with it.'

Veek's eyes held his for a moment, and then, with the tiniest tilt of her head, she moved away and out of the brig.

Kikker watched her go, doubts surfacing in his mind. Had he gone too far from the way of the hunter? Was this time machine really a trap?

He walked over to where Ruvis stood with the Doctor, flanked by two Vale Guards. The human had a strange, sterile smell, totally devoid of fear. Kikker had to admit to himself that he was finding it hard to deal with prey that just wasn't scared of him.

He turned to the Vale Guards, giving instructions to bring in the orbiting skirmisher that contained the strange blue box. Now he knew it posed no threat, it could be brought into the ship.

Kikker began to feel a thrill of excitement. His destiny was moving ever closer, he was sure of it. His destiny – and his apotheosis.

Chapter Sixteen
Contact

Deep inside the Valethske ship, a vast machine worked, boring down into the earth of the Garden. A gigantic cylindrical column of machinery over a hundred feet high, its surface was streaked and scarred with the dirt of countless worlds.

Clouds of coolant steam obscured its heights, and its bulbous metal torso dwarfed the figures working at its base. Over all rose a continual, calm thrumming sound, like the meditation of a machine god.

In its initial survey, the ship had detected a network of artificial underground chambers, a mile or so beneath the surface of the planet. It had located the point where the crust was at its weakest and had settled itself there, extruding the excavator into the surface of the planet like an enormous mechanical parasite. While the hunters in their copter-packs drifted across the surface of the Garden, the excavator churned its way slowly through the earth, coring out a section wide enough to take an army through.

The process was largely mechanical, and mostly automatic. A drill-head worked down through the loam and earth, while a series of powerful pumps removed the excess material, sucking it up through the skin of the excavator and ejecting it into waiting hoppers that whisked it away along a mechanised monorail to dump it outside the ship in a growing mound. But the excavator was centuries old, and often the excess material would be spilled on the enclosed area of ground within the ship, or on to the monorail, or even inside the workings of the machine itself. To prevent the whole thing from clogging up and stalling, an organic element had to be introduced into the process – the Valethske themselves. Hunters and Vale Guards alike worked to keep the excavator going, keeping the monorail free from mud, lubricating the machine's many moving parts, maintaining the flow of coolant, scooping up the copious excess of spilled material. None complained, as the work was all to the good of the Great Mission. There was a palpable excitement in the air, for many believed that this time, the legends were true and the Gods slept below the surface of this world.

And this time, the Valethske had a little help. Three human prey, which the Vale Commander had spared in exchange for the secrets of the blue box, about which rumour was rife, toiled alongside them.

Peri's arms felt as if they were going to fall off. She dug the shovel in, heaved out a chunk of wet mud and staggered with her load over to a rattling conveyor-belt that took clanking buckets up from the pit towards the waiting hopper above. Gasping, she upended the shovel so that the mud slid with a wet slap into the bucket, and then staggered backwards, glad to be free of the weight. Then it was back to the mounds of crud that were dotted like molehills around the looming presence of the machine, another shovelful, back to the conveyor-belt...

Athon and Taiana worked nearby, seemingly without complaint. Athon still wore his expression of distraction, which made Peri worry that something had gone seriously wrong with his head.

Peri hefted the shovel again and set to work, gritting her teeth against the pain, against the fetid odour, against the indignity, against the futility. She didn't even know why they were doing this.

They'd been given uniforms to wear, one-piece garments of a dark-brown suede-like material that buttoned up the sides. Nothing like the gleaming black close-fitting uniforms the Valethske themselves wore. The fabric was repulsively greasy to the touch, cold and clammy against the skin. They fitted the two Eknuri well, but even the smallest they'd been able to find hung loosely on Peri, the ends of the sleeves coming way past her fingertips, the legs rucking up against the clumpy boots they'd given her. She felt like a bizarre clown, condemned to perform the same actions over and over for the amusement of some cruel king. And the smell – it was so bad, Peri could almost chew it. It –

and now, she herself – smelt like the contents of a dumpster that had been open all day in the sun.

She'd gleaned the reason why they had been spared, from the Valethske that had thrown the uniforms at them and gruffly ordered them to dress. Apparently, the Doctor had bought their lives at the cost of the TARDIS. She knew, however, that he wouldn't give up the TARDIS so easily, and hoped that this was all part of some grand plan of escape.

So while she waited for that to kick in, Peri worked on, aware that all around her hungry eyes watched, pink tongues sliding over sharp teeth. She dared not stop working, dared not give them any excuse. She was under no illusion that the Valethske would keep their side of the bargain. They didn't look like the sort of creatures to keep their word – at least not with the likes of mere 'prey'. A mental image of the Valethske gunning the Doctor down and stepping over his body into the TARDIS kept playing in Peri's mind. With the Doctor gone, the TARDIS theirs, what was her life worth, or Taiana's, or Athon's?

The one that had shot her, some sort of senior Valethske as far as Peri could work out, was overseeing the excavation. Now and then Peri's gaze fell on the hunter's eyes, and hatred flashed between them, hot as fire.

The young Vale Guard stepped out of the blue box, whiskers twitching, eyes alight with wonder.

'Well?' growled Commander Kikker.

The Vale Guard uttered a few short, breathless barks.

'I think he's trying to tell you that it's bigger in the inside than it is on the outside,' said the Doctor, who stood nearby guarded by Ruvis and the other Vale Guard.

Kikker grabbed the young Valethske by the collar of its uniform. 'Speak, cub! Is it safe?'

Now fear glinted in its yellow eyes. 'Safe – yes, it is safe.' It blinked. 'But bright – so bright!'

Kikker shoved the Vale Guard aside and stepped towards the blue box – the TARDIS, as the Doctor called it. He stepped over the threshold into a blinding white void. He shielded his eyes and raised his gun, letting out a roar of anger.

Kikker stumbled as someone blundered into him – Ruvis, he didn't doubt, the old fool. Then he staggered forwards, his legs butting up against something solid. He took his hand away from his eyes to reveal a blurry image of a hexagonal bank of controls, surrounded by walls patterned with a recurring circular motif.

He whirled round, levelling his gun at the Doctor, who was standing in the open doorway, arms crossed in front of him, an expression of insolent amusement on his fleshy face.

Beyond him Kikker could see the dark passageway of his ship, and his mind reeled.

'That won't work in here,' said the Doctor, indicating Kikker's gun.

In answer, Kikker raised his gun and fired over the Doctor's head. A bolt of energy crashed into the distant ceiling of the TARDIS.

The Doctor stared up at the resultant scorch-mark. 'Well, that shouldn't have happened.'

Ruvis was walking around the console, muttering to himself, his whiskers twitching.

'Impressed?' said the Doctor.

'Oh, yes!' said Ruvis, licking his lips.

Kikker was also impressed, but didn't want to show it. He sniffed in disdain. 'All I'm interested in is whether it works – or not.'

The Doctor went up to the control panels, rubbing his hands. 'Well, I think a quick demonstration is in order!'

Kikker barred his way. 'I think not!'

Ruvis whined in disappointment.

'Think, Ruvis! This is a strange, alien machine – who knows what tricks its owner might employ to trap us?'

Ruvis shrank back from the console. 'Indeed.'

'Now why would I want to trick you?' said the Doctor. His gaze hardened and Kikker caught a glimpse of power in his eyes. 'As long as I know my friends are safe, I'll co-operate.'

Kikker sniffed again. This place had no odour; it was clean, obscenely so, but Kikker couldn't even smell the chemical tang of cleaning agents. 'They're safe enough. I'll take the presence of this TARDIS on my ship as proof of its functionality.' He licked his lips. 'How did you manage to develop time travel technology? It is something we Valethske have always coveted.'

The Doctor looked from Ruvis to Kikker. 'Let's just say that the TARDIS is the product of an extremely advanced civilisation.'

'You're from the future?' asked Ruvis, his bloodshot eyes widening.

'Either that, or the distant past.' The Doctor smiled. He was obviously enjoying running rings around them.

Kikker would soon put a stop to that. 'So, using this "product of an extremely advanced civilisation" you followed us from the planetoid?'

The Doctor nodded. 'I intercepted your ship as it came out of warp.'

'And rescued your friends.' Kikker put as much sarcasm as he could muster into his words. 'But you have failed, Doctor. I have your friends, your machine, and you, in my power!'

The Doctor began to babble something about his companions, about leaving this world in peace, but Kikker wasn't listening. He was thinking about what to do with this strange machine. It complicated things, clouded the mission objective. If it worked, he could go back in time and confront the Gods before their abdication. But the excavations were continuing and he would soon know if the Gods had fled to this world. After so long, he couldn't stray from the objective that was his lifeblood. He had to see the survey of this planet through fully. And if it turned out – as it had done on hundreds of worlds previously – that the Gods were not there, then he could use this TARDIS.

He came to a decision. 'Guards, take this human, put it in the long sleep.'

The Vale Guards grabbed the Doctor's arms.

The Doctor didn't struggle – wisely – but his face became flushed, his voice agitated. 'You're pushing your luck, Kikker. I might decide not to co-operate after all!'

Kikker smiled. 'Then my hunters will enjoy your friends.'

The Doctor bared his teeth in a grimace, and tried to break free from the Vale Guards. Though they were young they were still stronger than most humans. 'Why are you putting me in the long sleep?'

Kikker smiled, beginning to enjoy himself again. 'Doctor, it's for your own good. You'll be out of the way of my noble hunters – who might be tempted to devour you if you remain at large.'

'At least let me see my friends first!'

Kikker waved him away. He hoped his hunters had managed to resist temptation. But what was the appetite of hunters against such a prize as time travel? 'They are safe – you have my word.'

'What's your word worth, Kikker? Someone once told me that you Valethske see people as meat, nothing else. What's to stop you from killing Peri the moment I'm safely frozen?'

Now Kikker had made his plan, the continued presence of the Doctor was becoming an irritation. 'Without them I would not have your co-operation. As long as I need you, they live! Take him away.'

The Doctor struggled as the Vale Guards hauled him backwards.

'Tell me one thing, Kikker – why are you doing this? Why are you travelling so far and for so long?'

Kikker considered, and decided there was no harm in the Doctor knowing. 'It is the Great Mission, Doctor, as decreed by the Great Vale herself. The noblest enterprise we Valethske have ever undertaken. We are searching for our vanished Gods.'

The Doctor raised his eyebrows. 'Interesting. What are you going to do when – or maybe that should be if – you find them?'

Kikker breathed hotly into the Doctor's face. 'Destroy them.'

After the green mouth had 'eaten' her, Aline had blacked out, waking to find herself being carried down a winding tunnel by one of the motiles that had taken the Gardeners' offerings of fruit. Strapped like luggage to the creature's carapace, Aline watched the moss-covered ceiling of the tunnel pass by overhead. It seemed close enough to touch – if she could have reached out, but she couldn't; her hands were bound tightly to her side. The only parts of her she could move were her feet and her head. She rotated her ankles from time to time, in a vain attempt to rid them of pins-and-needles, and the back of her head rested on the smooth carapace of the motile plant that carried her through the tunnel, downwards, towards – what?

Aline tried reaching out with her mind, projecting her thoughts ahead of the lumbering motile, to contact whatever lay in wait. But she found herself unable to keep it up – self-doubt and fear made it impossible to concentrate. One thing she was sure of: the presence that had lured her into the green mouth had gone. The only thing in her mind now was panic. And embarrassment – how had she let herself be fooled so easily?

As she listened to the scuttling footfalls of the motiles, Aline began to believe that it had all been her imagination – a fantasy manufactured by her own mind, a mind she had never really trusted since the Encounter. What was she thinking – going into the Tree, allowing herself to be harvested? She remembered how the Doctor had been flung aside, and his words: *There's no such thing as destiny*. He was right, of course there wasn't. She'd been mad to think there was. And she was still mad, she told herself with a calmness she convinced herself was born out of psychopathy.

She wondered what had happened to the Doctor and the others. Would they find Melrose? Would they come after her? Or would the Valethske turn up and butcher them all?

All at once the monotonous view of the tunnel ceiling dropped away into blackness. Aline was bumped about as the motile plant carrying her increased its pace, its legs rustling with a new urgency. She craned round to see where they were; as far as she could tell, a rock-walled cavern, tunnel mouths gaping around the perimeter, the ubiquitous phosphorescent moss bathing everything in a ghostly green glow. How far beneath the surface were they? She'd lost track of how long they'd been travelling, and she had no idea how long she'd been unconscious. With growing alarm, she became aware of a new sound, emanating from the direction they were heading. A high-pitched chittering, like speeded-up birdsong.

Something was waiting, on the far side of the chamber.

Fear goading her into panicked action, Aline struggled against her restraints, and this time, to her surprise and relief, they let go.

She slid from the shiny pod-like body of the motile to land with an undignified bump on hard ground. Her hands met the surface; it was smooth and black, flecked with lighter elements. Must have been worn smooth by the passage of the motiles, over hundreds, thousands of years, maybe even more.

The car-sized motiles – Harvesters, she decided to call them on the spur of the moment – scuttled around her, totally ignoring her just as the Gardeners had. She didn't have to try too hard to get out of their way. Strange. She had definitely been brought down here, but why? Did they think, in their vegetable minds, that she was a piece of fruit? The image made her titter. But if so, why just dump her?

The bird-like chittering had reached a crescendo and, a lump of fear forming in her throat, Aline turned to look in the direction the Harvesters were scuttling. The chamber was larger than that of the green mouth, like a giant inverted bowl. Stalactites the size of church steeples depended from the ceiling. And on the far side of the area, a herd of creatures moved, their jet-black carapaces shining in the green phosphorescence.

Aline stumbled towards the creatures, trying to make out individual forms in the seething mass. From a distance they looked like beetles, and as Aline got nearer she saw that they were the size of cows. Their carapaces were strangely serrated – plainly they were not wing-cases – and their six legs were long and spindly, ending in leaf-like scoops. Their heads looked almost like afterthoughts protruding from the thick, ridged thorax. Tiny, deformed-looking antennae curled above plate-sized compound eyes. Their mouthparts were the only bit of the creatures that seemed alive, mandibles working busily, producing the chittering sound that echoed all around the chamber.

Aline circled around the side of the herd, almost slipping a couple of times on the smooth rock. She felt excited, on the verge of a great discovery, just like the days before the Encounter. Only this time there were no colleagues with whom to compare notes, no back-up team, no contactable cruiser in close orbit, nothing but Aline, alone within an alien world.

She watched as the Harvesters arranged themselves in neat ranks before the herd of chittering insects. They looked like two armies massing for a battle – and for a second, Aline thought that was what was going to happen. Between the two species, plant and insect, there was an open area that bisected the cavern, slightly raised above floor level.

Then the first rank of Harvesters moved forward as one, stepping up on to the table of rock, upending themselves and opening up with a graceful, balletic movement that brought a gasp of awe from Aline. She was probably the first alien being to witness this ceremony. And she had nothing to record it with.

The fruit spilled from the Harvesters and rolled out on to the table, a sudden tumble of colour. The chittering of the insects reached such a volume that Aline had to cover her ears. The creatures scuttled forwards, scooping up and devouring the fruit. The first line of Harvesters, now empty, ran quickly from the cavern towards the tunnels, disappearing into who knew what other areas of the planet – maybe back up to the green mouth, to wait for the next harvest. The second line of Harvesters unloaded their offerings, and the scene soon lost any semblance of ritual as the cow-sized insects scrambled and skittered for every last scrap of food.

Aline sank down on her haunches. So one riddle of the Garden was answered – the fruit was to feed these mindless insects. Aline thought of the intricate and seemingly endless beauty of the Garden, the avenues of trees, the plantations of fruit. Was this what it was all for? To produce food for these brutes? It didn't make any sense.

And then something happened to her mind. A word formed, as if something deep within the layers of her unconscious was shouting, yelling for all its worth. The word was her own name, repeated over and over again, yearning, calling...

Aline felt her skin go ice cold, and sweat broke out on her forehead.

It was back.

And it wanted her.

Aline turned. All at once, the voice vanished – but a lurking presence remained, deep within the pit of her mind.

Behind her, she could see a glowing tunnel in the rock wall that she hadn't noticed before. The light that spilled from it wasn't the ubiquitous green phosphorescence, but a pale golden glow like summer sun captured in a glass of wine. It played across the polished rock floor of the cavern, reaching out to Aline.

As if in a dream, she turned to face the light, took a faltering step towards it, booted feet skidding forwards slightly on the stone. She knew that if she walked through the tunnel of light, she'd come face to face with something too large for her mind to gather in, and it would be just like the Encounter all over again, only this time the effects would be irreversible.

But Aline wasn't scared. She was certain. She wanted to go, she wanted to know. She was a student of alien life, veteran of countless first contacts, a cataloguer of the galaxy's incredible diversity. She wanted to know alien minds. She wanted them to know her. The Encounter had been the first stepping stone towards whatever lay in wait for her now. She walked into the tunnel, the light bleaching out her vision, hands outstretched, thinned to skeletal silhouettes by the intensity of the glare. It was as if a sun was trapped within the planet. She could almost feel the rays buffeting around her, as if the light itself was intelligent, probing her, investigating her.

After a time, she came to the source. She stepped from the tunnel into a seemingly borderless space swimming in golden light, more diffuse now she was out in the open. As her eyes stopped throbbing she began to take in what was before her.

The light was coming from a strand of matter that began some way below Aline and disappeared high above her, its midpoint swelling on a level with where she stood. It had a textured, organic quality, like wax or mucus; within it, dark, fibrous shapes twisted and turned. As her wondering gaze took it in, the golden strand called her once again.

Aline.

She found herself moving towards it, through the golden void. There seemed to be no floor beneath her, but her feet were connecting with something. It felt like walking on glass. Some sort of energy field?

The strand expanded before her, filling her mind with its intonations, calling her over and over again, a tone of urgency creeping into its soundless voice. As she got closer she thought she could see patterns in the dark shapes twisting inside: great wings, enormous eyes and limbs twisting in fire. A small part of her cried out and cowered in fear, but Aline ignored it, consumed with the need to know.

And then, when she was close enough to reach out and touch the alien strand, the voice in her mind vanished, and she was herself again. Her normal, human, self.

She stared up at the tapering strand, and – worryingly – down past her feet where it disappeared in a distant twist of matter. Once again, she got the feeling that she was being duped. It had brought her all the way down here, using her mind, using her memories of her previous Encounter, but for what? Just to dump her here, all questions unanswered?

She turned around, and saw with a shock that she couldn't see any tunnel entrances. There was nothing but the golden void, seeming to stretch away to infinity.

She turned back to the strand, beginning to resent it. 'Well, is this it, then?' Her voice sounded muffled, as if her ears were blocked. She held her nose and blew; this eased the pressure a little bit. She waved her hand through the golden light that surrounded her. Was it some sort of fluid? A gas? Or some other state, previously unknown to science?

She began to panic. How the hell was she going to get out of here? Was she doomed to wander this void for ever, driving herself mad trying to work it all out?

She tried to reach out with her mind to the strand – to no avail. Perhaps this was the eye of the storm – too close to feel the effect. Maybe physical contact would help.

Slowly, curiously, she reached out to touch the alien matter.

She didn't even have time to scream as its surface ballooned outwards and engulfed her.

Chapter Seventeen
Dreams of Deicide

To his astonishment, Vale Commander Kikker found himself enjoying the Doctor's company. This was nothing to do with any attribute the Doctor might possess – to Kikker, he was still a walking, talking lump of meat – but because he was someone to whom Kikker could expound the glory of the Great Mission.

The Doctor easily kept pace with Kikker as they walked through the ship, seemingly unconcerned, despite the two Vale Guards immediately behind him, guns cocked and trained on his head. Kikker had concluded that the Doctor must be suffering from some sort of mental disorder that made it impossible for him to feel fear. He'd seen it himself in certain types of genetically altered soldier. Maybe, once the Doctor had served his purpose and Kikker was fully versed in the operation of the TARDIS, Ruvis could dissect him and find out.

They were walking along the ship's main artery, passageways and tunnels leading off, the sound of the excavator thrumming through the earth floor and the soles of Kikker's boots, a constant reminder of the Great Mission.

'We have been searching for centuries,' Kikker explained. 'Following every hint, every legend, the tiniest scent of the Gods. We have traversed vast tracts of the galaxy – though I estimate we have barely begun our search. There are still thousands of possible locations. Thousands more planets to survey. More centuries of searching – centuries until I can taste meat again!'

The Doctor regarded him curiously, and Kikker realised he'd got carried away. 'I have vowed not to touch meat until the mission is successful.'

The Doctor's eyes widened. 'You're that convinced of success?'

Kikker considered. 'Yes, I am – now. There are many things about this world that tally with the legends. The garden-retreat of the Gods, the distance from the sun, the actual *size* of the sun itself, the presence of artificial chambers underground – I can feel it, Doctor! The Gods are here!'

'Hardly seems worth all this effort, if all you're going to do is kill them.'

'You do not understand the concept of Valethske honour!' snarled Kikker.

The Doctor regarded him with mocking eyes. 'No, you're right – I don't.'

Kikker bunched his fists, but reined in his anger. If the Doctor's insolence was the only price he had to pay for the glory of bringing the gift of time travel to the Valethske, it was a small one.

'Then I will tell you,' said Kikker, 'and maybe you will understand.'

He walked on in silence for a while, searching for the right words. He had never needed to explain the Great Mission to anyone. His crew – the Vale Guards, the hunters, the technicians – all knew the purpose well. Perhaps this Doctor, in his travels through time, had encountered the Gods himself. Maybe he could offer new clues.

'Many thousands of years ago, the Gods ruled the galaxy,' began Kikker. 'They called themselves the Khorlthochloi, or the Korlevalulaw, or a number of other names – but to us, they were always the Gods.'

The Doctor stopped walking, the Vale Guards almost crashing straight into him. 'Those names – I've heard them before.'

Kikker licked his lips. 'Have you ever encountered them?'

The Doctor ran a hand through his fair hair. 'No, but I've heard of them – in myths, legends, travellers' tales and various religious texts. They're supposed to be one of the oldest species in the galaxy, acting as shepherds to the younger species, making sure no one of them gets too big for its, ah, boots.' He stared down at Kikker's feet.

Kikker felt a thrill of excitement – what the Doctor said fitted exactly with the legends. 'Do you know any more?'

The Doctor regarded Kikker with a strange distant look in his eyes. 'You know, if the Khorlthochloi were your Gods then that must make you an incredibly long-lived species.'

'Our creation myths date back hundreds of thousands of years,' said Kikker. 'Your facetious remark about boots – I now understand what you mean. Many thousands of years ago, the Gods decided we were becoming too aggressive, too dominant. We swarmed across the galaxy, colonising system after system. So they smashed our warfleets out of space, and introduced a great plague that affected only Valethske. They wiped most of us out. The few that survived had to rebuild our civilisation right from the beginning.'

'I wonder what made them think they had the right to do that,' said the Doctor, his eyes gleaming, his face in shadow. 'Not even my lot are so judgemental, so harsh.'

'As we slowly rebuilt our empire, in myth the Khorlthochloi were transformed into vengeful Gods, who envied our power.'

'Interesting. No concept of wrongdoing on your part.'

'Of course not,' growled Kikker. 'We exist to reproduce, to colonise, to hunt – we fear nothing. Not even the Gods. After thousands of years of rebuilding, we had re-established our empire, though it was only a mere shadow of its former glory. We began gathering intelligence on the Khorlthochloi, encountering other species who had heard of them, who had been husbanded by them and had developed legends and religions around them. We discovered one thing common to all those legends – shortly after they all but wiped us out, the Gods vanished. Absconded.'

'Died out?'

Kikker shook his head. 'How could beings as powerful as the Gods simply die out?'

'You'd be surprised.'

'Some believed they had traversed the intergalactic gulfs, moved on to a new galaxy. Others, that they had evolved into a higher form of life.' Kikker looked sideways at the Doctor. 'I'm no scientist, I do not know of such things. One legend persisted – that the Gods had gone senile, and had retreated from the younger races, hiding themselves away inside a planet of their own manufacture.'

'And so you set out to look for them,' said the Doctor.

Kikker stopped walking. They'd come to a nexus point, a shaft that ran from the control chamber at the top of the ship to the engines at the bottom. The sleep cells weren't far away. 'Yes, Doctor – to scour the galaxy, find and finally destroy the Gods!'

'So it's all about revenge,' said the Doctor. He sighed. 'Of course, you must realise how ridiculously impossible this Great Mission of yours is.'

Kikker stepped towards him, snarling.

The Doctor backed away. 'Or perhaps you don't.'

'As we speak, machines are digging down through this wretched planet. If the Gods are here, we will find them.'

'And if they're not?'

Kikker shrugged. 'Then we move on.' It was time to check on the status of the excavations, prepare to take the search underground. 'This has been most interesting, Doctor. I have never conversed for so long with a human being before, outside of torture sessions. The next time we speak will be when I need you to pilot the TARDIS.' He motioned to the Vale Guards. 'Take him away.'

'What about my friends? At least let me see them before you put me in the deep-freeze!'

Ignoring him, Kikker turned away, listening to the receding footsteps of the Vale Guards and the Doctor's imprecations echo down the tunnel.

When he was alone once more Kikker ran over their conversation in his mind. Something the Doctor had said was bothering him. Something about the pointlessness of the Great Mission. No one had ever dared say such a thing before. But now, when Kikker thought about it, to chase about the galaxy after shadows of legends was –

– Was a glorious, righteous thing to do!

And he'd almost let the words of a mere human shake his faith!

Must be the lack of meat, Kikker told himself as he strode off towards the lift that led to the control chamber, tail swishing in agitation. All this synthetic flesh was turning him soft.

* * *

The Garden was changing.

A light blue bloom dusted the peach-like fruit on the trees in the acres and acres of orchards. In the endless miles of neat hedgerows, thorny growths sprouted, giving them a dishevelled, neglected appearance. All the flowers had closed up, the petals folding over their pistils, as if they were covering their faces, averting their gaze from a massacre.

Which, in a way, they were.

For the biggest change of all was happening to the Gardeners.

In their pods deep within the Tree – and hundreds of others like it all over the Garden – they mutated. Their beautiful, orchid-like heads (which weren't really heads at all) retracted inside their compact, gourd-like bodies, which swelled and pulsed. Their limbs and appendages thickened, growing thorns and spikes flowing with poison.

As the rising sun brought daylight to each part of the planet, the Gardeners emerged from the Trees – hissing, crackling creatures of death. Within the pods they vacated, more grew.

Silently, beneath the blinded Garden, a plant army amassed.

Captain John Melrose was the only living thing to witness the emergence of the transformed Gardeners. He spent the night hiding from Valethske patrols in the depths of the hilltop forest where he had carried out his initial mission briefing.

To mask his scent, he removed and buried his uniform, smeared himself with the dark, peaty soil of the planet and squirmed his way into the middle of a large bush in the darkest part of the forest. He slept fitfully, at times hearing the distant sound of Valethske copter-packs, and once, a distant scream, definitely human. Dawn broke, bringing with it clammy light filtering down through the pale yellow leaves. Melrose emerged from the bush, shivering in the cool morning air, alert for any sign of movement, any sound of booted foot on twig. But there was nothing, just a sense of stillness and anticipation.

He breakfasted on the little water he'd brought with him from the canal in his hip-flask – one of the few items the Valethske had left him when they had first captured him – and some sloe-like berries from the bush in which he'd spent the night, half-expecting a Gardener to come crashing through the forest at this transgression.

But he was allowed to enjoy his meagre breakfast in peace, unmolested by either motile plant or vulpine hunter. The berries tasted sharp, and burned his throat as they slid down, but at least it was something. Overnight, the mud had dried on his body, so he dug into a fresh patch of soil and anointed himself once more. Then he unearthed his clothes – which after a night in their shallow grave were clammy and damp – and dressed, grimly pleased. Now he smelled as if he'd been reborn out of the peaty earth, a thing of the Garden, his human scent totally obscured.

Melrose moved cautiously through the regular ranks of silver-barked trees towards the edge of the forest, gun ready to blast anything that leapt into his way. His head felt clearer this morning, and he remembered his self of the preceding day with a scornful amusement. He felt calm, in control, able to put things right. As he had slept, his plan had become clearer in his mind. Obviously he couldn't tackle the Valethske on his own; he had to proceed in small steps, count himself lucky each time he achieved an objective.

First objective: secure the Valethske shuttle.

Melrose emerged from the forest, getting his bearings. After escaping from the Valethske ship, they had landed in a fallow field about a mile distant. As he set off, he noticed a movement on the horizon, west to east. A horde of – was it Gardeners? – was spreading through the Garden. From this distance they looked like streams of ants pouring from a nest.

Melrose shuddered, a feeling of disquiet denting his new-found confidence. He realised that he knew nothing of the workings of this strange planet. There could be creatures here inimical to all alien forms of life. Melrose smiled grimly, the drying mud on his face cracking, a few flakes borne away in the morning breeze. If that was so, the Valethske were in for a surprise. As far as he could tell, the distant columns of creatures were sweeping in the general direction of the Valethske mothership, which had landed at some point over the horizon.

Concentrating on his first objective, Melrose jogged around the perimeter of the forest until the fallow field came into view, an apron of dun grassland that only made the fields and gardens on its border appear all the more verdant and colourful. There, in the middle of the field, was the Valethske shuttle, at the end of a line of scorched grass. Pleased that it was still there, Melrose increased his pace, keeping his eyes peeled for any sign of Valethske. He half-hoped to see the Doctor and company waiting nearby – that would solve the problem of the control chip – but there was no sign of them. Perhaps the Valethske had already caught them. In which case they were already dead. He hoped Lt Meharg had taken a few down with her.

He reached the bottom of the slope and waded into the brittle thigh-high grass that whispered as he passed through, frail blades crunching under his mud-encrusted boots. Suddenly, he froze, senses jangling. From above and behind him came the unmistakable droning clatter of rotor-blades.

Melrose threw himself to the dusty earth, pulling armfuls of dead grass over himself. He cursed his stupidity – surely they would see the broken stalks that indicated his passage through the field? He lay among the cool grass, trying to control a violent trembling that had taken hold of his body. But the sound of the copters passed overhead – he estimated about three or four – the downdraught from their blades setting up a great susurration within the dry stems.

The sound of their engines seemed to sink into the earth beyond him, and descended into a mechanical splutter as the hunters landed. They'd obviously been sent to retrieve the shuttle. Valethske liked their hardware and always salvaged as much as they could. Which meant that they must know about the escape from the mothership. Which meant that they must have captured and interrogated the others. Which meant that he was alone. But by sending hunters to the shuttle, the Valethske may have provided him with a means for revenge. Melrose pictured himself at the controls of the small ship, face contorted in fury, yelling out the names of the soldiers the Valethske had killed as he rammed the mothership's engines, aiming for maximum devastation. He might not get them all but he'd certainly give them something to remember him by.

Yes, that was it. That was the way he was going to die.

So, second objective: kill the three (or maybe four) Valethske, take one of their control chips and then the shuttle and then...

No, that was too much all at once. Melrose trembled, almost giving in to fear. Concentrate, hone down.

Second objective: Kill the Valethske.

That was better.

Slowly, carefully, he rose until he could see above the close horizon of stems. Not more than a hundred yards away was the shuttle, its sleek, brutal shape rising like a metal hummock. Next to it, three copter-packs, their blades stilled and drooping, sticking up from the sea of grass like strange metallic palm-trees.

And around the base of the shuttle, red-furred, black-eared heads of Valethske moved about.

Melrose ducked back down as one of them leapt up on to the shuttle, clambering on external access-rungs. Had it seen him? Melrose sweated beneath his twin coatings of uniform and mud. He had no choice. He had to assume the hunter had seen him, or scented him despite his camouflage. He checked his gun quickly, a grim smile twitching across his face – he was about to kill Valethske with their own weaponry.

With a yell he leapt up from the grass, opening fire, spraying bolts of energy in a tight arc across the side of the shuttle. Above the sizzling bolts he heard high-pitched screams. He kept on firing, seeing the copter-packs jerk and topple over. He kept his finger pressed down hard on the trigger until the gun spluttered into silence. Melrose stood there shaking, scanning the scene with wild eyes. The smell of burning leather and flesh reached him and he stumbled towards the shuttle, not quite believing that he'd got them all.

He came upon his first hit some distance from the shuttle,

sprawled out, arms reaching in his direction, fingers splayed as if in death it was still trying to grasp at him. It must have started running the moment it had seen him emerge. It had got almost halfway to him. Melrose was impressed despite himself. He prodded it with his boot – quite dead, its chest pocked with smoking holes.

Melrose tossed the now-useless gun aside and searched the body for weapons. There – a foot-long spike of shining metal. He took it from its scabbard at the dead hunter's waist and weighed it in his hands, testing the point of the blade. Deadly sharp. A good weapon, made for stabbing rather than cutting. Melrose stepped over the dead Valethske and walked up to the shuttle, teeth clamped tight to stop his jaw from chattering, knife held ready.

The second Valethske was also dead, leaning against the side of the shuttle, the left side of its head burnt away, the rust-coloured hull spattered with bits of cooking brain.

Melrose smiled. This was better than he'd expected, far better.

He turned to the third Valethske.

It was still alive.

He stood over it as it writhed in agony, its powerful legs curling in towards a smoking stomach wound. An idea formed in Melrose's mind, a way to pay the Valethske back for what they had done to his troopers.

The wounded hunter noticed Melrose and hissed, sending a cloud of saliva up at him.

The wound looked fatal. It would die soon.

He didn't have long.

Using all his strength, he heaved the dying hunter into a sitting position against the side of the shuttle. Its arms flailed at him but he absorbed its blows, intent on a new objective, one he couldn't quite put into words. He somehow managed to lift the Valethske into a standing position against the superstructure, its breath wheezing from it in desperate gulps.

He held it there with one hand and with the other drove the knife through its shoulder and into the hull of the shuttle, hammering it down with the ball of his fist. Its piercing scream of pain almost deafened him.

'This is for Private Wilding,' he said, 'and Private Helal...' He recited a litany of names, his voice choking, his mind filling with images of the faces of his troopers. Good men and women. Fighting the good fight. They hadn't deserved to die like that, used as playthings by the Valethske.

When he'd finished, Captain Melrose stepped back, admiring his work.

The Valethske hung there, blood oozing over its black uniform, hand clawing weakly at the hilt of the knife. It couldn't have much strength left now.

Its eyes fixed on his, yellow slits of hate. There was no fear in them – yet – but Melrose vowed there would be. Before it died, the creature would know some of the terror and humiliation its kind had inflicted on his troopers.

But then the Valethske started laughing, black lips sliding back from blue-white teeth, tongue lolling, body shaking. An unearthly cachinnation rent the air, almost drowning the sound of –

Melrose spun round, and gasped. He'd been so intent on his torture that he hadn't seen the hordes of Gardeners sweeping across the field towards him. But these creatures were different, masses of thick, spiky limbs. More like giant weeds than giant flowers.

He looked around frantically for somewhere to run – but there was nowhere.

He turned back to his captive, raining punches down on it – but still it laughed. Tears of frustration welled up in his eyes – this wasn't how he was supposed to die!

He screamed as thorned tentacles wrapped around him, digging into him, tearing, ripping. He fell to the ground, his body seeming to disappear into separate bursts of pain. The sun disappeared behind a mass of writhing tentacles. He couldn't breathe; blood gurgled in his throat.

Only three Valethske. He'd only managed to kill three.

As he died, Melrose hoped that the plant-creatures would get the rest.

Chapter Eighteen
Sacrifice

Peri slumped to her knees and dropped the shovel. Her back was on fire with pain and she ached where she never even realised she had muscles. Through the blood roaring in her ears, she could hear the thrumming of the excavator machine, the yelps and barks of the Valethske – and footsteps, heading towards her.

She gritted her teeth. Now she was unfit to work, they'd find other uses for her. She could already feel their teeth sinking into her flesh.

Hands on her shoulders, then moving underneath, hauling her to her feet.

She opened her eyes. Athon.

'You must carry on working, Peri. If you stop...'

He looked the most together Peri had seen him since their capture. She rubbed her aching arms, eyeing the muscles that bulged beneath his uniform. 'That's easy for you to say.'

'Come on.' Athon handed the shovel back to her.

She took it with a weary groan.

His mouth trembled. 'I don't want to see you die. I couldn't stand it.'

So his concern was for selfish reasons. Just like the old Athon. But Peri didn't remonstrate with him – instead she managed a brief smile. 'Yeah, well, you might not have any choice in the matter.'

Then his expression changed, eyes widening in fear and looking over Peri's shoulder.

Peri whirled round to see a Valethske stalking up to them. It was the one that had shot the Doctor – the one that had shot *her*.

Peri held the shovel across her chest, as if to ward off the approaching hunter.

It raised a hand. Peri saw that it was like a human hand, only with three fingers and a thumb; the palm was a pad of glossy grey-black flesh, and from the ends of the furred fingers, sharp claws protruded. 'Get back to work,' it said in gruff tones. 'I cannot vouch for your safety – these hunters lust continually after meat!'

'And what about you?' said Peri, defiance welling up within her. 'Aren't you hankering to take a bite out of us?'

She heard Athon catch his breath, felt his restraining hand on her shoulder. She shook it off and glared at him.

The Valethske stood above her. 'I am the Hunt Marshal, responsible for this pack of hunters. I must set an example, not fall to temptation.' A pink tongue ran over black lips, and blue-white teeth glinted. 'Believe me, it is not easy.'

'I get it,' said Peri. 'You can't harm us or you'll lose the TARDIS.' Getting bolder, she pressed the Hunt Marshal for information. 'Where's the Doctor? And what the hell is all this for?' She indicated the excavator and monorail with a tired sweep of her arm.

The hunter's ears twitched and it blinked, surprised at Peri's audacity. Before it could answer, a commotion broke out on the far side of the excavation pit. The Hunt Marshal swivelled round, tail scuffing against Peri's legs. Peri had time to notice that it was similar to a fox's brush, only thinner and shorter, its end tapering to a black spike of fur.

Then suddenly a wavering scream cut across the hum of the machinery.

'Flayoun – Burzka!' hissed the Hunt Marshal, loping across to where –

Taiana –

Peri heard Athon let out a cry of anguish.

She began to run forwards, but stopped as she realised there was nothing she could do to help.

Taiana was buried beneath a mass of Valethske, their black-tipped tails questing in the air as they fed. She could see Taiana's arm raised to fend them off, watched helplessly as a hunter sank its teeth into it. She could hear Taiana's voice, a low, shuddering moan fading to an unrecognisable gurgle. A hunter flung something wet and dark into the air, another leapt to catch it, jaws wide. Yet another had its teeth locked around her throat. More tussled with her thrashing legs, tearing great welts in the uniform and the flesh beneath.

The Hunt Marshal had reached the feasting hunters and was screeching at them to stop.

Peri shook her head, mesmerised by the scene. It would be her turn next. She couldn't move. She felt something tugging at her uniform. Athon. 'Now's our chance – they're not watching us.'

It was true – all the Valethske in and around the excavation pit were fixed on the gruesome scene.

Peri found herself tumbling after Athon towards the excavator. There was a square door in its side, secured by a locking wheel. His muscles bulging beneath his uniform, Athon spun the wheel, looking fearfully over his shoulder. With a hiss the door opened and he thrust Peri through.

Peri found herself on a narrow gantry, sandwiched between the inner and outer walls of the machine. There was barely enough room to turn around. Dim light spilled from grimy bulbs spaced along the outer wall. The air was thick and greasy, the walls and floor vibrating.

'What do we do now?' she cried over the noise.

After his brief burst of action, Athon was once again a cowering child. 'I – I don't know!'

Peri looked around. This was obviously some sort of access point. She figured the Valethske were after something that lay underground, so there must be a way for them to climb down the bore. Peri tried to imagine what was happening beneath her, wishing she knew more about drilling and mining. Obviously the drill-head would be remote, carving a shaft through which the Valethske could descend. Peri ran along the gantry, her legs almost giving way beneath her. Soon she found what she was looking for – a ladder.

She turned to speak to Athon, but he wasn't there. 'Athon!' she called.

He hurried around the curving wall, zipping up a pocket on his uniform, a distracted look on his face.

'What's wrong?'

'Nothing, nothing... they'll soon be after us.'

Peri started down the ladder. It was hard going. As well as fatigue making her head swim, her arms and legs feeling like they were going to drop off, the ladder was made for Valethske and its rungs were widely spaced. Peri had to place each foot with precision, stretching her aching legs. She began to sweat, droplets falling from her face into the blackness below. Above her, Athon was descending with greater ease and she had to work fast to keep out of his way.

The Valethske must have noticed that they were gone. They must have finished with Taiana by now. Peri felt too tired to grieve for the Eknuri woman.

Soon they reached a second gantry, and Peri rested gratefully.

Below, the metal walls of the machine gave way to glistening black earth. In the midst of the shaft, a thick network of cables and tubes descended into darkness, from which the drill-head screamed. Peri looked back up, realising that they had only come a short way down, through the initial stages of the machine itself. How much further the drill-head had penetrated, she had no way of knowing. And short of shinning down the cables in the middle of the shaft – which she couldn't reach anyway – there seemed to be no way to climb down.

Peri fought down a wave of panic. They'd been stupid, running blindly into probably even greater danger. But what choice did they have? To end up like Taiana...

Athon had noticed this too. 'We're trapped. They're going to climb down after us and kill us.' A sob squeezed itself wetly out of him.

'Hey, calm down,' soothed Peri. 'They need us alive, remember? If they kill us, the Doctor won't let them have the TARDIS.'

It sounded feeble to her and made no impression on Athon.

'They'll just kill him as well and take it anyway!' he moaned.

He was probably right. She tried another tack. 'You've done well, getting us this far.' She managed a smile. 'You're not the total coward I took you for.'

His dark eyes were full of pain, his mouth twisted in an ugly grimace. 'But I am, I am,' he wailed. 'I don't want to die. I don't want to die.'

He was bordering on hysterics again. Peri began to realise that as long as he was doing something – shovelling crud for the Valethske, clambering down into the depths of the planet – he seemed to be OK. She needed to find something for him to do, to take his mind off the situation.

Giving Athon a reassuring pat, she set off around the gantry, searching for something, anything, some clue as to what this was all for. Perhaps the Valethske were digging for oil... no, that made no sense. Above her head, spaced evenly around the walls, were cylinders of tightly bunched cable. Beneath them, racks of harnesses. From the reels, the cable ran along an arm which jutted out over the drop.

Peri called to Athon. 'Hey, come here!'

She picked up a harness and chucked it at him.

He caught it, blinking slowly.

'Strap yourself in – we're going abseiling!'

Veek grabbed Flayoun's shoulder and hauled him away from the carcass. 'Fool! We need them alive!'

Flayoun glared at her, no trace of guilt in his yellow-green eyes. He tossed her a length of intestine. Veek let it slap against her breastplate and fall to the muddy floor. The other hunters backed away from the stripped carcass.

Veek sighed. She could hardly blame them. 'Get back to your positions!' she snarled. 'The Vale Commander shall hear of this.'

Suddenly she remembered the other two humans and whirled round. They were nowhere to be seen.

She dashed over to where she had stood conversing with the small dark-haired female, eyes scanning the ground for tracks. There – they led to one of the access hatches in the side of the excavator.

Flayoun appeared at her side, ears flat against his head in apology. 'If they have entered the machine, there is no escape.'

A technician called out from the machine's monitoring post, a plinth set into the earth, cables snaking from it to the side of the excavator. 'Success! The drill-head is chewing air – we're through!'

Veek strode across to the technician, roaring. 'Stop the machine!'

The technician's hands flicked switches and the distant rumble of the drill-head subsided. Soon the only noise was the throaty whine of the extractor fans.

'The humans have escaped into the guts of this planet,' hissed Veek.

Flayoun licked his lips, eager to make up for his lapse. 'We had better get after them.'

Veek nodded, beckoning to three of the hunters to follow her, and loped towards the now-silent machine. 'Take weapons – but shoot to wound only. The Vale Commander wants this prey alive.'

Veek gnashed her teeth. They all thought she was doing her duty, out of loyalty to Kikker. But she had other, more personal reasons for wanting the prey intact. Like Kikker, she wanted the secret of time travel, but not for the glory of the Valethske...

The Doctor stopped walking. 'Take me to my friends. Now.'

The Vale Guard in front of him turned, extending its arm so the muzzle of its blaster rested on the bridge of the Doctor's nose. 'Keep walking, prey!'

The Doctor moved the gun out of the way. 'I can hardly comply with that thing up my nose, now can I?'

The Vale Guard lowered its gun, blinking.

The other Vale Guard prodded him in the back with the muzzle of its gun. 'No questions. Keep moving.'

But the Doctor remained standing where he was, arms folded, staring intently at the maze of conduits and pipes that wound their way along the ceiling.

The first Vale Guard reached out, seized the Doctor's arm and sent him spinning against the wall. 'You will obey!'

The Doctor rubbed his shoulder. 'Your Vale Commander needs

me alive. If you kill me, he won't be pleased.'

The Vale Guards looked at each other.

'You're not proper hunters, are you? You're just Kikker's lap-dogs!'

The first Vale Guard, who was more quick-tempered than his companion, stepped forwards to cuff the Doctor, but the other, a more taciturn beast, restrained it.

'We will be hunters, when we come of age,' said the second Guard. 'We will undergo the Ten Trials of Azreske, and –'

'Oh, I'm not interested in all your rites and ceremonies.' He fixed the Guards with an earnest stare. 'But think, when will you ever come of age? In the centuries you've been travelling, you've probably only aged a few months. You're doomed never to become hunters, to always be slaves!'

The first Vale Guard, who had a limited attention span, had started picking his teeth halfway through the Doctor's speech; but its fellow had taken it all in.

'Your words are heresy!' it growled.

'Hardly surprising, since I'm not one of you,' the Doctor groaned.

'We've wasted enough time here,' said the second Guard. 'You must be put in the long sleep.'

The first Vale Guard had completed its oral hygiene. 'Move!' it bellowed, brandishing its blaster.

The Doctor stood firm. 'No. Not until you take me to see my friends.'

The second Guard holstered its gun and cracked its finger-bones. 'Then we will break your arms and legs. They *might* heal during the long sleep.'

The Doctor backed against the wall as the two Valethske bore down on him.

As Peri helped Athon fasten his harness she realised that the distant screaming of the drill-head had stopped.

'What can that mean?' said Athon.

Peri swallowed, looking up. Could she already hear faint sounds of pursuit? 'It means we've gotta hurry up.'

She sat on the edge of the gantry, legs dangling above the drop. Warm air surged past her, caressing her face. This has got to be what the Valethske intended to do, she told herself. They were after something beneath the surface of the Garden – maybe the thing the Doctor had spoken about, that had taken Aline... She shied away from that line of thought. If they were after some as yet unspecified thing below, the shaft must lead somewhere. Right?

Right. She looked across at Athon, who was sitting on the opposite side of the shaft, just visible beyond the central mass of tubes. 'Ready?'

He nodded, dark shadows under his eyes.

'Right.' She'd not been totally correct – this wasn't abseiling, more like mechanically assisted bungee-jumping. The cable was attached to the back of the harness, and the rate of descent could be controlled from a small panel in the breastplate.

'I'll go first, you watch me, OK?'

Athon nodded again. The Valethske-sized harness fitted him well but, even with the straps done up tightly, Peri's felt dangerously roomy. She knew that for any climbing activity you had to be strapped in real tight for safety. But what choice did she have? She craned her neck and checked the cable, which led from the reel in the wall through the arm mechanism and down to where it was tethered in the harness at the small of her back. Holding her breath, she slid off the edge of the gantry, feeling the harness bite into her underarms and groin. She swung into the middle of the shaft, kicking her feet out to butt against the tubes in the middle.

She swung back again, looking around for Athon. 'Go on, it's perfectly safe.'

He heard him grunt, then cry out in surprise. There was a metallic clang as he hit the tubes and she saw his flailing arms and legs.

'Stay calm! Now let's try out the controls.'

She looked down at her panel, trying to ignore the spinning view of her own legs, the shaft and the silver tubes descending into darkness. She hoped she'd got it right – there was a red arrow which clearly meant 'down' and a black button which equally clearly meant 'stop'. Or so she hoped. Other buttons, she presumed, controlled the rate of descent.

Well, she'd soon find out.

She gritted her teeth and pressed the red button. Nothing happened for a few seconds, then there was a whine of machinery from above her and with a jolt she began to descend. She looked up. The cable was paying out slowly, making a sibilant grating noise as it slid through the arm mechanism.

She just hoped there was enough of it to reach the bottom of the shaft – whatever else they were, the Valethske seemed to be good engineers, so she was probably OK. She looked down between her legs, the updraught rippling and thwacking against her loose garments. Was that a faint green light far below?

She looked across at Athon. She could see the top of his head as he hung from the cable.

'You OK?'

He swung his legs down, bringing himself upright in a balletic movement. For one brief moment there was a gleam of enjoyment in his eyes. Then he looked up, fear returning to his face.

'They're coming!'

Peri looked up too. The gantry was a circle of silvery light, surprisingly far away. Peri could hear the clamour of pursuit, booted footsteps on ladder rungs.

'We're gonna have to speed up.' Her fingers fiddled with the control panel, hesitating over a likely-looking blue symbol. Holding her breath, she pressed it – and immediately began to descend at a faster speed.

'The blue symbol!' she called out to Athon.

It was definitely getting lighter; a green glow suffused everything. She looked down. Between her booted feet, there was a rough circle of green light framed by the end of the shaft. She could see the serrated bulk of the drill-head, its churnings now stilled, hanging like a giant silver fist.

She was going too fast – at this speed the impact would break her legs. She pressed the 'stop' symbol again – and began to go even faster, the updraught tearing at her clothes.

She screamed as the end of the shaft raced up towards her. The Valethske must have taken over the controls – what did it matter to them if she ended up puréed?

She stabbed at the controls again and again – and eventually began to slow.

Soon Peri emerged from the end of the shaft. Her feet hit something hard and unyielding, the impact hurting her knees. The cable carried on paying out, its silver coils snaking around her.

Athon alighted, legs braced for touchdown. He pointed upwards, grimacing.

Peri could hear a distant whine. She looked back up the shaft. Dark, angular shapes were plunging down towards them.

Peri scrambled out of her harness, stumbling against Athon as he did the same, looking about for somewhere to run.

But she couldn't make out anything distinct in the green-tinged gloom. Next to them was the drill-head, the size of a small house, its cutting edges thick with black mud, extractor-tubes coiled around it, mouths gaping. It looked like the head of some alien beast. It had stopped mere feet from the rock floor of the cavern. A bitter odour of burnt metal rose from the blades.

'Come on – we gotta run,' she gasped.

'No.'

Athon was holding a red cylinder, staring at her with wide, terrified eyes.

She heard shrieks and yells from above and moved out from under the end of the shaft.

But Athon still stood there, transfixed. 'There's no escape,' he said. His voice was flat, lifeless, reminding Peri of Taiana.

Peri looked around for somewhere to run. Dark entrances led off in all directions from the cavern. Could be tunnels, or dead-end caves. She hated to agree with Athon, but he was probably right. She sighed. 'We're gonna have to give ourselves up.'

His head turned slowly towards her, brown eyes widening. 'G-give ourselves up? To them? You saw what they did to Taiana –

they'll do the same to us!'

Peri looked up into his handsome face, his dark eyes, sensuous lips. She had once thought he was God-like. How wrong she'd been. 'Athon, think! They need us alive, the Doctor's made a bargain!'

He wasn't listening. He shook his head, bringing up the red cylinder to his chest, big brown hands caressing it as if it was a talisman. 'I'm not going to let them eat me. I'm *not* going to *let* them *eat* me!'

His voice echoed around the cavern and back up the shaft.

In response, Peri heard the cackling cries of Valethske.

'They're not going to!' she implored. 'You heard the Hunt Marshal – we're hostages, too valuable to kill. Hey, what is that thing?' She tried to snatch the cylinder from Athon but he was too quick, raising it above his head way out of her reach.

'I'm not going to let them eat me!'

In a flash Peri realised. 'Oh no. Athon, no!'

He looked at her, dark eyes shining. 'Yes. I'm going to do it. Whatever you say about the Doctor making bargains, they're going to kill us sooner or later and I'm not going to let it happen.'

His thumb passed over the silver detonation stud at the end of the grenade or whatever it was. When had he picked it up? Peri remembered their dash into the machine – now she knew why he'd lagged behind.

Her mouth dry, Peri pleaded with him. 'Athon, please listen to me. You don't have to do this! There's always a way out...'

She backed away as she spoke, tears of frustration stinging her eyes.

Athon had stripped off his Valethske uniform and his body looked even more statuesque bathed in the green phosphorescence. His eyes were fixed on hers, and his expression was the calmest she'd seen it since the first Valethske attack, back on the planetoid, back at his party.

'Run, Peri!' he cried.

For once, he sounded almost heroic.

Then his head jerked upwards, and he leapt aside as blaster

bolts sizzled into the floor of the cavern.

He dropped the grenade, which clattered to the rock and rolled underneath the drill-head...

Athon scrambled underneath the machine, hands reaching for the grenade...

Two Valethske slid into view, their legs flexing as they touched down...

Athon snatched the grenade and spun round on his back, screaming as the two hunters aimed their weapons...

Peri was screaming too, and one of the hunters turned, bringing its gun up to cover her...

Peri stumbled backwards, feet slipping on smooth rock, trying to propel herself towards the gaping cave-mouths –

Athon pressed the grenade to his chest, against his tattoo...

The other Valethske realised what was going on and yelped, staggering backwards...

And then there was a flash of white light, a giant hand seemed to pick Peri up and dash her against the wall, there was the merest instant of pain and she blacked out.

Chapter Nineteen
Betrayal

A red-furred hand clasped around the Doctor's throat, claws digging into his skin, clamping his head against the rusty wall. Other hands gripped his arms, pulling, twisting. He concentrated, cutting off the pain. The Vale Guards had underestimated his strength, thinking that he was human, and he was able to resist, but only for a time. His hands groped around, feeling for anything that could be of use – and his fingers closed round the butt of a blaster. Heaving against his assailants, he yanked the weapon from its holster and fired, sending a bolt of energy smashing into the far wall.

As he'd expected, the startled Vale Guards let go of him and stepped back.

He brought the gun swiftly up to his head, resting the muzzle against his ear, taking care to keep his fingers away from the trigger. 'Take me to my friends – or I'll shoot myself!'

The first Vale Guard let out a bellow of laughter. 'Do it! What do we care?'

'You're forgetting that your Vale Commander wants me alive.' The Doctor lowered his voice to an awed hush. 'Just imagine what punishment he might devise for two Guards who by their ineptitude deprived the Valethske of time travel.'

For the first time, the Doctor saw fear in the faces of Valethske. Their eyes widened, their whiskers trembled and their tails began to swish about.

Eventually the first Guard found voice. 'He's right.'

The second Guard sneered, revealing a set of sharp blue-white teeth. 'Very well, we will do as you say. But don't think you have outwitted us! Soon, you will be in the long sleep.'

The first Guard nodded and snickered.

The Doctor had no intention of letting them cryogenically freeze him. 'I will go willingly, as long as I can see that my friends are safe. Lead the way.'

The two Guards walked hesitantly up the passageway, glancing back every now and then to check that the Doctor was following them. They looked so perturbed that he kept the blaster held to his own head, and wasn't pointing it at them. The Doctor couldn't keep himself from grinning.

Suddenly, from somewhere below, there was a muffled explosion.

Veek gripped the railing as the shock-waves tore through the walls of the excavator. Her vision juddering, she saw the central array twist violently, cables flying loose like whipcords. On the other side of the gantry she saw Burzka clap his hands to his face as a frayed cable-end caught him. Blinded, he staggered and fell, down through the ballooning cloud of dust and grit that was rushing up the shaft. His dying shriek was quickly swallowed up in the thunderous cadences of the explosion.

Suddenly Veek was engulfed in the up-blast, a hot wind of gritty particles sandpapering her uniform and scathing her head and hands. Her eyes turned to slits of fiery pain and she was pressed back against the wall of the excavator, the breath torn from her lungs.

When the shock-wave had passed, Veek rubbed the grit from her eyes and opened them. She coughed, her throat rough with dust, particles gritting her teeth. The air was thick with smoke and she could hardly see. Akkia and Freela, the two vixens sent down after the prey, couldn't possibly have survived such a blast. But what had caused it? A malfunction at the drill-head? But it didn't contain any fuel or anything that would cause an explosion.

Veek ducked as mud and grit began to rain down on her from above, wondering briefly where it was coming from – then she realised: the explosion had sent a mass of stuff up the shaft, and what goes up must come down. She endured the choking downpour, snarling as more grit found its way into her eyes and mouth. When it was over she brushed herself off. She itched all over; some of it must have got into her uniform.

'Veek – help me.'

The voice came from below.

She walked around the gantry and saw Flayoun, clinging to the edge by his fingertips. She knelt over him, regarding his panting face, dust-caked tongue lolling sideways from his mouth, yellow eyes burning in the smoky gloom.

'Pull me up – can't hang on much longer.'

Because of Flayoun, partly, the Doctor's friends were dead, his bargain with the Vale Commander forfeit. Because of Flayoun, she would never be able to access the secrets of the blue box.

She should let him fall to his death.

She went to turn away, but images of Flayoun's handsome body as he slept by soft firelight came to her, and she hesitated. He was her mate – and, despite his lack of intelligence, foresight and judgement, she still wanted him. Above all, he was a true Valethske – a ruthless hunter, loyal and fierce. She could hardly blame him for giving in to temptation. It wasn't his fault, it was the Great Mission; it had warped everything.

She couldn't let him die.

Leaning over, she gripped Flayoun's forearms and hauled him bodily from the shaft.

He stood before her, panting, rubbing his arms.

'Thank you, Hunt Marshal. I'm not yet ready for the Hall of the Dead!' Despite his gruff, jocular manner, his head was cowed, his ears twitching. She knew exactly how he felt – he burned with the shame of being afraid of death. It was often the way with hunters. Brave as Azreske herself until the time came to face the end.

Veek turned away and activated the mechanism, reeling in Akkia and Freela's cables. There was a slim chance they would still be alive. But after a few minutes, all that came up was blackened, frayed cable-ends.

Flayoun hissed through his teeth. 'The Vale Commander will not be pleased.'

That was a major understatement. The excavator wrecked, the

prey killed, the Great Mission delayed – Kikker would almost certainly have them eviscerated and fed to the other hunters. Strangely, Veek felt a moment of pure elation. This was what she had been waiting for, a reason to cut loose, break away from the Great Mission. She was on her own now. Well, not quite.

'Hunter Flayoun,' she said, approaching him and brushing the dust from the fur on his face. 'You have always been my most loyal hunter. Now we are doomed, what say we make our escape? We could return home.'

Flayoun's ears flattened against his head and his eyes widened. His lips curled back from his teeth in a snarl. 'You are concussed!' he growled. 'For a Hunt Marshal to utter such heresy...'

Suddenly his hands were round her throat, claws digging into her windpipe. Veek lashed out with her feet, catching him across the shins and he fell, letting go of her neck.

Coughing away smoke, she drew her spike-knife and was on him in an instant, bringing the pin-sharp blade up through his uniform until it tickled his breast just below the heart.

'That was a test of your loyalty,' she whispered into a twitching ear. She knew him well enough to know he'd fall for it. She dug the knife in, just enough for it to draw blood. Then she pulled back, sitting on her haunches. 'You passed.'

He sprung to his feet, ignoring the blood that trickled down his uniform. 'A test of my loyalty?' he spat. 'No, Hunt Marshal – I saw the longing in your eyes, the yearning for home.'

She'd underestimated him. She slid the spike-knife back into its scabbard and spread her arms wide in a final appeal. 'Don't you feel it too, Flayoun? Don't you want to go back to Valeth Skettra?'

For the merest instant she thought she saw him waver.

But then he snarled. 'I do not, Veek. This mission is the greatest honour. To speak of abandoning it is worse than heresy.'

Veek sighed. He'd clearly been too well indoctrinated. 'Then we have no choice but to fight.'

Flayoun snarled, eyes narrowing to yellow slits, teeth bared.

Now she saw no trace of the gentle hunter she'd lain with.

Veek prepared to fight to the death, summoning up all her hatred for the Great Mission, projecting it at Flayoun, at what he had become. She couldn't let him live, now he knew about her heresy.

The two hunters flew towards each other, their bodies slamming together like colliding skirmishers. They clattered around the walkway, snarling and spitting, sometimes almost slipping and plunging locked in combat down the shaft. Flayoun was strong, but his instinctive regard for his Hunt Marshal made him hesitant, robbed his manoeuvres of conviction. Soon Veek had her former mate pressed up against the wall of the excavator, her jaws clamped around his throat.

She remembered their joke, after the long sleep, after every long sleep. *I'll take a bite out of you, hunter.*

Veek sank her teeth into Flayoun's neck, feeling the tension in the skin, the underlying solidity of the flesh. She could feel his heart thudding against hers, his whole body trembling. He was whimpering in terror, mewing like a new-born cub at its first sight of day. Staring death in the face for the second time in a few short minutes. One savage snap of her jaws and a twist of her neck muscles would be enough to rip the life from him.

But something made her stop, hold back from the kill. Not the image of Flayoun in the firelight, his body straining against hers. This time it was contempt, not compassion, which saved Flayoun. Veek grinned, a dark jet of cruelty twisting through her heart.

She unlocked her jaw from its death-clamp, trailing strands of saliva down on to his face, on to the white stripe she had once thought so attractive. She let go of Flayoun and let him slump to the walkway. His body curled around her feet, his face savage with pain. He fixed her with a bilious yellow stare. 'Finish me!'

Veek smiled. 'No. I'm going to let you live, knowing that I have bested you.' She kicked him in the stomach a few times, making him howl. His cries excited her, as if he was prey fit only for torture and consumption. 'You will say nothing of my so-called "heresy", or by Azreske's teeth I will gut you alive!'

Without even looking to see if he followed, Veek grasped the rungs and began climbing.

* * *

Veek emerged into the excavation pit just as a trio of Vale Guards were about to enter the inspection hatch. Hissing, she waved them away and they scattered like cubs. She wasn't surprised to see Kikker and Ruvis standing before her. The Vale Commander's head was tilted back, his teeth bared in a sickle-shaped sneer, the whites of his eyes gleaming.

Ruvis looked as aloof as ever. Veek hated Ruvis; his perverted experiments, his aversion to live meat, even his very appearance – the plain grey tunic of the scientific caste, his prosthetic leg and jaw – were anathema to her and all the hunters. His presence on the Great Mission, though necessary she grudgingly supposed, was a reminder of how far the mission had brought her from the true way of the Valethske – the hunter's way.

Apart from them, the Vale Guards and herself, there were no other Valethske in the excavation pit. That was odd – surely, with the excavations nearly complete, they should all be here, stupidly slavering to be the first – after Kikker, of course – to get their claws on the Gods?

'What has happened here?' bellowed Kikker.

Veek gathered her thoughts. She could hear Flayoun scrambling up the ladder behind her. She wished now that she had killed him. With his honour besmirched he had nothing to lose – what if he blurted out her heresy for all to hear?

She decided on the truth. 'Unnatural conditions, Vale Commander.'

He cocked his head to one side. 'Explain.'

'Hunters cannot work alongside prey, that is well known. A few of them gave in to temptation.'

Kikker clenched his fists in anger and hissed through his teeth.

Ruvis regarded Veek levelly. 'Did any of the prey survive the feasting or the explosion?'

Veek shook her head.

'My theory is they committed suicide,' said Ruvis, his jaw whirring. 'It's quite common among prey, especially humans. They cannot bear the thought of being eaten alive, for some reason.'

Veek growled. Ruvis seemed to be poking fun at herself, at

Kikker – but Kikker didn't seem to notice.

'Suicide – or sabotage! They may know of the Great Mission!'

'How could they possibly know?' said Ruvis. 'Besides which, a blasting-pack is missing from the complement inside the excavator. It's quite clear what's happened.'

Veek remembered the look of terror on the male human's face. Despite her hatred of Ruvis, he was probably right. Veek's lips curled in a sneer of self-disgust when she remembered that only recently she had entertained, however briefly, the notion of suicide as a way out of the Great Mission.

At that moment, Flayoun scrambled from the inspection hatch, and saluted Kikker.

'Hunter Flayoun,' purred Kikker. 'Did you give in to temptation?'

Flayoun met his enquiring gaze resolutely. 'I cannot lie, Vale Commander.'

Whyever not, thought Veek – Flayoun was letting his loyalty get in the way of his own survival. He was too stupid to live.

Kikker hissed. 'Then your actions have jeopardised the mission – and the glory of the Valethske!'

Flayoun's uniform was stained with his own blood, and he was limping, but there was a grim determination in his eyes that Veek did not like one bit. She cursed herself again for letting him live, and vowed that she would kill him the next chance she got.

'I have done nothing – compared to the vile heresies of Hunt Marshal Veek!'

If she ever got that chance…

'Heresies?' Kikker's eyes widened and his voice rose.

'She denounces the Great Mission! She wishes to flee from the Gods, back to Valeth Skettra!' cried Flayoun.

The three Vale Guards drew their guns and aimed them at Veek.

Veek realised that she should have challenged Kikker back on the barren moon, before the feast. Now it was too late.

Kikker's voice was smooth and calm, his eyes coolly appraising. 'Is this true, Hunt Marshal Veek?'

Veek couldn't think of a way out of this except bluff. 'Flayoun is delirious, Hunt Marshal – the explosion addled his mind – he misunderstood my words.'

Kikker looked from Veek to Flayoun, eyes narrowing. He sniffed the air. The iron taint of Flayoun's spilled blood was clear to Veek and would be to all the others.

'You have fought. Yet one has survived. How can this be?'

'I spared him, Vale Commander,' said Veek quickly. 'It was, after all, a misunderstanding – and he is a fine hunter.'

'No misunderstanding, Hunt Marshal!' hissed Flayoun. He made to lunge at her but Kikker stepped forward, restraining the hunter.

'Enough, enough!' he growled. 'Whatever your differences, forget them – for now. You can settle them later. I need both of you. The ship is under attack.'

Veek gaped. 'Attack?' This was a planet full of inert, passive plants! 'From whom?'

Suddenly a voice rang out across the excavation pit. 'Hello there! Is this a private party or can anyone join in?'

Veek whirled round to see the human called the Doctor descending the staircase leading down from one of the walkways that crossed the excavation pit. Two sheepish-looking Vale Guards shuffled before him. For some reason Veek couldn't fathom, the human was holding a blaster to his own head.

'I told you to put him into the long sleep!' growled Kikker as the two Vale Guards came up to him and saluted.

'He threatens to kill himself!' said the taller of the guards.

The strange human walked right up to Kikker. 'And with me the secret of time travel dies. Where are Peri, Athon and Taiana?'

Veek wondered briefly which name fitted which. To her relief, all the Vale Guards were now targeting the human. His pink, fleshy face didn't look at all concerned – but then Veek had always found prey to be inscrutable, except when in the extremes of pain and terror. She licked her lips, edging nearer the Doctor. This human, though seemingly deranged, was her ticket back home.

Kikker turned away, pretending unconcern, but Veek could see his lips curl in a wince of anger. 'I have more pressing problems than the fate of mere prey.'

All the Doctor's attention was fixed on the Vale Commander. Silently, swiftly, Veek lunged at him, shoving him to the floor and snatching the blaster away from him in one swift movement.

The human sprawled on the mud floor of the excavation pit, glaring up at Veek. For a second, Veek saw power in his eyes. Power, knowledge and deep wisdom.

Kikker nodded at Veek. 'Well done, Hunt Marshal.' He waved a hand and the two Vale Guards the Doctor had outwitted dragged him back to his feet, handling him roughly, snarling threats into his ears.

The Doctor repeated his question. 'Where are my friends? There was an explosion, wasn't there? Something's gone wrong with your little treasure-hunt!'

Veek pointed at the bulk of the now-silent excavator. 'They tried to escape, into the planet's interior.'

'And the explosion?'

'Suicide,' said Ruvis, nodding his grizzled head, with a level glare at Kikker. 'Quite common among prey.'

'Oh, I don't think Peri would take her own life. She's far too spirited!' Despite the lightness of his voice, his eyes looked haunted. He tried to crane round in the grip of his captors to examine the machine. 'Is there any chance they could have survived?'

'No!' roared Kikker. He glared at Veek and Flayoun. 'They are dead.' He had been pacing up and down before the Doctor, clearly preoccupied. Veek remembered his words about an attack.

'Then the bargain's off,' said the Doctor. 'You couldn't keep your side of it, so I'm not going to keep mine. You will never learn the secrets of time travel, not from me anyway.'

Kikker stopped pacing and went up to the Doctor, gripping his face in a gloved hand, sending spittle flying into his fair hair. 'I care nothing for any bargain! When the time comes I will tear the information from you!' He turned away. Veek could see that he was shaking with rage. 'Take him away – put him in the long sleep!'

Veek saw her chance. 'I will take him. He has no chance of outwitting me.'

Kikker didn't seem to hear, but at her command the Vale Guards shoved the Doctor over to her. She caught him and held on to him tightly.

The Vale Commander had already started walking away. 'Come, Hunter Flayoun, Vale Guards – we have much to do.'

'He seems rather worked up about something,' muttered the Doctor.

Veek realised he was addressing her. 'He says we're under attack.' She raised her voice. 'Who attacks us, Vale Commander?'

Kikker stopped walking and turned round. 'The plants of this cursed world! They have mutated and swarmed against us. They are threatening to overrun the ship!' His voice rose to an indignant bark. 'It would be the ultimate humiliation if the Great Mission were to be thwarted by –' he spat the word '– *plants*!'

The Doctor shuddered – Veek looked at his face and realised he was laughing. She squeezed his arm, not quite hard enough to break it. He struggled to break free from Veek's grip but she held him too tightly.

'It's the Garden,' he said. 'It sees you as a threat – it's defending itself against you the only way it can!'

Kikker snorted. 'Ridiculous. These creatures have been sent by the Gods as a final test of our strength. Only when we have defeated them will we at last confront the Gods.'

The Doctor sighed in exasperation. 'No! Listen to me – your only chance is to leave this planet, now. If my theory's correct the attacks won't stop until you're completely eradicated!'

Kikker came up to the Doctor, blue-white teeth bared in a sneer. 'That will never happen. Valethske technology is superior. We will prevail.'

His words reassured Veek, but the mad gleam in his eyes did not.

The Doctor smiled. 'We will see,' he said in a fair imitation of Kikker's sibilant growl.

Kikker drew back his hand and flicked the Doctor in the face with the fingers of his gloved fist. The Doctor flinched and cried out, writhing in Veek's grip.

Then Kikker strode away, flanked by Flayoun, Ruvis and the Vale Guards.

The Doctor's nose was bleeding, but his eyes were burning with anger. Veek let him go so he could clean up his wound and regain his composure.

'Who elected him leader?' he muttered.

'No one,' said Veek. 'He is Vale Commander by right of combat.'

'It was a rhetorical question.' The Doctor sighed and looked Veek up and down. 'Well, come on then, aren't you meant to be taking me to the freezer?'

'Yes.' Veek grabbed the Doctor's arm again, more gently this time, and grinned, letting him see her blue-white teeth, giving an outward show of ferocity.

But inside she was wondering if the threat of death would be enough to make this strange human help her escape the Great Mission.

Peri woke up coughing, her eyes streaming and her lungs on fire. She opened her eyes: blackness. She stood up, gasping as pain threatened to drag her back down. She felt like one huge bruise. She did a quick check, feeling along her arms, along her legs, her ribs, her head – nothing seemed broken. A miracle she was alive.

No. It would be a miracle if Athon was alive.

She peered into the gloom, but couldn't see much. She stretched out her arms, fingers touching wet mud. The explosion seemed to have brought down the roof of the cavern, smothering Athon, the pursuing Valethske and the massive drill-head in untold tons of mud. Peri, by sheer luck, had been blasted back into an alcove in the cavern wall, thus escaping being crushed by scarcely a few feet.

Great. A whole planet had fallen on her. At least things couldn't get any worse.

Peri felt her way around her prison, trying not to panic, trying not to notice how hard it was getting to breathe. She soon found that the wall of mud met a wall of rock in both directions. There was no way out. She was entombed. She wished she had never read that Poe story about the premature burial. It had been at a pyjama party back when she was thirteen. She'd read it aloud with glee, scared all her friends. Not giggly, huddle-together scared, but sleepless-night scared. God, she could remember whole chunks of it now. She began to panic, sweat pouring into her eyes.

'Can anyone hear me?' she yelled. Her voice vanished into the mud. Smothered.

Peri sank to her knees and buried her head in her hands, letting the sobs come, for once not really caring. There was no one here to see her anyway. After a while she stopped crying and sat blinking in the darkness, feeling sort of empty and not scared. It was as if the tears had released something in her, wiped away all her panic and terror. For a while, anyway. She could already feel it starting to build again.

She stared at the boots the Valethske had given her – clunky, heavy things like diver's boots.

Hang on, she thought – how could she see them, in total darkness?

Then she saw that they were reflecting a greenish glow.

Peri looked off to her left – there, near the floor, was a tiny gap, not much bigger than an upturned open book, through which the now-familiar green phosphorescence sent its faint green glow. Peri scrambled over to the gap on all fours and peered through. The green light illuminated a gap that was way too small for her to squirm through. She could reach all the way to the other side with an outstretched arm, but that was all.

For what seemed like hours she widened out the gap, hauling out great hunks of slippery clay-like mud and slapping it in the small space around her. The effort made her giddy and she had to rest her aching arms every now and then. Her veins seemed to pulse with pain, as if even her blood was tired.

But eventually she managed to widen the gap enough to be able to force her way through. She felt like toothpaste being squeezed from a tube. For one terrifying moment she thought that more mud was going to plop down on her, but she broke free and scrambled away, stretching herself out on the rock floor, panting with the exertion, staring at the moss-covered ceiling some ten feet above her.

She was just getting interested in the glowing moss when an ominous creaking and groaning sound broke out from nearby.

Fearing that the roof was going to come crashing down, Peri got to her feet and looked around. She was in a tunnel, refreshingly wide and high-ceilinged. It had a smooth floor and rough walls of chunky black rock covered in the green moss. Behind her, the tunnel entrance was blocked by a wall of mud. She could see the gap through which she'd squeezed; it was at the junction of rock wall and mudslide. Any further to the right and she really would have been entombed for ever.

Thankful to be alive, Peri tried not to dwell on the fact that she was lost in the bowels of an alien planet with no food and water. She walked along the tunnel, which led in a smooth curve so that she was continually on edge waiting for something to run round the corner at her.

Presently, she came out into a large cavern bordered with tapering pillars of rock. There were many other tunnels leading off, and her heart sank. How the hell was she ever going to get back to the surface?

Then she noticed that she wasn't alone. Sitting in the middle of the cavern was a figure. A woman with white hair, head slumped on her chest.

She was wearing an old leather jacket and khaki combat trousers.

'Hello? A – Aline?'

The woman looked up.

Peri gasped. It *was* Aline! Where her skin was pale before, now it was positively luminescent, glowing with an inner, ghostly light. Her once-black hair was now pure white, glowing like fibre-optics. Where the leather jacket and combat trousers hadn't suited her before, now they looked positively grotesque.

Aline looked up at Peri, then slumped down again. Peri ran to her.

'Are you OK? What the hell happened to you?'

Aline stared off into the distance. Her voice was barely a whisper. 'I've made contact.'

Peri frowned. 'What do you mean?'

Aline looked at her. Her eyes were discs of silver swimming in pools of milk. She grimaced, as if remembering a nightmare. 'It showed me – showed me what this is all about!'

Peri remembered what the Doctor had said – that the Garden had 'harvested' her... She became aware of a rustling and chittering. Beyond Aline, giant insects moved, their black carapaces gleaming in the green phosphorescence.

Peri stood up, taking Aline's hand, noticing with a feeling of nausea that the skin was flaking and white, the veins standing out like freeways on a roadmap. 'Come on – we've got to get out of here!'

Aline shook her off. 'No point.'

The insects were getting nearer, their claws scratching against the rock, deformed antennae probing the air. They seemed to be converging on Aline.

Peri hesitated. She couldn't leave Aline here. Could she? She looked sick, dying.

Peri tried one more time. She grabbed Aline by the shoulders. 'Come on!'

Aline stood up, seemingly compliant – then twisted out of Peri's grip. Her face was a white mask – she didn't look human any more. Peri shuddered.

Aline's voice was a strangled whisper. 'You don't understand – they're dead! They're all dead!'

Peri turned and fled from the cavern.

Chapter Twenty
Alliance

Veek hurried along the main access passage of the Valethske ship, taking long, loping strides. Her ears twitched continually and she was alert for any sign of movement.

In the distance, she could hear sounds of battle, and she grinned. With Kikker and all the hunters concentrating on the defence of the ship, she'd be able to escape unnoticed.

In front of her the strange human walked at gunpoint, pale clawless hands raised on a level with his head.

They came to a point where the passage branched into three. The Doctor made a dodge for the leftmost branching, but Veek lunged forwards, bringing her hand down heavily on his shoulder.

'No – the central way,' she whispered.

The Doctor half-turned as if to question her, but Veek gave him a shove and he stumbled on.

'Where are you taking me? This isn't the way to your cryogenic facility.'

'I know this ship better than you, prey,' she bluffed.

He was right – they weren't going to the sleep cells. Veek grimaced, glad that the Doctor couldn't see the tension in her face. She knew that her escape depended entirely on this human. When he had been strapped in the torture-chair she'd heard him say that he was the only one who could operate the time-machine. *Kill me and you'll be forever denied its powers.*

Suddenly the Doctor stopped walking, and Veek bumped into him, making him stumble. He ignored the impact and turned to address Veek. Again she saw the power in his eyes. Naked in his pink face, they seemed to resemble orbs of glass encased in wrinkles and folds of flesh, hard and challenging amidst all that vulnerable meat. Veek sensed the inner strength and intellect behind those eyes, a mental prowess qualitatively different from the natural instinct and cunning of a hunter like herself.

Something to respect. Something to fear? Veek flexed the muscles in her arms, taking comfort from her superior strength.

'I said, where are you taking me?'

His voice echoed up and down the passageway like a clarion call to all hunters in the vicinity.

'Silence, prey!' hissed Veek, deciding to play the loyal Valethske for a while longer in case anyone should pass by. She shoved the human into the service alcove behind the nearest bulkhead, a cramped space of shadows and dust.

'Well, this is all very cosy,' said the Doctor, his face upturned to hers. He was smiling, blunt ineffectual teeth shining in the pale light seeping down from above.

'We are not going to the sleep cells,' she told the human.

'Well that's a relief,' he said, shoulders slumping slightly. Then he backed away from her, raising his hands. 'Now wait a minute – not thinking of having me as a quick snack, are you? Because if you're hungry I know a nice little place –'

His voice was loud in the confined space. Veek reached out and clamped a hand over his jaw. 'Be quiet!' she hissed. She let him go and he slumped against the side of the chamber.

'So where *are* we going?'

'You will take me to your time machine,' she said, aiming her blaster at his face. 'Or you will die.'

The Doctor groaned. 'Not again.' Then: 'No. I cannot let creatures like you have access to time travel.'

'Then...' Veek brought the blaster up to his face.

The Doctor smiled. 'Then...?'

She brought her hand down, appalled. It was as she'd feared – violent coercion, even the threat of death, had no effect! She would have to – have to co-operate with this human. Gain his trust. A new and abhorrent concept.

'Then I... I want...' Veek couldn't frame the words. No Valethske had ever appealed to a human before, for anything. It was beyond heresy, a mockery of her hunter's heritage. But she had to do it, in order to preserve that very legacy. She let out a hot sigh that made the human take out a cloth from a pocket and clamp it over the lower half of his face.

At last Veek found the words her mind was groping for, her voice a tight growl through gritted teeth. 'I want your help.'

The Doctor removed the cloth to reveal a mouth hanging open in complete amazement.

'Well, this is a... this is...' Then his face twisted, dark crevices of anger seeming to slice into the flesh. 'After all the death you've dragged with you halfway across the galaxy, the utter contempt you've shown for anything that isn't yourself, you want my help?' His voice was the petulant snarl of a teething cub.

Veek brought the blaster up to his face, to remind him who was in control. 'Yes, I – I want to return home. I do not believe in the Great Mission. It is a perversion of the nature of we Valethske.'

'Which is presumably to hunt and kill all you see as lesser species,' said the human in more subdued tones.

'We are hunters. We exist only to hunt, to feed, to reproduce. We do not enslave races, or experiment on them, or get ourselves involved in pointless conflicts. We hunt to eat. That is all. That is why the Great Mission is so wrong.'

'Sounds a very circumscribed life to me. What about your soul? What about your culture?'

'Of course we have such things – but this isn't the time to discuss them! Will you help me?'

The Doctor's eyes glittered. 'You just want to go home? You don't want to give your species access to time travel technology?'

Again Veek sensed the power hidden behind the weak flesh. She thought of the glory that bringing such a gift to the Great Vale would bestow upon her, and realised she didn't care. The sweet rains of home were worth much more than that.

She nodded. 'Yes. I just want to go home.'

'Do any other Valethske feel this way?'

'They are all loyal to Kikker and dedicated to the Great Mission.'

'So you're the only dissenter.' The Doctor seemed to consider for a while. 'Well, it's a harmless enough request.' His voice changed tone, becoming questioning. 'Tell me, are you a creature of honour, hunter Veek?'

'I am.'

'And that if we make a bargain, here and now, you will not renege – as Kikker did?'

'I swear!' hissed Veek.

The Doctor looked doubtful. Then he said, 'All right, I agree – but you must agree to help me, too. I want you to help me find my friend Peri, if she's still alive.' He added as an afterthought: 'Oh, and to stop Kikker before he destroys this world.'

Veek nodded. The enormity of what she was about to say and do struck home. A hunter – making a bargain with a mere piece of meat! Insanity. 'Very well, prey – we have an alliance.'

He smiled again. 'It would help if you used my name. I'm called the Doctor.'

Veek opened her mouth as wide as she could and moved to lock jaws with the human.

He stepped back, a look of alarm on his face. 'What now?'

Veek closed her mouth and stepped back, feeling foolish. 'My apologies – that is our custom on sealing a contract.'

The human – the *Doctor* – looked relieved. 'For a moment I thought I was back on the menu... anyway, where I come from, and some other places, we have a very different and much more hygienic way of going about such things.'

The Doctor extended his hand. 'Come on, don't be shy. Take my hand.'

Curious, Veek reached out and took it. Her red-furred paw completely enclosed his pink flesh. She growled in surprise as the Doctor began jerking her arm up and down with a vigour that surprised her.

'There, far more civilised, don't you think?'

Veek hissed and snatched her hand away.

She would never understand humans.

Peri was beginning to wonder if she would ever see daylight again. After leaving Aline, she had run blindly through the twisting, glowing tunnels of the world beneath the Garden, trying not to think about what the giant insects might be doing to the sick woman. She stopped only when she ran out of breath, slumping to the rock floor, totally exhausted. Her body felt like a machine that had been driven way beyond its design specifications. A car that had crashed too many times, fit only for the crusher. She rolled into a corner, mind teeming with giant insects, humanoid foxes and walking plants, and despite everything fell into a dark, dreamless sleep.

She woke later, feeling heavy and woozy, and far from a hundred per cent, but at least partly refreshed, surprised at and grateful for a period of unconsciousness that had not been initiated by a Valethske stun-gun, an explosion or a crack on the cranium with something heavy and blunt. The pain in her muscles had receded to a distant pins-and-needles and her head felt remarkably clear. One thing that hadn't changed was the rancid smell of sweat and probably worse that permeated her ill-fitting uniform. Her own perspiration had now dried into the suede-like fabric and she could smell herself, a sweet and pure fragrance rising above the rank, rotten stench of the uniform's previous wearers.

Peri wandered along the tunnels, taking any turning that led her in an upwards direction. She had no idea how far she was below the Garden. The Valethske shaft could have been miles long, she'd been far too preoccupied to make any kind of judgement. Athon's death kept playing out in her mind, a pointless sacrifice. Why hadn't he listened to her? Or perhaps he was right, death was the only way out.

She couldn't, wouldn't believe that.

She had to have hope.

The narrow tunnel began to turn back on itself, until it formed a kind of uneven spiral staircase. Peri climbed, hope beginning to rise along with the tunnel. She had to stop and rest at frequent intervals, the energy she'd gained from her nap quickly ebbing away. As she ascended, the rock walls gave way to peaty, crumbling mud, its tart smell a welcome distraction. The phosphorescent moss was still present, but only in small patches, so Peri was sometimes climbing in near-darkness. Interwoven in the mud were myriads of hair-like strands, trailing down from the wall and sometimes barring her way, like a spider-web. Peri tried not to think of spiders but once she had the image wouldn't go away. As if she didn't have enough problems, what with ravenous fox-creatures and giant beetles. She told herself the hair-like stuff was just plant fibre.

Surely, this had to be a way back up to the surface. A kind of emergency exit for the Gardeners, though she had trouble visualising any of the giant, bloom-headed creatures negotiating such a narrow, twisting passage. Maybe there were other types of Gardeners, adapted for different purposes. She remembered the one she had seen mowing the lawn. The last thing she needed was to meet anything in such a cramped space, but in her time underground she hadn't met a single motile plant, only Aline and the giant insects. She remembered Aline's hoarse, whispering voice: *They're all dead.* What had she meant? The Gardeners – or something else?

As she climbed she found herself thinking of the Doctor. He was the one person on the planet she badly wanted to see again. She had no way of knowing if the Doctor was dead, alive, imprisoned, free, whatever. For all she knew he could have single-handedly defeated the Valethske and be waiting patiently on the surface for her. He could even have made peace with them and they could all be sitting around drinking tea and playing cricket. Images of Valethske in cricket-whites brandishing bats instead of guns spun around Peri's head, the Doctor patiently trying to explain the rules as they growled and prowled around him.

The Doctor would find a way, she had to believe it. The thought of seeing him again was the only thing that kept her climbing. She imagined his face as she rushed up to him and hugged him tight enough to crack a rib. Imagined the look of surprise on his young face that couldn't mask the smile of joy in his old eyes. Imagined him saying something stupid and witty and lovable. Imagined a nice, long, hot bath and a holiday somewhere the Doctor could guarantee wasn't about to be invaded by bloodthirsty aliens.

The passage began to level out, turning into a mud-floored ramp that led upwards at a shallow angle. It seemed to go on for ever, and Peri estimated she walked for a least a mile. The walls were now a twisted, knotted mass of bark that looked strangely familiar.

Eventually they began to close in above her head, making her crawl on hands and knees. As she moved along in this awkward fashion she became aware of a change in the quality of the light. The pale green glow from the ever-present moss was gradually being overtaken by an orange flickering that set shadows dancing on the walls. Firelight, unmistakably. For a moment Peri thought she was going to emerge back inside the Valethske ship, but after a few moments' frantic thought she worked out that couldn't be the case. Then she realised what the walls reminded her of – the giant Tree. Could she have climbed all the way from the interior of the Garden to the Tree? If so, that meant she was on, or at least near, the surface.

She increased her pace, glad for once of her rancid uniform, as its suede-like fabric provided some protection from the rough bark. Her knees still felt like the skin had been stripped from them and her spine, already aggravated by her work in the pit, felt ready to snap at any moment. But she kept on going, questions running round in her mind. Had the Valethske torched the Garden? What a waste that would be. But then they had no use for plants.

Eventually the end of the tunnel came into sight, a dark triangle of blue framed by orange-lit walls. Peri gritted her teeth and made one final effort, heaving herself across the rough bark. A smell of smoke began to tickle her throat, and she could hear screams and the crackling of fire.

Overcome by curiosity, Peri pulled herself to the edge of the tunnel, feeling cool grass under her fingertips. Keeping her body pressed into the shadows, she peered around the edge into a nightmare.

She'd emerged at the foot of the Tree, between two of its lesser trunks. The sky was obscured by thick masses of cloud through which she could glimpse snatches of brilliant blue. A ring of fire curved in a crescent, cutting off escape in every direction, the blue-purple trunks of the Tree reflecting the flames. Within this half-circle, half-a-dozen Valethske were ranged, their black-clad bodies picked out clearly against the wall of fire, ugly-looking guns firing blasts of white energy through the curtain of flame.

Peri buried her face in her hands and wept. Would she never escape these creatures?

Veek threw the door open and stepped through, swinging her blaster round in a wide arc. She felt the Doctor shove past her and watched enraged as he sauntered into the dimly lit laboratory with a carefree air. She holstered the blaster. There was no one here, she could see that now. Ruvis and his technicians would be assisting with the defence of the ship. But how had the Doctor known?

She followed him, trying not to look at the machines that lurked in the shadows. Apart from the sleep cells, Ruvis's laboratory was the only area on the ship that Veek hated. No one except Ruvis and his technicians knew what went on in here, not even Kikker. To Veek the machines looked like robotic beasts waiting to pounce, their polished metal and glass reflecting the soft blue strip-lighting, full of menace. And the *smell* – harsh, unnatural cleanliness that seared her nostrils and stuck in her throat. She shuddered.

Against the far wall stood the strange blue box the Doctor called the TARDIS. He stood beside it, one hand touching its blue panels, his face seeming to be lit up from within.

Veek looked around the lab, still on the alert, hardly believing that she would soon be leaving the confines of the ship for good.

The Doctor thumped the side of the TARDIS. 'Blast! I haven't got the key – and the spare's in my other pair of trousers.'

Veek kicked herself for not thinking that the TARDIS would need a key. Of course, Kikker would have taken it. She stared forlornly at the blue box, Valeth Skettra receding into the mists of her mind.

'Is this what you're looking for?'

Veek swung round.

Ruvis stood in the doorway, holding a golden key on a long chain that twinkled in the blue lab lights.

In his other hand was a standard-issue blaster, targeting her chest. A mundane weapon for a hunter to be killed with. She

212

shifted from foot to foot but Ruvis kept time with her, his aim never leaving her central mass.

Her own blaster lay useless in its holster.

'Yes, it is! Thank you very much,' said the Doctor, walking around from behind Veek right up to Ruvis, hand held open in front of him.

Veek was getting used to the Doctor's unpredictable nature by now and hardly batted an eyelid, but Ruvis didn't know how to take this mad human. For a split second he took his eyes off Veek.

Veek threw herself sideways, just as Ruvis fired.

The blaster bolt seared through the air where she had just been standing and slammed into the front of the TARDIS, where it exploded in a blinding diffusion of energy.

Veek rolled across the floor, past the Doctor who was scrambling for cover, and into Ruvis, grabbing his legs and bringing him down.

Veek lunged for his throat, smashing off his prosthetic jaw and sinking her teeth into the stringy flesh of his neck.

He was old, but strong, and put up a creditable resistance despite his ruined body. But Veek was younger and stronger and whole, and the old technician's struggles quickly subsided.

Veek stood up, looking down at his body, breathing heavily, a feeling of deep satisfaction coursing through her.

Ruvis wasn't the first of her own kind she had killed; trial by combat was a Valethske tradition. And there was always Flayoun, in the unlikely event that she should encounter him before she returned home.

'That was not necessary.'

Veek looked at the Doctor in mild surprise. 'He would have killed us!'

His eyes were hard as glass again. 'You don't know that! He's a scientist. He would have listened, he may even have agreed to help!' The Doctor was shouting now.

Veek ignored him, stooping to prise the TARDIS key from Ruvis's fingers. 'I know Ruvis. He's as blinkered as Kikker, totally dedicated to the Great Mission. He would not have helped me.'

'You don't know that,' said the Doctor.

Why was he so concerned over the death of a Valethske? He hated them; their alliance was born of necessity and that alone. Once it was over she might have to kill him – or she might not. It didn't bother her much either way.

'Give me that.' The Doctor snatched the key out of her hands and walked over to the TARDIS without another word.

He opened the door and entered without looking to see if she was following him.

Veek stepped over Ruvis's body and hurried into the blue box. There was a moment of disorientation, then she found herself inside a brightly lit space, patterned with a curious circular motif. There was something wrong. It was larger on the inside than it was on the outside. Impossible!

'Impressed?' said the Doctor.

Veek realised she was panting, her tongue lolling over her teeth. She suddenly saw the Doctor in a new light. She knew that certain humanoid races had developed impressive technologies, but this was something different. She sensed power, the ancient power of the Gods. 'What – what kind of human are you?'

The Doctor's smile was like that of an equal. Now they were two hunters squaring up for a fight. Only the Doctor had the advantage – this was his territory. 'I am a Time Lord, one of an incredibly advanced and incredibly ancient civilisation with immense powers. Not quite up there with the Khorlthochloi, though. But I don't tend to go around bragging about it.'

Veek had regained some of her composure. 'Now – take me to Valeth Skettra!'

The Doctor sighed. 'Veek, we have a deal. You help me find Peri first. And before you start waving that gun around, please remember that without me you cannot operate the TARDIS.'

Veek nodded. 'Very well.'

The Doctor moved around the control panels, flicking switches. 'Why do you want to return home, Veek? It must be centuries since you left. You might not even have a home any more. The Valethske fell to the Khorlthochloi once, they may have fallen again, to another powerful enemy.'

Veek gestured at the control panels. 'You can take me back through time, to a point just after I left.'

The Doctor seemed to consider this. 'Yes, that's feasible. There will be little chance of you meeting yourself so the timelines will be safe. But how are you going to explain your presence at home if you're supposed to be off on the Great Mission?'

Veek frowned, watching the glass column in the centre of the control panel rise and fall. It was soothing, like the heartbeat of her mother, back when she'd been a playful, vicious little cub. Time and distance seemed to blur in her mind, and she imagined she could taste the rains of Valeth Skettra on her tongue. The longing to return was a hard ache in the pit of her heart, more intense now that the means were within her grasp. How would she explain herself? It hardly mattered. Just being there was all she could think of. Anything beyond that was a blank whiteness like the ceiling of this strange vessel.

Suddenly a muted chime came from all around her and the central column came to rest.

'I will think of that when I get there,' she murmured.

'Yes, well, here's hoping all goes to plan,' said the Doctor, walking round the control panel towards her. 'We've landed.'

Chapter Twenty-One
Sea of Thorns

Through the blur of her tears, Peri noticed a number of dead Valethske prone on the grass, their bodies pierced by what looked like spears. At the edge of the crescent of fire lay burning pyres, which Peri realised was the remains of Gardeners. Two of the surviving Valethske were holding flame-throwers, making sure there were no gaps in the fire-barrier.

Peri squinted through the flames, trying to make out what was beyond. Hard to see how much was real and how much was her imagination making shapes out of the orange tongues of fire.

There seemed to be a wall of writhing, thorned tentacles, heaving like a pit of snakes. Gardeners? But these were nothing like the creatures she had already met. As she watched, a hail of spears shot through the flames and another Valethske fell.

The others screamed and turned their energy-weapons on the source of the attack. Something crashed through the fire, a morass of tentacles sprouting from a thickly armoured central mass. It flailed in the flames, crackling and hissing, and then was still.

What were these things? Perhaps the Garden had produced these monsters to fend off the Valethske, thought Peri in a flash of insight. A cloud of smoke descended on her and she began to cough uncontrollably.

The Valethske nearest to her turned, its gun swinging unerringly round to cover her. Peri shrank back down the tunnel but it was on her in a few strides, its free arm reaching down and grabbing her by the throat. Choking and coughing, Peri scrambled from the tunnel, falling into the arms of the Valethske, stifling her yell of pain in its leather-clad chest.

It held her by the shoulders, eyes reflecting orange sparks of flame. It had a stripe of white over one eye and ear, and there was a long scratch on its jaw.

'Let me go!' cried Peri, struggling in its grip. The creature hissed at her and shoved her away, probably keen to get back to the fight.

It raised its bulbous gun.

Peri backed away, eyes fixed on the black muzzle. The hunter grinned, enjoying Peri's fear, toying with her. Behind it she heard its comrades scream with triumph as another monster-Gardener was incinerated.

Peri stumbled over something. The body of a dead Valethske. A plan formed in her mind, crazy and hopeless but her only option. Keeping her eyes on those of the Valethske, she crouched down and put her hands on the grip of the dead hunter's gun. Slowly, she picked it up, surprised at its lightness, and stood, holding the weapon across her chest.

The Valethske cocked its head to one side, curious to see what she'd do next.

Peri brought the gun slowly to bear, not on the Valethske but on the writhing shapes through the curtain of fire. She found what she hoped was the trigger and pulled, gasping in shock as a white bolt of energy burst from the end of the gun. There was surprisingly little recoil and the energy-bolt sailed straight through the flames; there was no way of telling if she'd found her mark. Well, she hadn't even aimed.

She coughed again, the smoke stinging her eyes. Then she looked over at the Valethske and smiled, hating herself for doing this but it was her only chance of survival. 'United against a common foe, right?' she cried above the roar of flames and the shrieks of the other hunters.

The Valethske threw its head back and emitted a peal of piercing laughter. Then it strode over to her, moving with frightening speed, and dashed the gun from her hands. 'As if I would trust a human!' it snarled.

Peri rubbed her hands, hoping it hadn't broken a bone. She felt irritated more than afraid.

Another hunter trotted over, its eyes widening in surprise as it saw Peri. 'Flayoun, the odds are too great. We must retreat.'

Her captor – Flayoun – nodded, and kept her held tightly with one hand while it spoke quickly into a button-like device mounted on its collar. The other Valethske retreated until they formed a solid ring around Flayoun and Peri, keeping their weapons trained on the curtain of flame. Despite the desperate situation, she noticed they still had time to leer hungrily at her.

'What are you doing, saving me for a post-game snack?' she said to her captor.

'Where's the skirmisher?' it hissed, ignoring her.

'We should devour this human now,' drooled another hunter. 'Our last meal before our glorious sacrifice!'

Flayoun growled angrily. 'No more deaths,' he said. 'We must report to the Vale Commander.'

Presently a dark shape began to descend through the smoke. Peri recognised the blunt wings and sleek shape of a Valethske shuttle. Its rust-coloured hull gave no reflection to the flames that licked around it. The blast from its engines set up a typhoon of hot air that screamed around them, extinguishing the flames and sending the attacking creatures scuttling back.

Peri was pulled along with the hunters as they ran pell-mell across the grass through the still-burning cinders. She saw Valethske gathered around an oblong hatch in the belly of the craft, some ten feet above her head. The shuttle dipped a few feet lower and she felt strong arms lift her up. She caught a swaying glimpse of thorned tentacles massing at the gap in the flames.

She swung her legs up over the hatch, and felt a lurching sensation in the pit of her stomach as the shuttle lifted off and away. 'Neat bit of flying,' she said as she watched the flames recede through the open hatch.

As they flew higher, she could see more of the Garden, and she gasped. The crescent of flame was dwarfed beside the massive Tree. Its branches seemed to reach up into the sky, as if to snatch the shuttle back. All around the tree, the monster-Gardeners moved. She couldn't make out individuals, just a great, thrashing mass that surged like a sea of thorns across the Garden.

Then with a painful grinding the hatch closed. Peri stood up and turned round to see Flayoun and the other hunters all staring at her.

Flayoun licked his lips.

Peri backed away, looking around for somewhere to run, to hide. But there was nowhere. This time, there really was nowhere.

Veek stepped through the white, slab-like doors of the time machine into green-tinted darkness. A dry smell of stone hit her with an almost physical shock after the sterile, odourless interior of the TARDIS. Her ears twitched, picking up distant scuttling sounds. She drew her blaster, alert for any signs of movement.

'No welcome committee,' said the Doctor. 'But then I wasn't expecting one.'

His words made no sense to Veek, so she ignored them and took in their surroundings.

They were in a subterranean cavern, high-ceilinged, dome-shaped. The air was cool, crisp, and tasted of minerals. Light-emitting moss covered almost every surface except the smooth rock underfoot. Where the curving roof met the floor, thick stalactites and stalagmites provided plenty of cover for anything that might be lurking, waiting to pounce. Between these formations, Veek could see hundreds of tunnels leading off. It all tallied with the initial survey of the planet. A vast labyrinth of artificially constructed tunnels, just as the legends said. *And the Gods grew old and frail and frightened, and so they fled, seeking to hide their cruel faces from the fledgling universe.* Veek had known the words since she was a cub. Despite her complete loss of faith in the Great Mission, she had never doubted that the Gods had existed, and might still live in exile in some distant keep. So could they be here, beneath this garden-world? Could the Great Mission, against infinite odds, have at last succeeded?

Veek gripped her blaster. It would be useless against the Gods, but it made her feel better. She felt as if she was sinking in confusion, doubting her own doubts, like a whelp with the fever chasing its own tail.

'Look at all these tunnels,' came the Doctor's voice, strained with sadness and frustration. 'Peri could be anywhere.'

Veek glanced back at the TARDIS. Her way home. She thought of the honour of slaying the Gods, the exhilaration of revenge. She could almost taste it, rich and strong like well-salted meat. It fired up her blood. She could not deny it. She could not deny that the success of the Great Mission would be a thing of the utmost glory. Then she thought of the forests of Valeth Skettra, of running through the fields after prey, rain hammering on her naked back, her mate – another, new mate – strong and supple at her side.

The rains of Valeth Skettra washed the taste of revenge away and Veek knew what she wanted. What use were glory and honour, when you were so far away from home, so far away from the things that defined you?

Veek strode off towards the tunnel mouths. The sooner they found the Doctor's companion, the sooner she could get home. But like the Doctor she could see how futile it would be, searching miles and miles of tunnels for one lone human – and that was assuming it hadn't perished in the explosion.

She called back to the Doctor over her shoulder. 'Doesn't your time machine possess scanning devices?'

The Doctor looked offended. 'It most certainly does, but something's blocking them.' He rubbed his temples with his fingers. 'Something's trying to communicate with the TARDIS, interfering with its systems.'

A cold current of air slid around Veek's neck. She shivered, and then growled, angrily dismissing the feeling of unease. 'Legends speak of the mental powers of the Gods.'

'You think they could be here? That Kikker's insane quest has actually succeeded?'

Veek gritted her teeth, vowing to stick by her resolution. 'Even if they are, I do not care.'

At the moment she stopped talking, Veek saw something stirring out of the corner of her eye. She swung her blaster up and fired in one smooth action. The blaster-bolt was like a shooting star in the gloom of the cavern. It hit home with a deafening crack that echoed all around the massive space like a thunderclap. Flakes of stone detached from the ceiling and sprinkled down on Veek and the Doctor like snow.

'Don't shoot!' said the Doctor belatedly, trying to snatch the blaster away from her. He cast a nervous glance at the cavern roof. 'I doubt that energy weapons have ever been fired in here, and your excavations can't have helped. We don't want the whole planet crashing down on our heads. It would hurt, for one thing.'

Veek was getting used to the way the Doctor prattled on like a deranged battle-veteran, especially when in danger, and had already started across the smooth, dark rock to the source of the movement. She heard the Doctor's soft footsteps follow.

At the conical base of a ridged stalagmite, Veek saw that her shot had found its mark, and smiled in satisfaction, squinting as she tried to make out what it was she had killed. Some sort of giant insect, the size of a calf. She'd hit it square in the head, now a charred and splintered hunk of chitin, its dark tarry life-blood leaking out and dripping on to the cavern floor.

She knew what the Doctor was going to say. His eyes held that dark look of power again, of censure and disapproval.

'There was no need to –'

Veek waved him into silence, letting a hiss of anger squeeze through her clenched teeth. 'I am Valethske, Doctor – I kill instinctively. Please do not chastise me for it again, or I may forget myself and kill you!'

The Doctor stared at her. 'Sarcasm is the lowest form of wit, but for you lot it's clearly the height of sophistication.'

Veek knew she'd been insulted somehow but decided to ignore it. 'You talk too much, Doctor. Your opinions do not matter to me. I hunt, I kill, I eat. Nothing you think or say can change that.'

There was sadness in his eyes. 'Have you no sense of morality at all?'

Veek frowned. 'What is morality?'

The Doctor looked appalled. 'You mean you don't even know?'

Veek realised her tail was flicking about like a serpent and reached around to smooth it. 'This is not helping to find your companion,' she reminded the Doctor.

'I know.' The Doctor stooped to examine the dead creature, poking his nose right up to the smoking remains of its head. 'Some sort of subterranean insect species, obviously. Now I wonder...'

Veek turned away from the kill and scanned the cavern for more. There – a short distance away, a herd of the creatures was spilling from a tunnel-mouth, their black carapaces jostling against each other, antennae groping the air. They were making a high-pitched, bird-like twittering that made Veek's sensitive ears twitch.

She called back over her shoulder. 'Doctor – here. More of them.'

'So I see,' he said, wiping bits of carapace from his hands with the cloth she'd seen him use earlier. 'Let's follow them, shall we?'

'Why?'

'Why not? They could lead us to Peri – or the Gods.'

Veek hesitated, then set off after the Doctor. He looked as perky as a cub again. His sudden switches of mood seemed to indicate a deranged mind, but Veek had seen the intelligence peeping out from beneath his façade. By Azreske – was she beginning to find mere prey interesting? She imagined slicing the Doctor open and consuming his innards. He would probably hold on to life long enough to make some disparaging comment, and chastise her for killing him. The image made her grin widely.

They caught up with the slow-moving herd of insects as they filed into a tunnel. The creatures were either blind and deaf, or uninterested in Veek and the Doctor, because they made no sign of having noticed them. They were big, as big as the cattle bred back on Valeth Skettra for meat.

A thought occurred to Veek. 'These insects could have consumed your friend, Doctor.'

'Oh, I don't think so,' he said airily. 'From our dead friend's mandibles – what was left of them – it's plain that these creatures are vegetarian.' He grabbed Veek's arm, his words speeding up with enthusiasm. 'You see, I've worked it out – most of it, anyway. This whole planet is a garden, dedicated to producing fruit for these underground dwellers. You've seen the motile plants, yes? Well, they exist to tend the gardens and harvest the fruit.'

Veek remembered what the Doctor had tried to tell Kikker back at the excavator pit. 'And also to repel invaders?'

'Yes,' said the Doctor. 'I haven't seen these hostile plants yet, but I bet they're some sort of accelerated mutation, antibodies – "plantibodies", if you like – produced by the planet to keep hostile visitors out, to protect the subterranean colony.'

It seemed an elaborate, though effective, form of defence, thought Veek. She imagined a world full of savage plant-creatures converging on the ship, and felt a pang of regret that she wasn't there at the fight. She wondered if Flayoun was still alive – and if so, if he had managed to convince Kikker of her heresy. It hardly mattered now – she was going home soon. She wondered if anyone had noticed that she, the Doctor and his time machine were all missing. They must have found Ruvis's body by now. She imagined the look on Kikker's face when he found out. He'd punish someone for it, probably disembowel an innocent Vale Guard to vent his anger.

They were now deep within the tunnel; its walls were smooth, clearly machined by some sort of energy beam. It seemed to have been designed specifically for the insects; it was wide enough for them to walk three abreast and the curved ceiling gave plenty of space for their jostling carapaces. Veek tried to peer over the top of the herd to see where they were going, but to no avail. The tops of their carapaces were almost level with Veek's nose. Their hind legs looked capable of delivering a hefty kick, but Veek could sense that these creatures posed no threat. Mindless, lowly insects.

A thought struck her. 'So it's all for these bugs!'

The Doctor smiled. 'I wondered when you'd notice that.'

Veek struggled to make sense of it. 'This whole planet, just for them?'

'I think they've rather got it made, don't you? All they do is wait for the harvests, eat, reproduce and think chitinous thoughts.'

Veek let out a cackle of laughter. 'So this isn't the last retreat of the Gods after all! It's just a giant insect hive!'

The Doctor nodded, and then shook his head, and frowned. 'It doesn't make sense – the alien presence smothering the TARDIS couldn't have come from these simple creatures.'

They walked on in silence. Presently they emerged into another cavern similar in shape to the one in which they had landed, only much smaller and with fewer tunnels leading off.

Veek noticed that from one of the tunnel mouths, light flickered – not the sullen green glow of the ubiquitous moss, but a shimmering luminescence, like sunlight reflected on water. The herd of insects were milling about a flattened area that bisected the cavern, antennae groping the air. They seemed to be looking for something.

She heard the Doctor catch his breath, and focus his gaze on the far side of the cavern.

Veek followed his line of sight. There, lying on the smooth rock floor, was a human figure.

'Is that your companion?' said Veek, indicating the body.

The Doctor had already started towards it and she heard his voice echo around the rock walls. 'I don't think so!'

With a glance at the herd of insects, Veek ran after the Doctor. She reached him just as he was lifting the human into a sitting position, resting her head on his shoulder. Her skin and hair were white, bloodless, and she had about her the unmistakable aura of death. Her eyes were closed and her hands clawed the air before her.

The Doctor put his hand gently over the woman's, bringing them down into her lap.

'Aline,' said the Doctor. 'Oh, Aline, I tried to stop you.'

Aline. Not Peri. Veek sighed. How many 'friends' did the Doctor have? Were they all down here, roaming the caverns like lost cubs?

The human woman opened her eyes. Veek was surprised to see that the irises were silver, like mercury. 'Doctor?'

The Doctor smiled down at it. 'Hello, Aline.'

They talked while Veek paced up and down in impatience. Surely now he'd found one of his friends, they could leave?

She could see the Doctor intent on the woman's whispered words. Surely it would be better to dispatch her now, save her suffering and them some time.

Veek drew her spike-knife and began to sidle closer to the Doctor and the woman.

Chapter Twenty-Two
Sterilisation

The Valethske hadn't killed and devoured her on the spot. Peri had to be grateful for that. Flayoun had stopped them, saying that he wanted to use Peri to help restore the Vale Commander's faith in him. How, she had no idea, but the other hunters had reluctantly agreed. And so they had chained her to a stanchion below the flight deck and forgotten about her, getting on with the business of flying the shuttle. Peri hadn't even bothered trying to escape. What was the point? Savage aliens on board, savage aliens below, and a certain-death drop in between.

Peri braced her legs as they went into another dive, the Valethske screaming and howling above her. Her hands were cuffed either side of a vertical metal support stanchion, so she could only stop herself from falling by bracing her legs against the floor and pushing her body against the shell of the little ship. Her limbs ached so much she was dying to rest but she couldn't sit on the floor; hell, she couldn't even see the floor. Bits of equipment, boxes, weapons cases, circuit boards, dust and detritus – even the odd bone, she was alarmed to see – littered the area beneath the flight deck where they had tethered her like livestock. She had a limited view of the flight deck, of Valethske intent on the shuttle controls and viewscreens. If she stretched her arms right out in front of her and turned her head to the wall she could look through a triangular vent and catch glimpses of the planet's surface, every inch of it sprawling with teeming masses of mutated Gardeners.

The ship shuddered like someone shivering in their sleep as it discharged its arsenal of weaponry – all of it, as far as Peri could tell – down on to the moiling plant-life. The Valethske shrieked as they vented their anger. The ship bottomed and began to climb again, sending Peri's innards swinging about inside her. Then they began to level out, and the Valethske became quiet, except for the occasional shriek and burst of weapon fire.

Peri stretched out her arms, leaned back and looked out of the vent – and saw a mountain rising from the sickly greens and browns of the ravaged Garden. It took her a while to realise that it was the Valethske ship. Sitting on three bulbous tubular engines, like bloated, blackened cigars, the main body swept upwards in tides of jagged metal to a blunt nose-cone. It looked strikingly like the head of a Valethske, upturned to bay at an invisible moon. Its rust-coloured surface was pitted and scarred – it certainly looked as if it had been dragging its ass across the galaxy for centuries.

Centuries... Peri gripped on to the stanchion, hearing the jangle of her cuffs as if from across a great gulf of distance. That damn ship had been her home for a hundred years. The memories of a century of cold, dead sleep would gradually thaw through and infest her mind. She knew that it would haunt her dreams for years to come, perhaps for ever.

The Valethske began to yelp commands – she heard them running about on the flight deck above her.

Hell, 'for ever' in her case might only mean a couple of hours. Or minutes. She stared at the Valethske ship, summoning up all her anger. It was big, ugly, bristling with weapons and it damn well didn't *belong* here, in such a paradise, thought Peri.

Then she caught sight of the mutated Gardeners swarming around its engines, climbing *up* the superstructure, moving across the metal surface like a swarm of bugs. Well, used to be a paradise. Though if her theory was right, if the Valethske had never come here, the Garden would never have changed. Would never have had to make itself ugly to repel ugliness. *Battle ye not with monsters lest ye become a monster*, the Doctor had once said to her, revelling in the fact that all he did was battle monsters and avoided turning into one, so far. Well, it had happened to the Garden – it had turned itself into a whole horde of monsters. Maybe when the Valethske left, it would slowly change back into paradise again, as sure as spring followed winter. But Peri doubted she'd live to see that happy day.

They were now so near the Valethske ship that its bulk obscured the triangular vent, so Peri slumped against the wall, trying to disentangle her feet from a coil of greasy cable that was trying to wrap itself around her leg. Suddenly she was plunged into darkness, then deep red blood-like light. Tremendous metal clanging sounds shook the shuttle and as Peri was thrown about among the detritus she realised they must be landing somewhere within the mountainous mass of the Valethske ship. Landing quickly and not worrying about the paintwork. After a few minutes of this tumult they came to a halt, and the normal lighting of the shuttle resumed, which still left Peri ensconced in shadow below the flight-deck.

Footsteps clanged along the deck above her and she looked up in time to see a long black-uniformed body ease itself down beside her. Flayoun. Without a word he removed her cuffs and hauled her bodily on to the deck, then out through the hatch into the Valethske ship. Its sights and smells were depressingly familiar, and once again Peri felt that she'd never escape from the Valethske.

She was marched along the earth-floored passageways in the midst of the shuttle crew, who kept cackling and prodding her, making her stumble in the dust. She was convinced they were taking her to be frozen again so she was surprised when they all piled into a lift that took them rattling and juddering up through the innards of the ship. The Valethske had become quiet, snorting occasionally, their tails swishing slowly. Through the wire walls of the lift Peri glimpsed the hellish interior of the ship.

'Hey, where are we going?'

The only answer she got was a cuff around the head that made her ears sing. She decided she'd stay quiet until she knew the score. Her legs started trembling uncontrollably as she fought to ward off a mounting sense of fear.

The lift stopped with a jolt and Flayoun shoved Peri out into a passageway floored, for once, with metal. This led to a set of massive double doors flanked by two Valethske who saluted at their approach. The metal doors – which were inlaid with bas-relief figures of Valethske, Peri noticed – slid back with a hiss of hydraulics and Peri was shoved through them into –

She gasped. This must be the centre of things.

She was in a circular chamber of gleaming metal, a striking contrast to the stink and squalor of the rest of the ship. For a start the place had a relatively clean smell, a tang of machine oil and incense. The far side was dominated by an enormous backlit mural framed between two mighty pillars of granite-like stone. It was as breathtakingly detailed as the stained glass windows she'd seen in Bath Abbey on a childhood trip to England. Around the edges, various scenes of battle and bloodshed were illustrated but Peri's eyes were drawn to the central image, which depicted a winged creature picked out in dark purples and blues. Its slanted red eyes seemed to burn with helpless malevolence as it was held down by three Valethske, their naked bodies shards of brown, red and white, their faces twisted with hatred. A fourth stood over them, clad in flowing golden robes, its hand extended, palm upward, to reveal the dripping heart of the fallen creature.

It was so vivid that Peri was struck dumb for a few seconds until she got a shove between the shoulder-blades that sent her stumbling across the shining metal floor of the chamber. Through a daze she noticed gigantic buttresses, Valethske working at banks of equipment between them. There were incense-burners in the pillars framing the mural, from which pale smoke curled.

Then she was hauled to her feet and thrust towards the centre of the chamber, where a single Valethske stood, intent upon a circular screen which, though it couldn't compete with the lurid mural, was still pretty huge. It was split up unto segments like a spoked wheel, and each segment showed a different scene telling essentially the same story: Valethske battling the thorned, spiky Gardeners, either outside in the autumnal Garden or on the skin of the ship itself.

The shuttle crew shuffled nervously towards the lone Valethske, who had not yet acknowledged their presence.

Flayoun stepped forward. 'Vale Commander, we have returned.' His gruff voice was low, his tail between his legs.

The Vale Commander remained fixed on the screen. 'And?'

Flayoun licked his lips nervously. Peri glimpsed fear in his yellow-green eyes. 'We can confirm that the whole planet is overrun with these plant-creatures.'

'Did you find their point of origin?'

Flayoun shook his head. 'No, Vale Commander.' He looked down at Peri, narrowing his eyes at her. 'But we have brought you – a gift.'

Peri was thrust down on to the metal floor. So this was it. She put every ounce of defiance into her stare as the Vale Commander turned to look at her. She noticed that its black uniform was decorated with insignia of red and gold.

'Ah!' it said. 'You have found one of the escaped prey. Very good.' It began to walk over to her, eyeing her up and down.

Peri struggled in Flayoun's grip. She knew there was nowhere to run, but she wasn't going down without a fight. Flayoun grabbed both of Peri's hands and hauled them above her head, making her cry out with pain. She heard the hunter's voice, sibilant and hoarse in her ear.

'It is fine and fit, Commander Kikker. It has climbed from the interior of this world. Feel its muscles.'

Peri realised with disgust that she was being displayed like a rack of lamb. She twisted and struggled as Kikker, drooling at the mouth, reached down and pinched her thigh. Her cheeks burned with shame at her own powerlessness. 'Hey, get off, fox-face!' she yelled.

Kikker bellowed with laughter, sending spittle flying into Peri's face. 'A spirited one! I can't wait to savour it – but we have more pressing problems, hunter Flayoun.'

Peri gasped with relief as Flayoun let go of her hands and she dropped to her knees, rubbing her aching muscles and wiping her face. She didn't know how much more of this abuse she could take. Dully, she watched Kikker's boots tap up and down on the shining metal floor, heard his voice growling from somewhere above her.

'These plant-creatures are overrunning the ship. Many hunters have fallen. They will soon overcome us through sheer weight of numbers. We will make a strategic withdrawal and sterilise the planet from orbit. Then we will use the Doctor's TARDIS to travel beneath the surface and confront the Gods.'

'A cunning plan, Vale Commander!' roared Flayoun.

Mention of the Doctor brought Peri to her feet. 'The Doctor's alive?'

'He rests in the long sleep, a mere tool awaiting use.' Kikker turned away. 'Recall all hunters. Begin preparations for launch. And revive the Doctor.'

There was a flurry of activity at the periphery of the chamber.

'Chain it up over there,' said Kikker, pointing to the stone pillars that flanked the mural. 'I want it near, so at the moment of triumph I can at last taste meat again.'

'Why not take a bite out of me now?' said Peri. 'I go past my sell-by date in a few hours.'

Kikker bore down on her. There was madness in his eyes. Madness – and hunger. 'I have forsworn living flesh until the successful conclusion of the Great Mission,' he said in a low growl, almost a purr. 'That conclusion is now at hand. Very soon I will kill you, and suck the marrow from your bones.'

As threats went, it was pretty nasty, and entirely within Kikker's power to carry out, but it still sounded faintly ridiculous to Peri. She had no idea what all this guff about Gods was. She looked at the mural. The winged red-eyed thing looked like a fallen angel. Was that what all this was about? Some sort of jihad? Kikker certainly had the slightly crazed eyes of the religious zealot – there had been a lot of them about, the summer before Peri had gone to Lanzarote, proselytising from the TV and summer festivals. Then she remembered Aline. *They're all dead.* With a flash of intuition, she realised what the woman had meant.

'Hey!' cried Peri, as Kikker was about to turn away. She could hear the hunters growling behind her, and tensed. 'So you're on a quest to find your Gods, yeah?'

Kikker turned back, looking surprised that she had spoken again. 'That is so. We have spent centuries searching.'

And hunting and killing people like Athon, Taiana, Lornay... Peri closed her eyes briefly. Gotta keep it together. 'Well, I've got news for you, Reynard. I have it on good authority that they're dead.'

Kikker snorted in amusement. 'What can you possibly know about the Khorlthochloi, the ancient Gods, the ebon ones?' He flicked a hand at her, dismissing her. 'Tether it, Flayoun, and if it speaks again, snap off its jawbone.'

Peri clamped her mouth shut and Flayoun dragged her over to the pillar to the right of the mural. There was a metal ring embedded within the stone, to which he manacled her with brisk efficiency. As he strode away she saw that the smooth mottled-grey surface was splashed with old, dark stains. Bloodstains.

A curl of smoke reached down to her and her head swam as the incense crept up her nose and into her mouth. She dared not cough and watched Kikker and the others through stinging tears, realising how close she'd come to being butchered on the spot. Valethske weren't the sort of creatures you could taunt and get away with. It was only because she was certain she was going to die that she'd done it. She was Peri Brown and she was gonna die as Peri Brown, not some whimpering lump of meat.

She watched the hunters file out of the control chamber, all except Flayoun, who stood beside Kikker.

At least she'd get a grandstand view of the 'sterilisation' of the planet. From the way Kikker had said it Peri knew it meant the end for the beautiful Garden-world.

She tried to work up some grief, but she couldn't. Despite everything she felt a sense of excitement fluttering inside her. The Doctor was alive! They were thawing him out! And they were gonna use the TARDIS to get inside the planet – surely this was her chance for escape. Peri felt a sense of power building up below her and watched the screen as the ship began to lift off. Curiously, she felt no sense of acceleration.

She saw one of the technicians – a smaller, slimmer Valethske than Flayoun and the hunters – scurry over to Kikker. They talked for a few moments and then Kikker exploded in fury, flinging the hapless technician across the control chamber with one flick of his muscular arm. She heard him bellow the Doctor's name.

Then he caught sight of her and stormed over, gripping her face in a gloved paw. 'The Doctor is not in the long sleep! Where is he? Answer me, prey!'

Peri shook her head, alarmed at this new development. 'I don't know!'

'Vale Commander!' called Flayoun. He was bending down, listening to the cowed, terrified technician. 'There is more – the time machine is gone, and Technician Ruvis is dead.'

Kikker looked as if he was going to explode, and then a sly expression stole over his long face. 'Who took the Doctor to the long sleep?'

Flayoun thought for a while. 'Hunt Marshal Veek!'

Kikker slammed his hands together. 'You spoke of her heresy – I should have listened.' He waved his hand at the receding view of the planet. 'This cursed attack distracted me. So Veek has taken the Doctor and his TARDIS and robbed the Valethske of the secret of time travel.'

Peri could hardly believe what she was hearing. The Doctor wouldn't abandon her, she knew it. She remembered the Hunt Marshal, her cruel eyes. It was obvious what had happened – Veek had taken the Doctor and the TARDIS and gone, for whatever reason. Peri sank down on the cold metal floor, tired, terrified, and feeling more alone than she ever had before.

Aline knew she was dying, but somehow it didn't seem to matter. She had touched the minds of the Khorlthochloi, one of the most ancient and mysterious species the galaxy had ever seen. No one knew anything about them – until now. Now Aline knew everything. Coming to the Garden once more seemed part of her greater destiny, however much the Doctor might scoff at such a concept. She knew what the Khorlthochloi had looked like, as they bestrode the stars thousands of years ago. She knew what they had aspired to, what they had become. And she knew where they were now...

Her only regret was that she wasn't going to live long enough to publish. She knew more than enough to write the definitive work on the shepherds of our galaxy. But 'The Khorlthochloi Revealed' by Dr Aline Vehlmann would never see light of day.

She lay with her head on the Doctor's lap, his hands encircling hers. Although she felt weak, she was drawing strength from his proximity. There was so much she wanted to say, but she didn't know where to begin.

'Doctor... the Khorlthochloi...'

'Shh,' said the Doctor. 'Let's get you back to the TARDIS.'

'It's here? Where's Peri?'

'That's who we came down here to look for,' said the Doctor, glancing up at someone standing just behind Aline's field of vision.

Then she remembered. 'Doctor – I saw Peri!'

He leaned closer. 'When? Where?'

Aline struggled to remember. 'It was shortly after I...' She sighed. Everything that had happened after the strand had engulfed her was a daze. 'I can't recall exactly, but she was here. I think. It could have been a hallucination.'

The Doctor frowned down at her. 'Aline, what happened to you?'

She struggled to find the words to express her experience, her second Encounter. 'I've made contact.'

'Contact?'

'We are wasting time!' came a gruff voice from behind her.

Aline sat up to see a Valethske towering over her. So the hunters had tracked them down to the Garden. She struggled to stand, fear enervating her. 'Doctor!'

'Don't worry,' said the Doctor, helping her to her feet. 'This one's a friend, in the loosest possible definition of the word. Her name's Veek. Oh, put the knife away, will you?'

The Valethske narrowed its eyes and snarled at the Doctor. It was the closest Aline had ever been to one of the creatures. It was huge and looked savagely powerful. It was holding a needle-sharp knife that caught the green phosphorescence. Its ears twitched and it slid the weapon away, turning its gaze to Aline. There seemed to be no intelligence in its eyes, its green-yellow irises and slitted pupils, just hunger and a kind of insane, sneering glee. How had the Doctor befriended it – and why? It looked ready to kill them both in an instant.

'Doctor... what's going on?'

'No time to explain now, this might be important,' he said impatiently. 'You said you made contact?' He seemed completely at ease despite the presence of the Valethske.

'Yes,' said Aline, 'and you're not going to believe what with...'

The Valethske ship placed itself in a stable orbit, its engines keeping time with the planet's rotation. It was an old ship – most of its systems were automatic and self-repairing, leaving the important business of hunting and killing to its occupants. Its arsenal was impressive, to those impressed by that sort of thing, and terrifying to anything possessing even the most meagre intelligence. It possessed enough destructive capability to knock out entire planets. It had a store of A-bombs, Q-bombs and Z-bombs and the capacity to manufacture more from raw materials gathered during its lengthy travels. It had biological and chemical agents that could unleash plagues and pestilences of biblical proportions. It was, to anyone other than the Valethske, a ship of death.

As it was bidden by its masters, it prepared and launched a hundred and fifty-one Scourblaze missiles. These were usually used only to purge planets that had been ravaged by diseases caused by germ warfare, or as a last resort when outnumbered – as was the case here, though Kikker's impatience to find the Gods was probably the overriding factor in the decision to deploy them.

Once free from the ship's missile-tubes, the Scourblazes did as they were programmed and spread out evenly in the planet's upper atmosphere. They cruised for a while, their sleek, finned shapes like metallic sharks in the rarefied air, and then they plunged down through the clouds, down towards their destiny, and that of the planet they encircled.

What happened when they hit the ground looked beautiful from a distance. The pea-green ball of the Garden planet suddenly blossomed with new flowers, yellow-white petals bursting across the surface, expanding to meet each other until no green remained. Then the Garden blazed as brightly as any star in the sky – but far more briefly.

Everything on the surface of the world was burned to a crisp in a matter of minutes. The Valethske engineer who had named the Scourblaze missiles hadn't been very imaginative, but made up for this lack with pinpoint accuracy.

To Peri, chained up on the Valethske ship, unable to tear her eyes away from the screen, it was a devastating sight. All the more so because it was so silent. Explosions were things she had only seen on TV or in the movies and they were always loud, always dramatic, even cathartic. But this, the destruction of a whole planet, was just a flare of yellow light on a screen, accompanied only by the gruff cheers of the Valethske.

She remembered waking up in the Garden, being amazed by its vast diversity. The silent, strange grace of the Gardeners. The toe-curlingly delicious taste of the fruit.

All gone now.

The Valethske were cheering and frolicking around each other like a pack of mad dogs.

Peri turned her face against the stone wall and wept for the death of the Garden, certain that she was the only being in the whole universe grieving its passing.

Chapter Twenty-Three
A Warning to the Curious

Veek stood before the Gods, and for a moment she believed. They were in a chamber of golden light that seemed to stretch into infinity. When Veek looked between her booted feet it was as if she was standing on nothing. Before her was something she couldn't comprehend, couldn't even begin to describe. A glowing column of matter like twisted glass in which dark shapes moved. She could hear voices at the edge of her mind, wordless and ancient like the wind.

Beside her stood the Doctor and the dying human woman. The Doctor had wanted to get her back to the TARDIS to minister to her in her final hours, but the woman had insisted on showing them this.

Veek stumbled towards the mass of matter, only half-aware of what she was doing. Through it, she was sure, dwelt the Gods, frail and frightened in their senescence. Now, as at the beginning of the Great Mission, she believed. She'd been a fool to doubt it! A fool to want to return home. Soon, the glory would be hers.

A hand came down on her shoulder. She flung it off, carried on. Then arms around her waist, pulling her back. The Doctor. Veek, once again surprised at his strength, shook him off and drew her spike-knife.

'Veek, stop!' said the Doctor, hands raised as if to ward off an evil spirit. 'Think about what you're doing.'

Veek hesitated. Her mind felt fogged, as if she'd been drugged. She dropped the knife and put her head in her hands.

'I – I am lost in confusion,' she whimpered. 'What is this place?'

She looked up to see the Doctor and Aline staring down at her. Embarrassed at her own show of weakness, she stood, reaching for her blaster. But then she hesitated. She was beyond the point where killing would make a difference.

'Time for a few explanations, I think,' said the Doctor, frowning up at the column of matter. 'A form of semi-sentient plasma, I shouldn't wonder. Aline, you say you actually went inside it?'

Aline nodded. 'It bonded with me.' Her pale, bloodshot eyes turned to Veek. 'I now know everything about the Khorlthochloi. I know that they were – still are – your Gods. You came here to find them, didn't you?'

Veek nodded. 'And to destroy them.'

Aline smiled. 'Such arrogance.'

Veek nodded again. 'I know. I no longer have a part in it.'

Aline looked from Veek to the Doctor. 'Is this true?'

'Veek helped me escape in return for her safe passage home,' explained the Doctor hurriedly. He was more interested in the strand of matter. 'Obviously, that was the presence you sensed. I sensed it too, but I was able to resist its call.' His eyes widened in realisation. 'And Kikker – he must have been able to sense it on some primal, instinctual level. That's why he was so certain the Gods were here. Oh, Aline,' he shook his head sadly. 'It thought you were a higher evolutionary, because of your Encounter. But you're only too human... contact with it has destroyed your cells.'

Aline leaned against the Doctor for support. To Veek's surprise she was smiling. In Veek's experience humans never smiled when faced with death. 'I don't mind dying. The things I have seen...'

'You're not going to die, not if I can help it.'

'It was worth it. I know everything about the Khorlthochloi now. I've touched the mind of something so alien I can't even begin to describe it – and this time I've survived with my sanity intact.'

'But not your body,' said the Doctor. 'Come on, let's get you back to the TARDIS.'

They began to move off.

Veek stared up at the plasma strand. There were so many unanswered questions. She couldn't leave for home now, not without getting answers to at least some of them.

'Wait!' said Veek, moving to bar their way. 'What about the Gods? You must tell me all you know!'

The woman's face looked up at her, and Veek could see the knowledge behind the silver discs of its eyes. Just like the Doctor, this frail human frame contained ancient wisdom.

'Your species came here to kill the Khorlthochloi,' she said, her voice barely more than a whisper. Her lips twisted in a pallid grin. 'But you're too late. They're already dead.'

Vale Commander Kikker closed his eyes and imagined that he could feel the heat of the burning world on his face, drying his eyes and singeing his whiskers. It was a risk, he knew, deploying such a high percentage of ordnance. It would take months of real-time to restock the Scourblaze arsenal. If he was wrong and the Gods were not within this world, he would look foolish, very foolish indeed. He opened his eyes and averted them from the glowing sphere on the viewscreen, looking up with reverence at the mural of Azreske defeating the Gods. When the time came to slay them, Azreske would live again through Kikker, and his glory would be complete. His gaze ran from the mural down the right-hand pillar to the prey chained at its base. He licked his lips. And his stomach would be full of fresh, succulent meat.

He realised that Flayoun and the others were looking to him for guidance. He could see the same fervour in their eyes. The same almost-disbelief: after centuries of searching, have we found the last resting place of the Gods?

He walked over to Flayoun and placed both hands on the young hunter's shoulders. He could feel the supple strength of Flayoun's body, see the absolute devotion in his eyes.

'In the absence of Veek, and on the authority of the Great Vale herself, I promote you, Flayoun, to Hunt Marshal.'

Kikker felt Flayoun's body rise beneath his hands.

'This is a great honour, Vale Commander! I will not fail you.'

Time would tell about that, of course, but for the moment Kikker bared his teeth and hissed at Flayoun in the ceremonial manner. 'Assemble your hunters, Hunt Marshal. Prepare them for battle, and for glory.'

Flayoun saluted and scampered away, his tail stiffening with pleasure. A little too enthusiastic, thought Kikker. Vixens always made better Hunt Marshals, but his best vixen hunters Akkia and

Freela lay dead, smashed at the bottom of the shaft.

This turned Kikker's thoughts back to the penetration of the planet. With the plant life now comprehensively destroyed, the way lay open to the system of underground chambers. And though the bottom of the shaft was blocked, the rest was clear. All they had to do was blast their way through the rubble and mud, and start their search for the Gods. Kikker gave orders to this effect, and then went over to where the prey was tethered against the wall of the control chamber.

There was defiance in its eyes, a defiance Kikker could hardly wait to turn into terror.

'You are privileged, prey; you are about to witness scenes of unsurpassable glory.'

The human woman wrinkled her nose and her smooth face creased in a frown. 'You call this privileged? You've just destroyed one of the most beautiful planets in the universe!'

Kikker had seen this behaviour before, in human prey. When they knew death was certain, sometimes they became arrogant, reckless even. Either that, or they lapsed into catatonia, or helpless paroxysms of weeping. Kikker preferred it this way, when they faced death with anger. It made the transformation into terror all the more drastic and gratifying.

'What use is beauty to me?' he whispered into the prey's ear, running its silky black hair through his fingers. The sweet scent of its oils made Kikker feel giddy. He couldn't wait to sink his teeth into its pink flesh. Flayoun was right; it was a fine specimen, fit and young and meaty. Unable to control his urges, he licked the woman's face, lapping up as much of her salt sweat and tears as he could, his body pressing hers to the wall, subduing her struggles and screams.

Not long now before he'd be able to feast on her.

Then he caught the eyes of the Vale Guards, all of whom had turned to look at him, and he released the woman, letting her slump to the floor.

He barked at them. 'Get back to your duties!'

He turned to utter more threats at the woman, but was taken

aback by the sheer look of hate that twisted her face into a snarl. She spat, the saliva flinging through the air and landing on the breastplate of his uniform.

A Vale Guard called. 'Vale Commander, we're coming in to land!'

Kikker turned away from the woman, absently wiping her spit from his breastplate and, licking his fingers, went to oversee the landing procedures.

Aline could feel her strength slipping away again and clung to the Doctor's arm as they walked through the chamber of the plasma strand. Veek had been stunned into silence by Aline's revelation and listened intently as she told them what she had learned.

'The Khorlthochloi were an extremely long-lived species,' she began. 'And like many such, they began to evolve beyond the physical plane, becoming creatures of pure mind.'

'I've seen it myself,' said the Doctor. 'It's supposedly the pinnacle of evolution.'

Aline nodded, fighting down a wave of nausea. 'But the Khorlthochloi needed to keep their physical forms alive, as insurance in case they needed to return to them. So they created this world to nurture their bodies while their minds roamed new realms. They created a race of motile plants to feed and tend their bodies. They created a defence system – any hostile beings coming to the Garden would be repelled by the plants themselves. They hoped that people would think the Gardeners were the true inhabitants of the planet, and not look beneath the surface.'

'For superior beings that's rather naive of them,' said the Doctor, 'but I'm beginning to understand now. Those herds of insects – they're the Khorlthochloi, aren't they?'

Veek growled at this. 'Nonsense – the Khorlthochloi are ebony giants, with eyes of fire, the size of mountains!'

'They may have been once,' said the Doctor, 'but over hundreds of thousands of years they must have devolved to this primitive, insectile state.'

To Aline's surprise Veek started laughing – short, sharp barks of mirth. 'So the Great Mission is for nothing after all!'

'What happened to their minds?' asked the Doctor.

This was the greatest tragedy of all, and Aline spoke with a heavy heart. 'The plasma strand told me – it contains some sort of recording, a memory trace. It's also a source of great power that the Khorlthochloi intended to use when they returned.'

'So they tried to return?' asked the Doctor.

'Many thousands of years ago. They encountered a threat, in the dimension of thought their minds occupied.' Aline frowned. 'I'm not sure what it was, but to threaten the Khorlthochloi it must have been pretty powerful. Anyway, when they tried to re-enter their physical forms they found that their autonomic systems had developed to such an extent that they rejected their minds.'

The Doctor grimaced. 'That is ironic.'

'What is – autonomic system?' rumbled Veek.

'The section of the nervous system that regulates breathing, sleeping, digestion; all the processes of life,' said the Doctor. 'Obviously the Khorlthochloi had rather more advanced versions than most species, and as their higher minds had been away for so long, these autonomic systems had grown independent. They didn't want to let the Khorlthochloi back in.'

'And so, trapped between the material universe and the dimension of mind, they were destroyed by the thing they were trying to escape.' Aline shuddered. 'Luckily the plasma strand was able to prevent the enemy from crossing to the material universe.'

'Which is why it must be left alone,' said the Doctor. He snapped his fingers. 'So that's why the plasma strand wanted to make contact with higher evolutionaries, to warn them not to try the same thing. To warn them of the dangers of abandoning their physical bodies!' Though his voice was excited, his face was grave. 'Hubris.' He glared at Veek. 'Something you lot should be wary of, especially Kikker.'

'The Vale Commander will not be pleased,' said Veek. 'To have searched for so long, only to find the Gods have been dead for thousands of years.'

'They were probably even dead before you left Valeth Skettra,' said the Doctor cheerfully – and rather unwisely, thought Aline. 'You never know, he might even be pleased that they're dead.'

Veek snarled. 'Kikker is after revenge, honour and glory, Doctor. He wants to kill the Gods with his bare hands, if he can. Who knows what he's going to do when he finds out there are no gods to slay?'

'Probably go completely insane,' said the Doctor thoughtfully. 'Now there's a cheering thought.'

They passed through the hidden exit from the chamber of golden light – which Aline could see now, as could the Doctor – and walked along the tunnel to the cavern where Aline had seen the Harvesters deliver their fruit to the insects, the remnants of the Khorlthochloi. There were only a few of the beetle-like creatures now, poking forlornly among the rocks. Aline regarded them in a new light now. Who would have guessed that these creatures once housed the minds of one of the greatest races of beings the galaxy had ever seen?

The Doctor and Veek led her across the cavern and, after a brief debate over which was the correct way, through a tunnel on the far side. This led, in turn, to another cavern, far larger than the previous one, with a greater number of other tunnels leading off from between stalactites and stalagmites that bordered the area like rows of giant teeth. On the far side, dwarfed by a massive pillar of rock, Aline could just about see the TARDIS lurking in a patch of gloom. Its familiar blue shape, she knew, signified unimaginable technology. Time Lords could regenerate, couldn't they? Perhaps, after all, she wasn't going to die.

The Doctor stopped walking, causing Aline to stumble against him.

'Sorry,' he said. 'I thought I heard something.'

Aline strained to hear, but couldn't make out any sounds above her laboured breath and the slow thudding of her failing heart.

'I hear it too,' said Veek. 'They're coming.'

Aline was about to ask who, when a herd of insects – of former Khorlthochloi host bodies, she told herself – burst from one of the tunnels at the edge of the cavern. They were screeching shrilly, scrambling over the rocks and each other, in panic to get away from –

Aline heard the sizzle of blaster fire and the shrieks of the hunters before she saw them. Valethske. Dozens of the red-furred, black-uniformed creatures suddenly poured from the tunnel entrances and swept across the floor of the cavern. Some of them caught sight of Aline, the Doctor and Veek and stumbled to a halt.

They were completely cut off from the TARDIS. So she was going to die after all. She felt oddly indifferent about it.

'Oh dear,' said the Doctor, with a sideways look at Veek. 'Any chance of putting in a good word for us?'

More Valethske had seen them and a circle of the hunters was closing in, brandishing blasters and knives, their faces alight with lust and hunger.

Veek stepped forwards to meet them. 'They may know of my heresy,' she hissed to the Doctor and Aline. 'I will soon find out.'

'Hunt Marshal Veek – or should I say, former Hunt Marshal Veek,' came a gruff voice. The advancing hunters parted ranks to let through a tall Valethske in a more elaborate uniform than the rank and file hunters. 'And the Doctor.'

'Vale Commander Kikker,' said the Doctor graciously, though his eyes were cold. 'So nice of you to drop in. I'm afraid I've got some rather bad news for you.'

Kikker bared his teeth. 'And I have something for you.'

He gestured to two hunters, who stepped forwards holding between them a human woman wearing a one-piece mud-coloured uniform, her face grimy, hair matted.

It was Peri, Aline realised.

Her eyes lit up like beacons of hope when she saw the Doctor.

'Let her go,' said the Doctor, stepping towards Kikker.

Kikker barred his way. 'Not until I have your guarantee of total co-operation.'

'All right, all right, yes,' said the Doctor impatiently.

Kikker gave an order and the two Valethske released Peri. She fell into the Doctor's arms, shuddering with relief.

She looked over at Aline. Through her tears, her eyes were hard, dark hollows beneath them. Aline could almost read her thoughts. *It's great to see the Doctor but we're not out of the woods yet.*

Aline looked at the massed hunters. Not by a long chalk.

'What is this "bad news" you have for me?' said Kikker, looking at the Doctor with amusement.

'Oh, just something you really should know,' said the Doctor with obvious relish. 'It's about your Gods, the Khorlthochloi.'

He motioned for Peri to go and stand with Aline.

Aline gave her hand a reassuring squeeze and was heartened to feel her squeeze back.

Kikker leaned towards the Doctor. 'They're here? You've seen them?'

'Not quite,' said the Doctor, with a look at Aline. 'You see, they're dead and have been for countless centuries.'

Kikker sneered. 'A pathetic lie.'

Aline backed the Doctor up. 'It's true. I've made contact with some of the technology they left behind. The Khorlthochloi no longer exist.'

'Why should I believe you?' hissed Kikker.

'Because she's telling the truth.' Now the Doctor had the attention of all the hunters. 'See those insects over there? They're all that remains of your Gods.' She could see him struggling to dumb down the explanation for the benefit of the Valethske. 'Their minds evolved beyond the need for their bodies, and died. The bodies they left behind carried on their mindless existence, tended by this garden world.'

There was a babble of comment from the hunters.

Kikker drew his blaster and fired at the ceiling.

'Do not listen to this human!' he cried. 'The Gods are here – I know it!'

'Doctor,' whispered Aline. 'Take him to the plasma strand. Maybe then he'll believe.'

'Good idea,' said the Doctor. 'Vale Commander, I can show you proof of this.'

Kikker eyed him suspiciously. 'How?'

'Through there.' The Doctor pointed at the tunnel that led to the cavern of light. 'They've left some of their technology behind. As a warning to the curious.'

Kikker seemed unimpressed. 'Trickery,' he said. 'How can I trust the word of a mere human?'

'You can trust him, believe me,' said Aline. She had no fear of the Valethske now, and she could tell that Kikker could see this. 'I've made contact with the thing in there. It told me the truth about the Khorlthochloi. Maybe it will tell you.'

She could see the calculation behind Kikker's eyes. One part of him wanted to slaughter them all right there on the spot – but another part seemed to recognise the truth in what she was saying.

There was an agonising silence, broken only by the snarls and growls of the Valethske.

'Very well,' said Kikker at last. 'Take me to it.'

'What about us?' said Peri.

The Doctor put an arm protectively around his companion.

'Yes, they'd better not come to any harm, or else I won't show you how to operate the TARDIS.'

Kikker beckoned two hunters over. 'Guard these two humans.' He turned to face the crowd of Valethske, raising his voice. 'Hunters, do not harm these humans – for now, anyway.' He gestured to the Doctor. 'This human tells us that the Gods are long-dead.'

There were hisses and howls of bemusement from the massed hunters. They seemed more ready to believe their leader than the Doctor.

'I do not believe him. However, I will return with proof, or otherwise.'

The Doctor led Kikker away, giving Aline and Peri a smile and a wave of reassurance.

Peri and Aline allowed themselves to be ushered away so they were standing at the edge of the cavern. Aline had no illusions that the hunters would obey their Commander and fully expected to be torn to ribbons at any second.

The Valethske hunters – there must have been a hundred or so – started checking their weapons, sharpening their claws or engaging in one-to-one mock-tussles. Aline had never been this close to so many Valethske and the musty smell coming from them was almost overpowering. As was the sense of feral power she could see in their rippling muscles, the hunger in their eyes. Aline could just see the TARDIS over the heads of the hunters. They'd never be able to reach it. It may as well have remained on the Valethske ship.

She saw Veek approach the two beasts guarding them. They stepped aside to let her pass, hissing at her behind her back. Spurning her. Aline realised that Veek must have sacrificed a lot to help the Doctor.

'I recognise that one,' muttered Peri. 'It's their Hunt Marshal or something. It's the one that shot me back at the party.'

'She's called Veek. She's friendly – as far as a Valethske can be,' whispered Aline. 'The Doctor's formed some kind of alliance with her.'

Peri stared at her as if she was mad. 'No *way*!'

Veek stood in front of them, arms folded, eyes narrow, calculating. 'You are Peri? The Doctor's friend?'

Peri scowled at her. 'Yeah, what of it?'

Veek crouched down. Aline could smell her rancid breath. 'We must leave as soon as the Doctor returns. I will help you reach the TARDIS –'

'Veek!' came a hoarse cry. Aline looked beyond Veek to see another Valethske approaching. This one had a white stripe across its face.

'That one's called Flayoun,' muttered Peri. 'He rescued me – sort of. Wanted me as a gift for Kikker.' Peri smiled tightly. 'And he's no way on our side.'

Veek stood up and whirled round. 'Flayoun!' Her voice was sibilant with malice. 'Still following Kikker around like a lost cub?'

Flayoun drew himself up proudly. 'I am now Hunt Marshal.'

Veek growled. 'Not while I'm still alive.'

Flayoun drew a blaster.

'Not this way,' said Veek. 'I challenge you to single combat. To the death.'

There were shrieks and howls of enthusiasm from the other Valethske.

Veek and Flayoun prowled to the centre of the cavern, growling at each other. The Valethske scrambled aside to form a ragged circle around the two combatants. Peri and Aline were herded back into the shadows by the two hunters Kikker had ordered to guard them.

'Ringside seats,' said Peri. 'Great.'

Vale Commander Kikker stood before the plasma strand, the Doctor's voice a distant buzzing in his ears, and felt nothing. No sense of victory, no feeling of triumph swelling his heart, no fanfares, no calls to glory. Just this golden void and the looming mass of alien matter. The sense of desolation was so great that Kikker knew that the Doctor had been speaking the truth. The Gods were dead, and in death they had evaded the vengeance of the Valethske.

It had all been for nothing.

The Doctor's babblings were beginning to annoy Kikker.

'And so you see, poor Aline thought she was going to make contact with a higher evolutionary, when all it actually is, is a machine. An immensely sophisticated and powerful machine, I'll grant you that, but a machine nonetheless.'

'Be silent!' hissed Kikker. 'Have some respect for this moment, Doctor. I have searched for centuries only to have victory snatched from my jaws. Have you any conception of how that feels?'

'Have you any conception of the trail of suffering you've left across the galaxy?' said the Doctor calmly.

Kikker sneered. 'I care nothing for that. They were only prey.' He drew his blaster and levelled it at the Doctor's chest. 'As are you.'

The Doctor showed no fear. Instead he sighed and turned away, his face bathed in the glow of the plasma strand.

A surge of anger rushed through Kikker's blood, and his finger tightened on the trigger.

'Killing me won't make an iota of difference, Kikker,' said the Doctor. 'Oh, it will make you feel better, for a very short while. But it won't bring the Gods back.'

He was right, of course - but his words sparked an idea in Kikker's mind. His back-up plan, of course! He'd been so blinded by anger that he had forgotten about it. So he would get his revenge and his glory after all.

'Won't you please go now, leave this beautiful planet in peace?'

Now he had a plan, Kikker found himself grinning. 'Beautiful no longer, Doctor - we have sterilised the surface with fire!'

'I was wondering how you'd got past the plantibodies,' muttered the Doctor. 'Do you realise that now you've destroyed the Garden you've cut off the insects' only source of food? That you've committed double genocide?'

Kikker sneered. 'Yes, Doctor, I realise. Do you really expect me to care?'

The Doctor turned his gaze on Kikker. 'I've met many murderous alien species in my time but you Valethske take my breath away. Is there nothing you care about other than satisfying your own grotesque appetites?'

Kikker stared up at the plasma strand. 'No, Doctor, there is not. We are Valethske.'

'As if that explains everything.'

Kikker reached out and grasped the Doctor's upper arm, relishing his cry of pain. 'I will soon sate all my appetites, Doctor - for you are going to take me back through time, to when the Gods lived, so I can destroy them!'

Chapter Twenty-Four
Superiority Complex

Veek was glad she hadn't killed Flayoun when she'd had the chance. It would have denied her the honour of dispatching him in single combat. They had discarded their guns, knives and uniforms and now faced each other naked across a makeshift arena. The only weapons they had now were tooth and claw, backed up by strength, agility and determination. Veek circled Flayoun, keeping her eyes locked on his, ready to spring. The hunters Veek had travelled with for centuries stood around her, baying for blood.

Veek forced all memories of Flayoun as her mate from her mind. Now he was just an enemy, an enemy she had to destroy. She forgot, for the moment, all about the Doctor and the TARDIS, all about going home. All that mattered, for now, was this fight. Veek licked her lips, mentally mapping her opponent's weak spots: the white-furred, tautly muscled belly, the soft triangle of the groin, the skin under the jaw, the tendons at the backs of the legs.

Suddenly, Flayoun lunged for her. Veek sprang to one side in a feint, reaching round and clawing at his back. He stumbled, but rolled over and was back on his feet in a flash, facing her once more, the pain drawing a snarl from between his bared teeth.

Before he could regain his balance Veek threw herself at him, coming in low, claws outstretched, reaching for his belly. He stepped aside – as she'd anticipated, and she swung a foot up sharply into his stomach. In an instant she was on him, her powerful knees pressed into his guts, arms raised to keep off his slicing blows. Wincing as he raked her forearm with his sharp claws, she lunged forwards, trying to lock her jaws around his throat. But this movement put her off-balance and he twisted beneath her, sending her sprawling to the smooth rock floor. She landed face-down, rolling over just in time to avoid his lunging body.

Veek scrambled to her feet, breathing hard, her arm-muscles spasming where he'd cut her. Flayoun stood and faced her again, his chest rising and falling with exertion. She saw his legs tense for a leap, and at the same moment she sprang. They slammed together in mid-air like a thunderclap, claws slashing savagely at each other, hissing and screaming. Veek slashed and hit and bit, feeling as if she was dissolving in a whirlwind of fury, oblivious to the blows he rained down on her. With a final lunge she bore the hunter to the ground and sunk her teeth into his neck, biting hard and twisting. She pressed down and down on to him as if she was trying to get through him to the rock beneath, his gargling screams sending a thrill of pleasure through her. She worried at his throat, dimly aware of his increasingly feeble body-blows, and then ripped out his larynx, leaning back and shrieking in triumph as a fountain of her former mate's blood splattered over her white-furred belly. She rubbed it in with both hands, her fingers running over her teats, exciting her. She drank down the cheers and howls of the hunters.

'I triumph!' she screamed, glaring around the circle of bared teeth and gleaming eyes. About half the hunters were howling and clawing the air; the other half looked sullen. She had to try to win them all over to her side, strengthen her position.

'Hunter Trenex – throw me your knife.'

Veek reached out and caught the blade that flew through the air towards her. She spun the blade deftly on her fingertips, tossed it upwards, caught it by the handle and in a smooth movement slit Flayoun's abdomen from groin to sternum. Blood seeped rapidly from the incision into his white chest-fur.

Flayoun was almost dead. She bent down and whispered in his ear. 'I'll take a bite out of you, hunter.' She'd said it many times in jest. How strange that it had actually been a premonition...

Veek slipped her free hand into Flayoun, her fingers finding purchase on his slippery innards, and tugged free a loop of intestine. Trenex's knife was good and sharp and she quickly and smoothly cut free a length of purple gut.

As she did this she kept her eyes locked on Flayoun's, and fancied she could see the exact moment when life went from him.

Veek stood over the corpse, raising the knife high in one hand, the portion of intestine in the other. She could smell her own sweat rising from her body, mingling with the metallic tang of Flayoun's blood and the steamy, tropical odour of his exposed guts. She raised her head and slipped in the morsel, chewing and swallowing with exaggerated movements. This was the worst thing a hunter could do to a defeated enemy, reducing them symbolically to the level of prey.

She swallowed and wiped the blood from her lips. 'I am Hunt Marshal now.'

She glared at the ring of hunters, daring any to challenge her.

Veek's victory had an unforeseen side-effect. The two hunters guarding Peri and Aline had been performing their duties with relish, keeping their guns trained on the women and one eye on the fight. But when Veek had eviscerated Flayoun, they had turned to watch, their whole attention taken up by the grotesque spectacle.

Seeing their chance, Peri and Aline edged slowly along the cavern wall and slipped inside the nearest tunnel entrance. Once they were a good way in, and the curve of the tunnel blocked the entrance from view, Aline sank down against the smooth rock wall. She coughed, doubling up, her whole body shaking in a fit.

Peri crouched down beside her. 'Hey, you OK?' she whispered.

'No, I'm bloody well not.' A trickle of blood ran from the corner of Aline's mouth and Peri could see a vein pulsing in her throat like something trying to escape.

Peri looked along the dimly glowing tunnel. 'We've got no idea where this leads.' It wasn't the tunnel the Doctor and Kikker had taken.

'Away from the Valethske,' gasped Aline, in between struggles for breath.

'And away from the TARDIS,' muttered Peri. The Doctor would

probably be back with Kikker quite soon. What happened then, she couldn't guess, but she wanted to be with the Doctor when it did.

'Come on, let's go back.' She moved to help Aline stand.

'No,' said Aline, shrugging off her assistance and standing up by herself. 'We go on.'

Peri sighed. 'Look, I wanna help the Doctor. We're doing no good by running away.'

'On the contrary,' said Aline, her haughty tones setting Peri's teeth on edge. 'I have a plan. Come on.'

Aline set off, leaning on the mossy tunnel wall for support.

Peri sighed, went up to Aline and made the woman lean on her instead. Together they went on down the tunnel. Peri could see that it was getting lighter – up ahead, was that sunlight? Couldn't be – they were underground.

At the sight of this Aline seemed to relax. 'It's close. Thank heavens. More than one tunnel must lead to it... I don't think I can go on for much longer.'

Wary of what the light might signify, Peri made Aline stop. 'Any chance of telling me your great plan?'

'No.' Aline smiled. There were big hollows below her eyes and her white hair was beginning to fall out. 'If I tell you it might not work.'

'Superstitious crap,' muttered Peri.

Aline coughed, the sound echoing up and down the tunnel like a gunshot. Peri winced, expecting the clatter of pursuing Valethske at any second.

They moved off again. 'What the hell happened to you, anyway?'

'There's something below the surface of this planet,' whispered Aline. 'Something ancient, something wonderful.'

'Yeah, the Doctor mentioned it. Can't be that wonderful if it did that to you.'

She felt Aline glance sideways at her. 'You wouldn't understand.'

Peri was about to give the woman a verbal lashing but she

figured that as she was dying she'd let her off. By now the golden glow was all around them, consuming the walls of the tunnel, and Peri had to squint to stop her eyes from hurting.

Suddenly they emerged into a seemingly limitless space filled with golden light. In the centre was an enormous strand of matter, like a giant thread of candlewax.

'Wow,' said Peri. 'So that's what it's all about, huh?'

Aline looked even more alien in the strange light. 'Yes. Help me to it.'

Peri took a tentative step into the golden void. It didn't seem to have any floor, but Peri could feel something underfoot, as hard and unyielding as stone. As they drew nearer the strand she thought she could hear voices muttering in her mind. 'So that thing is the presence you sensed? Is it alive?'

'Not in any sense you'd understand.'

'Don't patronise me,' said Peri, for the moment forgetting how ill Aline was. What made this woman think she was so superior?

Soon they were close enough to the strand for Peri's liking. She had hold of Aline's hand and could feel the woman trembling like a sick animal.

Aline turned to face Peri and she saw the fear in the woman's silver-white eyes.

'So, what do we do now?'

Aline's lips parted in a half-grimace, half-grin. 'Now we say goodbye.'

'Huh?'

Aline let go of Peri's hand and gave her a little wave.

'Goodbye, Peri. Give my love to the Doctor.'

Aline stepped towards the strand. Its surface seemed to contain wisps of smoky matter, which writhed and churned like dark ghosts.

Peri suddenly realised what Aline meant. 'You're not going in there?'

Aline nodded. 'I've done so before, and I'm dying anyway. What have I got to lose?' She took hold of Peri's hand. 'Believe me, it's the only way. It's my destiny.'

Peri had no idea what the woman was babbling about. 'But why?'

Aline let go of Peri's hand and stood back, swaying slightly. 'You'll see.'

The leather jacket seemed to hang loosely on her body like a shell. Peri fought down a perverse desire to ask for it back, and said instead, 'Look, this is nuts. Whatever it is you're gonna do it's probably dangerous – why don't we wait until we can find the Doctor?'

But Aline just shook her head and smiled. Her eyes were drawn towards the strand. Part of its surface was bulging outwards, a distended stomach of syrup-gold matter, elongating towards Aline.

'See – it knows. It wants me.' Aline turned away from Peri to face the advancing mass of matter.

Peri backed away. Although she didn't particularly like Aline, the prospect of another death was almost too much. Apart from herself and the Doctor, everyone had died. Everyone human, that is. 'Pity we never got the chance to know each other better,' she found herself saying, as Aline walked towards the bulging strand.

But Aline hadn't heard her.

Peri watched aghast as she stepped into the belly of matter. There wasn't even any sound as the golden stuff closed around her and the bulge sank back into the main mass.

Peri was left alone in a golden void, whispering voices tantalising her mind.

She folded her arms and stared up at the column of alien matter. 'What the hell happens now?'

Veek stood victorious before the hunters. Her body registered pain from the multitude of cuts and blows she had received, but it felt good to her. Her flesh sang with victory. She could see Trenex's eyes glinting with lust as he observed her nakedness. Maybe she'd take him as her new mate. He certainly seemed lithe and strong, and his eyes shone with an intelligence Flayoun had lacked all the way to his inglorious end.

Veek felt giddy with power. The Gods were dead, the Great Mission over – more, it had never stood any chance of success – so now they could all go home.

'I will now speak freely the thoughts that have been gathering in my mind throughout this Great Mission. The Gods are dead – accept it. I have seen proof of this. The Great Mission has reduced us all to a state of mindless slavery. Our ancestors, Azreske's cubs and vixens, were cunning, inventive – they survived the wrath of the Gods and rebuilt Valeth Skettra. It was a folly to go leaping across space to try to find and destroy the Gods. It has been over a thousand years since we left Valeth Skettra and it's time we returned. Are any of you with me?'

There was silence. They were all staring at her.

Hunter Trenex stepped forward. He was blinking quickly, tongue lolling from his mouth. 'Hunt Marshal Veek,' he growled. He licked his lips and made as if to speak again, but then his gaze shifted over Veek's shoulder and he snapped his jaws shut.

All the hunters' eyes followed the line of his gaze. Veek swung round.

The crowd had parted to reveal Vale Commander Kikker, the Doctor held in a tight grip at his side. In his other hand was a blaster, and it was pointing at her.

'Stirring words, vixen,' he spat. He shoved the Doctor down to the ground. 'Take him!'

Two hunters sprang forward and hauled the Doctor to his feet.

Veek looked around for a gap in the crowd, but she could see nowhere to run. Now the exertion of her fight and the wounds she'd sustained began to throb with a new pain, the strength-sapping ache of defeat.

Kikker strode up to her, blaster in one hand, spike-knife in the other. Though he kept his eyes on her he raised his voice so all the hunters could hear.

'The Gods are dead,' he cried, 'but we still have the means to complete the Great Mission.'

Veek glanced beyond Kikker to the Doctor, held tightly by two snarling hunters. His head hung in defeat and realisation dawned.

Veek groaned.

Kikker was now standing before her, teeth bared, eyes alight with bloodlust. 'But before we do, I will eviscerate this heretic!'

Aline found herself, as before, floating in a thick, syrupy mass. She could feel it all around her body, fuzzy and tingling. Somehow she could breathe, and to move around all she had to do was think. She looked down at her body and wondered how much longer she would need it.

She could see Peri through the surface of the strand, a dark shadow against the glare. She should have told the girl what she planned, but she hadn't wanted to breathe a word of it in case Peri had stopped her. It occurred to Aline that Peri might also die, and she wished she could tell her to try to make for the TARDIS. Well, she still could. She struggled back towards the surface of the strand, but it was no good. Its currents had snared her.

She fell deep within its golden core, to the thing that lived within. Somehow, one of the Khorlthochloi had been able to project a telepathic message to the strand before it died, programming it to warn all other higher evolutionaries of the dangers of transcending the physical plane.

But the strand was much more than a mere recorded message. It controlled the Garden, regulated the seasons, fed the Gardeners with nutrients, performed a thousand million tasks. Furthermore, it was a massive store of energy, an untapped potential ready for the Khorlthochloi to use when they returned, an event that would never happen now.

The energy remained locked within the strand, ready for release. All it needed was a little mental nudge...

Aline drew near the centre and, as before, its terrifying beauty took her breath away. It was a coil of dark matter, like fused metal and stone, arranged in a double-spiral. Its size was impossible to guess. Along the length of the spiral was threaded the core of the plasma strand, a line of pure light, pure power.

Aline floated down towards the spiral. She knew what she

wanted from it, but would it understand? Would it recognise her as a higher evolutionary, as it had done before, and obey her commands?

She felt as light as a feather, her body was almost an afterthought. She closed her eyes, delving deep within her mind, projecting her thoughts at the core of the strand.

Aline felt something stirring within her as the parts of her that had been touched by her Encounter began to wake. It had happened the first time she'd entered the strand and she was prepared for it now – she wouldn't let it swamp her own being as it had before.

She smiled with gratification as the immense spiral began to turn, and the column of light began to pulse in time with her heartbeat.

Peri was beginning to realise that Aline wasn't coming back. Whatever she'd planned clearly wasn't happening. She turned back, intending to head for the tunnels and find the Doctor. But she couldn't see the way out – there was nothing to see around her except this shimmering golden void.

'Hey!' She turned back to the strand, raising a fist as if to batter upon its surface, but hesitated. She didn't want to touch the stuff, end up like Aline. 'Hey, Aline!' she called, feeling slightly foolish. 'There's no way out!'

No answer came, not that she expected any.

Then she glimpsed something deep within the golden matter. Nodes of white light were forming in its amber depths, like stars. And they were getting bigger. As they grew, the muttering in Peri's mind grew in volume until her head was filled with screams.

Peri screamed too, but she couldn't hear her own voice. She sank to the invisible floor, hands clasped over her ears, and watched as the nodes of light grew bigger, and bigger, until all Peri could see was their dazzling, shimmering forms.

And then with a roar of energy, they burst from the surface of the strand.

Kikker drew his knife-hand back, ready to plunge it into Veek's guts.

Veek closed her eyes.

Through the purple mist behind her eyelids she pictured the rains of Valeth Skettra for the last time.

Then she heard a voice. A human voice. 'I wouldn't do that if I were you.'

The Doctor's voice.

Veek snapped her eyes open.

The Doctor had struggled free of his captors and was approaching Kikker, hands held behind his back. He looked so unconcerned that Veek had to fight down a bark of laughter.

Kikker swung round with a hiss. 'Give me one good reason why I should spare the life of this heretic!'

'One good reason,' said the Doctor brightly, his eyes glittering, 'is that I will refuse to show you how to operate the TARDIS if you harm Veek. There's also the question of Peri and Aline,' said the Doctor, looking round. 'Where are they? You haven't killed them, have you? Because if you have we're going nowhere.'

While the Doctor spoke a growl had been building up within Kikker's chest, his whole body trembling with anger. He let out a screech of rage and raised his blaster. 'I will work out how to operate the TARDIS myself! Give me the key!'

With a look of resignation, the Doctor held out the key.

With a triumphant sneer Kikker snatched it from his hands and turned towards the TARDIS, which was only a short run away at the edge of the cavern.

At that moment a ball of white energy crackled from a tunnel mouth on the far side of the cavern. The size of a short-range skirmisher, it was like a miniature sun, and it hurt Veek's eyes to look at it. The whole cavern was lit silver-white, the green phosphorescence totally overwhelmed.

Everyone turned to look at the manifestation, and many hunters screamed, falling to their knees in terror, shrieking that the Gods had arrived to destroy them.

The mini-sun paused at the edge of the cavern as if watching them, and then it swooped forwards, crackling and hissing, on to the hunters nearby. Veek could see them twist and burn, their death-screeches echoing round the cavern.

Another ball of energy followed it. And then another.

Veek realised that no one had hold of her any more. The terrified hunters were fleeing for their lives.

Veek dived for the floor as the ball of energy crackled above her, landing by the Doctor. Sounds of incineration and the screeches of the dying were everywhere.

The Doctor was injured: blood poured from a wound on his forehead. He was shouting something but she could hear nothing, her ears full of the sizzling roar of the mini-suns.

Booted feet stumbled into her as blinded hunters tried desperately to escape.

The Doctor put his mouth to her ear and yelled. 'Don't look at it. Stay low. Make for the TARDIS!'

He scrambled to his feet and shoved his way through the hunters, Veek following close behind. Despite the Doctor's words she wanted to look behind her but kept her eyes front, on the silver-lit walls of the cavern, on the TARDIS, dwarfed by the stalactites –

And Vale Commander Kikker standing in front of it, key in the lock, gun aimed straight at the Doctor.

Veek slid to a halt and ducked down behind an outcrop of rock, hoping that Kikker hadn't seen her. She risked a quick look behind; the mini-suns were streaking about the cavern like trapped meteors, bouncing off the walls and roof, causing great chunks of rock to break off. Those that weren't incinerated by the white-hot energy were crushed beneath the falling slabs.

She looked back at Kikker and the Doctor. It wouldn't be long before the mini-suns ricocheted into their corner, and that would be it. Fortunately, Kikker hadn't seen her and was screaming at the Doctor, his voice inaudible.

Veek calculated the distance between them and leapt, propelling her body at the Vale Commander.

Kikker saw her at the last moment and turned, eyes widening in surprise. He swung his blaster round – too late. Veek slammed into him and they both fell. He still had the blaster in one hand and the golden TARDIS key-chain in the other.

A flash of energy to her left. She didn't have time for an honourable kill.

As Kikker struggled beneath her, she drew his own spike-knife from his belt and thrust it into the soft flesh beneath his jaw, up through the roof of his mouth and into his brain.

The Vale Commander died instantly. Veek smelled and tasted his final breath, his body arched into a bow-shape and she tumbled off. She reached for the key-chain – but it had gone – in their struggle Kikker had flung it into the cavern.

It lay several metres away, directly in the path of a speeding ball of energy. There was no time to reach it. She heard a yell from behind her, stood and turned – to see the Doctor at the TARDIS door, face a mask of blood – and the TARDIS door was open!

Not understanding how this was possible, Veek leapt at the Doctor and bore him and herself into the bright, white interior of the TARDIS.

Chapter Twenty-Five
Final Destiny

Veek and the Doctor fell together in a heap on the floor of the console room. The doors closed behind them, cutting out the sounds of screaming and the sizzling of the mini-suns.

They extricated themselves from each other, both panting heavily.

Their eyes met.

'You saved my life,' said Veek, at the same moment the Doctor said the exact same words.

She helped the Doctor to his feet and he all but fell on to the console.

'That has to be the closest escape yet,' he gasped.

'How did you open the door without the key?'

'I didn't.' He held up the small golden object, smiling triumphantly. 'You intervened just in time – it was already in the lock; must have snapped off the chain.' He operated a control and the scanner screen came to life.

It showed a cavern full of fleeing hunters, pursued by blinding white spheres of energy.

The Doctor's face was a mask of pain. 'I do hope Peri and Aline are well out of the way of that lot.' He moved around the console, operating more controls. 'Now I wonder where it's coming from?'

Veek stared at the screen. She saw Trenex running towards the TARDIS, and was about to ask the Doctor to open the doors when a ball of energy descended upon him, frying him in an instant. Now she'd never know if he was on her side. Never have the chance to mate with him. All the hunters were dying, and there was nothing she could do about it.

'Can't we help them?' she said. 'What is that strange energy?'

'The last defences of the Garden?' muttered the Doctor. 'There's nothing we can do. The only safe place is here in the TARDIS.'

Veek looked helplessly at the screen. Few hunters remained

alive. Was this the price they paid for the folly of the Great Mission? Was her survival her reward for staying true to her nature?

The Doctor operated a lever and the column in the centre of the console began to rise and fall.

'Where are we going?'

The Doctor mopped his forehead with the once-white cloth. 'To the source.' He frowned as he looked at the cloth, his own red blood mingling with the dried stains of the blood of the insect Veek had killed. 'I've got a disturbing idea about what's causing all this.'

Peri curled into a ball, trying to block out the screaming maelstrom of light. Whatever Aline had planned, it had gone horribly wrong. Peri expected at any second to be fried by the whirling spheres of energy. A hot wind tore about her, like the aftermath of a nuclear explosion, she imagined. She peered between her fingers now and then, but all she could see was a whiteness that hurt her eyes. Why wasn't she being harmed?

Then inside the howling wall of sound, she became aware of another noise. A grating, trumpeting sound, somewhere off to her left.

She sat up and squinted through her fingers. There, in the middle of the gale of light, a familiar shape was forming.

Peri leapt to her feet, staggering as the energy roared around her, and ran towards the TARDIS. As she ran the door opened and the Doctor stepped out. He saw Peri and made for her, struggling against the energy storm.

Somehow they managed to scramble into the TARDIS.

Peri stood gasping in the console room. It seemed almost gloomy after the dazzling display outside.

'Oh Doctor, thank God you...' she began, but her voice tailed off when she saw what was standing on the other side of the console room, regarding her with yellow-green eyes.

'Doctor, what the *hell* is that thing *doing* in here?'

'Don't worry, Peri – Veek won't harm you, will you, Veek?'

Veek glared at him, snarled, and gave a curt nod. Peri saw with disgust that she was naked and plastered with blood.

'Doctor, that thing almost killed me. Almost killed you! How can you say it won't harm me?'

The Doctor put his hands on her shoulders, trying to calm her. 'Peri, Veek's on our side. She killed Kikker – saved my life. All she wants to do is go home.'

'Yeah, well, I know how she feels.' Peri shook him off, stomping away across the console room. She felt shaken and angry and couldn't understand why the Doctor had let Veek on board after all she and her kind had done. She didn't even *want* to understand. 'I'm gonna have a bath and clean up, and then you can take me right back to Earth. I've had enough of all this crap!'

She didn't look back to see the Doctor's expression, because she could picture it clearly enough. She'd offended him, hurt him probably – but right now she couldn't care less.

Veek watched the human woman go through the interior door, and briefly wondered how large the TARDIS was. Perhaps the blue box contained a whole world.

'A spirited creature,' she said. 'A worthy companion.'

'I'll miss her,' said the Doctor. 'And I haven't really got to know her yet.' He turned to Veek, his tone hardening. 'But I understand how she feels. Humans will never be able to forgive your kind, Veek. Do you understand? Do you even care?'

Veek shifted uncomfortably. 'Humans are our prey. You will never change that.'

The Doctor turned away in disgust. 'Those cuts and scratches must be smarting. There's a medical kit around here somewhere but, you know, for the life of me I can't quite remember where it is at the moment.'

Veek didn't care. She relished the pain, it told her that she was alive. The only hunter left alive.

The Doctor activated the scanner screen again. It showed a square of white light. The Doctor twisted a control and the image changed, to show the other cavern. Spheres of energy raced around it, illuminating the bodies of the hunters that littered the cavern floor.

The Doctor closed the screen.

'They're all dead,' he whispered. 'All your fellow hunters, Veek. Do you care about that?'

If they hadn't embarked upon the Great Mission, they would still be alive, hunting in the fields and forests of Valeth Skettra. 'Yes, Doctor, I do care. But I doubt that will make you feel any better about me.'

His glass-like human eyes blinked. Again she saw the power behind them. But now she felt sure that physical strength was always superior to mental prowess.

'And now for your side of the bargain, Doctor,' said Veek, walking around the console to tower over the human. 'We have found your friend – now take me back to Valeth Skettra!'

The Doctor stared at her.

Peri struggled out of the grimy uniform, bundled it up and hurled it into the furthest corner of her room. The boots followed, bouncing with a hollow clump off the roundelled walls. She looked down at her body. It was grubby and muddy and her legs were covered with bruises. And she *stank*. Inside, she felt knocked hollow. She tried to remember how many times her life had been in danger since arriving on the Eknuri planetoid. The skyboat – the Valethske ship – the shaft – the Tree – Kikker – the energy storm – it all whirled around inside her mind, a jumble of images, sounds, sensations and emotions. But she had survived. She wanted to cry with relief, leap around her room and yell for the sheer joy of life.

But she was way, way too tired. And *hungry*. Thoughts of coffee and doughnuts filled her head. She grabbed a towel, wrapped it around herself and headed for the bathroom, which was more often than not the third door down from hers. But when she swung it open she found herself staring at the entrance lobby to the wardrobe. She tried the next door along. Potting shed. Then the next. Room full of bicycles.

Cursing under her breath, she returned to her room and scrubbed off as much of the muck as she could with the white fluffy towel. When she'd finished, it was no longer white nor particularly fluffy so she hurled it over her discarded slave-clothes, hiding them from view. She found some perfume in her dresser and sprayed herself liberally, then rooted out trainers, blue jeans and a black T-shirt.

Beneath her anger and tiredness, guilt lurked. She went over her outburst in the console room, wincing as she remembered how she'd yelled at the Doctor. She knew he would never let anything dangerous into the TARDIS, not deliberately anyway. Maybe Veek *had* had a change of heart, and was now a good Valethske – no, she couldn't convince herself of that, however hard she tried. But she was convinced that the Doctor would never put her in danger.

She sighed. She was gonna have to apologise. He had just saved her life – again! For God's sake! Biting her lip, she ran back to the console room.

She saw Veek standing over the Doctor, blue-white teeth bared.

'What's going on?'

'Veek wants me to take her home,' said the Doctor. 'I have no choice. We made a bargain.'

'To hell with your bargain!' cried Peri. 'I want that creature out of here.'

The Doctor glared at her. 'Peri, don't make things more difficult than they already are.'

Peri folded her arms. 'No way. It's her or me.'

She could feel Veek's glare on her, but she held the Doctor's gaze. His face was impassive, and her heart missed a beat. Surely he wouldn't...? Not after all he'd done to save her.

At last the Doctor turned away and stared down at the console. His voice rang out clearly over the subliminal hum of the console room.

'Put those claws away, Veek. Violence won't work, you've learned that much.'

Veek hissed and leaned over the Doctor. Peri saw saliva

bubbling on her lips.

She looked around for a weapon, then remembered that there weren't any in the TARDIS.

The Doctor lifted his head and met Veek's snarling face. His eyebrows were raised, his jaw jutting. 'We've been through all this before. You can't force me to do anything.' And then, to Peri's surprise, he smiled and clapped Veek on the shoulders. 'You have a ship, have you not? And presumably all those poor Vale Guards are still on board waiting to hear the outcome of the Great Mission?'

Veek stepped back, brushing the Doctor's hands away from her. 'So?'

The Doctor's voice rose with enthusiasm. 'So what do you say I go to your ship, plot a course for Valeth Skettra and make a few adjustments? Soup up the engines a bit, so it can go faster than just a bit above light-speed. You'll be home in no time! Well?'

Veek folded her arms. 'That was not our bargain.'

'Our bargain was that I would help you get home,' said the Doctor sternly. 'I have every intention of honouring that bargain but I can't take you back to Valeth Skettra in the TARDIS. You're the only half-decent Valethske as far as I know. Your fellows will skin Peri and me alive.'

Veek stepped back from the Doctor. 'Very well, very well. I accept.' She licked her lips. 'Anyway, it would be foolish to leave such a fine ship on this world.'

Peri realised she'd been holding her breath and let out a long sigh.

The Doctor visibly sagged with relief. 'Now let's see what's been going on outside.' He operated the scanner.

Peri pouted at Veek and went to stand beside her, wanting to show the hunter she wasn't afraid of her.

Veek turned, her nose wrinkling. 'That odour - it is overwhelming!' she gasped, fixing Peri with a malevolent yellow stare.

Peri wished she'd brought the perfume bottle with her so she could spray it right in Veek's face.

On the screen, Peri was pleased to see a cavern full of dead Valethske, residual white energy crackling around their bodies. So Aline had succeeded. Good for her – but at what cost?

She felt the Doctor's hand on her shoulder. 'I wonder if you could tell me what caused all this?'

'It was Aline,' Peri stammered. 'At least, I think. She said she had a plan. Doctor, I'm sorry about –'

'No time for that now!' said the Doctor. 'Tell me exactly what happened in there.'

He wouldn't even let her apologise, but Peri was too tired to be irritated by this. She told him what had happened to Aline, or as much as she understood.

As she spoke the Doctor's face became shadowed with sorrow.

'The energy – it is dissipating,' said Veek.

Peri looked at the scanner screen. The residual energy had now all fizzled out, and the cavern was back to its normal murky fish-tank green. The Doctor flicked a switch, and the image changed to show the plasma strand, also back to what passed for its normal.

'Oh no. Aline,' breathed the Doctor, and in a flurry of movement opened the doors and fled out into the golden void.

Peri looked at Veek, who stared back at Peri. There was no way she was ever gonna trust those feral yellow eyes. Peri ran from the console room, after the Doctor.

He was making straight for the plasma strand.

'Doctor!' called Peri. 'What are you doing?'

She stopped dead in her tracks as the Doctor walked right up to the strand and stepped into it, vanishing without rippling the golden surface, just as Aline had done.

Peri walked up to the strand, tears springing into her eyes. This was too much. Why couldn't he just leave it?

Then just as she was about to drop to the invisible floor, the Doctor stepped from the strand, holding a pale, emaciated body. Peri gasped. It was Aline, she assumed, but the woman was barely recognisable. Her clothes were gone and her pale skin was stretched tightly over her body. Most of her white hair had fallen out, and the skin on her face was cracked like a dried-up river bed.

It was plain to see that she was dead.

The Doctor, face aghast with sadness, stumbled forwards and dropped to his knees, setting Aline's body gently down on the invisible floor.

Peri stood over him. 'Doctor? Are you all right?'

She was alarmed to see tears running down his flushed face. He wouldn't look up at her and was trying to wipe his face surreptitiously with the sleeve of his coat.

'It should have been me,' he mumbled. 'I could have withstood the forces within the strand.'

Peri knelt down before him. 'Hey, don't blame yourself. It was her choice.'

The Doctor shook his head. 'Not entirely. The shape of her life determined her decision.' He looked up at Peri, his eyes shining. 'She deluded herself into thinking it was her destiny. Well, unfortunately, it was in a way... her final destiny.'

Peri looked down at the wizened figure, outlined in a shimmering aura of gold. 'No wonder she didn't tell me. I would have tried to stop her.' She remembered the energy storm. 'Hey, how come I wasn't hurt while all the Valethske were killed?'

'Aline again,' said the Doctor. 'She guided the energy around you. It was that still point the TARDIS homed in on. She saved your life.'

Peri felt tears coming to her eyes. 'And I never even got to say thank you.'

She heard the Doctor's voice trembling with suppressed emotion. 'I told her there's no such thing as destiny. No such thing as fate. We make our own choices. There are only the patterns we see in the universe around us.'

Only the patterns we see. His words echoed in Peri's mind. *We make our own choices.*

She moved closer to the Doctor and hugged him to her.

Chapter Twenty-Six
Ashes

The surface of the planet was knee-deep in fine, grey ash that lifted with the wind, rising into the sky like swarms of insects. The sun was a white blob hanging behind this stifling grey veil, giving scant heat and only a diffuse, baleful light. It was a monochrome landscape, funereal and desolate. Smoke still rose in columns from the scorched ground. The only point of colour was the small blue box that stood embedded, its roof developing a pyramid of the wind-blown ashes.

Two figures stood a little way off from the blue box, a man and a girl, their arms around each other's waists, their heads inclined in an aspect of mourning at a point in the grey-white surface in front of them.

In the distance, through the grey haze, a mountain which wasn't a mountain stretched upwards into the sky.

Later, when the ineffectual sun had risen to its zenith, Peri stepped out of the TARDIS once more, cursing as some of the ash piled against the door collapsed and fell into the interior of the time-ship. Kicking it aside, she walked out on to the surface of the Garden. She was wearing wellingtons and a thick parka, the furred hood encircling her face, goggles over her eyes to keep out the drifting flakes.

She waded up and down through the ash in front of the TARDIS. She was angry, annoyed, on tenterhooks. She was waiting for the Doctor.

She was going to have to think of another name for this planet now. Hard to believe it had ever been the Garden. What should it be? Cinder-world? But then she changed her mind. It should always be called the Garden, as a testament to its former beauty and an indictment of what the Valethske had done.

The Valethske. Peri stopped pacing and gazed over at the

rearing hulk of the Valethske ship. Covered in ash, it looked even more mountainous than ever. The Doctor had told her he wasn't going to be long. That was three hours ago. Time enough for Peri to find the bathroom, have a good long soak, a pot of coffee and a whole plate of doughnuts. Time enough for her to become really, really worried about him.

To take her mind off things, she tried to locate the spot where they'd buried Aline. Might be a good idea to mark it with a flag or something. She struck out through the ash in the direction that seemed right. They'd buried her in a coffin the Doctor had produced, to Peri's alarm, from the room next to hers. There was nothing to mark where Aline now lay, nothing but a featureless expanse of grey ash, and Peri felt that was wrong.

But would the shifting ashes support a flagpole? Surely if the Doctor could conjure up a coffin from out of nowhere he could equally easily produce a headstone or something. Peri stomped around the ash, realising with a sinking heart that she had absolutely no idea where Aline lay.

She looked over at the Valethske ship. 'Oh come on, Doctor. Why couldn't you have just left the damn things alone?'

It wasn't her fault that she couldn't see the good side of the Valethske; there just *wasn't* a good side to them. They were evil. That was that.

At last Peri made out two figures in the grey murk, making their way back to the TARDIS. As they got nearer Peri could see that it was the Doctor and Veek. Veek had cleaned up her injuries and donned a new uniform. The Doctor had on a pair of green wellies that clashed horribly with his stripy trousers, and instead of goggles had his hat jammed well down over his fair hair.

Peri waited, arms folded, as they came up to her. The Doctor's mood had brightened – always did when he had something practical to do – and he was chatting to Veek as if they were old buddies.

He smiled as he saw Peri, as if to say, there you are, told you I was never in any danger.

Veek gave Peri a curt nod. Peri scowled back at her.

'Sorry I was so long, Peri – there was a lot of work to do on the guidance systems, and plotting a course back to Valeth Skettra was a bit more tricky than I thought it would be.'

'You have done me a great service, Doctor,' said Veek. She looked embarrassed. 'Thank you.'

She held out her red-furred hand, ears twitching.

The Doctor took it in both of his, his pale flesh totally enclosing the red fur. They shook.

'Veek intends to return home and denounce the Great Mission, tell the Great Vale that the Gods are dead.'

'Great. I'm so pleased for you,' said Peri.

The Doctor frowned. 'So you should be. Veek is a rarity among such a savage pack species. She can actually think for herself. Could even be persuaded to take up cricket.'

'Are you gonna stop hunting humans for food?' said Peri to the Valethske hunter. 'Make that small step towards decency?'

Veek shook her head, and growled at Peri. 'No. That is our way.'

Peri glared at the Doctor. 'Let's get the hell out of here.'

'Yes, well, I think it's high time we said our goodbyes. Goodbye, Veek – and good luck.'

Peri turned away as they shook hands again, and only began to relax when she heard Veek's footsteps swishing away through the ash.

Then she stood in silence, looking at the devastated landscape. If she closed her eyes she could see the Garden in all its colours. That was the only place it would ever exist now, in her memory.

'You know,' said the Doctor, 'there may be some hope for the Valethske if there are more of them like Veek.'

'So what? I don't care. I hope they die out.'

The Doctor looked offended. 'There's good in everyone, Peri.'

Peri couldn't believe she was hearing this. 'You know sometimes I – I just don't get you, Doctor! Look what they've done to this planet! And remember Athon, Taiana, Lornay? All those other poor people on that ship?'

'And Captain Melrose. Don't forget him. Must be out here somewhere, what's left of him...'

The Doctor looked away from her, hiding his feelings again. 'This planet was a closed system, Peri. Stagnant for thousands of years. It was going nowhere. An evolutionary dead end. Even the beings it was created for were long gone.'

Peri stared at the Doctor. Right now he seemed so alien, so cold. 'But it was – it was so beautiful! And it wasn't doing anyone any harm.'

'I know, Peri. I know,' said the Doctor gently. He sighed. 'Even taking the long view doesn't make things any better.'

He bent down and picked up a handful of ash. He opened his fingers and let the wind take the grey-white flakes.

Peri watched them flutter into the blank sky.

'So much death, so much destruction. So... so *pointless*.'

She could hear the pain in his voice, see it in his face, however much he tried to hide it. Then he turned to her. 'In the TARDIS you said you'd had enough,' he said. 'You wanted me to take you home.' The brim of his hat hid his eyes from view. 'So, shall we go?'

Without waiting for an answer he took out the TARDIS key and put it in the lock.

'Wait!' Peri touched his arm. 'I don't wanna go home... I was just angry.'

He turned round again. He was looking at her with an intensity that unsettled her, and Peri glimpsed a deep sadness within him that made her feel as if her insides were weeping.

'Are you still angry?'

Peri shook her head.

'Well, you sound and look very angry to me.'

Now he sounded like a little boy. A stray flake of ash settled on his nose and she reached up to brush it off.

'I'm not angry, Doctor – not with you.'

He smiled, but uncertainty remained in his eyes. 'You still want to stay with me?'

Somehow Peri knew that there was a whole lot riding on her answer. For the first time she wondered how many others had travelled with the Doctor. How many had left him, scarred by the things they had been through. How many – and this hit her with a cold shock – had died...

Maybe she would ask him. But then again, maybe she wouldn't.

She smiled up at the Doctor and said, 'Yeah. I'll stay. The TARDIS is my home now – just don't try to lose it again.'

The Doctor smiled, his relief abundantly evident. 'I'll do my best,' he said, putting his arm around her shoulders. 'Come on. Let's go somewhere... uneventful.'

Peri smiled up at him. 'That'll be the day.'

Arm in arm, the two friends went into the TARDIS.

Moments later, the blue box excused itself from reality, leaving behind a square depression in the ash. A few more moments later even this was gone, its shape blown into obscurity by the sighing wind.

Acknowledgements

Writing is a lonely process – it is only when the book is out there being read that you reap the rewards of knowing that people are being entertained (hopefully) by your work. Proof of pudding in eating, and all that. But along the way, during the months of dreaming, planning, research, plotting, panicking and writing, there are people who help make it less lonely. These are they:

Paul Vearncombe and Paul Leonard, whose insights made this a better book than it would otherwise have been, and whose friendship I truly appreciate.

Justin Richards, helmsman of literary Who, for guidance and encouragement, and for liking the book more than I dared expect.

Bristol Fiction Writers – Paul Leonard again, Christina Lake, Mark Leyland, Simon Lake, Mark O'Sullivan, and – sometimes – Jim Mortimore, for support and encouragement.

Bristol SF Group – far too many to list, but a special mention must go to Ken Shinn, Dr Who fan extraordinaire and dead ringer for Fitz, for voting me top Who writer of the year (bribery always works!) and for being there every Thursday night, even when I couldn't make it.

All my friends and family.

And hello to everyone I met at Gallifrey One in LA this February, my fellow writers and Doctor Who auteurs, and the fans, who were wonderful. Got a feelin' I'll be 'going west' again...

About the Author

Nick Walters lives in Totterdown, Bristol – location of the steepest street in Europe, fact fans. (Curiously, it's called Vale Street...) Thankfully for cyclist Nick, he doesn't live on this street, though he has walked up and down it in wonder a few times. *Superior Beings* is his third Doctor Who book for the BBC. He has also written a New Adventure for Virgin (with Paul Leonard), plus many short stories, a few of which have found their way into various compilations.

ALSO AVAILABLE